Paddle
into my
Heart

Jenny Dutton

ISBN: 978-1-0687432-0-7

I hope this book makes you laugh, inspires you to pick up a paddle, and have lots of fun.

If you find romance along the way, that'll be like catching the perfect wave!

This book is dedicated to
my amazing Nan,

Daphne Moore
(5.5.1922 – 14.7.2022)

Although you are no longer here, I know you're with me in spirit.
You never doubted me, and proudly told your friends I was writing
a book. You were the first person to hear my stories, and I'm so glad
I made you laugh. You held my hand on the day of my birth, and I
sadly held yours on the day of your passing.

Miss chatting to you every day.

Love you, Nan x.

In memory of my Angel cats.

Meg
Daisy
Purdy
Bailey
Willow
Jasmine

Acknowledgements and thanks

To my parents Wendy and Frank

Thank you for your help and believing in me. I have time to do the dishes now!

To my sister Karen

Your face was a picture when you awoke in the middle of the night covered in baked beans! Happy Times!

Bristol Mecca Ice-Rink Friends.

To all my old friends, Karen and I had the best years of our lives skating at the rink.

Canoeing and Kayaking Friends

Without all of you, past and present, I would have been unable to write this story.

Calvert Exmoor

At last I have finished! I hope this book makes you laugh.

Lastly to anyone thinking of writing a book.

Please don't think about it, just start writing. If I can write a book, so can you!

Make Dreams Happen!

Canoeing and Kayaking Terms

Canoe: An open boat in a variety of sizes and lengths. One, two or three seats or a kneeling thwart. Paddled with a single blade either sitting down or kneeling.

Kayak: Closed cockpit in a variety of sizes and lengths. Paddled with a spraydeck sitting down with legs in front, knees slightly bent and feet against footrest. Paddled with a double blade.

Sea kayak: A longer narrower kayak, often fitted with a rudder or skeg. Most have several hatches for overnight camping gear.

Sit-on-top kayak: A kayak you sit on top and can get quite wet! Excellent fun, especially on hot summer days.

Canoe paddle: A single bladed paddle.

Kayak paddle: A double-bladed paddle.

Bow: The front of your boat.

Stern: The back of your boat, or the look my mum used to give me when I sneaked home at three a.m.!

Draw stroke: Used to move your canoe or kayak sideways.

Ferry glide: A way of moving your boat sideways and fairies do this without fluttering their wings!

High/low brace: Support strokes used to prevent you taking a dunking.

J-stroke: A combination of paddling forward and twisting the paddle to act as a rudder. Once learnt you can paddle in a straight line without swapping sides.

Kayak/ Eskimo roll: Following a definite dunking, a method used to upright your kayak using a hip flick and paddle.

Lining a canoe: When the going gets tough, the tough get lining! This method transports your canoe on water rather than struggling portaging on land. With experience you can use a stern and bow painter or set up a bridal on the keel line. It's like taking your canoe for a walk rather than your dog!

Pry stroke: It's used to push the canoe away from the paddling side.

Stern rudder: A steering stroke used to control your direction. Commonly used in surfing, or small gaps.

Gunwales: The upper edge around the canoe.

Kneeling thwart: A strip of wood you perch your backside on whilst kneeling in a canoe. Mainly used in whitewater paddling, it lowers your centre of gravity and helps you to connect with your canoe.

Painters: The ropes attached to the stern and bow of your canoe to either tie or tow your canoe. Or someone holding a paintbrush!

Spraydeck: A cockpit cover fitted to prevent your kayak or canoe from becoming a bathtub.

Throw line: A rescue bag containing an attached rope with a loose end. Used to rescue a paddler who has taken a dunking!

Eddy: A current created behind an obstruction, or your mate.

Chapter One
Famous Last Words

Men are like buses; you've waited ages for the right one, and when you've turned your back, four are paddling into your life at once! Though, knowing my luck, the first would cause my head to spin whilst driving me around the bend. The second would be a joyride that lasted less than a weekend. The third would lead me up the garden path before dumping me at the end, and the fourth would be a mystery tour, believing he had a girlfriend.

How on earth was I going to cherry-pick between the four of them? Especially with my indecisive nature. It reminded me of holding up the queue in an ice cream parlour choosing between a soft Mr Whippy, sleek Magnum, Screwball, or a Feast, where once you've devoured the nutty outer layer, the best bit is waiting to be nibbled.

I peered over my shoulder as four kayakers emerged from within the phantom grey mist, and just like buses, three passed without stopping. The fourth kayaker released one hand from his paddle and held it towards me. I tried to reach his hand, but a huge wave see-sawed my canoe from port to starboard and catapulted me into the stern. When I scrambled to my knees and regained my composure, the kayakers had paddled back into the mist.

'Help. Please don't go. Please don't leave me. Wait!' I screamed after them. Though no matter how loud I screamed, my cries for help were carried away in the fangs of the wind.

The waves continued ricocheting my canoe, making me feel as green as the frog who was kissed by the princess in *The Frog Prince*. Crikey, was I about to croak it before experiencing the magic of true love? My mum would be seething when she heard I'd popped my clogs without following her golden rules. I visualised her glaring above the rim of her glasses, waggling a finger and gesticulating her commands.

'Oakley, remember, under no circumstances are you to leave home without following my three golden rules.

- ♥ Always wear clean presentable knickers.

- ♥ Ensure your legs are as smooth as silk.

- ♥ Leave your house sparkling clean.

(You never know when you might bump into the man of your dreams and have overnight company!)' Though on recollection, the final comment was from my nan!

Do you think my makers at the pearly gates would mind me being a tad late? I seemed to be late for everything these days. Perhaps they'd grant me a little longer so I could put my house in order before my mum arrived to find:

- ♥ The dishwasher hadn't been emptied for days, and trying to find a piece of crockery in the sink was akin to playing a game of Jenga.

- ♥ My washing basket had spewed up its contents like an erupting volcano.

- ♥ A stalagmite of ironing had risen on my bedroom floor.

- ♥ You could have written a whole book in the dust.

- ♥ Shortly, I'd be able to open my own recycling company.

Suddenly, my thoughts were obliterated as I began gurgling and spluttering. When I lifted my head, and opened my eyes, Coco Pops were running down my face onto my dressing gown. Dammit! My daydreaming was going to be the death of me, and instead of drowning in the river, I was drowning in chocolate milk.

Cinnamon, my Ragdoll cat, sprang onto the table and before I could stop her, began lapping the spilt milk. On discovering it was chocolate, she twitched her fluffy bum in my face, swished her tail across my nose, and jumped down. My kitchen clock displayed, 6.40 a.m. Oh my word, I'd been daydreaming for ages. If I didn't get a wiggle on, I'd run out of time to change into my fairy outfit, for the charity Christmas fancy dress paddle.

Jasmine, my Chinchilla Persian cat chased Cinnamon upstairs with me hot on their tails. I raced into the bathroom, and with no time for a shower, spritzed myself head to toe with Romantic Spark Impulse. Cinnamon popped her head around the corner, sniffed, sneezed three times, and scurried out of the room.

Images of my canoeing friends sprang into my mind. I had a sneaky suspicion that following the boys' night out, there'd be plenty of garbled banter flowing out of my impulsive friends' mouths.

I dashed into my bedroom to find something to wear. Though considering the height of the clothes in my laundry basket, I wasn't surprised to find only one clean item in my drawers. Glistening, and beckoning me to wear them, was last year's unworn Christmas present from my best friend, Ruby. Despite my reservations, Ruby was adamant that a black glittery thong with hipster silver chains would help me find a boyfriend, but I wanted to find a boyfriend before that stage of a relationship! The thong wasn't the most comfortable attire to wear canoeing, and reminded me of flossing my teeth, however my thermal knickers were packed in the boot of my car, so for now the thong would have to suffice.

After riffling through the laundry basket and stalagmite of ironing, I managed to find enough layers to hide my modesty, though where my socks were was anyone's guess. Cinnamon had a habit of hiding them, and although my excuse for wearing odd socks was to blame it on the cat, I would have preferred it if she learnt to hide them in pairs. One of my many bugbears was wearing odd socks, so for now I'd go barefoot, perhaps I'd find a pair in my wellies. Another bugbear was drivers who don't thank you after you've reversed half-way down the road, or people who don't thank you when you hold the door open for them. I could go on forever, but I have too many bugbears to list!

Cinnamon returned and sniffed my clothes; yep, they were a bit pongy. I spritzed myself with another can of Impulse and read the label – Rock and Love – cripes, I hope I wasn't going to be finding love with any rocks today.

I stepped into my trousers, and my hands skimmed down my legs, stumbling upon a lawn of sprouting new shoots. Blinking heck! I'd failed my mum's rule number two as the lawn was in desperate need of mowing. Peeping into the mirror, I was surprised to see my hair gleaming like a fresh conker, freckled with golden streaks of caramel amongst locks of chocolate brown. I tied it into a ponytail and ran a flannel over my face before applying moisturiser, and several layers of foundation. The remainder of my face painting could wait until later, I couldn't possibly travel with my face fully made-up; I might scare the other drivers. Yesterday my niece Willow witnessed me rehearsing, and said I looked more like one of Cinderella's ugly stepsisters than a fairy. Well at least no one would recognise the fairy paddling down the river.

The past month had been hectic. In addition to covering another vet's shifts, I'd also been making my fairy fancy dress outfit. What with babysitting my nieces and nephews, and organising the family Christmas Day dinner, there wasn't a lot of time for anything else. And to top that, my brothers had asked me to buy Christmas presents for their wives. Today was the first day of my ten-day-staycation holiday ... and tomorrow, the washing machine was going into overdrive.

Nutmeg, my tortoiseshell Manx cat, laid spreadeagled on the

top step guarding any escape routes for Cinnamon and Jasmine. Nutmeg twisted onto her tummy and meowed, announcing she was the head of the household, and everyone could follow behind her. I scaled over her head, and shadowed by Cinnamon and Jasmine, we bounded downstairs before her. I dished out salmon cat food onto plates, while three cats purred and flounced in and out of my legs.

The answerphone was working overtime, flashing seventeen new messages. I pressed play whilst making two flasks of hot chocolate. My next-door neighbour, Molly, who doubled up as my sister-in-law, demanded I looked after her three boys tomorrow. Apparently, her husband, Harrison, the eldest of my five brothers, was too busy to watch the kids while Molly finished the Christmas shopping. The remainder of the messages were demands from my family to help with the kids over the holidays; so much for catching up on my washing tomorrow.

With no time for another bowl of Coco Pops, I bit the end of a Snickers bar and sipped a mug of coffee as my mobile chimed.

'Morning, Mum.'

'Morning, love. We've been desperate to get hold of you, everyone's left loads of messages on your answerphone.'

I nibbled a bit more Snickers bar. 'I was listening to them before you rang.'

'Oakley, don't speak with your mouth full, it's rude.'

'Sorry Mum! You're up early, it's only seven o'clock.'

'I'm preparing the food for this afternoon's Christmas party at the Forever Spring Chickens' care home.'

I gulped the remaining Snickers bar and slurped my coffee. 'I thought you were only making the starters?'

'I am, despite a hitch with your dad. Anyway, why didn't you listen to your messages when you got in? Everyone's been frantic with worry.'

'Sorry, I didn't realise anyone would be worried about me. I was working until two-thirty this morning as I carried out an emergency caesarean on a dog.'

My mum chuckled, ignoring my comments about the dog. 'No

dear, they weren't worried about you, they were panicking they'd have no one to look after the kids in the holidays.'

I took a deep breath and sighed. 'Oh! I'll call them when I'm home from canoeing.'

'Don't worry, I've told them you'd love to help during your holidays.'

I bite my lower lip. 'You did? I was hoping to have a few days to myself.'

'Whatever for?'

'It doesn't matter, Mum,' I said, opting not to come clean about the state of my house.

'What time are Harrison and Molly's boys arriving tomorrow morning?'

'Eight-thirty, now going back to the problems with your dad, I need twenty bags of frozen prawns, and twenty boxes of Christmas crackers.'

'Mum, after forty years of marriage, six children and sixteen grandchildren, how on earth are prawns and crackers going to solve Dad's problems?'

'Your dad's driving me crackers, and I'd happily throttle him with a bag of frozen prawns. Would you believe it, yesterday I asked him to do three things to help me out at Christmas, just three simple things!'

'Nothing is ever simple with Dad, what's he done wrong now?'

'All he had to do was pop to the supermarket to buy twenty bags of frozen prawns to make cocktails, and twenty boxes of crackers, then pop to the craft shop and buy twenty packs of bunting and drop them into Forever Spring Chickens. Hardly rocket science is it love?'

'Seems like a simple task, though we are talking about Dad. I'm a little surprised you asked him to shop for three items in one morning!'

'Providing he remembered the number twenty he couldn't go far wrong, though I should have known better. Sometimes I think your dad needs a rocket stoving up his posterior.'

I interrupted and raised my voice, 'I'm in a hurry, Mum, what has Dad done wrong?'

My mum tutted before continuing her saga. 'I've opened the freezer, and would you believe it, he bought twenty bags of prunes! Love, what the dickens am I going to do with twenty bags of prunes? I searched everywhere for the bunting and boxes of crackers. Do you know what he brought?' Before I had time to answer, my mum rabbited on. 'Twenty bun tins and twenty boxes of Jacob's crackers. So, I asked what he was playing at, and do you know what he said?'

A bout of giggles almost choked me as I slid onto the sofa suppressing them. 'No Mum, please tell me.'

'He had the audacity to tell me I talked as if I had a prune in my mouth!'

'I think the saying is plum in your mouth, not prune.'

'Well, whatever. He said my voice was too posh, and my pronunciation of prawns sounded like prunes, especially as I was making cocktails for the elderly folk. Love, who's heard of prune cocktails? Oh my god, love, your dad lives in cloud cuckoo land.'

Sometimes I thought my dad wished he lived in cloud cuckoo land in preference to listening to my mum's ramblings. How they had six children was a complete enigma.

My bout of giggles exploded as I slid off the sofa and landed on the rug.

'Nan told me she's been scoffing a lot of prunes lately, as they made her regular. Why not use the bun tins to bake the residents prune cupcakes? I'm sure everyone would be regular then. I'd hate to think how long the queue would be for the loos!'

There was silence before my mum inhaled and snapped, 'Oakley, I thought you would have been more supportive; you're just like your dad and brothers.' she sighed and raised her voice. 'Oakley, stop laughing. It's high time you reined your spirit in. It isn't funny. The party is at three o'clock and your dad's borrowed my car.'

I tried to regain my composure. 'Sorry, Mum, how can I help?'

'Before you spend the day sailing your little dinghy thing, be a dear and spare me a few minutes to pop down to the supermarket to buy the prawns and Christmas crackers, and then deliver it here.'

'It's a sixteen-foot canoe, Mum, not a little dinghy thing, and you don't sail it, you paddle it, unless of course, you're on open water and can rig a sail. What about the bunting?'

'The residents are making the bunting out of old Christmas cards.'

'Good idea. Can you meet me at the entrance with a couple of trolleys?'

'Yes. Phone me when you're on the way.'

'Okay, bye Mum.'

'Oakley, hold on a tick, your nan is shouting something.'

My mum bellowed down the phone, 'You want what, Mum?' My mum paused before speaking to me. 'Oakley, you still there? I'm working in a madhouse! Have you heard of extra-large tuna knickers?'

'I think Nan means Tena knickers, you know, the pull-up disposable pants.' With all this chuckling I could do with a pair of Tena knickers myself. My mum continued to yell at my nan who was staying in respite at the home following a hip replacement.

Once again, my mum screamed, 'Mum, do you mean Tena knickers?'

'Well, that's what I asked for!'

Oakley, the phone is on loudspeaker, did you hear that?'

'Yes, Mum, Nan wants extra-large fishy knickers. Ask her if she wants chips with them.'

The roar of laughter from my nan was enough to scare the other residents to death.

'Let me speak to my favourite granddaughter. Hello sweetheart, you're a naughty girl, I'll have plenty of chips and don't skimp on the salt and vinegar. I wanted to tell you something, your grandad's been touching me.'

Now I really needed a pair of Tena knickers!

'Grandad passed away years ago, Nan, what have you been doing, having a séance?'

'Of course not, silly. They say if you find a white feather close by, you have a guardian angel. You'll never guess where I found a feather this morning.'

I was hesitant to even ask.

'Where, Nan?'

My nan had a fit of giggles. 'In my red silky knickers. I went to pull them up, and there it was, a small white feather. So, I said to myself it could only have been my old man, he was the only one who had ever tickled my fancy.'

I could hear my mum grappling with the phone, and my nan.

'You still there, Oakley?'

'Yes, Nan, that was too much information. I thought you wore Tena knickers?'

'Only in bed, love, they're a lifesaver. I wouldn't be without them as I don't always make the loo in time, but with this new hip, I should be bouncing around like a spring chicken.'

'Watch out for any cockerels chasing after you. I hear there's a special one called Ken Tucker who has the hots for you?'

'Don't make me chuckle, love, Ken is a hundred and one. By the time he catches me he'll be Ken-tuckered-out fried chicken. Isn't it time you found a fella to tickle your fancy? What happened to Trent? The one with the cheeky grin, like your dad.'

Before I had the chance to reply, I could hear my mum still attempting to wrestle the phone back from my nan.

'Mum, you know Oakley doesn't have time for a boyfriend, she's too busy working and taking care of the kids. Now let me have the phone.'

'But they're not her kids, Vi! You need to give her breathing space or you'll lose her.'

My mum raised her voice towards my Nan. 'Mum, it's none of your business. Oakley loves helping with the kids, and she doesn't need a boyfriend. Give me the phone back, now!'

My nan started barking like a dog. 'Woof, woof, woof, I'm not a dog you know.'

'No Mum, a dog is more obedient.'

'What like Oakley, who must obey your every word.'

'Hello, Mum, Nan, I'm still on the end of the phone.'

'Oakley, sorry, your nan is like your dad, a pain in the posterior. I'll see you shortly. Oh, and make sure you get large prawns – can't abide by the little shrimp things.'

'Okay. Say goodbye to Nan.'

My nan shouted, 'Bye favourite granddaughter, stand up to your mum and go and find yourself a fella to tickle your fancy.'

The line went dead. Then immediately chimed; it was my best friend, Ruby.

'Hi Ruby, I'm on my way.'

Hi Oakley, I'm at Exeter Services, where are you?'

'In my kitchen.'

Ruby raised her voice. 'You're where? Why are you so late? You should have left ages ago.'

'I didn't get home from work until 2 a.m. I got up early, but lost track of the time daydreaming about four kayakers ...' I paused, '... would you believe it, I was paddling my canoe into a storm, when four kayakers appeared. One tried to rescue me, but I couldn't reach his hand, so he gave up and left me to face the storm on my own!'

Ruby sniggered down the phone. 'You're nuts. Let's hope you don't need rescuing today.'

'Don't worry, I'll be fine; I've never swum whilst paddling on the River Dart.'

'Don't jinx it! Remember what Trent used to say? "Never say never!" How long are you going to be?'

I ignored the mention of the name Trent.

'I'm nearly ready. I was listening to loads of answerphone messages when my mum rang. She's asked me to pop to the supermarket to buy prawns, Christmas crackers and Tena pants.'

'That's an odd combination, and let me guess, your family want you to look after their kids during the holidays.'

'Sounds about right.'

'You can't keep being at everyone's beck and call. You need a life of your own or you'll never get a boyfriend. Stop trying to please everyone.'

'Rubes, they'd be useless without me.'

'No, Oakley, they're useless, full stop. They're taking advantage of you because you're so kind. I hardly see you anymore, and when did you last go on a date?'

'Not sure, must be over a year ago. Remember Basil? He was lovely until he stood me up. Told his mate I was too nice and reminded him of his ex-wife.'

'You only saw him for a week. Didn't I tell you to brush him aside?'

'Very funny, Rubes. Remember the guy in the Navy? I really fell for him, until true to form, he did have a girl in every port, what was his name?'

'Twat!'

'Nope, I think I called him something stronger. And of course, there was Scott, who was two-timing me with his best friend. Oh, I nearly forgot Rupert, wearing his mum's awful handknitted, brown-and-orange jumpers. Oh my word, Rubes, what's wrong with me? Why can't I find a soulmate?'

'Define a soulmate.'

'Oh, I dunno, I'm not too particular. He's got to love animals and children, make me laugh, treat me like an equal and not expect me to do all the housework—'

Ruby interrupted: 'What housework? Emptying the dishwasher would be an improvement on you.'

'Okay, point taken. Maybe we could eat out more. He's got to be a positive thinker, and I'd love him to be a dreamer like me. He must love canoeing and kayaking, and the outdoors. It would be great if he loved Christmas and had smiling blue eyes with a hint of cheekiness.'

'Oh my god, Oak, and you're not particular? No wonder you only daydream about a man. You're far to pernickety; the man you're looking for is only found in fairy tales.'

'I'm paddling as the Christmas fairy, perhaps I'll bump into him on the river. You never know, Rubes, maybe fairy tales do come true. Anyway, what do you look for in a man?'

'A tight bum and a ginormous w—'

I jumped in. 'Ruby, don't be so crude, I wish I hadn't asked, all you think about is sex!'

'What else is there to think about? I was going to say a ginormous wallet.'

'Yeah, right, I'm more worried about our connection.'

'Stuff the connection, Oakley, we're young, you're too much of a dreamer, time to wake up to a bit of reality.'

'I suppose so.' I mumbled.

'I heard a rumour that Trent's paddling today.'

I raised my voice. 'What? I thought he was living in Cornwall with his girlfriend.'

'They've split up and he's rented a house around the corner from you.'

'Seriously, he's living by me?'

'Yep, with his new girlfriend.'

'He doesn't waste time. Has he ever paddled a canoe?'

'No idea, though he's an excellent kayaker.'

'That's a different kettle of fish. I wish you'd told me earlier.'

'If I had you wouldn't have agreed to come paddling.'

'I'm not sure I want to go now.'

Ruby screamed down the phone. 'Oakley! Don't you dare back out now! If you see Trent, paddle out of his way.'

'I suppose, though you know Trent, that's like throwing a ball for your dog and telling him not to chase it.'

'Maybe if you'd gone on a date with Trent, he'd have realised what you're like and stopped chasing after you.'

'Thanks. Maybe you should have gone on a date with him.'

'It's not me he's fancied for god knows how many years.'

'Rubes, are you forgetting he was engaged to Scarlett?'

'He was eighteen! Anyway, they split up two weeks later when he caught her with a waiter. Oakley, he's not had a serious, long-term relationship for years.'

'I'm not surprised, he's such a pain in the backside.'

'Yep, so you should get on like ice-cream and hot chocolate sauce. Maybe he can melt your icy exterior. Now you'd better get your arse into gear, or we'll paddle off without you.'

'Thanks, Rubes, now I know who my friends are! If you stopped gassing, perhaps I could get my skates on.'

'You might need them today, it's freezing. And don't drive like a maniac, and Oakley ...'

'Yes, Rubes.'

'I still think you're nuts. See you later my bonkers best friend.'

'See yer, Rubes.'

Ruby and I met twenty years ago in a lake on a freezing March morning. We were attending an interschool water sports day, and although our lives were separated by only a mile, our paths had never crossed. Ruby attended a private girls' school, whilst I attended the local primary. My memories were still vivid. Ruby appeared self-conscious, shuffling from foot to foot, and dressed to perfection modelling the latest cerise-pink and black wetsuit with matching boots. She stood out amongst kids tripping over the ankle cuffs on old, faded, black wetsuits while struggling to pull up worn-out zips. A group of boys jumped up and down in front of Ruby, threatening to push her in. Scarlett and Cordelia, my nemeses from school, stood on the edge of the lake jeering the boys on. A glass-shattering scream echoed around the lake as Ruby disappeared under the surface. Ten-year-old Trent, the ringleader, and the most annoying boy at my school, stood gloating at the side of the lake. A thunder of applause exploded, while his grin had the appearance of a coat-hanger stuffed inside his mouth. Boy, was I hopping mad, with my fists clenched and head held high, I marched towards him and pushed him out of the way. He promptly fell against the next boy, who then knocked the next boy, and the next and the next, it was like watching a human chain of dominoes, and one by one they fell into the water taking Cordelia and Scarlett with them. I waded into the lake, grasped Ruby's hand, and hauled her to her feet. We linked arms and snubbed Scarlett and Cordelia while they screamed, they'd get me back one day. I didn't care, I'd just met my best friend.

The kitchen clock read 7.20 a.m. Strewth, time I got cracking, I still had to go shopping and meet my mum at Spring Chickens. In haste, I stepped back onto the plates of leftover salmon cat food, and now it was oozing between my toes. With no time to wash my feet, I flicked a tea towel over them before snatching a pair of socks out of my wellies. Nutmeg's gaze ping-ponged from the floor, and then to me.

I pulled my socks on and peeped under my arm at Nutmeg. 'Sorry, Megs, I'll clean it later.'

She glared down her nose and meowed, no, you'll do it right now young lady! Nutmeg was worse than my mum.

Loaded with the flasks of hot chocolate I stepped out of the door. It hadn't stopped raining for weeks, and the last thing I expected was a million frozen raindrops adorning my car. They sparkled under the streetlamp, and it just my luck, there was no sign of my ice scraper. No doubt it was hidden in my unorganised garage, where my brother Harrison had been storing his tools for the past year. When I'd asked him to move everything into his own garage, he'd responded, 'All in good time, sis, all in good time.'

A shiver spiralled down my back and my fingers tingled, as I scrapped the windscreen with my library card. Furthermore, my driving skills were tested while completing a three-point turn on an ice rink. Harrison had begun parking his vans opposite each other on the corner of my drive, leaving me a minuscule gap to squeeze through. Big brothers could be so annoying, and I had five of them!

After popping to the supermarket and loading my mum's shopping into my car, I phoned her before driving to Forever Spring Chickens.

I was shocked to see a stack of bun tins and lunchbox sitting beside her.

'Sorry, Mum, I couldn't find any bags of prawns, so I bought twenty pots of readymade prawn cocktail. If you spoon it into glasses, add chopped lettuce and tomatoes and decorate the glass with a slice of lemon, no one will realise you haven't made it.'

'Thanks, love, what a good idea. Here's a lunchbox, I've filled it with all sorts of goodies. I was in the deli yesterday and spotted a long-maturing cheese called Beaufort. It's quite pungent, and reminded me of washing your dad's socks, however it tasted delicious. I bought far too much, so I've slipped some in with the sandwiches and added it to a few chunks of pineapple on cocktail sticks.' My mum paused. 'Nearly forgot, I've made some sausage rolls and shortbread.'

'Wow! Thanks Mum, you're amazing, though you needn't have gone to so much trouble for me.'

Mocking me, my mum sniggered. 'It's not for you, love, it's for Flynn and his mates. Flynn went out with the lads last night as Poppy and Blossom are staying with their mum for Christmas. Almost forgot, your nan gave me this to give to you.' My mum handed me a bag of Freddo chocolate frog faces. I couldn't speak as I was still digesting how my twenty-nine-year-old brother Flynn could still twist our mum around his little finger. My mum never appreciated anything I did. She continued her ramblings. 'Nan said maybe if you kiss the whole bag of frogs your Prince Charming will appear. Oakley, both you and your nan are as mad as a box of frogs.'

I summoned the strength to find the words to answer her.

'Nan's crazier than me.' I paused and raised my voice. 'Why are you giving me the bun tins?'

My mum handed me the receipt. 'Sorry, love, be a dear and return them. Your dad paid cash for them, keep the money towards Christmas dinner.'

I gritted my teeth. 'I haven't got the time to take the bun tins back today.'

'I'm sure you can fit it in during your time off, I have so much to do for Christmas.'

I clenched my jaw and folded my arms. 'Like what? You've given everyone money for Christmas, and I'm organising and preparing Christmas dinner.'

'This and that love, this, and that. Say hello to any nice sailors you meet.'

My muscles tensed as a heaviness crept over my body.

'They're called canoeists and kayakers!'

'Oh well, love, whatever floats your boat, it's all the same to me. Must dash, busy, busy, busy! Oh, and Oakley, you will remember to follow the golden rules, won't you?'

'I'm wearing my best clean knickers!'

'Good, you never know when you might be involved in an accident.'

'Hopefully not today.'

'You can't predict the future love; remember the motto, always be prepared.

My mum used to be a scout leader, being prepared was ingrained into her.

'I'm always prepared. Bye Mum.'

'Bye sweetheart. Watch out for the sailors.'

Oh my word, my mum could be so annoying and condescending, and she really didn't understand canoeing.

Although my head felt like an exploding party popper, my spirits were lifted when I glimpsed my fairy costume on the passenger seat. My heart was set on winning first prize for the best fancy dress costume, but there was no chance of me ever winning the prize for the first swimmer. Though I prayed those weren't my famous last words!'

Chapter Two
Magic Wand

A string of obscenities rattled off my tongue as my car skidded into a lay-by beside the River Dart. After narrowly missing a group of kayakers, a ginormous Christmas pudding leapt out of my way and landed on the embankment. Phew, at least I hadn't been responsible for turning the Christmas pudding into mincemeat. I stopped and checked my rear mirror. Three kayakers had their backs to me as the Christmas pudding rolled down the embankment and landed at their feet. A fourth kayaker stepped forward and hoisted it up. Oh my word, the Christmas pudding was Ruby! Unimpressed with my driving skills, she tossed her curly locks over her shoulders and rested her hands on her hips. She looked in my direction, and modelled a frown that was scary enough to frighten every ghost and ghoul at Halloween.

I continued driving to the end of the lay-by, crunching through frozen puddles that reminded me of cracking the top of my first and only attempt at a crème brûlée. A chisel and mallet would have been more appropriate than a spoon. With my eyes screwed shut, I held my breath as my car slid in a direct collision-path towards Ruby's new car. On opening my eyes, it had stopped a whisker away. I breathed a sigh of relief, though my next breath was short-lived as the Christmas pudding stomped towards me. With the radiating heat, I could have sworn someone had poured brandy over it and struck a match.

Holding my hand above my eyes, I squinted in the winter sun, observing a blanket of freezing fog hovering above the river. Sunbeams cast eerie pillars of light through the naked trees while fog weaved through the treetops engulfing everything in its path. I shivered at the thought of stepping out of my nice warm car, and the notion of Ruby's sharp tongue made me wish I was still tucked up in bed.

On opening the car door, dank air engulfed me as I stepped out and zipped my coat up. I pulled my gloves on and tucked my ponytail under a beanie. Cottonwool clouds circled my head as I impersonated *Puff the Magic Dragon*. With a frosty reception on the horizon, I was prepared to receive my rollicking, though Ruby's appearance was more akin to a dragon breathing fire than puffing clouds of cotton wool.

'Oakley, you almost hit me and my car,' hissed Ruby.

'Sorry, Rubes, the car skidded on ice. Don't worry, I was in full control and missed you both by miles.'

Ruby crossed her arms as she stood in front of me. 'Your definition of control and miles is slightly different from mine.' Although Ruby boasted a temper as smouldering as her amber sunset curls, the flames were soon extinguished. She hitched up her Christmas pudding outfit. 'You took your time to get here.'

'Sorry, my ice scraper was in my garage, the cul-de-sac was like an ice rink, and I had to manoeuvre between Harrison's vans before going to the supermarket.'

'I don't know, Oak, you used to be so organised. I thought you were going to speak to Harrison about parking his vans on the corner, and I bet he's still storing his gear in your garage.'

'He is. I've asked loads of times to move his vans, but he just takes the mickey out of me and says you could drive an HGV through.'

'An HGV? Who's he kidding? There's barely enough room to swing one of your cats. I'd like to see him drive an HGV through.'

'There'll be no swinging of my cats, thank you very much. You know men, always exaggerating about the size of things.'

'I can see who you take after; you don't know the difference between an inch and a mile.'

'I do know when my best friend is flirting with a cute kayaker.'

'He was simply helping me standup after an idiot tried to run me over.'

'You'll have his number by the end of the paddle.'

'Who says he hasn't already given it to me? Now, do you want a hand lifting the Beast off the roof or not?'

Ruby was such a flirt; a guy only had to smile at her, and she was worrying about whether there were clean sheets on the bed. Guys rarely smiled at me; laughed yes – having five older brothers, I was always good for a laugh.

I untied the straps and threw them over the Beast. 'Thanks, Rubes.'

Ruby reached for the bow. 'I'm surprised you brought your tandem canoe, the Beast, instead of Peewee, your solo canoe.'

I grasped the stern as we lifted the Beast off the roof bars. 'I've got a bow paddler this year, so needed the extra seat.'

Ruby peered into the back of my car. 'I can't see anyone.'

'You'll meet later. Where is everyone?'

'Most of the lads travelled down in a minibus; it's parked in the next lay-by. By the sound of it, they lost quite a lot of money at a casino last night.'

'I guess there'll be plenty of banter flying around today.'

'Yep, and I've already seen a hipflask doing the rounds.'

'Enough gassing, I'd better change before everyone paddles without me.'

After unloading my car, I threw everything into the Beast, and two seconds later the contents of my dry bag began flying over my shoulders. A muffled shriek erupted from inside me.

'Knickers! You won't believe it, Rubes; I've forgotten my thermal knickers.'

'What's wrong with the knickers you're wearing?'

'It's not going to be too comfy wearing the thong you gave me for Christmas last year.'

'Ouch, doesn't bear thinking about, imagine all that readjusting. Best go commando,' Ruby sneered, failing to sound the slightest bit sympathetic.

'What if I end up swimming, have to go to hospital, and I'm knickerless?'

'Oakley, you are such a pessimist. Wear the thong. Anyway, why are you wearing the thong I gave you on a canoeing trip? You were meant to wear it on a date.'

'A date, who are you kidding? I guess that's why it was the only clean item of underwear in my drawer.'

Ruby pulled her buoyancy aid over her head. 'Sounds like your washing machine will be working overtime tomorrow?'

'Maybe, but I'm looking after Harrison and Molly's three boys for the day.'

Ruby fastened her white helmet, which was sprinkled in holly and berries. 'Why didn't you say you were busy?'

'I couldn't, my mum told them I was free,' I mumbled, gripping my towel between my teeth, and attempting to hide my modesty. I pulled my thermal leggings up, as yet another vehicle sped by while the driver tooted his horn.

'Oak, you really should change inside a dry robe, rather than scaring everyone.'

'I haven't got one. Maybe Santa Claus will bring me one.'

Ruby hovered, then sniffed the air like one of my cats. 'I'll have a word with him. What's that strange fishy odour?'

I pulled my dry trousers up. 'Sorry, I stood in salmon cat food, it's squashed between my toes. I'll try and fish it out.'

'Oakley Breeze! You're revolting!'

I hitched braces over my shoulders and pulled a lime green cag over my head. 'Sorry. Do you like my homemade legs? They're sewn onto the tutu. Willow helped me make them from an old pair of tights, which we stuffed with foam.'

Ruby sniggered. "Your dangly legs are hilarious, and I love the baby shoes on the end, but why aren't you wearing a dry suit? You'll freeze your arse off if you swim.'

'It's easier to visit the ladies, and I'm not going to swim.'

'Where you gonna find a ladies on the riverbank?'

I heaved my olive-green buoyancy aid over my head. 'I'll rephrase it. Trying to be discrete squatting behind a huge tree.'

'It'll take a humongous tree for me to squat behind in this Christmas pudding costume.'

'It's all right for the lads, they line up along the embankment and no one blinks an eye.'

Ruby helped me attach my Blue-Peter-inspired fairy wings made from coat hangers and clingfilm. 'There might be a few raised eyebrows if the women squatted on the embankment.'

I squinted in the sun. 'We wouldn't dare! Talking about raised, have you seen how high the river is?'

'Not yet. It hasn't stopped raining for days, although it's turned to snow now. Let's hope the river hasn't risen too much. Are you going to be much longer? I'm getting frostbite waiting.'

'Sorry, I've still got to apply my make-up. Why don't you check the river level, there might be a certain kayaker down there who'll melt the frostbite.'

Ruby poked her tongue out at me. 'Okay, I'll be back shortly.'

After clambering across everyone, I popped back to my car and jumped into the passenger seat. I reached for my huge make-up bag, pulled down the sun visor and flipped open the vanity mirror. Within five minutes my face was a picture that even I didn't recognise. Who knew bright red lipstick looked so good smudged into your cheeks, and sunflower yellow and blue eyeshadow could be smeared above your false eyelashes? I just hoped they survived the paddle.

After tucking my hair into the back of my dry cag and fastening my helmet, my attached blonde plaits dangled over my shoulders. I reached towards my bow paddler's bottom, inserted a nozzle, and plugged the other end into a pump and power point. Before long, Mr Frosty, the inflatable snowman, was raring to go.

Ruby waddled back from the river as I twirled my tinsel-covered wand in the air.

'I'm granting you a wish, my lady, what do you so desire?'

Ruby's Christmas pudding was quaking so much it could have curdled the cream.

'Oh, my word, Oak, I hardly recognised you. You look like a cross between a pantomime dame and the Tooth Fairy. I love your bow paddler. Please grant my wish for the river level to drop.'

I spun my magic wand in the air. 'Wish granted. Now what wish do I desire?'

Ruby nearly rolled over giggling. 'Oak, you're as mad as a hatter. You can't grant your own wishes, but if you could, I suppose you could wish for one of the kayakers in your dreams.'

Once again, I twirled my magic wand and chanted: 'Magic wand, please send me a mysterious kayaker from my dreams.' I twiddled the wand around my head, slipped backwards on the ice and landed in the Beast. My wand spiralled into the air in a direct path towards three kayakers.

With her legs crossed, Ruby bent double crying with laughter. 'Oak, all this gigging has made me need the loo. You'd better ask for your wand back while I find a humongous tree.'

'Rubes, look it's three of the kayakers I was daydreaming about. This is so embarrassing. Remember when we were little, and my brothers kicked their football next door and sent us around to retrieve it? I feel like a nine-year-old again.'

Ruby was jiggling on the spot with her legs crossed. 'You were acting like a child. You might find the three kayakers are not quite the men in your dreams. Oak, I can't talk, I have to go!'

Ruby waddled into the woods as I shuffled through the mist towards the kayakers, and on closer inspection, I could see Ruby had a point. The kayakers were about fifteen.

'Excuse me, lads, sorry to disturb you. Has anyone seen my wand? It flew over your heads a few seconds ago.'

The kayakers about-turned, looked me up and down and burst

into spontaneous laughter. My rouge-red cheeks glowed even brighter. One of the kayakers leant over an orange kayak, retrieved my wand, and swished it around in front of me.

'Look lads, it's Harry Potter's cousin. Anyone got a mirror? I think she's had a make-up malfunction.'

What a rude boy. Before I had chance to reply, their boom of laughter drew the attention of a much older kayaker.

'Lads, what's so funny? I could hear your cackling from the riverbank.' He said in a deep croaky voice that sounded like rubbing with sandpaper.

The younger kayaker hid the wand behind his back. 'Nothing, Woody, having a bit of fun with a fairy godmother.'

'I have eyes in the back of my head. Now please give the wand back to the lady and apologise.' He said as his voice tapered out at the end.

The younger kayaker passed the wand back to me. 'Sorry, your make-up doesn't look like you've had a make-up malfunction.' He paused and giggled as another lad joined the conversation.

'More like she fell headfirst into a tin of paint.' The lads snorted with laughter and ran into the woods.

Woody twiddled his beard and pushed his sunglasses back. 'Apologies about the lads, they're very rude. Sorry about my voice, I spent yesterday shouting at them on the river, so I'm a bit hoarse today. I'm not sure I'll have any voice left by the end of today.'

'There's no need for me to wave my wand and turn them into toads, it looks like I've already succeeded. Perhaps instead I can wish for your voice to return, though a gargle in lemon and honey might work better!'

Woody chuckled and lifted his orange kayak onto his shoulder. 'Sounds perfect. Maybe you could cast a magic spell to get them down the river unscathed. Though after their comments, a dunking in the river would be more appropriate.'

I twirled the wand in the air. 'Wish granted. You can choose who has the first dunking. Enjoy your paddle.'

'Thanks. I hope it's not me.' Woody waved and headed towards the river.

Ruby hobbled out of the mist. 'I see you got your wand back, are you ready yet?'

'Yes, Mr Frosty is getting impatient.'

'Oak, has anyone ever said you have a screw loose?'

'Yep, you, all the time. Come on, pudding, we have a river to paddle.'

Chapter Three
Tinker Bell and Cupid

Milling around the riverbank were a mixture of Christmas characters, including my friend Nick dressed as Santa Claus. To be honest, he didn't need to dress up, he already had the long white beard, large round belly and a Mrs Claus at his beck and call.

We climbed over the canoes and heard the roar of the river before witnessing a torrent of turbulent water, the colour of cappuccino. A heaviness washed over me as I stepped away speechless and gazed at Ruby, who was hugging a tree like a security blanket.

'Not sure about this, Oak, the current's quite fast.'

'You're telling me! Look at the colour, I'd rather spend the day drinking cappuccino than swimming in it.' I spun around and addressed the group.

'Are you sure we should be paddling today? The river is awfully high.'

A voice drifted from behind me. 'Of course, what are you? A chicken?'

Clucking Trent, dressed as a reindeer, proceeded to prance around me flapping his arms, followed by Perry, a well-fed gobbling turkey past its sell-by-date.

The reindeer bellowed, 'Oakley is a chicken!'

The turkey looked me up and down. 'It looks like Oakley's had a bit of a glitch in the wardrobe and make-up department.'

I ignored the reindeer and frowned at the turkey, a close family friend who should have grown up by now. Worries about the velocity of the river were put on ice while my eyes followed the reindeer and turkey as they meandered back to the canoe trailer.

'Trent's so immature. I can't believe he danced around me clucking like a chicken.'

'He's only trying to get your attention. Two minutes ago you were waving a magic wand and dancing like a fairy. You're like two peas in a pod.'

'I'd rather be a runner bean than a pea in a pod with Trent.'

'Oakley, you do make me laugh, why a runner bean?'

'Because anywhere Trent's been, I'm running as far away as possible.'

Ruby chuckled. 'He's more mature since he accepted the job as a PE teacher. You must admit, he's rather cute and handsome, he looks a bit like Danny from McFly.'

I guess to an outsider he was tall and muscular with dark brown hair and cheeky blue eyes, though I hardly noticed; he was still the annoying boy who'd teased me since I was four years old.

'Trent is more like an annoying fly from the muck heap. Buzzes around your head, getting into your hair, and when you thought you'd seen the last of it, the familiar buzzing starts again and all you want to do is swot it. Come on, that's enough about Trent, let's drop the canoes at the water's edge.'

We portaged our canoes above everyone's heads and left them beside the edge of the river.

'Oak, does the water look even higher to you?'

'Not sure, though it looks more like a latte than a cappuccino. Let's wait and see what Nick says. It takes at least at hour to complete the car shuttle; the river level may have dropped by the time we return.'

'Okay.'

Trent and Perry returned from the trailer carrying their canoes.

They positioned them either side of me, and I wondered what nonsense was about to spout out of their mouths as they began talking over my head.

'Dude, the waters stonking, I'm gonna get the stuffing knocked out of me.' said Perry.

'Time to rename you Paxo Perry,' honked Trent as he readjusted his antlers.

Paxo Perry made a gobbling noise as loud as the river. 'What about Oakley?'

Trent looked up and using hand gestures encouraged his audience. 'Erm … what shall we call Oakley?' He paused awaiting a reaction.

'What about the Sugar Plum Fairy?' shouted an angel.

Trent hesitated. 'Let me think. No, the Sugar Plum Fairy is too bitter and devious.'

'How'd you know that? Next, you'll be telling us you like ballets,' said Paxo Perry.

Trent sniggered. 'Bud, how'd you know the Sugar Plum Fairy was in a ballet?'

'Missus took me to see *The Nutcracker*. Thought Sugar Plum would be a cracking name for Oakley.'

Trent crossed his legs, squirming. 'Think I'll call Oakley Tinker Bell, who is a much kinder fairy.'

I looked up while clipping a stern painter. 'Trent, I'm gonna name you Prancer, as you're always prancing around.'

'Nope, he's Rudolph. If he doesn't behave, someone might give him a shiny red nose.' said Paxo Perry as he pulled out a feather.

Nick, alias Santa Claus, ambled down and joined in our conversation. 'No, he's Dasher, by the expression on Oakley's face he should make a run for it.'

Trent stood up, smirking, enjoying all the attention. 'You're all wrong. I'm Cupid, though you peasants can call me the god of love.'

The group groaned as Trent ducked, avoiding the throw bags hurtling towards him.

Watching angels, Sam and Simon, swigging from the hipflask, didn't appear politically right, though what did today?

Once again, I addressed the group. 'If the river level keeps rising, we're going to be shouting "watch out for the sheep and cows" instead of rocks and trees.'

'Listen, everyone, it's Tinker Bell, the voice of doom. Don't worry if you swim, I'll jump in and save you.'

'I've never swum in the Lower Dart and have no intention of changing my track record. You should have dressed up as Peter Pan rather than Cupid, as you've never grown up.'

'Erm ... Peter Pan, then you can be my Tinker Bell.' Trent's eyes sparkled as he winked at me, or maybe it was because another throw bag hit him in the face. I clasped my hands together; he was so irritating and always had an answer for everything.

Angel Sam passed the hipflask to Angel Simon. 'Trent, watch Oakley doesn't wave her wand and turn you into a frog.'

Simon slurped the contents. 'Bet Oakley has kissed a lot of frogs, maybe she'd settle for Peter Pan while she's waiting for her Prince Charming.'

I gulped, trying to think of a witty comeback.

'Looks like Oakley has a frog in her throat,' chuckled Paxo Perry.

'Ooh, wouldn't I like to be that frog.' croaked Trent.

Nick clambered over the canoes and sneaked something into Trent's hand. Trent sauntered towards me and held his hand above my head.

'Tinker Bell, look above you, I have a piece of mistle-toad, fancy a quick snog?'

He really was the most annoying and exasperating man I had ever known.

'Forgive me for declining the offer. Not every amphibian turns into a prince, some will forever remain toads.'

'I ribbit somewhere that Oakley's favourite food is toad-in-the-hole,' gobbled Paxo Perry.

With his hands on his thighs, Trent leant forward cackling. 'I'd give anything to be the toad-in-the-hole.'

Nick stepped forward. 'Will you lot stop your ribbiting, Trent, I've toad you before, stop bugging Oakley. I'd suggest you hop along and Kermit yourself to getting ready.'

Once again, everyone dissolved into laughter while I trudged back to my car. As my boot door swung open a familiar voice sounded from behind me.

'All right, sis? Am I glad to see you,' shouted my brother Flynn who was dressed as an elf riding on Santa's shoulders.

'Hi Flynn, love the outfit.' I twiddled my mock fairy legs in the air. 'Seems we had the same idea.'

'Cool legs! Not sure about the make-up though. I have a bit of a problem behind me.' Flynn twisted and revealed two, four-foot sparkly Christmas trees.

'Surprise! Hi Auntie Oakley. Mum's spending Christmas with boring Billy the boyfriend so she dropped us off in the lay-by,' said Poppy as she wrapped her arms around me.

'Sorry, sis, I told the girls they could stay with you tonight as I'm going out with the lads and staying at the YHA.'

Blossom spun around. 'Do you like our costumes?'

'They're amazing. You both look very festive. Why don't you say hello to Ruby and Perry?'

'Okay,' said the girls as they scaled the rocks.

I turned to Flynn. 'Of course the girls can stay with me, though I'm not sure they should be paddling today, have you seen the height of the river?'

'Not yet, you've seen how excited they are, I can't tell them they can't paddle.'

'Why not? You'd rather two eight-year-olds drowned?'

'Oh, don't be such a drama queen, look around, they're better paddlers than everyone else. Besides, if they were to swim there's plenty of people to rescue them. You worry too much, sis.'

I spun around, glancing at our friends. 'I think you have more confidence in everyone's abilities than me.'

'If it makes you feel better, one can paddle with you and the other with me.'

'Okay, though I can't say I'm happy they're paddling. You'd better put their bags in my car. Mum has given me this lunchbox for you, she's included her homemade sausage rolls and shortbread. You do have a way of twisting Mum around your little finger.'

Flynn pulled my fairy plaits. 'I guess it's a mum-and-sons thing. We'll always be her little boys, and you'll always be our little sis. You take the lunchbox in your canoe, and you can share it with the girls.' He waved at the girls. 'Poppy, please will you paddle with Auntie Oakley, and Blossom, you're with me.'

Poppy had her bossy head on. 'No, Dad, it's sorted. I'm paddling with Santa Claus. Blossom is paddling with Perry, he's funny, Dad, he's dressed up as a turkey and keeps flapping his arms and making gobbling noises.'

Flynn waved to Paxo Perry, his best mate and the girls' godfather. 'He does look rather silly, doesn't he? If you're sure it's okay with them, then it's fine by me.'

Nick returned from the riverbank rubbing his hands. The expression on his face was similar to when he opened his lunchbox and found Mrs Claus had swopped his Cornish pasty for rice crackers, and his hipflask for a Brussels sprout and broccoli smoothie. She left a note saying it would give him more energy and wind in his sails. It certainly did the job!

'Gather round, everyone. As you can see the river is quite high. It's not in flood and will have dropped off and run clear by the time we return from the car shuttle. Earlier, I thought about cancelling, however, I think most of you are capable of paddling at this level, though I still have doubts about a few. I'd like the less experienced paddlers to double up with someone more experienced. It's going to be a rollercoaster of a ride and most of the drops will have been washed out. It's a case of sitting tight, sticking to the middle of the river, and keeping an eye out for submerged rocks. Follow the canoe in front; unless of course it's upside down, then you can practise your rescuing skills. Trent, Ruby, I would prefer it if you both paddled with someone more experienced.'

Ruby wandered towards me. 'Oak, I was hoping Nick was going to call it off rather than telling me to double up with someone.'

'Paddle with me, if it becomes too gnarly, we'll get off and take the girls too. Rubes, watch out, Trent's heading our way.'

'Tinker Bell, as Nick said we need to double up, you can kneel in front of me, and I'll keep an eye on you behind.'

Nick piped up. 'Trent, did you say you're keeping an eye on Oakley's behind?'

An army of quivering shoulders were trying to suppress their laughter until the muffled chorus of sniggering erupted. There was no way I was paddling with Trent.

'Nick told you to double up, not me, anyway, Ruby is paddling with me.'

Nick slipped down the rocks and joined us. Ruby, I think it would be better if you paddled with Flynn. Trent you can be Oakley's bow paddler in her canoe.'

Trent's face had the appearance of a severe bout of constipation. 'What's wrong with paddling my canoe?'

'Sorry, Trent, Oakley's canoe is better for tandem paddling.'

'Why the bow?' Trent questioned like a spoiled five-year-old.

'You'll be the engine and provide the power, although you won't need much today. Oakley can be the stern paddler, keep you in a straight line, or maybe I should say straight and narrow.'

Paxo Perry creased over laughing. 'Looking at Oakley's face, stern paddler is quite appropriate. There's no way Trent is going to bow down to anything. And as for keeping the canoe in a straight line, Trent's going to drive Oakley round the bend.'

Gritting my teeth I growled, 'I'm not paddling with Trent! Tandem paddlers are meant to paddle in harmony. Trent's not going to listen to me, this'll be a disaster.'

Trent glared at me with his hands on his hips. 'I have paddled a canoe before.'

Paxo Perry shook his head while chewing his lower lip. 'Yeah mate, in a swimming pool.'

Trent wagged a finger in Paxo Perry's direction. 'Dude, the wave machine was working!'

'Anyone want to swap? I already have a bow paddler,' I pleaded gazing at Mr Frosty the Snowman sitting proudly in the bow of my canoe.

'Nope,' came a unanimous reply.

'Why can't Flynn and Trent paddle together?'

'Because I'd end up tipping him out, sis, you're far more patient than me.'

'Thanks, Flynn, now I'm the one who is likely to be tipped out.'

'Sis, don't be a sourpuss. We know you love Trent, and you never swim. So, what's the problem?'

With my lips drawn in, and hands on my hips, I snarled at my annoying brother. 'I do not love Trent. He is the most annoying man I have ever known.'

'Yeah, yeah, yeah, sis, whatever.' said Flynn as he gave me a brotherly push.

Chapter Four
Tinkering Under the Bonnet

We returned from the car shuttle to see everyone doing star jumps; talk about ten lords a-leaping! Santa Claus waved his arms and with every bounce, his huge imitation belly smashed into his face. I almost had my eye taken out by Trent's antlers. Ruby lost her footing and rolled down the bank taking out Paxo Perry, who fell backwards knocking over the angels. Two little Christmas trees jumped up and down sending baubles zooming in every direction.

Having warmed up enough, I retreated to the Beast, secured my dry bags, and moved Mr Frosty to the middle. Trent followed me and threw two dry bags over my head into the bow.

'I can't see over Mr Frosty, so you'll need to let me know if you see any rocks. Remember any draw or pry strokes you make to manoeuvre the Beast; I will follow and try and keep the Beast in a straight line.' I said surprised at my assertiveness.

Trent stood to attention and saluted me. 'Yes ma'am.' He relaxed and inquired, 'What strokes? By the way, I have been kayaking for years, I'm not a complete novice.'

'The Beast hasn't got a spraydeck, if it fills with water, it will feel like paddling a bathtub.'

'Now there's a dream I can't get out of my head; imagine us lying in a bath together.'

'Sounds more like a nightmare to me. Remember, when paddling tandem we need to paddle in unison and complement each other.'

Trent rubbed his head. 'I've never understood women, now you want me to pay you compliments. By the way, your hair looks lovely and your bum— '

'Not that sort of compliment, you knucklehead! We need to synchronise our paddling. Not too fast, and no sudden strokes or else we'll turn sideways, capsize, and Trent ...'

'Yes, Tinker Bell.'

'Communication is very important.'

'Well, if you stopped rabbiting, I might get a word in edgeways!'

'You really do know how to push my buttons.'

'Not all of them, I'm still trying to find the mute button.'

'I'd like to press the power button and turn you off.'

'You could never turn me off, Tink. You turn me on too much.'

Nick was ambling back to his canoe. 'Can't you two ever get on? Remember, tandem paddlers make their canoe dance and glide down the river, like a swan from *Swan Lake*.'

Paxo Perry stepped into his canoe shaking his head and laughing. 'What a load of rubbish. They're going to be more like the ugly ducklings.'

Trent waved his finger at Perry. 'Don't forget, Paxo, reindeer and fairies can fly through the waves, unlike big fat turkeys. Now, as I'm the power in the engine, I must be firing on four strokes, right?'

'No, mate, you're a reconditioned model, hoping to fire on four strokes but only managing two. Looks like you could do with a good service,' chirped Nick.

'No reconditioning here, Santa, classic vintage model. Though a winter service wouldn't go amiss, it was a demanding summer. Tinker Bell, fancy finely tuning my engine?'

Nick replied before words escaped my mouth. 'Oakley's not into vintage models, I'm sure she'd prefer a turbocharged sports model accelerating from nought to sixty in under four seconds.'

'Not a problem, Santa, pretty sure I can perform in under four seconds,' said Trent.

Paxo shouted from his canoe, 'Mate, heard you didn't last that long! Have you asked Oakley to check your undercarriage and make sure your piston is in working order?'

'My parts are in excellent working order, but she's welcome to tinker with my piston anytime.'

'Mate, by the look of Oakley's face, she's blown a gasket and is about to throttle you,' replied Flynn.

Watching me for a reaction, the group erupted into spontaneous laughter. I was about to retaliate when we were interrupted by Ruby.

'Remember, everyone, there's a prize for the first swimmer.'

'What's the prize, Rubes?' Trent hollered.

'Something that will come in handy if you swim again!'

Trent attempted to climb into the Beast while I held onto the gunwales.

'That's one prize I've never won, and I intend on keeping my losing streak.' I said.

Trent sniggered. 'There'd be nothing losing about you streaking, Tink.'

Accidentally on purpose, the gunwales slipped from my hands, causing Trent to lose his balance and step back onto the embankment.

'Oops, sorry Trent, I seem to have butterfingers, and the only thing I'm losing is my mind for agreeing to paddle with you.'

'Hold the canoe steady, woman!'

Nick stood above us sniggering. 'Trent, you seem to be having a problem getting your leg over.'

'Tell me about it, Santa. If Tinker Bell stopped toying with me, I might get both legs over!'

Trent paused and glared at my two huge dry bags and lunchbox. 'We're not paddling for a week! How much kit have you got?'

'Enough to cover every eventuality. What are you moaning about? You have two dry bags!'

'My two are pint-sized!'

'I'd guessed as much, though I'd keep that to yourself, Trent! And if you're not happy, jump ship!'

'No jumping ship here, I can't think of anyone else I'd rather paddle with.'

'Please, don't make me laugh, no one else would have you!'

'Ah, you love me really.'

Chapter Five
Love With A Rock

Daylight gleamed beneath us as we flew over wave after wave. When Trent ducked, a deluge of freezing water nearly drowned me.

Pushing my fairy plaits over my shoulders, I hollered, 'Trent, we need to slow down!'

Trent peered over his shoulder. 'Why? This is so much fun.'

'Because I'm going to need a snorkel and mask at this rate!' I was wasting my breath, as for the umpteenth time Trent plunged his paddle into the waves. I drained another bailer of water over the gunwales. 'Trent, slow down, I can't steer and bail at the same time!'

'I thought women were multiskilled?'

There was no time to reply as I spotted the tip of a submerged rock. Dropping my bailer, I back paddled. 'Trent, river left.'

Trent plunged his paddle into a wave. 'River what?'

'Left!' I bellowed, as we were magnetised towards the line of rapids.

I unhooked my feet from under the seat and peered over the top of a deflated Mr Frosty.

'Reverse ferry glide!' I screamed. 'Trent, reverse ferry glide, we're heading straight towards a rock.'

'You what?' Were the last words that escaped Trent's mouth. The Beast performed an emergency stop as it hit the rock, and although Trent remained seated, I wasn't so lucky. Like a cork being released from a bottle of champagne, I was propelled over his head. Gripping my paddle with my left hand, and with my right hand trailing behind, I resembled a cross between Superman and a flying squirrel. Seconds later, a humungous splosh echoed as I entered a torrent of freezing water. I gasped for air as the numbing cold gripped my heart. With my tutu skirt wrapped over my head, my only sense was hearing, and my ears were picking up an impending deafening roar in the distance. With my arms and legs tangled like spaghetti, I managed to unravel them with seconds to spare before a huge wave swallowed me. It spat me out and spiralled me towards a rock in the middle of the river. I threw my body over the top of the rock and clung fast like a limpet, praying the force of the water didn't reveal a knickerless bottom. Why oh, why, hadn't I worn my dry suit?

I crawled onto the top of the rock which formed a love-hate relationship with me, and it was going to take a lot of persuasion for us to ever part company. Voices resonated behind, and every time I twizzled my head, my fairy plaits slapped me across my face.

A croaky voice hollered, 'Swimmer on the rock, are you waiting for the canoeists to rescue you?'

What the hell did he think I was doing, waiting for a number ten bus? On swivelling my head, I let out a deep breath. Paddling towards me were the four kayakers from the magic wand incident, and just like my daydream, three zoomed past without stopping.

'Hi, grab the end of my kayak and I'll tow you in,' said Woody the fourth kayaker.

Who was he kidding? There was no way I was going be dragged down the river with my dry trousers around my ankles while exposing my nether regions! Woody paddled past me and broke out into the next eddy. He scaled the embankment with feline grace and sprinted along the bank towards me. He was impressively fit, and despite wearing a dry suit, I could see the outline of a toned physique.

Above the roar of the river, Woody called, 'Miss Fairy, get ready to catch the throw bag.'

Without speaking, I released my grip on the rock and caught the throw bag.

'Brilliant.' He sounded relieved. 'Everything's going to be fine. I'll pull you in.'

Despite having a husky voice it was composed with a hint of assertiveness, which triggered a sense of calm within me. Bewitched by his powers, I unshackled myself from the rock and floated into the fast-moving current. Swiftly, the line became taught, and with the strength of Goliath, Woody hauled me into the eddy. With one hand he grappled with the back of my buoyancy aid, and with the other he swept me off my feet, as I clung onto my dry trousers!

Woody helped me to my feet. 'Are you ok?'

For once I was speechless; what did I look like? My sodden, or sodding, fairy legs had stretched to at least four feet long and water trickled out of my nose. My teeth were chattering and my whole body was shaking; to be honest, I didn't have a lot going for me. I gazed up and noticed his lips, as soft as petals. Overcome with emotion, I wanted to throw my arms around his neck and kiss him, but the respectable side of me replied, 'I'm fine, thank you.'

'You look freezing! I'll find something to warm you up.'

Images sprung into my head of Woody searching for his emergency bothy shelter, pulling it over us and sharing body heat before I became hypothermic. Though, disappointment prevailed as he handed me a fleece.

'Why don't you jump up and down while I find you a thermal blanket.'

A few minutes later, he wrapped me tightly in the blanket, removed my helmet, pulled a woolly hat over my ears, and handed me a pair of thermal gloves.

'Better?' he enquired, as he passed me a towel to wipe my face.

'Toasty, thanks,' I murmured as warm tears of shock streamed down.

'No worries.' He handed me a cup of hot chocolate and smiled. 'I have to say you're the first fairy I've ever rescued. Couldn't you have cast a spell with your magic wand?'

'Why didn't I think of that as I was catapulted into the river?' I said throwing my fairy legs over my shoulders. I crossed them behind my neck and let them dangle over the front my buoyancy aid as our eyes connected and we giggled simultaneously.

'That's better – a smile. Seriously though, are you okay?'

'I'm much warmer, thank you.'

Woody held up a large bar of mint crisp chocolate. 'I don't suppose this will make you feel better?'

I removed my gloves, and he passed me the chocolate. Our fingers touched, sending an electrical spark from my fingertips to my toes, although, it could have been a result of the metallic thermal blanket I was wrapped in!

'Thank you so much, you know the way to a woman's heart.' I snapped off a couple of pieces and handed the bar back.

Woody returned it to me. 'Keep it, I think you may need it more than me.' He paused. 'Sorry, that didn't sound right, I wasn't implying you're going to swim again.'

'I don't intend to. Did you see two little girls dressed as hyperactive Christmas trees?'

'Yes, they were having a whale of a time, there seemed to be a lot of laughter.'

'The hipflask is responsible for that! The lads are on a Christmas jolly, leaving their partners to run around trying to finalise everything for Christmas.'

'That explains the laughter. I love Christmas shopping, though keep that to yourself; wouldn't do my street cred any good. How are you feeling now?'

'Roasting, I'm wearing three thermal tops under this get-up. My ego's a bit bruised though, it's years since I swam. It'll be all over social media before we're off the river.'

'Tell everyone you're Santa's new helper and were practising your flying skills!'

I removed the thermal blanket, folded it, and passed it back to Woody.

'By the time everyone gets off the water with the empty hipflask they'll probably believe that story, although with my flying skills, I wouldn't be surprised if Santa gave me the sack.'

Woody's sniggers were drowned out by the drone of an approaching group of noisy canoeists. 'I trust you won't be requiring my services again?' He said.

'I hope not. I'm very grateful you rescued me. I'd return the favour, though doubt you ever swim.'

'Never! Although if I did, I wouldn't mind being rescued by a pretty fairy with a face smudged in the colours of the rainbow.' He grinned as he stuffed his dry bag behind his seat.

'Oh no! I must have smudged my make-up with the towel. Are my false eyelashes still intact?'

He slid into the cockpit and secured his spraydeck. 'Yes, though your yellow, and blue eye shadow has smudged into your red cheeks, looks very artistic. Stay safe, Miss Fairy, and keep your little Christmas trees safe too.' And with that final word, he paddled into the distance.

Chapter Six
Santa Train

'Tinker Bell, you, okay?' Trent shouted attempting to ferry glide across the river. Paxo Perry and Poppy paddled over with ease, closely followed by Nick and Blossom.

'What's taken you so long?'

Paxo Perry stepped out of his canoe and said, 'When you performed an amazing exit, old Cupid over there turned your canoe sideways into the angels. They capsized, taking out the elf, and Christmas pudding.'

'Are Flynn and Ruby all right?'

'Yes, the girls rescued them.'

'Auntie Oakley, everyone was laughing so much that they couldn't get out of the river,' said Blossom.

Poppy giggled and pointed to my fairy legs. 'What happened to your fairy legs? They look like aliens' legs, and your make-up has smudged.'

I rubbed my face with hands. 'The foam stuffing has soaked up so much water my legs have started to grow! The kayaker that rescued me lent me his towel to dry my face, I must have smudged my make-up. Are you both warm enough?'

'We're warm enough, aren't we Poppy?'

'Yeah, though we haven't been swimming. Aren't you cold, Auntie Oakley?'

'I'm fine thanks. Did your mum pack you any snacks or lunch?'

Poppy opened her lunchbox. 'Only crackers and an apple.'

'Is that all? If Trent manages to ferry glide here, there's plenty of food in my lunchbox. For now, here's the remainder of my chocolate.'

'Ooh, mint crisp, our favourite!'

Trent had no intention of joining us, as he edged the bow of the Beast onto the crest of a standing wave. He stood up pretending to play air guitar on his paddle while singing a heavy rock song about a sinking feeling; he was such a show-off.

'Perry, please can I borrow your canoe for a few minutes?'

'Depends on what you're up to.'

'Trent is singing about a sinking feeling, and any minute now he's going for a swim, I'd like to offer my assistance.'

'In helping him swim or rescuing him?'

I raised my eyebrows and screwed up my nose. 'What do you think?'

Paxo Perry chuckled. 'Be my guest!'

I hopped into Perry's canoe, ferry-glided across the river, and positioned myself directly behind Trent. With a little nudge, there was an almighty splash as he tumbled out of the Beast and grabbed the gunwales on Perry's canoe.

'Handy you were behind me, Tink. I was having problems getting my angle right.'

'I'd heard a rumour about that. Hold on to the gunwales while I reach the painter on my canoe.'

Trent the showman always had to do things his own way. He let go of the gunwales and the current whisked him down stream into the next eddy where he scrambled up the embankment. With the Beast in tow, I ferry-glided back across the river. I climbed out of Perry's canoe, and hauled in the Beast, as Ruby approached gripping two black bin liners.

'Oakley, do you want the good news or the bad news first?'

'Good news first please, Rubes.'

'Congratulations, it was a unanimous vote, you've won first prize in the fancy dress competition. It had something to do with positioning your legs behind your ears! Here's a voucher for your favourite pizza takeaway.'

'Thanks, Rubes, that's brilliant, what's the bad news?'

Ruby handed me the black bags. 'You've also won the prize for the first swimmer. You have to wear these for the rest of the paddle.'

'Thanks, that was one prize I was hoping to avoid.' I groaned as I opened the bag to find a pair of inflatable unicorn armbands and rubber ring adorned with the head of a unicorn. My audience were in stitches as Trent rushed towards me, pushed the armbands onto my arms and yanked the rubber ring over my head.

Poppy stood behind me. 'Your wings are in the way; you'll have to stand in it.'

Trent tugged the rubber ring back over my shoulders. 'Tinker Bell, I'll deflate it before you stand inside.'

After Trent released the air, I stepped inside the rubber ring before he twisted it up to my tutu. He then knelt down and reinflated it using his surplus hot air.

'Auntie Oakley, you look like you're riding a unicorn,' said Poppy giggling.

Blossom squealed, 'Oh, Auntie Oakley you look so funny. Your make-up matches the colour of the unicorn.'

I caught sight of a circle of lads peering into Trent's phone. 'What's so funny?'

A sonic boom of laughter exploded from the lads as Flynn passed Trent's phone back to him.

'Sis, you don't want to know!'

Alarm bells rang in my head as I marched towards them and snatched Trent's phone. The recording was of the back of me and every few seconds Trent peeped out from under my tutu. His face mirrored a beetroot as he gasped for air and a grin spread across his face quicker than butter melting at one hundred degrees.

Poppy meandered towards me. 'Why's everyone looking at Trent's phone?'

'Nothing for you to worry about. Please sit down and I'll pour you a cup of hot chocolate. Help yourself to one of Nan's homemade sausage rolls.'

'We'd rather look at the phone,' said Poppy.

I raised my voice. 'Poppy, that's not like you to turn down a sausage roll. Now please sit down.'

'Okay.'

'Girls, here's your hot chocolate. I'm off to find the ladies, don't get up to any mischief while I'm gone.'

Poppy stuffed a sausage roll into her mouth and spluttered, 'Us? Of course not.'

I traipsed along the riverbank in search of a secluded ladies, though returned crossing my legs.

Trent pointed to a huge oak tree at the top of the hill. 'Tinker Bell, climb to the top of the hill, no one will see you behind that old oak tree.'

'Thanks,' I said, though I trusted Trent about as much as I trusted Ruby to stop fantasising about jumping into bed with every guy that smiled at her. The oak tree would have to suffice as I couldn't hold on much longer.

When I reached the tree, I attempted to remove the unicorn rubber ring, but it was tangled in the back of my tutu skirt. With time of the essence, I yanked my dry trousers and thermal leggings down and felt a wave of relief while squatting behind the tree. A penetrating gust of icy wind blew through my legs causing me to shiver; boy was it cold in the nether regions. Blimey, how much water had I drunk? I must have swallowed half the river! Ominous black clouds gathered in the distance as a ribbon of white, ragged clouds spiralled into the horizon. I reached out towards the tree as the ground began to shudder, and a rumble of thunder boomed. Crikey, what was that high-pitched shrill in the distance?

'Oh, come on, for goodness' sake, stop weeing,' I said to myself.

Then to my utter astonishment from within the ragged clouds was the silhouette of – no! Really? Why was Thomas the Tank Engine chugging towards me?

A sudden coldness spread throughout my body as the voice in my head screamed, I thought the steam line was closed for winter! In a frantic panic, I grappled with my trousers, lost my balance and tumbled headfirst into a molehill. For a second I lay motionless, not daring to look over my shoulder. Talk about being caught with your pants around your ankles, though in my case it was lack of pants! Right now I wished I were a mole and could tunnel underground, or maybe I could impersonate a hedgehog, curl up into a ball and no one would notice me.

The screams of laughter told another story, as brakes screeched, and the train chugged towards me at a snail's pace. When I peeked over my shoulder, hundreds of children were hanging out of the carriage windows. Santa Claus pulled the whistle and waved. Of course, it was the children's Christmas Santa train. I had two choices: remain lying face-down on the ground until the train chugged into the distance or pull my dry trousers up and run like Usain Bolt. I chose the latter, jumped up, and readjusted my tutu to cover my modesty. I bowed to the little kids snapping photos on their phones and ran down the hill.

The rumbling of the train diminished, and the children's screams faded. Once again, the only sound was the northerly wind whistling through the trees.

On reaching the bottom of the hill, Trent's braying filled my ears to bursting.

'Did Santa wave to you?' he said in a voice like corn exploding into popcorn.

My head felt like it was going to detonate into million pieces.

'You could have told me the Santa train was running today.'

Trent's head was buried in his phone. 'Oops sorry, Tink, forgot about the train.'

'What's so funny? Did you know anyone on the train?' I said, leaning over him trying to catch a glimpse of his phone.

'My brother and his kids, they've already texted me the photos. Look.'

Displayed on his phone was a picture of me lying on my front with my trousers around my ankles. My tutu skirt and fairy legs were tangled in my wings and a unicorn's head was poking out of my bottom. Blimey, surely this day couldn't get any worse!

'Look at the positives,' Trent said and chuckled.

'Positives? You complete doofus, what positives?'

Trent spun around with his phone in full view for everyone to see. 'Doofus, I like it. At least you weren't wearing Bridget Jones knickers.' He paused as everyone crowded around the phone. 'Would you believe it; Tinker Bell has gone commando. I should have named you Miss St Knickerless instead of Tinker Bell.'

'At least I don't think the sun shines out of my own backside. There's so much shining out of yours I'm surprised you don't blind everyone.' With that I sauntered towards the Beast.

Trent roared with laughter as he shouted after me, 'There would never be enough sunshine to melt your icy exterior. You know your problem, you're frigid, and too high and mighty to let anyone near you, except of course Mr Frosty.'

I could feel the tears welling up as I reached the Beast. No, I wasn't going to let Trent get to me. How Flynn could think I even liked Trent let alone loved him was beyond me. I carried Trent's dry bags to the edge of the river and dumped them; he was fortunate I hadn't tossed them in.

'Tinker Bell, don't get your knickers in a twist, oh no, of course you can't.'

'Time for you to jump ship, mate.'

'Who am I going to paddle with now?'

'You can drown for all I care.'

Nick ambled towards Trent. 'I think you have well and truly blown her gasket. You'd better paddle with me, unless you'd prefer to walk.' Nick paused. 'Poppy, would you mind paddling with your auntie please?'

Trent picked his bags up and threw them into Nick's canoe while Poppy ambled towards me with a sheepish look etched across her face.

'Sorry Pops, you don't mind paddling with me, do you?'

She beckoned me to bend down and whispered in my ear: 'No, but we've done a terrible thing.'

'It can't be that bad, surely?'

'It is! Trent let us see the video of him under your tutu skirt.'

'Do you two ever do as you're told? I asked you not to look at it.'

Poppy stood astride with her hands on her hips. 'Well, if someone tells you not to do something, don't you want to do it?'

'That's not the point. I'm an adult and you're a child and you shouldn't have looked at it, we will forget it for now.'

'That's not all! While we were looking at Trent's phone, he left his phone with us and went to look at Nick's phone. A text beeped and I know we shouldn't have looked at it, but we did. We think it maybe crude as everyone was laughing at Nick's phone.'

'What text?'

Both girls held out their little fingers. 'We're only going to tell you if you pinkie promise not to tell anyone, especially Trent and Dad,' said Blossom.

I held out my hand. 'Okay I promise.'

'Have you watched "Send to All" on *Michael McIntyre's Big Show*?'

'Oh my god, what have you two done?'

'Trent has had lots of girlfriends, hasn't he? said Blossom.

'Yes, loads.'

'We wanted his current girlfriend to see what he is like, but we didn't know which one she was, so we pressed send to all. We think we've sent the text to you as well.'

Blossom smiled and said, 'Don't worry, no one will know it's you, as you can only see the back of you.'

I was dumbfounded. I reached for my phone and opened the text with a photo of Trent on his knees peeping from under my tutu skirt. Below the photo the text read:

After blowing his doe at the casino, Santa's reindeer, Cupid, erected his unicorn head while going down in the fairy's garden!

Oh my word, who wrote that? Everyone on Trent's phone must have seen it by now. It was time to make a sharp exit before Trent's contacts replied, and the effluent hit the fan!

'Are we in a lot of trouble, Auntie Oakley?' said Poppy.

'You shouldn't have sent it, though it's no more than Trent deserved, at least it doesn't show my face. I think it might be a good idea if we leave, as any minute now Trent's phone is going to start beeping and the two of you will be in a lot of trouble. Do you fancy walking across the fields to the road and going to the coffee shop?'

Poppy jumped up and down on the spot.

'Ooh, will you buy us a hot chocolate with cream and marsh-mallows?'

'Only if you're good.'

'We're always good.'

'That's debatable.'

Poppy giggled. 'We love acting, pretending we're cold will be easy.'

Nick strolled towards us as the girls jumped on the spot.

'Are you two cold?'

Poppy giggled while waving her branches up and down. 'Don't worry about us, Santa, Christmas trees are used to not feeling their limbs in the winter.'

Nick raised his eyebrows and chortled. 'I think I'd better have a word with your dad.'

He returned with Flynn and Ruby.

'Nick says you're both cold,' said Flynn.

Poppy winked at Blossom. 'We're fine, Dad.'

'Blossom is shivering! Time to get off the water. We can follow the footpath back to the road and walk to the car park.'

'And then what, Dad? You didn't drive here,' said Poppy.

'Of course not.' Flynn twisted around. 'Maybe Auntie Oakley can walk with you to the road, and I'll meet up with you later.'

'Sounds like a good idea of yours, Dad. Shall we meet you in the coffee shop?'

'Sounds good. Is that okay with you, sis? You can't carry your canoe on your own, I'll ask Trent to help.'

Both girls squealed, 'No Dad!'

'You can't carry Auntie Oakley's canoe across the fields on your own.'

Ruby peered into her phone. 'They won't have to. I'm getting off the river too.'

I quizzed Ruby. 'Are you sure?'

Ruby held her phone up. 'Yep! After the text I've received from Trent, I don't want to be anywhere near him.'

Oops, it appeared Ruby was one his contacts too.

Flynn returned to his canoe with Ruby and handed her two dry bags. They lingered a bit longer than usual. I'd have to keep an eye on those two.

'Bye, Dad, see you in the coffee shop,' shouted Blossom.

Poppy pretended to do the breaststroke. 'I know you enjoy doing this, Dad, try not to do it in the river.'

'Cheeky monster! Keep warm, and no mischief, and under no circumstances are you to sing, or you'll scare the animals away.'

'Okey-dokey, Dad, whatever,' shouted Poppy.

Now all we had to do was follow the river, find the path through the forest, cross a railway line, amble across several fields, and find the road. How hard could that be?

Chapter Seven
Woody

What did we look like? A Christmas pudding leading the way, two mini-Christmas trees clinging to either side of the Beast, and a fairy riding a unicorn at the stern. And of course, we couldn't forget a rather deflated Mr Frosty.

'Oakley stop, I can't believe the text message Trent sent me.' Ruby paused, lowered the Beast, and turned her head like an owl. 'You do know where we're going, don't you?'

'Ignore the text. Have I ever got us lost?'

'I can't ignore the text, and yes, you've got us lost heaps of times.' Ruby dropped the bow and began typing her reply. 'There, that'll show him, I've replied—'

Poppy butted in: 'You haven't sent it, have you?'

'About to.'

Poppy let go of the middle of the Beast and tried to grab Ruby's phone.

'No! Don't send it.'

Ruby raised her phone above her head. 'Whyever not?'

'Because we sent it, not Trent. Nick sent it to him, and we forwarded it to his contacts.'

Ruby gazed in my direction. 'So he didn't make up the rhyme about you?'

I stepped towards her. 'No. Maybe it was Nick or Perry. You know what they're like.'

Ruby smirked. 'So Trent's not as bad as I thought.'

'He is, despite not sending the text.'

Ruby held her phone up. 'Okay I'll delete it. Come on I'm dying for a slice of chocolate cake in the coffee shop.'

After trekking half a mile along the river, Blossom dropped the Beast and pointed towards the embankment.

'What's that caught in the trees at the bottom of the ravine?'

Poppy let go of the Beast and pushed Blossom out of her way.

'I can't see anything, what yer looking at?'

'An orange kayak.'

'Girls, stay with Ruby, and I'll scramble down and check.'

While descending, a clatter of rocks tumbled behind me hitting the backs of my legs. I peered over my shoulder.

'Don't you girls ever do as you're told?'

'No,' they said giggling.

In my most authoritative voice, I said, 'I'm being serious. Please wait here while I check the kayak, and do not move an inch!'

I tried to reach the kayak, but it was out of arms reach and tangled in overhanging willow branches.

Ruby shouted from the top of the ravine, 'Do you need my help, Oak?'

'Yes, thanks Rubes. The kayak is caught in willow branches. I'll send the girls back up, please can you lower the Beast, then I'll paddle to the kayak and untangle it.'

'Okay.'

The girls raced each other to the top and helped Ruby lower the Beast. I paddled to the kayak, untangled it, and tugged it into the Beast. When I paddled back to the shore and stepped out, the girls had traipsed down again.

Poppy leant over the kayak. 'We can't carry it as well as the Beast.'

Blossom climbed over the Beast and lifted the kayak.

'Yes, we can, it's not that heavy, we can carry it between us.'

Despite being twins they rarely agreed on anything.

I pointed upstream. 'Look, there's a kayaker carrying a paddle on the opposite side of the river. It looks like Woody who rescued me.'

Woody spotted us and waved.

'Hi, I wasn't expecting to see the fairy again quite so soon.' Woody paused and chuckled. 'And I see the fairy is now riding a unicorn.'

'Hi, it's my award for being the first swimmer. Unfortunately, I've become attached to it, literally.'

Woody laughed. 'I don't suppose you've seen my orange kayak? I hate to admit it, but I've swum too.'

'Thought you never swam!' I shouted across the river.

'Only on rare occasions when I'm not paying attention. I was surfing a wave when Santa Claus and that reindeer friend of yours landed on top of me. I rolled up and was finished off by a pair of angels at the helm, and if that wasn't enough, a turkey landed on top of them. I bailed out of my kayak and in all the commotion it was swept downstream.'

I lifted the kayak out of the Beast. 'I don't suppose it could be this orange kayak we found in the trees?'

A smile stretched across Woody's face. 'Seriously, you've found my kayak, thank you so much. Where did you find it?'

I pointed to Blossom. 'My mini-Christmas tree spotted it while we were walking back to the road.'

'Is my dry bag behind the seat? I left my car keys in it, and don't have a spare key.'

I reached behind his seat. 'Yes, it's still here.'

Woody gazed at Blossom. 'Thank you, darling, you should have dressed as an angel instead of a Christmas tree, you've saved me a lot of grief. I'll swim over to you.'

I stepped into the Beast. 'No! I'll paddle over to you instead, there's been enough swimmers today.'

'Okay, guess that means we're even. I rescued a pretty fairy, and now she's saving my bacon.'

I couldn't believe it, I thought I'd never see him again. Now all that lay between us was for a fairy to ferry glide across the river.

Woody grinned as I reached the eddy. 'Wow, you made that look easy.'

'I've been paddling a long time. Can you paddle a canoe?'

Woody lifted his kayak out of the Beast. 'Yes, though not as good as you. Don't tell my mates, they think canoeing is for old gits.'

'Canoeing and kayaking is for everyone, though I'm not sure some of my mates could climb into the cockpit of a kayak. I love both as much as each other.'

Voices could be heard as two kayakers approached on the footpath.

'Woody, mate, you found your kayak.'

'Yep, a little Christmas tree spotted it.'

The two kayakers grinned at Blossom and Poppy. 'You're life savers, he was in for some real earbashing if he'd lost his car keys. Hurry up mate, or we're going to be late for the train.'

Woody hitched his kayak onto his shoulder. 'All right, all right, I'm ready.' He handed me two KitKats. 'Please give these to the girls.'

Poppy shouted across the river. 'Thank you, that's our favourite chocolate. We used to have a cat called KitKat.'

Woody grinned. 'Do you know what, when I was your age, I sneaked Snickers bars for breakfast and named my cat Snickers.'

'Woody! Stop chatting up the ladies, everyone's waiting for us.'

'Jeeze, lads, I'm coming! Thank you, ladies, you're my guardian angels.' He waved, before following his mates along the path.

Within minutes of ferry gliding back, Poppy was already washing her chocolate-covered hands in the river.

'Woody was nice wasn't he, Auntie Oakley? Aren't you glad Blossom spotted his kayak?' said Poppy, her mouth stuffed with KitKat.

'I am, now it's getting late, and we'd better get a move on.'

Blossom pointed to my fairy legs. 'The stuffing's come out of one of your legs, and you've lost a shoe.'

'Oh! What a shame, it must have fallen into the river while I was untangling the kayak. Never mind, I'll take my costume off now. Come on, poor Ruby must be fed up, sitting at the top of the ravine.'

We'll collect the dry bags and I'll line the Beast down to the next eddy.'

Blossom was still nibbling her KitKat. 'Why? We can carry it back up.'

'Do you always have to question everything? It's far too difficult to haul the Beast up the ravine.'

Blossom wiped chocolate down one of her branches. 'Why do you need all the bags?'

'The bow needs to be heavier than the stern.'

Poppy shouted from halfway up the ravine. 'Can we line the Beast down?'

'I don't think so, it will be quicker if I do it.'

'Please, we've lined a canoe before, it's like taking your canoe for a walk in the river.'

I hesitated for a moment. What harm could they come to? We were only lining the Beast to the next eddy.

'I guess it's not far, but remember, no fighting.'

Ruby questioned me. 'Oakley are you sure it's a good idea for the girls to line the Beast?'

'They'll be fine, why don't you wait at the next eddy for us.'

Ruby didn't look convinced. 'I guess it will be okay, though I'll take my dry bags with me.'

'No, we need them for ballast.'

Ruby raised her voice. 'You had better not lose them!'

'Don't be silly, of course I am not going to lose them!'

Rather than leaving their dry bags in the Beast, Poppy and Blossom hitched them onto their backs. My confidence was dwindling in their ability to line the Beast.

'What about the lunchbox?' said Poppy as she grasped the stern painter.

'I'll make room for it in my dry bag.'

'Good, we wouldn't want soggy sausage rolls.'

'You're not going to if you line the Beast correctly.'

Blossom gripped the bow painter while I pushed the Beast into the current. Blossom jerked her line.

'Poppy, your line is too long.'

'No, it isn't, your line is too short.'

This continued for at least ten minutes as the Beast glided in and out of the current. Poppy yanked the stern, then dropped the painter shouting, 'I'm not doing this anymore.' She sulked off down the path to join Ruby. Before I could reach the stern painter, Blossom yanked the bow. The Beast swung into the current, hit a rock and began tipping sideways. I grabbed the painter from Blossom, but it was too late, the Beast overturned onto the gunwales.

I screamed down river, 'Ruby, the Beast has capsized.'

Ruby raced up the track and confronted me with her dragon face, a look that was becoming familiar today. She waded into the river and caught the other painter, and we dragged the Beast around a rock and into the eddy.

A feeling of relief spread throughout my body.

'For a minute, Rubes, I thought we'd lost the Beast.'

Ruby's dragon face evaporated as she let out a huge sigh of relief. 'So did I!'

As we up-righted the Beast, her face needed a fire extinguisher to dampen the flames.

'Oakley, where the hell are the dry bags?'

'I'll find them, they can't have gone far. Watch the girls please, Rubes.'

Spurred on by the fear of Ruby skinning me alive, I sprinted back up the ravine in the hope of outrunning the pace of the river. Below me, a huge expanse of white water hurtled through a valley, shrouded in overhanging trees. I continued running until I spotted a fallen conifer spanning the river. Phew! At least the dry bags couldn't have floated any further as the tree was acting as a strainer. I shimmed down to the riverbank, but they were nowhere to be seen.

I backtracked along the ravine towards a crop of rocks where my senses were awoken by the familiar aroma of coffee. Like a mountain goat, I scaled the rock face and peered over the top. Sitting on a rock, holding a cup of coffee in one hand and sausage roll in the other, was

Trent. Nestled beside him were four dry bags, an empty lunchbox and Ruby's flask of coffee. What a toerag, was a polite expression. I stepped forward and snapped a twig, revealing my presence.

Trent twisted around. 'Tinker Bell, what the heck are you doing up here?'

'I trust you enjoyed our lunch, and coffee?'

'Delicious, I'd offer you a cup, but ...' Trent tipped the flask upside down. 'Oops, all gone. The sausage rolls and shortbread were delicious, though next time, could you add a few chocolate drops to the shortbread, or maybe a squeeze of lemon?'

I felt like a tomato cooking on high power in a microwave, and the only words I could conjure were, effing arsehole!

'You've got a nerve! Why aren't you paddling?'

'Nick said I was a liability when I paddled into a kayaker. He told me to walk the rest of the way. I haven't got any lunch as I left it in his canoe, so when four mysterious dry bags floated towards me, it had to be fate as one of them was full of food.'

Gripping hold of a branch I reached over the ledge. 'Didn't you think of phoning someone or searching for the owner? They may have been in trouble in the river.'

'Thought about it, but I've left my phone in Nick's canoe. When I opened one of the mysterious dry bags and it contained everything but the kitchen sink, I knew it had to be yours. So, I sat here waiting for you to find me.'

'I guess you've riffled through my kit?'

'You know me well. Found a nice glittery thong, which I'm keeping as a souvenir.'

My muscles stiffened as I leant over the ledge to give him a piece of my mind.

'You've stolen my thong! Give it back now! Of all the—' were the only words that escaped my lips as the branch snapped sending me spiralling down the embankment and straight into his arms. He caught me with ease, and as her eyes met, we had a moment. What the hell was I thinking? I pushed his arms away and he dropped me like a sack of potatoes into the river. I scrambled to my feet and stuffed everything into the dry bags.

Trent's laughter echoed through the valley, and as I opened my mouth to tell him what I thought, I paused thinking I was wasting my time.

'The earth sure moved for you, Tink. How on earth are you going to carry four dry bags? I'm going your way, need a hand?'

I really wanted to wipe the smugness off his face.

'No thanks. What you mean is ...' I paused and raised my voice. 'You don't know the way back!'

'I do actually. But do you?'

I hitched one bag onto my front and glared at him. 'Yes, I do, and no, you are not walking with us.' I said throwing another dry bag over my shoulder. I gripped the other two in each hand and could feel Trent's eyes boring into the back of my head. No doubt he was waiting for me to fall flat on my face.

He leant back on the rock sniggering. 'Bye, Tink, thanks for lunch, must do it again someday.'

I had a sudden compulsion to push him into the river. However, I resigned my spirit in, bottled my anger, and ignoring him trudged to the top of the ravine. I was relieved to see Ruby and the girls waiting for me.

'Auntie Oakley, you've found them!' exclaimed Blossom.

'Technically, Trent found them, and I found him eating the sausage rolls and drinking Ruby's coffee.'

Poppy giggled. 'We didn't tell you, but I dropped the container of sausage rolls in the dirt. We brushed them off and stuck them back in the container.'

'Poppy! I'm glad Ruby and I didn't eat anymore then.'

Ruby grinned. 'Serves Trent right if he has a bad stomach. Did he say anything about the texts?'

'No, he's left his phone in Nick's canoe, but I have a nasty feeling he'll be trailing us as he doesn't know the way back.'

Ruby glared down her nose at me. 'And we do?'

'Of course! Come on, surely nothing else can go wrong.' I paused and pointed to a path through the forest. 'I bet that path leads us to the railway crossing.'

Ruby grabbed the bow. 'If you knew the way, you wouldn't need to use the word bet.'

'Have faith, Rubes, I've never been lost.'

Ruby shook her head. 'You and your adventures, Oak. One day you are truly going to get us into trouble.'

'Why do you think I'm prepared for every eventuality? Look ahead, thee of little faith, it's the railway crossing. We're nearly back, safe and sound.'

'Erm ... I'll reserve judgement until a large chunk of chocolate cake is sitting in my hand.'

Chapter Eight
Run, Run, Rudolph

Ruby encouraged my tastebuds to tingle at the thought of devouring a slice of cake.

I licked my lips. 'Not long now, girls, can't you smell the aroma of fresh coffee and hot chocolate?'

'Ooh yes,' cried Poppy.

We lifted the Beast over the stile, crossed the railway track, and waited for Ruby to climb over the next stile; however, she froze.

'What's up, Rubes? Why have you stopped?'

'The field is full of cows ... and I hate cows.'

I lowered the stern and ambled around the Beast for a better look. 'Don't worry, Rubes, they're Highland cows, we'll be fine.'

'Look at the size of their horns!'

'I'm sure they'll be friendly; they look like cuddly teddy bears.'

Ruby spun around. 'They don't look that friendly to me! You're right about Trent, he's hiding behind a tree.'

'Is he still wearing his reindeer outfit?'

Ruby peeped over her shoulder. 'He is.'

'Maybe the cows will follow him rather than us.'

'I thought you said they were friendly.'

'They are, though out of curiosity they may follow a reindeer.'

Halfway round the field, Ruby dropped the Beast. 'Oakley, the cows are heading our way. Shall we make a run for it?'

'No, they can outrun us. Girls, remember your dad told you not to sing or it will scare the animals away?'

'Oh yeah, so he did,' said Poppy.

'Do you ever do as you're told?'

Poppy giggled. 'Never!'

Ruby dashed behind me. 'The cows are right behind us; I think now would be a good time for the girls to sing their hearts out.'

'What shall we sing?' said Blossom.

I caught sight of Trent stepping out from behind the tree.

'Seeing as Trent is dressed as a reindeer I think "Run, Run, Rudolph" would be quite appropriate.'

Blossom rubbed her hands together. 'Ooh yes, we love that song.'

As we continued walking and belting out the lyrics, the cows stopped in their stride, and so did Trent. He pretended to play air guitar while standing in the middle of the field. When the cows focused their attention on him, he legged it to towards the top right-hand stile. A few seconds later, like a snooker ball bouncing off the cushion, he ping-ponged back to the left-hand stile. In one almighty leap he cleared the stile, proving reindeer really could fly. The cows spun around, bellowed, and fixed their attention back on us.

Ruby's voice was shaking. 'Oh my goodness, Oakley, what do we do now?'

'Keep walking and sing as loud as you can, we're almost there. Don't worry they're only inquisitive, they won't harm us.'

Blossom screamed: 'Stop! It's a bog. That's why Trent ran to the other stile. Now what do we do?'

I unclipped the stern painter and clipped it to the bow. 'Ruby, lower the Beast please; girls jump in, and we'll drag you across.'

The girls jumped in, and Ruby and I grasped the bow painters.

'Everyone ready?' I shouted.

'Yep,' screamed the girls as Ruby and I sank up to our calves in the bog.

Ruby huffed. 'Oh, for Pete's sake, Oakley, this is not going to work, and now I'm filthy.'

Blossom leant over the side of the Beast and sniggered. 'Ruby, you're almost as funny as Auntie Oakley. Guess what? Dad doesn't mind mud; I overheard him saying to his mates, maybe he should consider going out with filthy women.' Blossom paused and gazed at Ruby. 'Perhaps Dad would like to go out with you.'

Ruby was lost for words as it appeared she was trying not to laugh.

'I'm sure Ruby is just his type of woman. Now back to our little problem, I think the Beast is too heavy with six bags, the lunchbox, and the twins. I'll carry the dry bags and lunchbox to the stile. Once on firmer ground we can slide the Beast across the mud by pulling the painters.'

With the first dry bag secured onto my back, I impersonated a grasshopper while jumping from one clump of grass to the next.

Poppy handed me another. 'This is the final bag, Auntie Oakley, you're doing so well.'

With my legs and back tiring, the grasshopper had metamorphosed into a kangaroo.

'Almost there, girls, one more clump and we're home and dry.'

When I was mid-air, one of the cows let rip a huge bellow. Momentarily, I lost concentration, missed the clump of grass, and landed on my knees. The girls screamed with laughter as they wiped smelly bog water off their faces. With mud dripping down Ruby's face, her dragon impression told a whole different story. As I knelt up and tossed the dry bag towards the stile, my mobile chimed; it was Molly.

I switched my phone to loudspeaker. 'Hi Moll, I'll call you back. I'm on my knees in a slightly awkward position.'

Molly giggled. 'Ooh, any males involved?'

'They smell, pant, snort, and chase after women, so I guess you could say there are males involved.'

Molly giggled. 'Sounds like your brother. I'll be quick, I'm shopping with Isla and my friends.' Molly paused. 'What's that noise? Is everything okay?'

The cows were licking the back of the Beast. The girls screamed and sprung over the bow like a pair of gazelles.

'Sorry, Moll, it's hugely intense, Ruby and I were pulling painters, with six bags and a huge lunchbox.'

Molly shrieked and shouted to the rest to her friends. 'Oakley and Ruby are with Hugh and Lee in tents; a couple of painters they've pulled, who have six-packs and huge lunchboxes.'

We could hear a roar of laughter from Molly's friends.

'Oh my word, Molly, I didn't say that!'

'Oakley, the line crackles every time you speak. Can you have the boys for a few hours tomorrow morning?'

'Yes, fine.'

'Brilliant, thanks. Good luck with the painters, they sound gorgeous. Bye, Oakley.'

'Bye, Molly.'

My phone chimed again.

'Hi Mum.'

'Hello, darling, isn't it wonderful, Flynn texted me and said the girls are home for Christmas. They can stay overnight with me tonight as I have five tickets for *Cinderella*. Can you be here by seven-thirty?'

'That's amazing, Mum, how did you manage to get tickets? I thought they'd sold out.' I said in a high-pitched voice full of excitement.

'It's a thank you from Forever Spring Chickens, they said my prawn cocktails were the best they'd ever tasted.'

'You let them think you made them yourself?'

'Well, I did add lettuce, tomato and a slice of lemon to each dish.'

'Guess it's a strain cutting up lettuce, tomato and a lemon.'

'Oakley, sarcasm doesn't suit you. And I didn't cut up the lettuce, it was from a bag. Make sure you are here before seven-thirty.'

'Okay, bye Mum, and thanks for the tickets, I can't wait to see *Cinderella*.'

'See you later, love.'

The girls were beaming. 'We're the only ones at school who haven't seen it yet, but what about Ruby?' said Blossom.

'Don't worry about me, my mum and I saw *Cinderella* a few days ago. You're going to love it. We'd better get a move on, or you'll miss the start.'

'Okay, but first we have to get out of this bog.'

Loud burping and squelching noises radiated while we pushed and pulled the Beast over the bog. We hauled it over the stile to a round of mooing from our spectators.

'Girls, do you think you can behave while I jog back to the car?' I said, whipping mud off my face and smearing my make-up even further.

Poppy stood in a stream, and splashed water over her legs. 'We always behave. Auntie Oakley please don't accept a lift from a stranger.'

'Good advice, Pops, you do have to be careful, you should never get into a stranger's car.'

'I was more worried about the person's car; you smell awful.'

I peered down my nose at Poppy. 'Thanks Pops.' I turned to Ruby. 'Do you mind keeping an eye on the girls, Rubes? I won't be long.'

'Of course, stay safe, Oakley.'

Chapter Nine
Pulling Painters

With every step the mud in my boots squished between my toes, although I guess it made a change from salmon cat food. I stepped onto the verge as a car approached from behind. The car pulled alongside me and when I peered over my shoulder an orange kayak was leashed on the roof.

The window wound down and a voice said, 'Jeeze, what happened to you? Do you want a lift to the car park?'

Three pairs of cornflower blue eyes, set within angelic, cheeky faces, glared at me from the rear seats.

'Thank you, a lift would be lovely, but I'm covered in mud, and a bit pongy.'

'We have seat covers, and the back of the car doesn't smell too good either.' Woody turned and glared at the children, who had chocolate around their mouths, and a stench of coal soot wafted in the air.

I hopped into the front seat and peeked over my shoulder. 'Hi, you look like you've had a fun day.'

The oldest boy replied, 'We've been on the Santa train with our school.'

Woody turned his head towards me, and his sunglasses reflected in the winter sunshine.

'Their mum dropped them at the station this morning, and I agreed to pick them up after my paddle. I think they're going to be in the bath for a long time.'

My heart sank, oh, how disappointing, Woody had a wife and kids. Why were all the lovely men always taken? I just prayed the kids hadn't seen me from the steam train.

'Was it fun on the Santa train?' I asked.

A red-haired little girl with a face full of freckles leant forward in her seat. 'It was so funny and—'

She was interrupted by an older boy. 'We saw a fairy weeing behind a tree, and then she fell over with her trousers around her ankles. She had funny wings, and dangly legs and—' the boy paused when his sister interrupted.

'And a unicorn's head sticking out of her bum.'

The kids screamed with laughter while I sank as far into my seat as possible.

Woody peered into his central mirror and addressed the kids. 'Are you making stories up again? You know what your mum says about telling fibs.'

'No, it's the truth,' replied the older boy.

Once again, Woody addressed his kids. 'I hope you didn't laugh, that would have been very unkind.'

The older boy giggled. 'No, we were too busy taking photos and videoing her.'

'You were told to take pictures of wildlife.'

'We did, we took pictures of the unicorn sticking out of her bum!'

Woody tilted his head towards me as I sank further down in the seat and looked the other way.

'I'm sorry, I bet you wished you'd walked now. I don't suppose you'd like to join us at the coffee shop?' Woody said.

'We're having toasted teacakes and jam,' said the little girl.

I turned around to see her older brother putting his hand across her mouth.

'No, we're having fudge cake.'

She pushed him away and whined, 'I wanted toasted tea cakes.'

The younger boy joined in the conversation. 'No, we're having the Christmas chocolate Yule log. The one in the window covered in flakes.'

Woody raised his voice and croaked. 'Enough! Stop squabbling, you can choose what you want when we get there.'

I giggled at the thought of all the children's bickering I had refereed over the years.

Woody gripped the steering wheel and staired straight ahead. 'I'm sorry about them, it's been a long day.'

'That's okay, I'm used to it.'

'Of course, the little Christmas trees. I bet they're angels.'

'On the contrary, they argue nonstop. Thank you for the invite, we're already going, so we'll see you inside.'

'Great, look forward to it.'

The older boy held his phone over the headrest. 'Du wanna see the photos?'

Woody braked and switched the engine off. He leant over the back seat and snatched the phone, before shoving it into the glove compartment and driving on.

'You will not be showing the photos to anyone, because as soon as we stop, I will be deleting them.'

The little boy kicked his feet against the back of my seat.

'Doesn't matter, they're already on Snapchat, TikTok, and Instagram.'

'Look a pirate ship, let's have our picture taken,' shouted the younger boy pointing to a huge wooden ship with cut-out pirates' faces.

Woody stopped in the entrance to the car park.

'Which car is yours?'

I pointed to my car, and he parked alongside as the kids piled out and ran to the pirate ship.

'Come and take our picture,' they screamed as they stuck their heads into the pirates' faces.

'Sorry about the kids, we'll see you in the coffee shop.'

'They're fine, I'll see you inside.'

'Don't worry, I'll delete the pictures, assuming they were of you? Can't have been many pretty fairies riding unicorns on the river today.'

'They were, and it was a bit of a shock to see a train full of kids and Santa waving to me.'

Woody shook his head, chortling. 'I bet it was, and the mud?'

'Long story, I'll tell you about it in the coffee shop.'

'Great, see you shortly.'

As I drove past the pirate ship Woody poked his head out of a porthole and grinned. Why did I always want what I couldn't have?

Ten minutes later, the girls climbed into my car while Ruby and I loaded the Beast onto the roof bars. After returning to the car park and dropping Ruby beside her car, the girls and I dashed into the toilets to wash and change. When we returned, Flynn was leaning against the bonnet of my car.

'Hi, Flynn, how was the rest of the paddle?'

'Fine after we ditched Trent. I'd keep out of his way, he's in a foul mood, ranting about someone sending a text message to his contacts. He's had an earbashing from his mum, his boss isn't too happy with him, girls all over the county are heartbroken and his latest girlfriend has threatened to leave him. He's on the warpath as he wants to know who sent the text.'

I bit my lower lip and peeked at the girls whose heads hung low.

'Maybe we'll give the coffee shop a miss and head straight home. We don't want to be late for the concert do we, girls?'

'No,' they muttered simultaneously.

'Good idea. Mum managed to get hold of you then?'

'Yes. You know how much I wanted to see *Cinderella*.'

'Yep, well now's your chance. Mum said she's too busy to make the girls tea. Can you stop at the McDonald's drive through? Order them whatever they want, and they can eat it in the car on the way home.'

'They've eaten loads today. They might be sick in the car if they eat anymore.'

'Sis, don't fuss.'

'It's not your car they're going to throw up in.'

Poppy turned her nose up. 'That's gross, of course we're not going to be sick. Dad, can we have chocolate milkshakes and a McFlurry?'

I mouthed the words 'no' to Flynn, though he ignored me.

'I suppose as it's Christmas. Here's thirty pounds, which should cover it. Thanks, sis, don't know what I'd do without you. I'll be home tomorrow afternoon. Enjoy the concert, girls.'

Poppy buckled herself up next to Blossom. 'Always, Dad. Love you, Bye.'

'Flynn, Ruby is changing in the toilets, would you mind waiting for her and telling her I've had to leave. Maybe she could go to the coffee shop with you?'

'Of course. Enjoy the concert.'

'I almost forgot; I'm meant to be meeting a kayaker in the coffee shop. His name is Woody, he'll be with his children, two young boys and a little girl. Could you please apologise and tell him I had to take the girls home?'

'No worries. Girls, behave for Auntie Oakley.'

'Aw, Dad. Why does everyone tell us to behave?'

Flynn blew the girls a kiss. 'I wonder why?'

Poppy leant out the window. 'Bye, Dad, behave yourself tonight.'

'Always. Enjoy the concert, love you both.'

Chapter Ten
Opening My Eyes

'**R**ight, girls, next stop McDonald's, then *Cinderella*. Are you as excited as me?'

Poppy leant forward in her seat. 'Yes, how long until we eat? I'm starving.'

'Oh my god, Poppy, I'm starting to think you have worms.'

'It's all the exercise, it's made me hungry.'

'Most of your exercise involves using your mouth muscles, I would have thought they could have done with a rest.'

Blossom giggled. 'That's funny. I'm always telling Poppy to shut up.'

Poppy ignored her sister. 'Auntie Oakley, did you like Woody? He'd be perfect for you.'

'He was nice, wasn't he? But he has three kids and is married.'

'That's a shame. Well, if you get desperate there's always Trent, especially as his girlfriend might be leaving him now.'

'I think there's more chance of you telling me you're not hungry than me going on a date with Trent.'

Blossom roared with laughter. 'That's funny, Auntie Oakley.'

We stopped at McDonald's and ordered two meals including chocolate milkshakes and McFlurrys. The girls finished their meals, and when I checked my rear mirror, they were sound asleep.

My mind was whirling like a spinning top, and I couldn't shake off the magnetic sensation of Woody's hand reaching towards me as he swept me off my feet. Maybe it wasn't the most romantic version of my daydream, especially with water pouring out of my nose. It felt so real, except there was a sting in the ointment, he was someone else's dream man and not mine.

When we arrived at my parents' house, Molly's car was parked outside. That was odd, why would Molly be visiting on a Saturday evening?

'Wakey, wakey, girls we're at Nanny and Gramp's house. After I've dropped you off, I'll nip home to feed the cats and get changed.'

Poppy rubbed her eyes. 'How long have we been asleep?'

'About an hour and a half.'

'Seems like seconds ago I was sipping my milkshake. Wake up, Blossom, we've got to get ready to go out.'

Blossom stirred and stretched her arms above her head. 'Okay, but my tummy hurts.'

I swivelled around in my seat. 'That's because you've eaten too much. We don't have to leave for an hour. Why not have a snooze on your bed. I'll take your bags upstairs while you say hello to Nanny and Gramps, and I think Auntie Molly might be visiting.'

Blossom yawned. 'I'm not sure I can stay awake. We didn't go to bed until late last night as Mum had a party.'

'That's news to me, what time do you call late?'

'Oh, I don't know, Poppy what time did we go to bed last night?'

'It was after midnight. Don't worry, we'll try to stay awake.'

'Girls, you don't have to go if you'd rather go to bed. I'm sure Nanny will understand.'

Poppy unbuckled her seatbelt and shuffled out of the car, followed by Blossom.

'We want to go, don't we Blossom?'

Blossom yawned again. 'I suppose.'

'If you're sure, go in and say hello, I'll be there is a minute.'

After dropping the girls' bags in their room, I overheard Molly chatting on her phone in the bathroom.

'Imagine their faces when they hear the news, I'm expecting twin boys. It's lucky Oakley lives next door and doesn't have a boyfriend; she can look after the five boys for us.' She paused. 'No, I haven't told your mum and dad yet. Let's keep it a secret for a few days. Enjoy the ice hockey, your mum's invited me to see *Cinderella,* see you later, darling.' Molly opened the door, and I scooted back into the girls' bedroom.

Was that all I was to my family, a readymade babysitter? How did my mum manage to get another ticket for *Cinderella*? I snuck downstairs to find her making the girls' drinks.

'Hi, Mum, how did the girls seem to you? I'm not sure they should be going.'

'They're excited, that's all. You worry too much.'

Molly's head appeared around the door. 'Hi, Oakley, how'd it go with the painters?'

My mum squinched her eyes and cocked her head. 'What painters?'

'It was nothing, Mum, I've going home to get changed.'

Molly, nosey as ever, giggled. 'Ooh, you off out with them tonight?'

'No. You look smart, going anywhere nice?'

'The concert, silly. Harrison has taken the boys to an ice hockey match and Willow is at her friend's. Your mum invited me to the concert as I was going to be on my own.'

Grabbing my elbow, my mum ushered me to the front door as Molly retreated to the living room.

'How did you manage to get another ticket, Mum?'

'I didn't, love, I gave her your ticket.'

'How could you? You knew how much I wanted to go.' I said with a sinking feeling in my heart.

'You're going to have a long day tomorrow looking after the kids. Come on, love, Molly was going to be on her own tonight.'

I gritted my teeth. 'I'm going to be on my own too, and they're Molly's kids.'

'I know, love, but you're used to being on your own and Molly isn't. There will be plenty of times you can go next year.' My mum's voice sounded muffled while I comprehended what she was saying. 'Don't say anything to Molly, love, she'll be upset if she knew she had your ticket.'

'I'm sure Molly knows she has my ticket.'

My eyes were as hot as pokers, and my heart was lying on the ocean floor, but I wasn't going to let my mum see how upset I was. I jammed my hands into my pockets, held my chin high, pushed my shoulders back and marched towards the open door. I twisted around, and for the first time ever perceived my family in an entirely new light.

'Fine, Mum, say goodbye to the girls for me.'

'Have a good night's sleep, love. I'll tell you all about the concert tomorrow when I drop the girls off.'

I peeped into the living room where Molly had settled back into my dad's armchair. She peered towards me, smirked, and pushed herself back with her heels.

'Night, Oakley, enjoy your night out with the painters, we'll tell you about the concert tomorrow.'

I didn't reply as I held the tears back, closed the door, and headed home.

The security light flashed brightly across my drive as three cats tore through the cat flap to greet me. My phone pinged – a text from Ruby wishing me a lovely evening. I didn't reply. Tickets for *Cinderella* were like gold dust, how could my mum be so thoughtless?

The answerphone flashed – fourteen new messages, and without listening I pressed delete all, and sank into a chair. Ruby was right, I'd been letting everyone walk over me. A change of scenery was called for, though first, I needed something to eat. Gripping the voucher I'd won for the best fancy dress outfit, I touched speed-dial on my phone.

'El-lo, bestest piz-zas in town, Carlos is a-speking.'

I loved his Italian accent, although it always made me giggle as he sounded as if he was saying they were the best pissers in town.

'Hi, Carlos, it's Oakley Breeze, could I have my normal please?'

'El-lo Ms Breeze, so nice to 'ear from you, you'd like to try de special, no? As a regular client I let you 'ave money off, Sounds good? No?'

'Sounds great, what is it?'

'Ground-a-beef, shakioi mooshrooms, black olives, black poodding, black cheddar cheese and 'ot chilli to give it a bit of heat, and you a bit of a kick.'

'Sounds wonderful, I need a bit of a kick, what's the special called?'

'We' ave named it Cindois, all de ingredients are black except for de chilli, which represents de 'eat of the embois. We are celebrating de last poiformance of *Cindorel-la*, you can ave it for 'alf price.'

Was I hearing right? He had named the pizza Cinders, and they were celebrating the last night of *Cinderella*. Talk about rubbing salt into a wound.

'Great, make mine a large please, though can you leave off the black pudding, and can I have beef tomatoes instead of beef?'

'Okey-dokey, it will be with you in a jiffy, signoria, grazie.'

'Thank you, Carlos.'

I had no idea what to expect; knowing my luck someone had accidently burnt the pizzas and renamed them Cinders. It seemed like everyone was trying to give me a kick somewhere today.

It was time to branch out on my own. I picked my laptop up and googled veterinary positions, but there were so many to choose from. With an old, dog-eared map laid on the floor, I beckoned the cats to choose.

'Where shall we move to, girlies?'

Cinnamon, sat on the map and clawed at the dog-eared pages. I slid my fingers between the pages, tipped her off and opened it.

'Cornwall – let's see what vacancies there are.'

One position stuck out like a sore thumb:

Rural practice requires a mixed veterinary surgeon.
Must love the outdoors, canoeing and kayaking.
Accommodation may be available.
Please email madigan@madhatters.co.uk.
Whispering Pines, Cornwall.
Closing date: 18 December.

That was today. Time to google the practice.

Whispering Pines was a small Cornish village overlooking a picture-perfect harbour; it looked idyllic. Within half an hour my CV was on its way to Madigan and the disappointment I'd felt an hour ago was transformed to anticipation combined with a hint of warm fuzziness.

The doorbell rang, and a lad on a bike handed me the pizza. I gave him my voucher and opened the pizza-box lid. Carlos was right when he said it reflected cinders. Layers of mushrooms and peppers were interspersed with black olives, tomatoes and loads of gooey black cheese topped with red-hot chillies. Boy did it give me a kick, and I found myself reaching for a glass of almond milk to extinguish the flames roaring inside my mouth. Despite the heat, it was divine and the best pizza I'd ever eaten.

Nutmeg sniffed the air disapproving of my new cologne, Odour de Pizza, combined with bog water. She gazed at me and meowed. Woman seriously, you need to take a bath.

I stepped into my bath of soothing lavender bubbles, and within seconds was sound asleep dreaming of Woody. Just as Woody was about to take my hand, I was woken abruptly by the ringing of my phone.

'Hello, Oakley speaking.'

'Hello, Oakley. My name is Madigan Hatters of Madhatters veterinary practice. Thank you for your CV, I hope it's not too late to call?'

I sat bolt upright; thank goodness it wasn't a Teams or video call.

'No, that's fine, Mr Hatters.'

'Call me Madigan, only my wife calls me Mr Hatters when I'm in the doghouse.'

I chuckled to myself; he sounded lovely. 'Okay, Madigan.'

'That's better. I was impressed with your CV and wondered when you're free for a coffee and a chat?'

'Is Monday too soon? I have Christmas week off. If Monday is not convenient then Tuesday, or Wednesday or any day next week other than Saturday of course, as it's Christmas Day.'

Madigan was sniggering at my ramblings. 'Monday will be fine, shall we say around thirteen hundred, after morning surgery?'

'Yes, that's perfect.'

Madigan chuckled. 'Sorry, Oakley, my wife is calling me for dinner. I look forward to meeting you on Monday, have a nice evening.'

'Thank you, Madigan, I look forward to meeting you too, enjoy your dinner.'

With a smile etched across my face, I sank back into the bubbles until a text from Molly disturbed me.

> I'm going home. The girls threw up in my car on the way to the concert. It's revolting. We didn't see Cinderella. I'm shopping early 2mor, can you pop round and clean it for me? I can't stand the smell.

I replied:

> Sorry Mol, tied up with the painters. X

A few seconds, later my mum rang.

'Oakley, tonight has been a disaster, what on earth did you feed the girls?'

'Sausage rolls, shortbread, Beaufort cheese, sandwiches, KitKats, hot chocolate, burger and chips, a chocolate milkshake and a McFlurry.'

'No wonder they were sick. How could you let them eat so much?'

'I told Flynn they would be sick if they ate that much, but as usual, no one takes a blind bit of notice of me. Sorry, I'm busy, Mum, I'll see you tomorrow.'

'Oakley, what's got into you? That's no way to speak to your mother. Molly is terribly upset. I want you to drop what you're doing and clean her car; the smell is making her feel sick.'

'Well tell her to put a peg on her nose. Goodnight, Mum.' For the first time in my life I hung up on my mum, switched my mobile phone off, and ignored the ringing landline. With the doors locked and the lights out, hopefully Molly would think the painters had picked me up.

My doorbell chimed several times, no doubt it was Molly. I was lying in my bath ignoring everyone and dreaming of a new life in Whispering Pines. I closed my eyes where Woody was still waiting to rescue me.

Chapter Eleven
Cat out of the Bag

The following morning I was up early, and soon the washing machine was working overtime. I settled down to wrap several sets of lingerie for my brothers to give their wives. Last Christmas, Brenden bought Isla lingerie that made my mum's eyes pop out, and Isla cringed with embarrassment. So, this year I'd been nominated to help my brothers choose the gifts for their wives, but as usual they'd left it all to me.

The front door flew open, and a whirlwind whooshed through the hall as Blossom and Poppy announced their presence.

I sprung up to shut the door. 'You're early, it's only eight-thirty.'

Blossom twiddled her plaits. 'Sorry Auntie Oakley, Nanny said she had a lot to do so dropped us off at the end of your drive.'

'I see, well do you think you can both keep out of mischief while I finish wrapping the presents?'

'Yes of course. Where are the cats?' said Poppy.

'Jasmine and Cinnamon are asleep, and Nutmeg is in the kitchen eating her third breakfast, somehow, I think she is related to you. How are you both feeling today?'

Poppy poked her tongue out. 'We're fine, but I don't think Auntie Molly was happy with us. Where did you go?'

'I had to rush off to work, so Auntie Molly went instead of me,' I lied, though I'm not sure the girls believed me.

Blossom held her finger on the ribbon as I tied a bow around a present. 'It was lucky you didn't go, or it would have been your car we threw up in.'

'That's what I thought,' I said, giggling.

The girls ran towards the kitchen shouting, 'Meg.'

Nutmeg came tearing through to the living room wagging her stumpy tail from side to side.

'Girls, it's going to be a while until your cousins arrive, do you both want a drink?'

Poppy walked into the kitchen. 'I'll make them, are there any Christmas cookies?'

'No, not at half past eight in the morning, you can have a banana each and a glass of strawberry milk.'

When Poppy returned, she almost dropped the glasses.

I jumped up and snatched the glasses from her. 'What's so funny?'

Poppy pointed to one of the carrier bags of ladies' undies. 'Look in the carrier bag.'

I peeped inside as a paw slapped me across my hand; Nutmeg had made herself at home amongst the bras and knickers. I reached in and tried to pull her out.

'Meg, you silly puss, come out.'

Like a rumble of thunder, the front door sprang open, and three boys charged in like cows skipping on spring pasture. Panicked, Nutmeg leapt up while attempting a getaway. She caught her stumpy tail on a bra fastener, stuck her head through the bag handle and dashed towards the open door with the carrier bag still attached. I leapt up to stop her, but my rugby tackle failed.

'Boys, shut the door.' I screamed. Too late, Nutmeg hotfooted it through the doorway and tore down the drive. 'Kids stay here. I'll find her.'

A jingle-jangle ricocheted off my neighbour's walls announcing the early arrival of Santa's sleigh. When I peered down, a pair of green-

and-red striped elf's slippers, covered in bells, were still attached to my feet. I peered over my shoulder to see the clan of giggling kids following me, as usual, completely ignoring my instructions.

Leaning over a car bonnet, and defrosting the windscreen, was a rather dishy-looking neighbour who I'd never met before. Boy did I feel stupid in my elf slippers.

'Hi, terribly sorry to disturb you, did you see a cat running in this direction?'

He walked around the side of his car sniggering. 'Was that a cat? All I saw was a carrier bag running along the ground scattering ...' he paused and picked something up, '... I don't suppose this belongs to you?' He held up a lacy black bra with embroidered red roses, and as he handed it to me, I felt my cheeks glow as red as the roses.

I studied the paving slaps and muttered, 'Yes, thank you.'

'Nice slippers by the way.'

'Thanks.' Although by the tone of his voice he was being sarcastic.

The kids and I followed a trail of bras and knickers along the drive until we found the empty carrier bag hooked around the end of an exhaust pipe, but there was no sign of Nutmeg.

Armed with handfuls of lingerie I beckoned to the kids.

'Let's go home and see if Meg has returned a different way.'

We wandered back up the drive and spotted a quivering Nutmeg peering around the side of the garden wall. I picked her up and checked her.

'She's fine kids, other than a slight manicure. With a few broken claws clipped she'll be back to her normal self.'

Harrison and Molly's eldest son, ten-year-old Reuben, grasped a thong and bra set and ran his fingers through the lace.

'You have a lot of sexy underwear, Auntie Oakley.'

I was shocked he even knew what the word sexy was. My nieces and nephews seemed to know far more than I did at their age. I snatched the underwear out of his hands.

'Reuben Breeze, you are a cheeky boy. Now you mustn't look or touch ladies' underwear until you are at least ...' I paused for a few seconds, '... thirty!'

He burst out laughing. 'You're joking, thirty! You sound like my mum.'

'Your mum would probably have said forty.'

I glanced at the time, 9 a.m. What the heck was I meant to do with five kids for the day? Then an idea flashed through my mind.

'Have you got coats and gloves with you?'

'Why?'

'Fancy going ice-skating and then a pizza?' You could never eat too much pizza. There were nods and cheers all round as they raced to grab their coats.

'I'll nip upstairs to find my skates.'

The doorbell chimed while I searched for my skates.

Poppy yelled upstairs, 'I'll answer it.'

A couple of minutes later Poppy bellowed, 'Auntie Oakley, can you hear me? It's Uncle Lando.'

Crikey, that child had a fine pair of lungs; she'd make an excellent town crier. I hurried downstairs. Voices in my head were screaming, please no more kids, five is enough.

'Hi sis, sorry to ask, but I've been called out to fix a burst pipe. Mum told me to drop the kids off with you, but I can see you have your hands full.'

'Keep calm,' I said to myself, nothing was going to faze me today.

'She did, did she? We're about to go ice-skating and maybe a pizza afterwards. Would you mind dropping your three off at the rink and taking Blossom or Poppy with you?'

Lando reached for his wallet. 'Of course, I'm going that way. If I finish the job early, I'll join you on the ice. Here's some money to pay for the kids to go skating and a pizza, I think that will cover it.'

'One hundred and fifty pounds. That's far too much.'

'Sis, not for eight kids it isn't. Anyway, one of my clients gave me a Christmas bonus. I'll try and be at the ice rink for around twelve-thirty. I hear you met the guy of your dreams yesterday.'

'Yep. He was perfect; cute with a good sense of humour, just a shame he was married with kids.'

'Don't worry, I'm sure there'll be another fun guy around the next corner. Maybe you'll bump into someone at the ice rink.'

'Doubt that, but if I bump into him, you'll be the first to know.'

Lando smirked. 'I'll follow you to the ice rink.'

He turned to the twins. 'Blossom or Poppy can one of you jump into the front seat please?'

'I'll go. Blossom, you go with Auntie Oakley,' said Poppy with her bossy head on.

Funny how the girls did exactly as they were told by Uncle Lando.

Chapter Twelve
Bulldog

Eight excited kids piled through the entrance to the ice rink while I waited at the booth to pay. The queue seemed bizarrely quiet for a Sunday morning. I pressed the bell on the counter and a lady appeared. She had long black hair tied back in a ponytail and wore an old-fashioned ice dance tunic. I recognised her immediately as Daphne, the lady who taught me to skate when I was a kid.

'Do you want tickets to the Christmas party, love?'

'Christmas party? Of course, it's the last Sunday before Christmas. That would be lovely, thank you, please could I have nine tickets, plus eight skate hire.'

'The Christmas party doesn't start until the ice hockey match has finished, but seeing as your children are so well-behaved, you can watch the remainder of the game for free.'

'Thank you so much. I'd have no idea what to do with this lot for another hour.'

Daphne smiled. 'All yours love?'

'Crikey no. They're my nieces and nephews. Do you know if there will be a game of Bulldog during the party?'

'I should think so, but you need your own skates.'

'I have my own skates, although I haven't skated for years.'

'Didn't you used to skate here? Let me think, are you Oakley Breeze?'

'You remembered me.'

'How could I forget your pretty face. You used to fly around the rink like a fairy.'

Poppy giggled and nudged me. 'Do you know what? Yesterday Auntie Oakley dressed as a fairy for our canoeing fancy dress paddle, but her swimming was better than her flying.'

Daphne chuckled. 'It seems your Auntie Oakley likes being near water. She used to spin around the ice as if she was floating on air.'

'She was floating on air when she was torpedoed out of her canoe.'

'Oh dear, sounds like an adventure. Did you give up skating, Oakley?'

'No, we couldn't afford lessons anymore, so I joined the hockey team until I went to uni and studied to become a vet.'

'A vet, how lovely.' Daphne smiled and addressed the kids. 'Your auntie used to outskate the boys.'

'Thank you, though I wasn't that good.' I handed the entrance money to Daphne. 'It was lovely to meet you again, wish me luck with this lot.'

The kids jostled their way through, and Daphne handed me my change and cackled. 'Kids, you'd better be on your best behaviour for your auntie, no shenanigans!'

Blossom spun around and piped up, 'We're always good.'

I shook my head. 'You're only good in your dreams.' I smiled at Daphne. 'Thanks, for letting us in early, you're a lifesaver.'

'You're welcome, remember, don't let the lads outskate you.'

'I won't.'

The skate hire booth wasn't open, so we settled down to watch the remainder of the hockey match.

Poppy stood up obscuring my view.

'Auntie Oakley, I'm hungry, and thirsty.'

'You're always hungry.'

Blossom joined her sister. 'I guess we're making up for throwing up our tea.'

'So, I guess it's hot chocolate for everyone?'

A chorus of 'yes please' echoed in the rink.

'Reuben, I'm leaving you in charge while Blossom, Poppy and I fetch everyone drinks.' I addressed the kids: 'So you had better all behave.'

'Yeah, or I'll trip you up on the ice,' Reuben said giggling.

'Reuben Breeze, you will do no such thing.' I said trying to be the grown up and not succeeding.

When we reached the café, I could still hear the kids chattering. Ten minutes later, the twins and I returned laden with cups of hot chocolate with marshmallows and fresh, hot, sugared ring doughnuts.

'Promise me you won't tell your parents I let you eat doughnuts at quarter to ten in the morning?'

Eight sugared faces nodded as the intensity of the match increased and the noise from the crowd became deafening. Several players were sent to the penalty box for fouls, but one player seemed to be spending a lot more time there than the others.

Blossom leant over the barrier. 'Auntie Oakley, why has that player been sent off?'

'Because he's causing the fights. He'll be eliminated if he doesn't follow the rules.'

Reuben piped up, 'It wouldn't be any fun if everyone kept to the rules, Rules are there to be broken.'

'Don't let your nan hear you say that.'

'I love the fights; I can't wait to join the juniors' team.'

Blossom pointed to the player in the penalty box who was removing his helmet.

'He's got a terrible temper; he keeps banging his stick on the back of the chair. Oh my gosh, you won't believe it, it's Trent!'

'It can't be. he's with your dad on the lads' weekend.'

'No, Dad texted me this morning. Trent didn't stay at the YHA as he had to go home to calm his girlfriend down.'

The referee waved his hands and Trent picked his bag up and

headed our way. Yikes, he mustn't see me, he'd think I was following him. I sank into my seat and withdrew my head like a snail sensing danger. With any luck, Trent would walk straight past without noticing me; but my luck was about to run out. The backrest tilted backwards throwing my legs into the air, and my bum slide through the gap. I'd been snapped up by the chair like a crocodile catching its dinner. If my feet had been bare, I could have trimmed my toenails with my teeth. A feeling of warmth was spreading in my groin area as hot chocolate seeped through my jeans. I attempted to lever myself up with my elbows and noticed my doughnut wedged inside my bra. I scooped it out and dropped it onto the floor as the kids screamed with laughter. I had as much chance of being inconspicuous as I did of the kids listening to me. This crocodile wasn't releasing its prey without a fight. Poppy grabbed one of my arms.

'Blossom, pull Auntie Oakley's other arm, and Reuben can pull her legs.'

Blossom pointed down the aisle. 'Poppy, it's not working. Look, Trent is walking this way, I'll ask him to help.'

'No, not Trent!' I screamed; but it was too late.

Trent appeared trembling with laughter. 'Fancy bumping into you, Tinker Bell. You are aware this is an ice rink and not a yoga session? You must get out of the habit of trying to get your legs around your ears.'

'I'm in an ice rink? You're kidding me. With the amount of clowns surrounding me I thought I was at the circus auditioning for a job as a contortionist!'

Trent roared with laughter. 'So, I suppose you want me to give you a hand?'

'No thanks, I'm sure I can wriggle my way out.'

'This is one time I don't think even Tinker Bell can wriggle out of. I'll help you, but what's it worth?'

'I am not going on a date with you if that's what you're planning.'

'For once we agree on something. I'm not going on a date with you either, I know you too well; how boring would that be?'

'I'll pay for a drink from the bar if you would kindly pull me out.'

'Nope, I'm driving, that's of no interest to me. What else can you offer?'

Reuben, who idolised Trent, piped up, 'I know, you can join us for a pizza after skating, and Auntie Oakley can pay.'

'Now you're talking. Pizza sounds great, What time?'

Reuben checked his watch. 'Auntie Oakley, is one o'clock, okay?'

Before I had time to say anything, Trent butted in: 'Sounds great. Kids, want me to show you some moves on the ice?'

Reuben's eyes lit up as if Christmas had come early. 'Yeah, that would be great, Trent. Can you help us with our skates?'

'I can do better than that, there are several pairs of hockey skates you can try out. Come on, let's get you lot kitted out.'

The children jumped up from their seats, left their rubbish, and followed like a bunch of ducklings waddling after their mother.

I wriggled my elbows up and down and clapped my hands to get their attention.

'Hello. Have you forgotten something?'

The children twisted around, exploded into laughter, and began performing the chicken dance.

With a grin stamped onto his face as if he'd won the lottery, Trent returned to my chair and reached under my arms. Following a couple of failed attempts he yanked me out of the chair and dropped me on top of the doughnut.

'Look at all the rubbish, woman, the ice stewards will have a field day if they see this mess, you'd better clean it up. I'll take the kids to get their skates and we'll see you on the ice. By the way, you might want to clean yourself up a bit.'

Trent strutted towards the changing rooms displaying a definite swagger. He glanced behind and winked, as eight besotted kids, who had nothing but admiration for their rule-breaking hero, followed him to the changing rooms. Keep calm, I told myself, tomorrow may be the answer to my prayers.

After disposing of the rubbish, I retreated to the ladies and glared at my reflection in the mirror. My blue fleece had a streak of hot chocolate down one side that corresponded to the streak down the inside of my leg. I sank onto a bench and sponged the hot chocolate; my phone beeped three times.

Ruby: Hi Oakley, what u up 2? How was the concert? X

Me: Hi Rubes, I didn't go to the concert, long story. @ ice rink, want to join us? X

Ruby: Love to, on my way. X

Flynn: Hi sis, Mum said you have the girls. Left YHA early, will pick the girls up in ten mins. Taking them ice-skating.

Me: Hi Flynn, already at the ice rink. C u later x

Flynn: Great. On my way.

Lando: Finished with client early. B there shortly.

Me: C u later x

I tottered towards the rink while the Zamboni resurfaced the ice. Ten minutes later, Lando and Flynn arrived carrying their hockey skates.

'Hi sis, where are the kids?' Lando sounded anxious.

'Trent's helping them lace their skates in the changing room.'

'Why aren't you helping? How could you have left poor Trent to look after eight excitable kids by himself.'

Sometimes, brothers could be so annoying. I stood up and faced Lando.

'I didn't leave, he left me. Anyway, you left me to look after them on my own, so what's the difference? He's a teacher, he must have some experience with kids.'

Neither of my brothers uttered another word as they impersonated a pair of guppy goldfish to a tee. Trent returned from the changing rooms followed by eight pairs of wobbly legs.

Blossom hobbled towards Flynn. 'Dad, Uncle Lando, you've both got your skates, this is going to be so much fun. Trent is going to show us some moves. Auntie Oakley, the stains hardly show.'

Flynn glared at me. 'What stains?'

'Auntie Oakley spilt her hot chocolate when a chair snapped her up, it was so funny, she had her feet around her ears. Don't worry though, Trent rescued her, and while she wiped the stains off, Trent helped us lace our skates.'

Lando and Flynn's facial expressions reminded me of when the local pub ran out of beer. Great, now I sounded like a damsel in distress. Trent's smirk brought back memories of the gloating ten-year-old boy who pushed Ruby into the lake. The DJ played the music and the gates opened on the barriers.

I turned to my brothers. 'I'm off for a spin, trust you can look after your own kids for five minutes?'

'Of course, sis, we'll join you in a minute.'

I could feel everyone's eyes eating away at the back of my head as I stepped onto the ice. Although my legs felt like jelly, I pretended not to be the least bit scared. There was no need to worry – it was like getting back on your bike. I was in a world of my own, lost in the moment whilst feeling the music. That was, until someone grabbed my hand and refused to let go. Before I knew it, Trent was gliding around backwards and skating faster and faster. I tried to break free, but he gripped me even tighter. My heart was in my mouth as a small boy tripped in front of us.

'Trent, watch out!' I screamed.

Trent pivoted, tripped, and landed face-down on the ice. I dug my toe pick into the ice and performed a toe loop over the boy. I landed just in time to see Trent, whizzing across the ice on his front. Seconds later, the hockey team circled him several times before performing hockey stops and showering him in ice. I spotted Ruby watching from the barrier. As I waved, her smile transformed into a dragon face.

'Hi, Rubes.'

'Oakley, after everything you've said about Trent, I can't believe you were holding hands while skating.'

'It wasn't by choice. He grabbed my hand and wouldn't let go. Can I detect a bit of jealousy?'

'Not at all, though sometimes I think you like the attention. Did you know he was going to be here?'

'Of course not, or I wouldn't have come.'

'Seems odd how you keep bumping into each other.'

'It's not intentional.'

'Didn't look like that to me. Anyway, why didn't you go to the concert?'

'My mum gave my ticket to Molly, so I went home. The girls threw up in Molly's car, so they missed the concert. Molly and my mum had the cheek to ask me to clean the car.'

'You didn't, did you?'

'No, told them I was out with the painters and had an early night.'

'Serves Molly right. Bet she wasn't pleased.' said Ruby chuckling.

'She wasn't.' I said giggling. 'I'm off for a quick skate with the kids, are you joining us?'

'I'll just lace my skates, then I'll see you on the ice.'

After spending a lot of time helping the kids up from the ice, I skated around the rink a few times to build my confidence up. When the DJ announced a game of Bulldog, my anxiety returned, and I joined the kids behind the barrier.

Poppy hobbled to me. 'Auntie Oakley, why don't you skate on Bulldog?'

'I don't think I'm good enough, it's mainly the boys that skate.'

Blossom placed her hands on her hips quizzing me. 'Why? You're as good as them, if not better. You taught us we were equal.'

'I guess I did.'

Lando strolled towards me. 'Sis, Flynn and I are skating on Bulldog. Please can you keep an eye on the kids?'

'Sorry, I'm skating too.'

Lando glared at me. 'You what? You can't.'

'Why not? Because I'm a girl and you're worried I'll beat you?'

'Maybe. Who'll watch the kids?'

Ruby butted in. 'Me! Go on, Oakley, show them how good you are. It's a long time since a bloke caught you.'

Reuben enquired, 'How do you play Bulldog?'

'It's a bit like catch. A few skaters stand in the middle of the rink, they're the Bulldogs. Everyone else skates from one end of the rink to the other trying to outskate the Bulldogs. If they're caught, they become a Bulldog too. The last skater standing is the winner.'

Blossom pushed me towards the ice. 'Go on, Auntie Oakley, I bet you can outskate the boys.'

Oh God, what was I letting myself in for?

Trent skated towards me. 'You're not playing, are you?'

'Why? Scared you won't be able to catch me?'

'I could easily catch you, I'm more worried you'll fall on your backside and make a fool of yourself.'

'I can do that without falling on the ice, and you seem good at making a fool out of me too.'

'Don't say I didn't warn you.'

'You'll never catch me, Trent.'

'Never say never.'

We formed a line at one end of the rink while Flynn, Trent and Lando volunteered to be the Bulldogs. The kids leant over the barrier calling out my name, as Fun Boy Three sang, "It Ain't What You Do It's The Way That You Do It".

Thirty skaters took off attempting to outskate the Bulldogs; I hid at the back and sneaked through with ease. Five skaters were pounced upon as Kool and the Gang sang, "Get Down On It". I hid at the back again, though when I took flight Trent made a beeline for me. The Rolling Stones sang, "You Can't Catch Me" as I switched sides, dodged Trent, and reached the other end. This was exhausting; however, I wasn't a quitter. I set off again, Trent skated towards me, and tried to grab my arm, but I leapt into the air and jumped out of harm's way.

The Bulldogs increased to twenty-five, and as seven of the remaining skaters raced towards the middle, the Bulldogs pounced.

The crowd chanted, 'Oakley, Oakley, Oakley' as I crouched down, and slid under a Bulldog's arms. With three of us left, the chance of me making it to the other end had the same odds as Trent ever being related to me. I circled my end of the rink a few times as Elton John sang, "I'm Still Standing".

Trent skated from one side to the other, waving his arms and egging the crowd on as he soaked up the ambience. He waggled a finger towards me as I attempted to dash to the other end.

'She's mine, lads, Tinker Bell is going down.'

With his attention wavering, I was off to the tune of Michael Jackson, "Beat It"

The crowd screamed: 'She's behind you.'

Trent pivoted, raced across the middle of the rink, and grabbed the arm of my jacket. A few seconds later, I was safely at the other end of the rink, leaving Trent holding my jacket. The rink erupted into applause as Trent skated towards me to the tune of Tina Turner screaming out, "Simply the Best".

'That was sneaky, I almost had you.'

'You'll never have me, Trent.'

He tossed my jacket towards me, skated off and about-turned shouting, 'Never say never!'

The DJ announced another round of Bulldog.

Flynn skated towards me. 'You were amazing. Now you can be a Bulldog and see if you can catch Trent.'

'Thanks, I have no intention of chasing after Trent. Would you mind looking after your kids? I've got a lot to do this afternoon.'

'Yes of course, thanks for bringing them.'

'That's okay, it was fun. Here's the remainder of the money to buy the pizzas. Enjoy the rest of the day.'

'See ya, sis.'

After changing my skates, I joined Ruby and the kids.

Poppy rushed towards me. 'Auntie Oakley you were brilliant, wasn't she Blossom?'

'Yep, and you should have seen how annoyed Trent was when you outskated him,' said Blossom.

Ruby's dragon impersonation was in full bloom. 'Oakley, you should have let him catch you.'

A frown spread across my face like butter running off hot toast. 'Why?'

'Because you humiliated him in front of the ice hockey team. Why do you always have to prove you're as good as the boys?'

'Because I am. He'll get over it. I call it tit for tat after what he did yesterday. All's fair in love and war, Rubes.'

'Well, you've been at war with Trent for far too long, men don't like women who show them up, and you won't get a boyfriend acting that way.'

'I have no intention of Trent being my boyfriend, so what does it matter? Enjoy the rest of the afternoon, kids. I'll catch up with you in the week, Rubes.'

Poppy shouted: 'Bye Auntie Oakley, thanks for bringing us skating, we thought you were brilliant.'

Ruby remained silent and looked in a different direction while I walked towards the door. I had no idea what her problem was, she had been acting a bit strange for the past few weeks; maybe she liked Trent.

I arrived home and loaded the fifth basket of freshly washed linen into the tumble drier as it groaned, no more please. Next was the mammoth task of wrestling the mountain of ironing. There was only one film this task could be tackled in front of, and although I'd watched the box set a hundred times, Bridget Jones was soon miming to, "All By Myself" as I accompanied her.

My body tingled with excitement thinking about my interview tomorrow, although it could have been the sensation of the electric current running through the iron. Like me, it was a bit rusty when it came to ironing out the creases and wrinkles in my life. A feeling of heaviness suddenly swept over me, awaking my indecisive head.

Was moving to Cornwall a step too far? I'd be on my own with no family to pop round if there was a problem. How would my brothers manage without me helping with the kids? Crikey, and what about my nan and parents? My indecisive head chastised me and voiced its opinion, that I was a very selfish person. As the iron spat limescale over my top, my decisive head awoke. Oakley, it's time you grew up and branched out on your own. If you don't, you'll spend your life looking after everyone else, and when they've moved on, you'll be all by yourself.

For the next few hours, indecisive and decisive fought inside my head, until for the first time in my life, decisive won the battle. The mountain of ironing had reduced to a molehill, and Bridget Jones was now pregnant. I switched the iron off and feasted on the remains of my Cinders pizza. A bath of lavender bubbles beckoned me where I was sure if I nodded off Woody would still be waiting for me in my dreams.

Chapter Thirteen
Interview at Madhatters

My stomach felt jittery, and my mouth parched, as I veered my car to a standstill. Ahead of me, a sign read: Welcome to Whispering Pines. I continued driving before pulling into a lay-by beside a single-vehicle arched bridge. With my window open, my car was engulfed with the acrid smell of decaying seaweed combined with a hint of a wood-burning stove. It evoked memories of childhood holidays spent by the sea, especially sharing a tent with five smelly brothers.

Water cascaded down a sequence of interconnecting ponds and rippled under the bridge into an enchanting harbour. To the right, a row of chocolate-box thatched cottages overlooked a shingle beach. The wind whistled through the rigging on yachts' masts as turnstones dashed to and fro, outrunning the ripples with amazing precision.

I continued driving over the bridge and turned into a car park, where nestled in the corner, overlooking the harbour, was my answer to quenching my thirst. A quaint café with mint-green walls painted with summer flowers was bordered by a landscaped garden. Within a pergola stood an iron gate, and hanging above it, swinging in the breeze, a sign displayed the name – The Lily Pad.

I glanced at my watch – it was far too early for my interview, but perfect for elevenses. Dressed to the nines in my four-inch heels and smart black suit, I hobbled under the pergola wondering if I was a little overdressed.

A bell jangled as I stepped through the cafe door, although the woman behind the counter hadn't heard me. She bobbed and frolicked to "Cold Heart" sung by Elton John and Dua Lipa, and when she twisted around, a rather red-faced woman, with auburn hair piled high in a bun, smiled at me.

She brushed a stray ringlet away with her floury hand. 'Ey up lass. Sorry about that, got carried away. You look bonny, what can I get you?' The strong Yorkshire accent didn't quite fit the ambience.

'Your dancing was amazing; I love that song. I'd like a strong black coffee please.'

'Ta lass, keeps me fit. Owt to eat?'

'I shouldn't really, but the aroma is difficult to resist.'

The women wiped her floury hands down her cerise-pink pinafore. 'There's a pan of bangers n' onions sizzlin. I could rustle up a butty if you're hungry.'

'You've twisted my arm. A sausage butty sounds delicious, though no onions please.'

'Right-e-ow, one banger butty coming up. Sure you want coffee? There's nothing like a proper brew.'

'Coffee will be fine, thank you. '

'You look mighty smart. Are you passing through?'

'No, I have an interview at the vets.'

'That explains the suit. Madigan said he was interviewing today. Travelled far?'

'Weston-Super-Mare.'

'Cor blimey, that's a long way, nothing much happens round here lass. What makes you wanna move to somewhere as quiet as this?'

'That's what I'm looking for. Far enough from the family so they can't pop round every minute, but close enough, so they can drive down within a few hours. Your accent doesn't sound local.'

'No love, born and bred in North Yorkshire. My brother is your potential new boss Madigan, he moved here when he was sixteen and has lost most of his accent. My husband is Madigan's business partner who may also be your potential boss. Can I give you a bit of advice?'

'Okay,' I said, wondering what on earth she was going to say.

'You're a tad overdressed for an interview with Madigan. Have you got anything else to wear?'

'Only a fresh set of work overalls in my car.'

'Madigan ain't much of a dresser, he'll respect you more in overalls.'

'Oh!' I said, feeling a bit offended.

'Don't take offence, but you look like you're about to step onto a catwalk. I'd think about dressing down a tad.'

Looking down I shuffled my feet. 'Thanks for the advice, I will give it a bit of thought.'

'Here's your butty and coffee, there's mustard and tomato sauce on the table.'

Reluctant to receive any further advice I asked, 'Is it okay to eat outside?'

The woman frowned. 'Of course, it's a bit parky today.'

'I'm used to the cold, and I want to breathe in the scenery.'

She smiled. 'Here, take this.' She handed me a cushion and laughed. 'Don't wanna damp behind.'

'Thank you.' If only she'd known how damp my behind was on Saturday.

I sat down on a bench by the water's edge. With my butty open, I squirted mustard and sauce over the sausage. The aroma titillating my nostrils was irresistible; this was heaven. I breathed in the tang of warm mustard and held it to my mouth, and within a split second, it had disappeared. I glanced up and knocked my coffee over, as two doorstep wedges plummeted towards me and skimmed off my nose. Their journey continued through my open jacket and ended on my crisp-white shirt. I sprang off the bench, fished them out, and an uninvited colony of gulls joined me for breakfast.

With her tea towel spinning in the air, the woman from the café charged towards the gulls. In a flash, a cackling herring gull swooped, grabbed the tea towel, and glided across the harbour. It landed on the railings on a veranda that was bordering a beautiful white house on the opposite bank. The gull seemed to be making fun of us as it shook the tea towel from side to side. I peered at my mustard-stained top as coffee seeped through my trousers.

A grimace was spreading across the lady's face.

'Ooh, blooming heck, love, those pesky gulls. I should have warned you about them. I'll make you another butty and coffee.'

'That's kind of you, but no thanks. I'd better see if I can clean this off before my interview.' I made a quick exit to the toilets in the car park. No amount of rubbing removed the stain, instead it made it worse. Ten minutes later, I sauntered back to the Lily Pad dressed in my overalls.

The woman rushed towards me. 'Perfect. Far more fitting for a role as a vet. I'm Lily by the way.'

'Thank you, Lily. I'm Oakley Breeze.'

Lily handed me a box of cakes. 'Enjoy these as a way of an apology. Good luck with the interview. I'm sure you will do well.'

'Hope so, I need to try one of your sausage butties again. Bye Lily.'

'Ta'ra, lass.'

I drove out of the car park and followed the road along the estuary. You couldn't mistake Madhatter's Veterinary Practice; the entrance was within a converted boat bordered by large, yellow-and-blue teacups planted with winter-flowering pansies. Porthole windows overlooked the harbour while to the rear, a raised glass walkway lead to a wooden structure on stilts.

After parking my car I strolled around the harbour absorbing the breathtaking surroundings. It was hard to imagine working and living in such an incredible place. I paused outside a quaint thatched pub called Reel Them Inn. The menu was mouth-watering, and a perfect excuse for not doing the washing-up. With a light step, and feeling on top of the world, I returned to Madhatters and opened the door.

'Good afternoon, Oakley,' said a woman dressed in vets' overalls.

'Good morning, how did you know my name?'

'A little birdie informed us.' She stood up, beaming, and offered me her hand. 'I'm Madeleine, Madigan's veterinary partner and wife, though people call me Madge. Tea or coffee, love?'

'Black coffee please, thank you. Sorry for wearing overalls, I had a mishap with a gull.'

A stocky man, who sounded like a trumpeting elephant, appeared in the doorway. 'Don't worry, lass, Lily was the little birdie who told us about your predicament. She felt guilty for not warning you about the gulls. You look very fitting in your overalls. Would you believe it, one women turned up for an interview in a smart black suit and four-inch heels.'

After Madigan shook my hand, I pulled my overall trousers over my boots hiding my four-inch heels. We retreated along the glass walkway to the office and chatted for ages. Madigan told me lots of funny stories and informed me of his plans. His nephew, Mackenzie, was working as a vet in Scotland and would be returning to the practice in June. Madigan was seeking a vet who could start in March and also help at the family's new water sports activity centre based on the estuary.

Madigan dunked a digestive biscuit in his coffee. 'Well what d'you think? It will be a lot of hard work and odd hours, but I think you'll love every minute.'

I tried not to snigger as the end of the biscuit snapped off into his mug and he said an expletive while fishing it out with a spoon.

'It's the most amazing opportunity I could imagine. I'd be too busy enjoying myself to notice odd hours.'

'Excellent. Are you available to start in late March?'

'Really? You're offering me the job?'

'Yes, I think you'll fit in perfectly.'

'In that case I accept, though I'll have to find somewhere to live.'

'I may have the answer to that. Are you or your family any good at DIY?'

'Yes. My family run their own building company.'

'Perfect. I've purchased a farm about a mile from here. The land borders the estuary and is ideal for my son and daughter to set up their activity centre. If you're interested, there's a large farmhouse that's surplus to my requirements. It has a huge garden, outbuildings and an adjoining paddock. I will only sell it to someone within the practice.'

'Sounds too good to be true. Is it habitable?'

'Structurally it's sound, though it needs modernising.'

'Doesn't your nephew Mackenzie want it when he returns from Scotland?'

'He already owns a house in the village.'

I could feel my heart racing. 'Would you mind if I viewed it now?'

'Of course not. I'll run you up there, let me find the keys.'

When we returned to the reception, Madigan began riffling through drawers.

'Madge, where are the keys to Catkins?'

'In your top pocket.'

'Of course, what would I do without you?'

'Stay in bed!' Madge said.

'Catkins, what a lovely name, I love it already.' I said.

'We'll take the Land Rover, the track's a bit bumpy, but I will arrange for it be resurfaced in the spring.'

We drove out of the village, up a steep hill, and turned onto a single-track road. Madigan indicated right onto a track that was little more than a bridle path. A loud moo emanated from within the glove compartment causing me to jump in my seat.

Madigan stopped the car and roared with laughter.

'Sorry to startle you, lass. There isn't a cow in the glove compartment, it's my ringtone for Farmer Gedin. There's always one catastrophe or another at World's End Farm.'

I passed Madigan his phone and listened to his concerned conversation with Farmer Gedin.

'Sorry, Oakley, I have to attend an emergency. Here's the keys to Catkins, which is at the end of the track. After you've viewed it, follow the path through the gate at the back of the garden. It will lead you to the estuary and back to the practice. If no one is in, pop the keys through the letterbox. I'll email you the contract later.'

'Do you need any help?'

'No love, but thanks. You get on and see Catkins.' Madigan paused and directed his gaze towards my feet. 'You won't get far in those shoes, borrow a pair of wellies from the boot. They might be a bit big, but better than ruining your heels.'

I jumped out and grabbed the wellies. 'I can't thank you enough.'

'That's okay, it's me who should be thanking you. We're going to get on like a house on fire. Can, I give you a bit of advice? Next time you eat at the Lily Pad watch out for Sidney, the seagull, though technically he is a herring gull.'

'Sidney. Who names gulls?'

'Mackenzie hand-reared him and released him back into the wild. Sid thinks everyone should share their food, and if they don't, he pinches it.'

'Mackenzie should have taught Sid manners.'

Madigan laughed. 'He does sometimes drop thank you messages, it's meant to be good luck.'

'Mackenzie or Sid?'

Madigan roared with laughter. 'Mackenzie is going to love working with you, a shame he missed your interview. Watch out for the spiders at Catkins.' He waved his hand out of the window and disappeared over the brow of the hill.

Chapter Fourteen
Snowball of Sheep

Excitement was exploding out of me like a shaken bottle of Coke, and although I was standing in the middle of nowhere, strangely it felt like home. A tapestry of fields was stitched together by hedges intertwined with oak trees, and a pine forest crocheted the horizon. What an awe-inspiring landscape. The air was draped with the odour of decaying leaves, the sweet aroma of pine needles, and whiff of a muck spreader. Surprisingly, it wasn't too offensive and reminded me of childhood visits to my grandparents' farm.

Despite a frosty chill hanging in the air and the wind slapping its icy hands against my face, I felt a lightness in my limbs. With a bounce in my stride and feet swimming in the oversized wellies I squashed my heeled boots into my bag.

Except for birds twittering, and a gurgling brook, the void was filled with an air of serenity as I began my ramble to Catkins. It was a complete contrast to the hullabaloo at home where new houses sandwiched me in every direction. When I purchased my house, it was surrounded by the countryside. However, the fields had long been transformed to row after row of tightly packed houses. The peace and quiet had been replaced by music blaring, car doors slamming, dogs barking and cats yowling. It didn't help either that my brother and his noisy family had moved in next door.

Living opposite my home was annoying neighbour Mr Popular, who was anything but. He wandered around his garden dressed in a bright yellow boiler suit, a motorcycle helmet and a jet-propelled leaf blower strapped to his back. I'm sure as a child he must have dreamt of becoming an astronaut. Throughout the year he blew dust and leaves into the neighbouring gardens, and especially enjoyed partaking in this daily ritual during BBQ season. When he was bored of the leaf blower he turned his hand to the weed zapper, woe betide any weed that emerged in his garden.

Then there was Mr Slugman, well that's what I called him, I've no idea of his real name. His garden could have been mistaken for the surface of the moon, as he topped up craters daily with beer to catch the slugs. During the summer, Mr Slugman emerged at 10 p.m. donned with a head torch and a bucket. He paced up and down like a sniffling hedgehog; it wouldn't have surprised me if Mr Slugman wasn't related to Mr Popular. And then there was sweet Mrs Rhymes, who couldn't hear the twenty annoying windchimes hanging metres from my bedroom window. I'd asked her loads of times if she would kindly move them, but she always said no, as she loved watching them swaying in the wind. For the past two years, I've been trying to get up the courage to climb over the fence and cut them down. With my house move on the cards, and my annoying neighbours consigned to history, maybe it was time to cite my revenge.

Around the next corner were an array of fungi growing on dead wood. I giggled to myself – Lando said I'd find my fun guy around the next corner. Perhaps I could take up foraging and have a dinner party, but I wouldn't want to poison anyone at my new home; that wouldn't make me very popular.

Lost in my thoughts, I continued down the track until my heart skipped a beat. From out of nowhere, a pheasant drummed a racket similar to Reuben practising his trombone; though the pheasant sounded like he had a bout of hiccups. A blackbird shrilled a warning of ping, ping, ping, ping, as a startled fox crossed the track in front of me. Crows cawed high in the branches, and in the distance, the bleating of sheep was accompanied by a long-drawn-out bellow from a cow. Maybe the countryside wasn't as quiet as I thought.

The low golden glow of December sunshine cast shadows across the fields while silhouettes of starlings fluttered on the horizon. As the track narrowed, overgrown clumps of grass were bursting through the broken tarmac. Towering embankments were shrined in skeletons of summer grasses entwined in brambles. It was lucky it was a dead end; I couldn't imagine reversing the whole way back.

A huge oak tree stood proud and tall with branches spanning across the track. Within the bark's gnarly cracks and fishers a face of an elderly man beckoned me to hug the tree.

I patted it saying aloud, 'Bet you could tell me a story or two.' Crikey, I was talking to a tree, people would think I was barking mad.

My pace fastened in anticipation of seeing my potential new home. The sheep's bleating intensified and glancing towards the next bend, I froze on the spot. A giant snowball of stampeding legs was rolling towards me, and any minute now I was going to be trampled to smithereens. Shit! Believe me, there would be plenty of that once this lot had trampled over me. With no escape routes, I grasped a low-hanging tree root and heaved myself up the embankment. Ten seconds later the root snapped, propelling me backwards onto my most prominent feature. I scrambled to my feet and impersonated a galloping shire horse to perfection, as I clip clopped back down the track. How the wellies remained on my feet was anyone's guess, and with no passing places I knew diddly squat of where I was galloping to. I peeped over my shoulder. Effing hell! The snowball had metamorphosed into an avalanche and was advancing quicker than Sir Mo Farah running a mile. With seconds to spare, the old oak tree came into sight, and without a moment too soon, I climbed up the tree out of harm's way. With my legs straddled either side of a branch, I appeared to be riding a horse, rather than pretending to be one.

The snowball halted a few feet away, and numerous pairs of eyes glared up at me as the remainder of the snowball caught up. Images of concertinaed sheep, with their heads up each other's backsides, sprang to mind. Satisfied the thing dangling from the tree was no longer a threat, the snowball melted and thundered past.

Above the hullabaloo, the drone of a quad bike was amplified by the constant yelping of a dog. The racket intensified until it was booming directly below me. Perched on the quad bike was the figure of a man wearing filthy bottle-green overalls and an even dirtier beanie hat. I prayed he didn't look up as I clung to the branch. His dog, a huge beast, resembled a wolf and was far too focussed on the sheep to have noticed me. A whisp of wind brushed a tiny branch across my nose. Swishing the branch away I released my hold on the main branch. In all the kerfuffle, I'd forgotten to keep my toes curled in the wellies. My left foot became bored of swimming around in gigantic wellies and thought it was time it surfaced. I tried re-curling my toes, but to no avail, the wellie slipped off and headed in a direct collision path towards the man's head.

Expecting the man to step sideways, I screamed, 'Watch out!'

Instead though, he looked up. 'What the f–' was all he said, as the wellie hit him squarely on the nose, and I fell out of the tree, landing in a heap at his feet.

I knelt up. 'I'm so sorry, are you okay?'

'Think I'll live, are you okay?' The man held out his hand and plucked me from the ground.

'I'm fine thanks. I'm very sorry my wellie hit you on the nose.'

He rubbed his nose. 'Don't think it's broken.' He gazed at me with puzzled eyes the colour of blue topaz. The concerned squint soon turned to anger, as he pulled his beanie back revealing a mop of blond curls.

'Don't you know this is a private no-through road? And what the heck were you doing up a tree?'

His good looks didn't camouflage what a rude and unpleasant man he was.

'Of course I know it's a private track. I was on my way to view Catkins when my climbing skills came in handy and avoided me being trampled to death by your sheep. I shimmied up the tree, but my wellies were too big and ... well, you know the rest of the story.'

The man threw me a cheeky smirk. 'I see, so what you're saying is you were so scared of the sheep you were shaking in your boots.' He snorted with laughter at his own joke before continuing. 'And what the heck are you going to look at Catkins for?'

'I'm thinking of purchasing it. I'm the new vet, and whoever heard of a vet fearing sheep?'

The man scratched his head. 'Purchasing Catkins! Are you kidding me? Guess you'll be working with Madigan. How was the old codger?'

I didn't care much for this man's attitude.

'That's a bit rude to call him an old codger, he's only in his fifties, that's not old. I'm going to be working with his nephew in the practice, and occasionally helping his son and daughter on canoeing and kayaking trips. Madigan was about to show me Catkins, when he was called away on an emergency, so he dropped me off at the end of the track.'

The man's eyes crinkled at the corners as he gazed at me and didn't say anything. I wasn't sure if it was astonishment or a bout of sympathy. Unexpectedly, he leant back before throwing himself forward, snorting like a pig. 'That sounds like Madigan. Did he tell you that the house is derelict, and the only residents for the past ten years have been the eight-legged kind. Not forgetting the bats, and it's gonna take a lot of touching up.' He paused and scrutinized me up and down. 'Do you even know how to paddle a kayak or a canoe? I doubt his son wants a novice helping him.'

With my legs planted firmly apart, I pushed my sleeves up and placed my hands on my hips before snapping, 'I've been canoeing and kayaking since I could walk. I'm not afraid of spiders, or bats and I'm prepared for plenty of touching up!' Yikes, that didn't come out right, though before he had the chance to say anything I continued. 'All my family work within the building and gardening trade so there'll be plenty of free hands.'

'I'd keep it quiet about being touched up around here or you might end up with guys queuing at your door. The only trade needed at Catkins is the demolition trade.' Once again, he leant back on his quad bike, chuckling at his own joke, before tossing the wellie back to me.

I hopped towards the wellie and slipped my foot inside.

'There will be no need for any demolition, my family can fix anything.'

'I'd reserve judgement until you've seen Catkins. If you do decide to buy the old ramshackle, we'll be neighbours, the name's Beau. I live on the farm over the hill.'

'Bow, like the front of my canoe?'

'Not Bow! It's Beau, short for Beaufort, it means beautiful, charming and embodies elegance.'

Now it was my turn to laugh. 'You mean like the Beaufort scale? Were you full of wind as a baby?'

'No, though after spending the night with me, many women tell their friends I'm off the scale, and a force to be reckoned with.'

I couldn't find any words, was this man for real, he was so full of himself.

'The truth is my mum named me after her favourite cheese as she had a craving for it when she was pregnant.'

'You're named after a cheese! I ate a chunk of Beaufort cheese at the weekend. It was nutty with a pungent aroma, took a long time to mature, and too much made you nauseous.'

Beau's sniggering lit up his face. 'Sounds about right, though I thought it was soft and smooth, without flaws or holes.'

'Beau Peep, I can see one big flaw, you've lost your sheep! You'll need plenty of wind in your sails to catch up with them. Sorry, must dash, before Catkins falls down.' I said continuing down the track.

Beau laughed and shouted after me, 'What's your name?'

Walking backwards, I shouted, 'Oakley Breeze. Though you can call me Dr Breeze.'

Beau slid back onto his quad bike and shouted, 'It will be a breeze to find my sheep, as they'll come home, wagging their tails behind them. *Ewe* had better get a move on Doc while Catkins is still standing.'

'Very funny. See *ewe* around, Beau.'

He started the ignition and waved as he sped after his sheep and I trundled along the track in search of Catkins, before it turned into a mound of dust.

Chapter Fifteen
Catkins

It seemed I'd been walking for an eternity by the time the end of the track was visible. With my fingers crossed, I prayed Beau was exaggerating about the condition of Catkins. Imagine bumping into such a gorgeous-looking farmer in the middle of nowhere, pity his ego was as large as his flock of sheep. He reminded me a little of Trent, cheeky with a glint in his eyes. I bet he had swarms of girls clinging to his every word, not really my type of guy. Though maybe Ruby was right, I was too pernickety and shouldn't view every man as a potential long-term partner. But then again, in six months I would be twenty-nine, it was time I grew up and settled down. Would it harm to have a little fun first? Oh, my goodness, Oakley, pull yourself together, I scorned myself. Far too many buts and maybes, however, the butt on Beau appeared to whet my appetite. None the less, he was probably taken, can't be many single men in Whispering Pines. Why was I born with such an indecisive nature?

At the end of the track a large turning circle was bordered by a wall taking a horizontal rest. To the left, an orchard peeped through a paddock of brambles, and to the right an overgrown rambling rose clung to a six-foot wall. Camouflaged within the wall an arched gateway supported a mammoth, rusty old iron gate strewn with thorny briars. Lifting the latch, I pricked my fingers several times. Crikey, was I going to fall asleep for a hundred years waiting for my Prince Charming to kiss me? I couldn't possibly wait that long to be kissed.

The gate creaked and swung open on one hinge almost falling off the support. I stepped back flabbergasted; the garden was gigantic, and I needed binoculars to see the end. Remnants of a veg patch were visible with twisted, dead runner beans hanging off bamboo canes. Nestled in the distance, surrounded by a sandstone wall, bordered by overgrown flower borders and a huge oak tree, was the façade of a dilapidated old farmhouse. With the amount of moss on the roof and twigs protruding from the chimney pots, it wouldn't have surprised me if a mustering of storks hadn't made themselves at home. The white exterior was stained in lichen and damaged gutters dangled over smashed leaded windows encompassed by rotten frames. Catkins was a skeleton of its former self. Though combined with a little love, a humongous amount of touching up, and a lot of imagination, I was positive it could be transformed to its former glory. Who said romance had to be between people? I had fallen head over heels in love with Catkins, and I hadn't even seen the interior.

A herringbone path of red bricks led up to a flimsy front porch that wasn't far off joining the wall in the horizontal position. Within the porch stood a solid oak door that must have been made for giants. I turned the key, and with a shoulder nudge or two, it creaked open. A whoosh of stale musty odour greeted me like a force twelve squall. The stench reminded me of living with my brothers and their festering football kits waiting for the laundry fairy. Hideous brown and green mosaic tiles covered the floors, and the pattern on the walls was not dissimilar. The sweeping central staircase was festooned with cobwebs hanging like lace curtains. A rainbow of dust particles danced in the sunlight, and when they penetrated my nose, my sneezing must have woken every eight-legged resident in Catkins. Amazing views dominated two living rooms, which both had inglenook fireplaces and moth-eaten window seats sitting in bay windows. The kitchen was huge, though except for a Belfast sink and solid fuel Aga, it was virtually bare. Leading from the kitchen was an additional door that opened into an amazing orangery that spanned the back of the house looking out to the sea.

Stepping gingerly upstairs I accidentally trod on every loose floorboard, reawakening the eight-legged residents, and on reaching the top, I was amazed to see eight doors. Five led to huge double bedrooms, and a master bathroom was dominated by the biggest rolled-top bath I'd ever seen. Two of the remaining doors were bathrooms, but the final door opened into a secret staircase twisting its way up to an attic bedroom with tiny round windows at either end. If I invested in a couple of skylight windows, the room would be flooded with light. Catkins was amazing, and despite the endless list of jobs poaching my brain, a sledgehammer most certainly wasn't included in my list of tools. I glanced at the time, it was late and time I headed home, but it felt like I was already home, and I didn't want to leave. Previously, Catkins had been showered in love, now it was time for it to be deluged in love; not forgetting the oodles of touching up.

Chapter Sixteen
The Herring Gull Rescue

By the time I locked the front door, the light was fading fast, though there was just enough time to explore the garden. After scrambling through undergrowth, I discovered a pond, which was big enough to paddle my canoe and even had a duck house in the middle.

I followed the path to a kissing gate that groaned as it swung open. The squeaking frightened a flock of fieldfares and redstarts gorging on the last of the autumn berries. After circling the field, they landed in the freshly ploughed soil, creating a repetitive rattling noise as they foraged for worms. I squeezed through another kissing gate, they certainly liked to do a lot of kissing in this neck of the woods.

Ahead of me, the incoming tide crept onto the mudflats, snaking and tiptoeing up the numerous channels and inlets. Glittering schools of tiny fish darted to and fro, followed closely by a flash of blue. A kingfisher darted along the surface, before perching on an old branch sticking out of the mud. A wooden bridge arched the estuary into a pine forest on the opposite bank. My lungs filled up with cold salty air as my ears were bombarded with the trill of blackbirds. I glanced at the time – half past three, time I kicked my heels up, though in the ginormous wellies it was best not to go too fast, or I'd end up in the mudflats.

The setting of the sun painted a palette of soft glowing salmon and tangerine, intertwined with wisps of lavender. The moon hung patiently waiting for its turn to shine and cast shadows across the valley. A flock of starlings gathered and chatted high up on the treetops, then like a clap of thunder, they took flight, forming silhouettes against the advancing twilight. They twisted, swooped and swirled, shaping a murmuration into an amazing heart. They were spellbinding, capturing my heart as they danced their aerial ballet, choreographed to perfection. Their constant hum magnified the stillness of the late afternoon as they disappeared over the horizon. With the light fading, I quickened my pace until my ears picked up the pitiful cries of a distressed gull. Tangled amongst pieces of driftwood was a mass of feathers and the outline of the gull, and if I didn't hurry, the poor thing was going to drown.

It was time I forged a plan. If I laid spreadeagled, redistributed my weight, and slithered across the mud, I could cut the gull free using the multitool I kept in my overalls. It was a treasured gift from an old kayaking friend, though like me, it hadn't seen a lot of action recently. Despite the temperature being bone-chilling cold, I left my coat and wellies alongside my bag and began impersonating a snake slithering towards the gull's cries. Ignoring the rustling in the undergrowth behind me, my mercy mission continued. Then, without warning, something grabbed the back of my overalls and began dragging me back, it felt like I was being dragged by a pack of wolves. A dog started barking as a huge pair of men's boots squelched in the mud beside my nose. My line of vision followed the boots towards a pair of legs, wearing dirty green overalls.

'Good boy, Wolf. What have we got here?' My eyes scanned further up the legs to see Beau staring at me. The noise that followed sounded like a cackling gull and caused his dog to bark incessantly.

'What have we got here? Doctor Oakley Breeze practising her doggy paddle. Oh my god, now what are you up to?'

'Hi, Beau, I'm trying to rescue the gull.' I lifted myself up onto my elbows and pointed to the driftwood. 'It's caught on a piece of driftwood, and it's going to drown if I don't rescue it.'

Beau stepped towards the driftwood.

'Beau, what are you doing? You'll sink in the mud, and then I'll have to rescue you too.'

Beau stopped and twisted around shaking his head and frowning. 'Do I look like I'm sinking? Why didn't you walk over and pick it up?' He marched through the mud, leant over the driftwood, and hollered with laughter.

'Is the gull all right?' I said feeling rather foolish and humiliated in three inches of mud.

Beau unravelled the fishing line and peered at me, chuckling. 'Sorry, even the new vet can't save this gull.'

'Oh no, I'm too late.' I squealed attempting to stand up.

Beau squelched towards me carrying the gull. He dropped it into the mud in front of me, revealing a deflated, inflatable, herring gull. 'They're tied all over the deck of the disco boat; this one must have escaped.'

'I was positive I heard it crying.'

'I could give it the kiss of life if you want?' Beau attached his lips around the gull's deflated beak and started blowing it up. 'Look, it's breathing, fancy a go? It could be your first patient.'

'Very—' was the only word uttered, as my legs and arms gave way spiralling me into a Bambi on ice position. The only sense left was my hearing, and all I could hear was Beau braying like a donkey. He grabbed the waistbelt on my overalls, swept me into his arms, and threw me over his shoulder before dropping me on the path.

'My ex would have paid a fortune to have a face pack like that, and you've had one for free.'

I wiped the mud from around my eyes, picking up on the point he said ex, and pointed to the mudflat. 'Looks like you might be having one too.'

'No, Wolf come here boy, Woolfey boy leave the gull. Wolf come here and leave the gull. Wolf ... leave ... the ... effing gull.'

Hysterical laughter brewed within me like a hose pipe with a kink. Wolf crawled towards us covered from head to tail in mud. Protruding from his mouth was the inflatable gull followed by a rope entwined in seaweed, a piece of driftwood and a buoy. Beau trudged through the mud and tried to wrestle the gull out of Wolf's mouth. Wolf thought it was a game of tug of war and refused to give up his beloved gull. Out of nowhere, a real gull nose-bombed him. Wolf leapt up, dropped the inflatable gull, and barked nonstop, warning it to leave his gull alone. Beau, who a few seconds earlier had been holding the other end of the inflatable gull, was now sitting in a mudflat. I couldn't keep quiet anymore as Wolf, who thought it was a huge game, jumped on top of Beau, flattening him.

'Get off me, you stupid mutt. Oakley, can you call Wolf please?'

'He's not going to come to me.'

'He will if you open my backpack and show him a sausage.'

I dangled a sausage in front of me. 'Here, Wolf, look what I've got, a lovely fat sausage.'

With his tongue dangling out of the side of his mouth, Wolf raced towards me. He sat down at my knees, gazed up with huge puppy-dog eyes, and rested a massive paw on my knee. What a beautiful dog. I held out the sausage and a mouth like velvet encased it as it disappeared from my fingers.

'There's a good boy, do you want another one?'

Who could resist those eyes as he peered up drooling for another sausage, and before I realised, the bag was empty.

Beau picked himself up and squelched through the mud towards me. 'Thanks for distracting Wolf, he likes you.'

I handed Beau the empty brown bag feeling great that I had connected with his dog.

'That's okay, he's gorgeous, like a huge teddy bear. What breed is he?'

'A Caucasian Shepherd.' Beau peered inside the paper bag and seemed annoyed. 'You haven't given him all the sausages, have you? They were meant to be for my tea.'

I looked at the empty bag. 'Sorry, I thought they were for your dog.'

'Excellent! Not only am I covered in mud, but my dog has eaten my tea!'

Somehow, impressing the local gorgeous farmer and my potential new neighbour wasn't going too well.

'I'm so sorry, it's my fault, I'll buy you some more at the café.'

'It's closed, that's why I had the leftovers. Forget about it, I'll go to the pub later.'

'At least let me pay for your meal in the pub.'

'No, you get off home. You can buy me a meal when you move down, that's if you're still moving here?'

'I am, and I'm buying Catkins.'

'Seriously, that rickety old place? Well good luck to you, looks like we're going to be neighbours. Though maybe I should keep out of your way, I hate to think what you might do to me next.'

'I don't normally get into so much trouble.'

'We'll see. I'd best be going, I've a mutt to bath as well as myself.' Beau took a huge bunch of keys out of his pocket and detached one of them.

'You can't go home looking like that. Madhatters is round the next corner, here's a key as there's no one in the reception for an hour. There's a shower in the utility room, and borrow one of the spare overalls, I'm sure my dad won't mind. Pop the key through the letterbox when you've finished.'

My jaw dropped. 'What do you mean your dad? Is Madigan your dad?'

Beau smirked. 'Oh yeah, forget to mention, I'm the son you're going to be helping at the water sports activity centre. So, Doctor Oakley Breeze, your paddling had better be as good as you said it was.'

'It is. I'm glad I said nice things about your dad.'

'Doesn't matter, we wind each other up all the time. Maybe we should rename you Miss Tornado as I think you're going to be stirring things up in sleepy Whispering Pines.'

'I have no intention of stirring things up. See you in the New Year, have a lovely Christmas, Beau.'

'You too, and congratulations on getting the job, see you around, new neighbour. Come on, Wolf, home boy.'

'Thanks. Bye, Beau.'

With my coat and wellies tucked under my arm, and my body tingling with happiness at the thought of spending time with Beau at the water sports centre, I trundled in my socks towards Madhatters for a shower before heading home.

Chapter Seventeen
Cutting the Apron Strings

My boss was disappointed when I popped into work the following day and handed her my notice, though she understood my decision.

I set off to my parents' house knowing they would not be very understanding. I hadn't spoken to my mum since she gave my ticket for *Cinderella* to Molly, and I wasn't sure if the reception would be frosty.

On arrival, several cars were parked on their driveway; maybe this wasn't the best time to visit. I drove past and Harrison waved. I reversed back and opened my window.

Harrison ran down to my car. 'Sis, you'll have to park around the corner.'

'Okay, why is everyone here?'

'Didn't you get the text?'

'No.'

'Tell you in a bit, you're holding the traffic up.'

I parked my car on the next street and hurried back to meet Harrison.

'When did you send a text?' I said while riffling through my bag for my phone.

'I sent it in the WhatsApp group, inviting everyone round to Mum and Dad's for lunch so Molly and I can give you our good news.'

I already knew their good news, maybe today wasn't the best day to scupper their plans.

I glanced at my phone. 'Sorry, Harrison, I switched my phone off yesterday. I must have forgotten to switch it back on.'

'Switched your phone off? That's not like you, why are you here then?'

'I wanted to give Mum and Dad my news, but it can wait for another day. Is everyone here?'

'Yes, other than Flynn, he had other plans. Trent is here too.'

'Why on earth have you invited Trent?'

'We bumped into him yesterday and Reuben invited his ice hockey hero. Don't worry, Mum's made a mountain of meatballs and spaghetti, they'll be plenty to go around.'

'I wasn't worried about him shuffling too much food in his mouth, more worried about the garbage he spouts out.'

'Don't sit by him then.'

After a few seating squabbles, we settled around the table and piled into the humongous mound of food.

'Come on, Harrison, we're waiting. What was it you and Molly wanted to tell us?' piped up my mum.

Harrison smiled at Molly. 'Shall I tell them or you?'

Molly, not one to keep quiet, blurted out, 'We're having another baby, or two!' Everyone dropped their forks and spoons and fell silent, except my mum.

'What do you mean, or two?'

'I'm expecting twin boys, isn't it wonderful? With Oakley next door to help, the timing couldn't be more perfect.'

What a relief I was escaping to Cornwall, I couldn't have timed it better. With the image of Catkins in my mind, I momentarily lost concentration. There was a rumble of laughter, and all eyes fixated on me as my mum tutted. The white tablecloth was splattered with tomato sauce as a result of the overzealous twisting of my fork. My mum gave me her best witch stare.

My dad stood up and raised his glass. 'That's wonderful news, let's raise our glasses and toast the new babies.'

While everyone held their glasses up and cheered, Willow's head hung low, and her glass remained untouched.

My mum placed her fork and spoon beside her dish. 'Your turn now, Oakley, what did you want to tell us?'

Using my napkin, I sponged the tomato sauce off the tablecloth. 'It can wait, Mum.'

'It must have been important for you to come round, so out with it.'

I took a deep breath and slowly exhaled. 'I've accepted another job.'

My dad bolted upright. 'You have? I thought you loved your job.'

'All I do is castrate pets; I need to do more, Dad. I've accepted a position within a mixed practice, plus I'll be helping at a water sports activity centre.'

Brenden piped up, 'Sis, that sounds wonderful, when do you start?'

'March, which gives me long enough to sell my house.'

My mum gulped her wine. 'What do you mean? Where's the job?'

'A remote Cornish village called Whispering Pines.'

Molly dropped her cutlery and spluttered, 'Cornwall! You mean you're not going to be living next door?'

'No, I'm buying an old farmhouse in need of renovation.'

'Are we not going to see you anymore?' said Poppy on the verge of crying.

'Of course you'll see me. You can stay whenever you like.'

Blossom wiped the sauce from around her mouth. 'Is it by the sea?'

'Yes, you can walk to the sea from the house.'

Poppy sucked her spaghetti up like a worm. 'But if you move, we'll miss the cats.'

'You can see them on your holidays, or when you stay at the weekends.'

My dad turned to me. 'When did this happen?'

'I was offered the job and house yesterday.'

My dad seemed annoyed. 'You've agreed to buy a house without speaking to me first?'

'Yes, I'm a big girl, Dad, but before I put in a firm offer, I've asked if my family could view Catkins to estimate the cost of repairs.'

'Offer what? Your house isn't even on the market. How are you going to pay for another house?'

Before I had time to answer, Brenden's five-year-old daughter Savanna interrupted.

'Auntie Oakley, what's castrating?'

My dad gulped, before popping another meatball into his mouth.

Reuben, eager to help his cousin blurted, 'It means Auntie Oakley is taking away the dogs' and cats' balls.'

'Auntie Oakley, that's mean. What will they play with if they have no balls? I play with my dog's balls. Daddy plays with his balls all the time, and my cat keeps getting his balls stuck under the sofa.'

The table erupted with laughter as all eyes were directed towards Brenden, but poor Savanna was none the wiser.

'Don't they take the balls away to stop them humping your leg, or the cushions?' enquired Reuben. 'That's what Ben did before he had the chop.'

Harrison ignored Reuben and turned to his niece. 'Savanna, the male dogs are castrated so they don't give the female dogs anymore babies.'

'I see. Mummy said Daddy didn't want any more children as we were a handful, can Auntie Oakley castrate Daddy?'

Brenden glared at me, shaking his head and mouthing, 'No.'

My dad was eyeing up his remaining meatballs. 'Somehow dear, I don't feel hungry anymore, what's for pudding?'

'Your favourite, plum crumble.'

'Think I will pass on that, anyone for coffee?' said my dad, placing his knife and fork on his plate.

We finished our tea and withdrew to the living room for coffee. My dad, fully recovered from his ordeal, parked himself in his favourite armchair, leant back and closed his eyes. Harrison and Molly disappeared outside and returned a few minutes later.

Harrison pulled a stool alongside me. 'Sis, Molly, and I have come up with a plan, we'll buy your house. We can knock through and make it into a detached house. The kids can have a bedroom each and there will be a nursery for the babies, and I won't have to move my gear out of your garage.'

'Oh, my word, Harrison, that would be amazing. Would you mind driving down with me to cost the repairs?'

'How much work does it need?'

'New kitchen and bathrooms, electrics, plumbing, windows, plastering, painting, chimneys repointing, tiles replaced and tons of gardening; though that can wait until the spring.'

'Is that all? Lucky you have five brothers in the trade.'

My dad opened an eye and added his two pennies' worth. 'What about me? It's not called Rob the Builder and Sons for nothing!'

'Sorry, old man. Five brothers and a dad; I'm sure we can come up with a plan. Is there a local pub?'

'Yes, It's called Reel Them Inn, it looks nice, and has a huge selection of food.'

'Sounds great. You pay for the materials and a meal in the pub and forget about the labour charges. I'm proud of you, even if we are losing our babysitter.'

Without saying a word, Willow left the room, with Poppy and Blossom in pursuit. How selfish of me, I'd forgotten about Willow's escape bolt in my spare room.

I called after her, 'Are you all right, Willow?'

She popped her head around the door, clearly close to tears. 'I understand you want to move, Auntie Oakley, but so do I. Where will I study now?'

Harrison peered towards his daughter. 'Love, don't get so upset, you can study in the same room, it will be part of our house instead of Auntie Oakley's.'

'Dad, you don't understand, it won't be the same. Now I'm going to have five annoying half-brothers! Before you married Molly it was just the two of us. Why do things have to change? I'm walking home, I need to think.'

Poppy followed her and reached for her coat. 'Willow, can you walk home with us? Dad should be there by now.'

'Yes, if that's okay with Nan and Gramps.'

My dad handed Blossom her coat. 'Let me check your dad is home first.'

I could hear my dad chatting to Flynn and a few minutes later the three girls slammed the door shut without saying goodbye. I sank into an armchair as pangs of guilt suffocated me. Should I run after the girls and shout I've changed my mind? Oh, but this was a once-in-a-lifetime opportunity for me, and maybe the start of a whole new life. In two years' time Willow would be getting ready for uni and the twins would be planning to move to a secondary school. They'd be so busy they wouldn't need their auntie, but even those thoughts didn't extinguish my guilt. Willow's mum died when Willow was four. Harrison remarried two years later, but Molly never gelled with Willow. Poppy and Blossom's mum left last Christmas and moved in with boring Billy the boyfriend; the girls needed me more than ever; how could I have been so selfish? I left everyone discussing knocking walls down, as I headed towards the door, followed by Trent.

'Oakley, you're really moving? Good for you. I spend a lot of time in Cornwall, I'll have to pop by and say hello.'

'I haven't given you the address. It's so remote you'd never find it.'

'I'll pop by the vets' then. My parents live about three miles from Whispering Pines.'

'Seriously? I thought they lived in Scotland.'

'Moved two years ago, though my uncle still lives in Scotland; runs a campsite on the West Coast by the Driftwood Islands.'

'Sounds lovely. Anyway, I've got to dash as I've got loads to think about. Bye, Trent, have a nice Christmas.'

'You too. See yer, Tinker Bell.'

I parked on Ruby's drive as she walked out of her front door laden with a box of papers.

'Hi, Rubes.'

'Oh, hi, Oakley. I was on my way out. Why does your face have the same expression as when your brothers replaced your Christmas Quality Street with Brussels sprouts wrapped in empty sweet wrappers? Is everything all right?'

'Yes, fine. I just wanted to tell you about my news in person rather than by phone.'

'News. What news? I can spare a few minutes; do you want to come in?'

'No, I can see you're busy. Just wanted to thank you for waking me up.'

'Oh my gosh, what have you done?'

'I was offered a job yesterday in a veterinary practice in Cornwall.'

Ruby dropped the box on the floor. 'Really? You're a dark horse. Are you taking it?'

'Yes, and I'm buying a farmhouse.'

'On your own?'

'Yes, but I want my brothers to see if first and give me a quote for the repairs. I'm hoping to go back on Thursday.'

'How exciting, can I come?'

'Of course you can.'

'Why are you so down then? I'd be jumping for joy.'

'I've upset Willow, Poppy and Blossom; they don't want me to move.'

'They'll adapt. It's time to live your own life.'

'I know, but it doesn't make me feel any less guilty.'

'That's because you're too nice. Sorry, Oak, I've got to dash to a meeting. I'm proud of you. Maybe you can stop dreaming about a man and find a real one. I'll see you on Thursday.'

'Hope your meeting goes okay. Bye, Rubes.'

That was strange, I thought she would have been more upset that I was moving over a hundred miles away. My phone chimed as I stepped back into my car.

'Sis, I think congratulations are in order.'

'Thanks, Flynn. Although I'm worried about the girls.'

'They're a bit miffed, but they'll get over it. It's not like there aren't any other relatives close by. Is the house near a blue sea, rather than a brown muddy one?!'

'Yes, walking distance.'

'Sounds wonderful. Harrison said you wanted our advice on Thursday, so count me in, and Perry too.'

'Great, thanks, Ruby wants to come too. What about the girls?'

'They're going to a party.'

'Okay, thanks.'

'Cheer up, this might be the best thing that has ever happened to you.'

'I know, but how can I feel happy when I am leaving the girls behind.'

'They'll be fine, think how excited they'll be spending weekends with their favourite auntie who lives by a blue sea. Have you told Nan?'

'On my way now.'

'You know she will want to come and live with you.'

'She can come down to stay for a bit, but she is not moving in permanently.'

Flynn chuckled down the phone. 'What's the expression Trent says? Never say never. You'd have no peace and quiet with Nan in the house.'

'That's why she is not coming to live with me. I'll let you know tomorrow what time we're meeting on Thursday.'

'Thanks, sis, and don't worry about the girls.'

'Night, Flynn.'

Ten minutes later, laden with a huge bunch of flowers from the local garage, I pushed the door open at Forever Spring Chickens. My nan was in the lounge playing poker with several of the male residents. I handed her the flowers.

'Hi, Nan.'

'Oh, hello, love. Are those for me? How lovely.' My nan turned to the men. 'Fellas, I want you to meet my favourite granddaughter, Oakley. Pull up a chair, love. Want us to deal you a hand?'

'No, you're all right, I can't stay long. Just wanted to stop by and tell you I've been offered a job in Cornwall and I'm moving home.'

'Seriously? Can you take me with you?'

'You can come and stay whenever you like.'

'Hear that lads, I'm getting out of here. Why are you so glum about it, love?'

'Because I've upset Willow, Poppy and Blossom.'

My nan addressed the men. 'They're my great-grandchildren. Would you believe it, I've got sixteen, plus another two on the way.' She turned to me. 'Don't worry about the kids, they'll be fine. Bet Molly and your mum weren't pleased. I think you've escaped in the nick of time.'

'Molly and Harrison are buying my house, then I can buy a farmhouse called Catkins.'

'What a lovely name, how exciting. Oakley, you're doing the right thing, time to cut the apron strings and follow your own rules.'

'You're right, Nan. Anyway, I'd best leave you to your game.'

One of the men stood up, coughed non-stop, and cleared his throat. 'You can take your nan away now if you like, my dear, maybe I'd have a chance of winning.'

My nan blew him a kiss, before pushing her chair back, leaning over, and hugging me.

She slipped a bag into my hands. 'Here's my winnings, you need it more than me.'

I peered inside the bag. 'Nan, I can't take all this chocolate.'

'I'm about to thrash these old codgers; look at that mountain of chocolate I'm gonna win.'

I giggled. 'Old codgers, Nan, they don't look a day over twenty-one. But as you seem to be on a winning streak, I'll gladly accept the chocolate.' I gave her a kiss on the cheek. 'See you Christmas Day, Nan.'

'See you Christmas Day, love.'

I winked at her. 'Bring a friend if you like.'

'No love, they're all coffin dodgers, I'm after a toyboy.'

I waved goodbye. 'You're too cheeky, Nan.'

My nan's chocolate did the trick and soon an idea popped into my head for last-minute Christmas presents to cheer Willow, Poppy, and Blossom up. After spending hours online I ordered three presents to be collected on my way back from Cornwall on Thursday. Later when I fell into bed, the feeling of guilt was transforming into a feeling of anticipation. I felt like pinching myself to check this wasn't just one of my daydreams. As I drifted off to sleep, Woody now had a rival as Beau pushed him out of the way and reached for my hand.

Chapter Eighteen
The Family Viewing

Madigan was more than happy for me to view Catkins with my family on Thursday. After letting everyone know the plans, we piled into three cars and set off to Cornwall. Three hours later, I nipped into Madhatters to collect the keys, and soon we were bumbling down the track to Catkins.

Ruby sat upright gripping her seatbelt. 'You can't live down here on your own, it's far too spooky.'

I opened my window. 'Don't worry, I'll be fine. Listen.'

Ruby opened her window. 'To what?'

'The countryside, isn't it wonderful?'

'Oakley, you're round the bend.'

'I know. Just one more bend and you'll see my potential new home.'

We parked in the yard, and as I pushed the gate open, everyone could have caught a swarm of flies in their open mouths. Lando, my green-fingered brother, was like a kid at Christmas.

'Oh my word, sis, look at the size of the garden! I'm off to explore.'

Ruby impersonated an owl. 'Oakley, it's like a jungle.'

Sniggering, I gazed towards my brothers. 'My family will feel right at home then.'

'Harrison, what do you think?'

'Blimey, sis, we haven't even walked through the front door, though I have an idea – we've been looking for a project to advertise on our website. It would be great to show the before and after pictures.'

I turned the key in the door, and everyone piled in.

'That's a great idea, Harrison, welcome to the before pictures.'

Flynn poked his head around the kitchen door. 'I know two little girls who are going to want to spend every holiday with their auntie. I may even consider moving down here myself.'

Brendon appeared at the top of the stairs and shouted down, 'Fantastic view from the bedrooms. Wonder if Isla would consider moving to Cornwall.'

Harrison followed Brendon down the stairs.

'It's amazing, I wonder if Molly would consider moving to Cornwall in a couple of years.'

Ruby sighed. 'Sorry Oakley, it seems like you may not be escaping your family after all.'

Lando appeared at the front door and shouted, 'Sis, the garden is amazing, think of all the parties we could have. I'll speak to the missus about selling up and moving to Cornwall.'

Perry and Spencer returned from viewing the orangery. They strolled towards me with huge grins plastered on their faces.

Spencer held his phone up to take yet another photo. 'I can't wait to show Mia the photos, this house is fantastic. Is there a local primary school? The kids and Mia will love it down here. We spotted a house for sale about a mile away and there was a large piece of commercial land for sale; maybe we can all relocate. What do you think, Perry mate? Fancy moving down here too?'

'Fantastic idea, could see the missus in her wellies, living the good life.'

My glare was so strong I felt my eyes watering. 'Give over the lot of you. Perry, I bet your wife doesn't even own a pair of wellies. You're all winding me up.'

Brendon reached the bottom of the stairs. 'Nope, we can't wait to move here too.'

My brothers exploded in laughter.

Flynn ruffled my hair. 'Got you a good'un, sis. Bet you were having kittens?'

'Erm, now there's an idea, I would love to have a couple kittens. I was going to treat you to lunch in the Lily Pad, but I'm not so sure now.'

'Come on, lads, looks like lunch is on little sis.' said Flynn.

Armed with a list of repairs, we headed to the Lily Pad and spotted an empty table in a corner.

I picked a menu up. 'My treat, order anything you like, you'll like Lily, the owner.'

A familiar voice appeared from behind the counter and shouted, 'Well if it's not the gull rescuer. Come back to see how much more trouble you can get into?' Beau wandered towards us looking rather fetching in smart black trousers and shirt, however, the pink-and-yellow pinny tied around his waist was hysterical.

'Beau, I didn't know you worked here; thought you'd be out searching for your sheep.'

'Very funny. Lily's popped to the cash and carry and asked me to fill in.'

A man in the opposite corner pushed his chair under the table and ambled towards us. He leant over my table and whispered, 'I'd go to the pub if I were you, service here is not up to much.'

Beau reached for a notepad and pen from the pinny. 'I heard that, Aidan. I've never had any complaints about my service, in fact, most women are bending over backwards for me to serve them!'

There was an air of joviality in the café while Aidan, along with the whole café erupted into spontaneous laughter. We could have charged them an entrance fee for this much fun.

'You're all mouth and no trousers, mate.'

'Some women like that. Oakley, I'd like you to meet Aidan, Lily's husband, fifty percent your new boss, one hundred percent my annoying uncle, and Mackenzie's dad.'

Aidan mooched around to me and shook my hand. 'Lovely to meet you, Oakley, welcome to the team. I'd watch yourself with this one, and don't believe anything he tells you about me.'

'That's a shame, he told me how lovely his uncle Aidan was, and how lucky I was to work with him.'

Aidan chuckled. 'Madigan was right, I think you and I are going to get on just fine. Enjoy the food, just don't order anything beyond page two. Have a lovely Christmas and we'll see you in the New Year.'

'Have a lovely Christmas too, Aidan. I'm looking forward to the New Year.' I opened the menu to see only beverages on the first two pages.

'Guess it will be coffees all round, unless you can rustle up bacon sarnies?'

Beau jotted some notes on his pad. 'I think I can manage not to burn the bacon. Are you going to introduce me to your friends?'

I pointed around the table. 'These ugly mutts are my brothers, and the ugly one on the end is my friend Perry.'

'And the beautiful young lady?'

'That's my friend Ruby.'

Ruby flirted her sweetest smile. 'Hi, Beau. I'm sure your bacon will be perfect.' Ruby never changed and always wanted first dibs on any good-looking boys.

Beau flirted back. 'Not as perfect as your beautiful smile.'

Ten minutes later, we were chomping doorstep sarnies, sipping coffee and chatting like a flock of chirping sparrows.

Harrison pulled another chair closer. 'Beau, why don't you join us? Oakley's shown us around Catkins so we can estimate the cost of repairs.'

Beau almost dropped his tray. 'That was a wasted journey. I could have lent you my sledgehammer for free.'

'Yeah, I guess it does need a lot of work, but we'll have it fixed in no time. Now what was this you were saying about a gull? I don't recall our little sis mentioning it. Maybe we could tell you a story or two of ours?'

Flynn wiped tomato sauce from his top lip and leant back on his chair. 'Beau, would you like to hear the story about Oakley's first and only Valentine's date?'

I kicked Flynn under the table. 'Beau doesn't need to know everything about my love life.'

'Don't you mean lack of love life?' said Flynn, sniggering.

Ruby threw me a look of sympathy and butted in, 'I think we need another round of coffees please, Beau.'

'I've just refilled the coffee machine; it needs a few minutes to warm up. So, what's this about Oakley's love life?'

Harrison began the story. 'The funniest date she had was the Valentine's card date. I popped home to see Mum and Dad and found a hand-delivered card addressed to O Breeze. I gave it to Oakley to open.' Harrison paused. 'I'm trying to remember the exact wording. I think it was along the lines of, I want to run my fingers through your beautiful brown hair and gaze into your sparkling eyes. Something corny like that. He wrote his phone number in the corner of the card, followed by a load of kisses. Wasn't the most romantic of Valentine's poems—'

I interrupted. 'I had no intension of calling him, but as usual, you had to interfere.'

Harrison chuckled. 'I was looking out for you, sis. You wouldn't call the number, so I did. I told him we had the card and that I was the big brother checking him out. His name was Simon, he seemed like a nice chap, so I arranged a date in the local café.'

'I didn't want to go.'

'Yeah, but sis, he sounded so sweet ... and after all, it was only coffee.'

Flynn continued. 'Despite not wanting to go, Oakley spent hours getting ready. When our dad saw her walking downstairs, he hit the roof.' Flynn put his hand on my shoulder and continued. 'You see, Beau, madam here had cut about two feet off her best skirt; it looked more like a belt and hardly covered her backside.'

Lando added his contribution. 'Dad told Oakley to put a proper skirt on before she went out, but she ignored him, climbed out the bathroom window and shimmied down the oak tree.'

Beau grinned in my direction. 'Now I see how Oakley gained her tree-climbing skills.'

'How do you know she likes climbing trees?' said Flynn.

Beau diverted his attention to me. 'You haven't told them about climbing the oak tree to escape a few sheep?'

'A few sheep! There were hundreds!'

Flynn piped up. 'When was this?'

'On my way to view Catkins. I climbed an oak tree to escape being trampled to death.'

Beau smirked. 'Oakley forgot to mention she booted me in the nose, fell out the tree, and tried to rescue an inflatable gull.'

By now the whole café was engrossed in my life and everyone dissolved into laughter.

Flynn jabbered, 'Sis, why didn't tell us any of this?'

'I don't tell you everything about my life.'

'We can see that now. Anyway, back to the story. We watched her hobbling up the road in her new heels while pulling her skirt down to hide her backside—'

Harrison butted in, 'Oakley didn't realise, but I was tasked with following her.'

'You mean you spied on me from across the road.'

'You were sixteen and on your first date that I'd arranged, if anything happened to you, Mum would have killed me.'

I continued the story. 'Simon told Harrison he would be dressed in a red top and sitting at the table in the window. I thought I looked fantastic tottering in high heels and my short skirt. I spotted Simon, he was gorgeous with hair as black as a raven. If he hadn't been so good looking, I may have lost my nerve. I walked straight up to Simon and said, "Hi, I'm Oakley," though he gazed at me as if I was from another planet.'

Ruby interrupted and sniggered. 'That's understandable.'

'Thanks, Rubes! I apologised and said I must have got the wrong boy. Simon said he was waiting for a boy from his carpentry class called Orlando. I explained he was my brother, and we thought the Valentine's card was for me as it was addressed to O Breeze. I'm not sure who was more embarrassed, me or Simon.'

Lando roared with laughter. 'Oakley explained I had a girlfriend. Despite being disappointed, Simon saw the funny side and asked Oakley to join him for coffee.'

Beau leant back on his chair, cackling like a gull. 'That's the funniest tale I've ever heard. Guess there wasn't a second date then?'

'No, but we became good friends. Lando introduced Simon to a friend of his called Sam. Lando was the best man at their wedding last year. During his speech, he reminded everyone how we met, but that's enough about my love life, we'd better hit the road, I still have a lot to organise for Christmas.'

Harrison quizzed me. 'You have bought the presents for our better halves, haven't you?'

'Yes, and I've wrapped them.'

He blew me a kiss across the table. 'Thanks, sis, shouldn't have doubted you.'

Beau cleared the mugs from the tables. 'I can see Oakley is going to keep us on our toes when she moves here. I can't wait to hear more stories. Lads, maybe you can help me build a jetty for my water sports centre.'

Harrison pushed his chair under the table. 'No problem, mate. Providing everything goes okay with the finances to purchase Catkins, we'll be back in the New Year to start work. Perhaps we can discuss plans over a few bevvies?'

'Sounds great. You can camp in one of my fields and make a night of it. I'm looking forward to Oakley waking up sleepy Whispering Pines.'

Harrison sniggered. 'There's never a dull moment when our little sis is around. Believe me, I think trouble is her middle name.'

I hit Harrison on the arm. 'Excuse me, I'm still here.'

'We know, how could we ever forget you?'

'Bye, Beau. Have a lovely Christmas.' I said.

'You too, Oakley. Hope to see you all in the New Year.'

Ruby placed her hand on Beau's shoulder. 'Was lovely to meet you, Beau. Hope to see you again really soon.'

Beau leant into Ruby as she was about to kiss him, but then pulled back. 'Lovely to meet you too, Ruby. Look forward to seeing you again too.'

As we ambled to the cars, I glared at Ruby who had the appearance of a lovestruck teenager. She caught my glare. 'What? Only window shopping. Needed to check the merchandise was in working order for my best friend.'

'You don't change, do you? Come on, we'd better hurry, we've got to pick up the presents for the girls before the shop closes.'

'I thought you'd finished your shopping,' questioned Harrison.

'I had, but I've bought Willow, Poppy and Blossom something extra.'

Flynn waved. 'Sis, you spoil those three. Ruby are you still picking the girls up in the morning?'

'Yes, around eight o'clock if that's okay?'

'That's fine, have a good trip back, ladies.'

I handed the remainder of my nan's bag of chocolate to Flynn and Harrison. '

Thanks for your help today. Pass these around on your way home, Nan won them last night playing poker.'

'Thanks, sis. They'll go down a treat.'

Ruby and I waved goodbye to my brothers and Perry before we headed off to pick up the girls' presents.

'Oakley, are you going to tell me what you've bought them?'

'No, you can keep guessing all the way to the shop.'

Two hours later we arrived at the shop, collected the presents, and headed home; I couldn't wait for the girls to see them on Christmas Day.

Chapter Nineteen
Christmas Eve

With so much to do, I was up bright and early on Christmas Eve. When I arrived at the village hall, Ruby, Blossom and Poppy were waiting for me.

'Morning ladies, glad to see you're here early.'

Blossom reached into the boot and lifted out a box of tree ornaments. 'Auntie Oakley, this is so exciting, but next year can we have a party at your new house?'

'We'll see.'

Poppys' smile slipped. 'Blossom, stop overloading me with boxes. I can't see where I'm going. Take that last box off before I drop everything. Auntie Oakley, what time will the Christmas tree be here?'

'Uncle Harrison, Reuben and Willow will be here at quarter to nine, which gives us fifteen minutes to unload my car.'

Blossom lifted another box out and dropped it on the floor sending decorations spiralling around the car park. This was going to be a long day.

'Oops, sorry, Auntie Oakley, I'll pick them up. I can't wait to see Willow, she's like a big sister to us.'

Gathering up the decorations I turned to Blossom. 'Don't you love Reuben?'

'Yikes no, he's a boy! We don't like boys do we Poppy?'

'No, we don't. There's an annoying boy at school called Theo who keeps chasing us and asking us both to be his girlfriend.'

'I'll remind you of that statement in a few years' time.' I said reaching into the box of decorations.

'Yeah, well I'm not going out with a boy who picks his nose all the time and he also fa—'

I cut in. 'I don't think Ruby wants to hear the details of his bodily functions.'

'Well, he does, and it's not nice.'

Ruby was giggling as she unloaded the remaining boxes. 'What's the plan for today, Oak?'

'We'll decorate the tree and hall first, and then wait for everyone to deliver the food orders I assigned them.'

'When are we going to bake the cookies?' quizzed Blossom.

'Once we've prepared the veg for Christmas dinner.'

Blossom sighed. 'I hate vegetables, especially Brussels sprouts, I'd prefer a buffet.'

'We're having one for tea. Try and eat one Brussels sprout, they're good for you.'

'It's not good for everyone else around me if I eat Brussels sprouts.'

'Remind me to stay away from you then,' I said, fumbling with the flaps on the end of a large box.

Ruby lifted the flaps on the other end. 'Oakley, what's in the box?'

'An electric wood-burning stove to make the hall appear more Christmassy.'

'I take it back about you being unorganised, you think of everything.'

'I wonder where Harrison is with the tree,' I said, pressing my contacts to call him as my phone chimed.

'Hi Molly, is everything okay?'

'Oakley, you're going to hate me.'

'Why?'

'The man from the Christmas tree farm rang yesterday checking when we were collecting our tree. I said we'd already collected it so we must have double-booked our order. I'd forgotten we'd ordered two trees. Harrison's just left the farm, and they've sold out of trees.'

'Please tell me you're joking?'

'No, sorry Oakley.'

'Is Harrison searching for another one?'

'No, he's had to go to work. That's not all – I thought I was only cooking the ham, but Harrison said we were meant to have ordered two turkeys, sorry I forgot.'

'Molly!'

'You don't need to raise your voice; I said I was sorry.'

'What time will Willow and Reuben be here to help?'

'Reuben has gone to his mates, and I've no idea where Willow is.'

'Aren't you worried about Willow?'

'She'll turn up when she's hungry. Anyway, must dash as I've loads to do.'

'Not as much as me. Please don't forget to cook the ham. Bye Molly.'

Ruby was tying herself in knots unravelling a box of fairy lights.

'What was all that about?'

'You won't believe it; we don't have a tree or turkeys!'

Ruby dropped the lights. 'No! What are we going to do?'

'Go shopping, I suppose.'

'Oh, Oakley, I'm sorry, nothing ever seems to go right when Molly is involved.'

'You're telling me. I have to call my new boss before we go shopping.'

Before I had chance to call Madigan, Isla, my sister-in-law rang.

'Hi, Oakley, I'm ever so sorry.'

'Why what's happened?'

'We ran out of dry rabbit food, so I told the girls to give them greens. They were meant to pick grass, but they've given their rabbits and guinea pigs the veg, and salad, but that's not all, I forgot to buy the dessert.'

'Are the rabbits and guinea pigs all right?'

'Yes, they think Christmas is a day early.'

'Don't worry, I'll add veg, salad and dessert to my list.'

'Thank you for being so understanding. Next year we'll have to stay with you.'

'We'll see about that. See you tomorrow, Isla.'

'Bye, Oakley, and thank you.'

Ruby glared at me as my phone chimed again.

'Leave it, Oakley.'

'I can't, it's my mum.'

'Hello, darling.'

'Hi Mum.'

'I'm sorry, I've been so busy with the Christmas food parcels I haven't had time to bake the sausage rolls, mince pies, or make the pizzas.'

I gazed at Ruby whose expression mirrored Poppy's scowl, after biting into a lemon.

'Don't worry, Mum, I'll add them to my ever-growing list.'

'Thanks love, what time are we meeting tomorrow?'

'I'll call you later, if that's okay?'

'That's fine, love, have a good day.'

'You too. Bye.'

At last, my phone was free to call Madigan. A soft speaking posh male voice answered the phone: 'Hello, Madhatters veterinary practice, can I help you?'

'Is Madigan available please?'

'I'm sorry, he's out on a call, can I take a message, or help?'

'Please could you tell him that Oakley would like to discuss purchasing Catkins.'

'Oakley, hi, it's Mackenzie, we're going to be working together. Sorry I missed your interview.'

'Hi, Mackenzie, that's okay, I thought you were in Scotland.'

'I've been staying at my sister's house for a few days before spending Christmas with my parents. Catkins is a wonderful house, though it needs an awful lot of work.'

'My family will help with the renovations, once I've moved in.'

'You can't live there while its being renovated.'

'I can't afford to live anywhere else, plus I have three cats.'

'I have an idea. The tenants moved out of my house a few days ago, I'm not looking for new tenants, so you'd be doing me a huge favour if you stayed there for a while; no charge of course.'

'That would be amazing, how kind of you. Where is it?'

'Do you know the Lily Pad?'

'Yes.'

'If you look across the harbour, you'll see a white house with gulls perched on the railings. It's called The Laughing Seagulls.'

'Wow, that's your house. I was admiring it from the Lily Pad, though I wasn't admiring the gulls. Maybe it should be called the Sneaky Seagulls.'

Mackenzie sniggered. 'Sorry to laugh, I heard about your encounter with Sidney, he can sniff a sausage from a mile away.'

'He did me a favour. Your uncle may not have offered me the job if I hadn't been wearing my overalls.'

Mackenzie roared with laughter. 'If you hadn't been wearing your overalls, he would have defiantly taken you on.'

'Very funny, you're as cheeky as your cousin Beau.'

'Thankfully, apart from our love of water sports, that's all we have in common. Why did you want to move to Whispering Pines?'

'Peace and quiet.'

'Whispering Pines lives up to its name, although it could do with a bit of livening up. The only real entertainment is the whispering gossips.'

'I can cope with a few gossips. Sorry to sound rude, as much as I'd love to chat all day, I'm organising the family Christmas dinner tomorrow, and everything is going wrong. We don't have a Christmas tree, turkeys, or any trimmings ... and my best friend is giving me the evil eye.'

'Sounds like you have a lot on your plate.'

I chuckled. 'We haven't anything for the plates yet!'

'Maybe the supermarkets will have last-minute offers, and you might be able to pick up a Christmas tree at your local garden centre.'

'Good idea. There's a garden centre about a mile away.'

'How many people are you catering for?'

'Thirty-three, although the village hall holds around four hundred.'

'Can't imagine catering for thirty-three let alone four hundred.'

'I'm struggling with thirty-three! What are you doing for Christmas?'

'Christmas dinner at the Lily Pad, then fall asleep in front of the telly. Should be eleven of us.'

'Sounds perfect.'

'Let me know when you want to stay at my house. It's fully furnished, so you can leave your furniture covered at Catkins during the renovations. I'll text you my number.'

'That's kind of you. Do you mind my cats staying?'

'I love cats, but keep an eye on Sid, he scoops water up and fires it at cats.'

'Crikey, who taught him that?'

'My tenants kept firing a water pistol at Sid, so he got his own back.'

'I'll warn my cats. Happy Christmas, Mackenzie.'

'Happy Christmas, Oakley. I'll let my dad know you want to buy Catkins, and welcome to Madhatters.'

'Thank you, Mackenzie, look forward to meeting you in the summer.'

I spun around to find a tornado of decorations strewn everywhere, and Ruby still trying to untangle the fairy lights.

'Is everyone ready to find a Christmas tree?'

Poppy jumped up. 'Yes, what about the food shopping?'

'Tree first, then the food shopping.'

We piled into my car and found one remaining tree at the garden centre, though why did it have to be sixteen feet tall?

Blossom lifted the bottom of the tree. 'If we put this on the roof, the car will swallow the wheels.'

I laughed. 'You're right. We'll leave the car here and carry the tree to the hall.'

Ruby produced one of her famous frowns. 'You're kidding, aren't you? It's at least a mile!'

'It won't take us long; we carried the Beast for over five miles.'

Ruby faced me with her hands on her hips. 'You owe me a huge slice of chocolate cake for this.'

'I'll buy you a whole chocolate cake while we're shopping. So, are we carrying this tree back to the hall or not?'

Ruby shook her head crinkling her nose. 'I suppose. Every time I spend the day with you, Oakley, I get roped into another escapade.'

'At least you can't accuse me of being boring. I'll pay for the tree, and we can begin our next adventure.'

'Girls, if you take the front, Ruby the middle and I'll carry the back. Everyone ready?'

'Yes, though I'm getting a déjà vu feeling,' Ruby said giggling.

'Me too, let's hope we're not followed by anything with horns,' I said.

We'd walked about half a mile, stopping several times for hand changes, before the twins dropped the tree and swopped sides.

Poppy rubbed her hands. 'Auntie Oakley, this tree keeps biting me, I've never had so many pricks.'

Ruby sniggered. 'Believe me, I've had plenty of pricks.'

'I believe you Rubes, though at this exact moment I have a prick right up my backside.'

'Auntie Oakley, too much information,' Blossom said, giggling.

'No really, look behind me.'

Everyone turned their heads to see a bright red sports car following us. The driver tooted his horn, pulled alongside, and opened the window.

I peered at the driver and addressed the girls. 'As I was saying, the biggest prick is now alongside us and he has a horn.'

'Morning, ladies, should have guessed it was you four. No Highland cows following you today then? What are you doing?'

A stupid question deserved a stupid answer. 'Morning, Trent. We're taking our Christmas tree for a walk, apparently, if it gets plenty of fresh air between its branches, it's less likely to lose its needles, and in return, we're less likely to encounter any annoying little pricks. So far though, it doesn't seem to be working.'

'Ha, ha, ha. Sharp as a needle as always, Tinker Bell. Here I was about to offer you my services.'

Poppy pipped up, 'What can you offer us, Trent? We're having a party at the hall and we're not sure if we can get the tree through the entrance.'

'Seems like you need the services of my big chopper.'

Poppy giggled. 'You have a helicopter to carry the tree?'

'Poppy, that's not a chopper, remember Dad's old bike, it was called a Chopper, but I've no idea how we're going to carry the tree on a bike.' said Blossom.

Ruby raised her eyebrows. 'I can think of other things that are called choppers, and you can keep yours tucked away, thanks.'

'Ruby, crude as always. Girls, I've lent my helicopter to Santa to help him carry the presents tonight. Sorry, you'll have to carry the tree yourselves, but I could nip home, pick up my chainsaw and axe and cut it in two. Plus, you're gonna need two stands, I think I've got a couple in the garage.'

Ruby and I glanced at each other. We'd forgotten about standing it up!

'That sounds great, Trent. What yer doing for Christmas?' said Blossom.

'Nothing now. Was meant to be going to my girlfriend's parents for Christmas dinner, but after she spotted an item in my dry bag ...' Trent paused, gazed at me, and stopped short of revealing he'd taken my thong. 'She told me ... well, I won't repeat it, but she isn't coming back, so I'm on my own for Christmas.'

Poppy looked at me. 'He can't be on his own at Christmas can he, Auntie Oakley? We have plenty of room, can he join us if he helps?'

It seemed I didn't have a lot of choice. 'I suppose.'

Trent's goofy grin shone brighter than the Christmas baubles. 'If you're sure, that would be fantastic. Are you going for a Christmas surf tomorrow? High tide is at four-thirty.'

'Yes. And I suppose you want to join us?' I said without a lot of enthusiasm.

'Would love to.'

Poppy's smile was splashed across her face. 'We love kayak surfing, don't we Blossom? Can we come too?'

'Of course, if your dad says it's okay.'

'Do you know what I asked Santa to bring us for Christmas? Sit-on-top kayaks, although they're quite expensive. Poppy asked for a karaoke machine between us; I'm not sure which present Santa is going to deliver.'

'It all depends on how good you've been, and I'm not sure how he'll get either of them down the chimney.'

'We're always good. I'll wait up all night and let Santa in the front door.'

Trent butted in. 'I don't think it's a good idea to let strange men in through the front door, and if you're not asleep, Santa won't leave you any presents.'

Blossom peered into Trent's car. 'A strange man comes down our chimney, surely it would be easier for him to use the front door?'

'Why do you have to question everything, Blossom? Trent, we'll make sure we're asleep, or we won't get any presents. Are you any good at making cookies, Trent? We're making some this afternoon,' said Poppy.

'I'm the best cookie maker ever.'

'He can help us, can't he, Auntie Oakley?'

'If he wants, though I'm sure Trent has much better things to do this afternoon,' I said hoping he'd get the hint.

'Nope, nothing planned. I'll see you at the hall in ten minutes.'

'See ya,' shouted the girls as Trent sped home.

Ruby smirked. 'Didn't I tell you Trent seems to be popping up everywhere, and he even admitted he had a big chopper.'

'It's a coincidence, and he can keep his big chopper. Come on, we'd better hurry as we've still got the food shopping to do.'

When we reached the hall, Trent was brandishing a chainsaw, and with his goofy grin, he had the appearance of Fred Flintstone.

Ruby and I left Trent and his little helpers positioning the two halves of the tree while Ruby gave me a lift to my car. We both headed out to different supermarkets in search of bargains.

On seeing the huge amount of reductions, an idea sprang into my mind, and I reached for my phone and called my mum.

'Hi, Mum, can you speak?'

'Yes, is everything okay?'

'Are you still packing the Christmas food parcels?'

'Almost finished, I'm writing the labels and your brothers, and the kids will be here shortly to deliver the parcels.'

'How many are they delivering?'

'About fifty. Why?'

'You know how you've always wanted to help people on Christmas Day?'

'Yes, what do you have in mind?' I could hear the excitement brewing in my mum's voice.

'I'm in the supermarket and the Christmas food has been reduced. Rather than a family Christmas dinner, do you fancy inviting the recipients of the food parcels to join us for a lunchtime buffet at the hall?'

'What a fantastic idea. I could attach an invitation to each food parcel. What time shall we say?'

'Is eleven-thirty, okay? We're going kayak surfing at half past three, do you mind staying for the afternoon? I'll be back around half past five.'

'That's fine, love, but who's going to clear up?'

'The hall is booked until Bank Holiday Monday. I'll clean it on Boxing Day.'

'That's good, love, couldn't bear to lose one of my new nails. Christmas Day will be so exhausting; I'll need Boxing Day to recover.'

'I understand Mum, chatting all day can be exhausting. See you tomorrow.'

'I've told you before, sarcasm doesn't suit you. See you in the morning, love.'

I dialled Ruby's number. 'Hi, Rubes, sorry but there's been a change of plan.'

'Oak, I've already filled my trolly, a lot of the food has been reduced.'

'It's reduced here too. I've just been chatting to my mum; rather than cooking a Christmas roast, do you fancy preparing a huge buffet for the single older folk who she prepares the food parcels for?'

'I love that idea. I'll put the Brussels sprouts back and see what other bargains I can find.'

'Don't buy too much, they don't eat much.'

'Don't worry I won't. See you later, Oak.'

After loading the shopping into my car, I headed back to the village hall. When I turned into the car park Trent and the girls appeared in the doorway. I couldn't wait for them to see the bargains I'd brought.

Trent opened the boot, twisted around, and scowled. 'How much food have you bought Oakley?'

'It was reduced by eighty percent, most of its use-by-date is tomorrow.'

'Yes, but that didn't mean you had to buy it all!'

'There's been a bit of a change of plan. My mum sends food parcels to lonely older people who don't see anyone at Christmas. Instead of our family Christmas dinner, we're having a buffet and inviting them to join us. There should be an extra thirty people, as I doubt everyone will turn up.'

Blossom gleamed. 'Does that mean we don't have to eat Brussels sprouts?'

'It does, but I've got a stalk at home, how about Brussels sprout rolls instead of sausage rolls?'

Poppy screwed her nose up. 'That's disgusting! Why have you got a stork at home?'

With my eyes wide and a frown etched on my face I stared at Poppy. 'It's what Brussels sprouts grow on!'

'They grow on birds! How awful, no wonder I hate them, the poor birds.'

'Do they not teach you anything at school? Where do you think Brussels sprouts come from?' I said failing to sound serious as I suppressed my laughter.

Blossom nudged Poppy and giggled. 'A bag in a supermarket. I thought storks delivered babies.'

'Seriously, I think I need to have a word with your dad. Storks do not bring babies, and Brussels sprouts grow on a stem in the ground called a stalk.'

'Do you know what? Miss Percy, our teacher, told us to bring stork margarine into school to make a cake. Is that made of birds or Brussels sprouts?'

I stared directly at Poppy. 'Are you kiddin' me? It's made of vegetable oils.'

Blossom squirmed. 'Yuk! Do vegetables have oils? I thought they were good for you because they didn't have oils. Now I'm definitely not eating them.'

Poppy bit her lip, frowning. 'I've never seen vegetables growing, they just come from a supermarket.'

'When I buy my new house, I will save you a patch of ground and we can grow our own vegetables.'

Blossom glared at me with her arms crossed. 'Auntie Oakley, I'm confused.'

I couldn't stop chuckling. 'Trent, you're a teacher, you explain.'

'Poppy, there are several ways of spelling stork, though they all sound the same, and mean different things.'

Poppy emptied another bag and looked up. 'Really? Do you know what, my friend at school told me she was delivered by a stork, just like in the film *Storks*. Ooh, look everyone salted caramel profiteroles.' She wrapped her arms around me. 'Auntie Oakley, this is going to be the bestest Christmas ever.'

Trent unloaded several more bags. 'Oakley, remind me how many we're catering for?'

'I've estimated about fifty to sixty.'

'I hope they're hungry, there's enough food to feed five hundred. We'll have to send everyone home with goody bags. Let's hope Ruby hasn't gone overboard like you.'

'I'm sure she hasn't. Wow! The hall looks amazing, I didn't realise you were so artistic. The snowflake bunting strung across the ceiling is incredible, and I love the cut-out snowflakes in the windows.'

Trent smirked. 'I do have some talents you know.'

Blossom peeked out a window. 'I can hear a car, it's Ruby, can we go and help her?'

'Yes, though I'm sure she hasn't brought that much.'

Ruby opened her boot revealing overflowing bags about to spill onto the drive. Not only was the boot full, but also the back seats and the front passenger seat. 'Sorry I was so long. I may have bought too much.'

'You're telling me. I think we need to send out more invites to eat this lot.' Trent said.

'Why do we need fifty French sticks?' I quizzed Ruby.

'They were reduced to twenty pence. We could always give people one to take home.'

'Most people leave parties with goody bags, but we're sending them home with a French stick! What's in these bags? Ruby, what the heck are we going to do with all these boxes of sandwiches?'

'We can make platters of sandwiches. When I told the assistant our plans she spoke to her manager, and would you believe it, they gave me them free of charge.'

'Really? How wonderful, though I haven't bought any platters.'

'Look in the bag Trent's holding.'

Trent opened the bag containing boxes of crackers, tablecloths, party plates and platters. He picked up another bag. 'Oh my goodness, Rubes, you've bought another three turkeys; Oakley has already bought three.'

'We'll have plenty then. I hope people have a sweet tooth, there are three more bags of cakes.'

The girls were licking their lips and I realised we'd forgotten to eat lunch.

I handed the girls a couple of packs of sandwiches. 'How about I put the kettle on, and we'll eat lunch, might even stretch to a bag of doughnuts.'

Trent licked his lips too. 'Now you're talking, Oakley. You ladies remain seated, I'll put the kettle on.'

'Is there any hot chocolate please?' said Blossom.

'Yes plenty,' shouted Trent, as he headed to the kitchen.

'What are we going to give our guests to drink?' spluttered Poppy with her mouth full.

'There's various non-alcoholic drinks, tea, and coffee plus hot chocolate, and I'll make a vat of mulled wine. No doubt your dad and uncles will bring plenty of alcohol,' I said while unwrapping the sandwiches.

Trent returned carrying a tray of drinks. 'Oakley, have you fathomed out how you're going to cook six turkeys?'

Ruby helped herself to a mug of coffee. 'Why don't you ring your brothers and ask each one to cook a turkey? That leaves one that can be cooked here in the morning.'

'Good idea, I'll text them.'

Within fifteen minutes, five turkeys had been collected.

I picked my phone up to text my brothers again. 'I've forgotten to check they know the length of time to cook the turkeys, as the turkeys will need plenty of time to rest.'

Poppy glared down her nose at me. 'I think they're quite rested, Auntie Oakley; they're not alive.'

Ruby and Trent were in a fit of giggles.

Trying not to laugh, I attempted an explanation. 'Allowing time to rest allows the meat to relax and reabsorb the juices. It makes the meat more tender and juicier, the last thing you want is a dry bird.'

Trent muttered, 'Yep, I like my bird to be relaxed with flowing juices. Last thing I want is a dry bird.'

Ruby and I glanced at each other, and before I had time to say anything, a jam doughnut flew out of Ruby's hand and landed on Trent's head.

Trent put on an innocent face. 'What did I say wrong?'

Ruby shook her sugar-coated hands. 'Trent, there are innocent children here, and Oakley.'

'Thanks.' I sneered.

Blossom butted in. 'When we were on the phone with Mum yesterday, we heard boring Billy the boyfriend making gobbling noises like a turkey. He shouted something about being hot and needing more basting. They must have been having their turkey early and couldn't wait until Christmas Day. I'm going to play some music, coming Poppy?' The girls disappeared to the main hall as Ruby was in hysterics, and Trent and I stared at her bewildered.

'What are you two staring at? The girls probably caught them doing the turkey.'

I was even more shocked than Trent. 'Doing what to the turkey? You don't mean having sex with the turkey? That's disgusting.'

'Oakley! Of course not, you ninny, the turkey is a sexual position; don't you know anything?'

Trent seemed as bemused as me. 'I can't believe you two haven't heard of it. Didn't your family discuss sex with you growing up?'

I was flabbergasted. 'Oh my word, Rubes, the only sex that was discussed was the life cycle of a frog. My brothers told me I was a tadpole and came from a pond, and when my mum told me I was delivered to her from a tiny package, my dad stormed out.'

Trent's laughing sounded like a chimpanzee swinging through the trees. I was surprised he hadn't fallen off his chair.

'That explains a lot, Oakley. Don't give me that look, for once we're on the same page, I haven't got a Scooby Doo either, though I'm keen to find out. Go on Rubes.'

'When I travelled to the USA for the school exchange it was Thanksgiving. The family I was staying with organised a party. As people were leaving, I overheard them saying they were off home to baste the turkey. I thought they were having another roast until someone enlightened me. You can look it up on the internet, I'm not going into details, I'm only telling you it involves a lot of gobbling.'

Trent reached for his phone, raised his eyebrows, and passed it to me as I stared at both Ruby and Trent.

'Oh my god, Rubes, do you think that was what Billy was on about? He seems so quiet and reserved and ... well, boring. Maybe that's what attracted Kate to Billy. Who would have thought it, Billy the boring boyfriend was a bonking turkey baster. I wonder if Flynn knows.'

Ruby giggled. 'Oakley, I think we will keep this to ourselves.'

Blossom snuck up behind us, picked up Trent's phone and glared at the pictures.

'Keep what to yourselves? Why are you looking at naked people? Do you know what, when we went to Theo's tenth birthday party, he told us they had sex education at school and learnt about the masonry position.'

Poppy tried to grab the phone off Blossom, but Trent was there in a flash. Poppy aimed her scowl towards Trent. 'We were shocked when Dad said he was looking on the internet at masonry positions. Why would Dad be looking at sex on the internet?'

This was turning out to be the funniest Christmas Eve ever. Ruby dashed to the loo, giggling all the way, and Trent held his stomach as I tried to gain my composure.

'Girls, it's not the masonry position, it's called the missionary position.' I said.

Poppy gazed at Blossom. 'Oops, so Dad wasn't looking at sex on the internet.'

Tears were trickling down my face. 'No! You haven't told anyone have you?'

'Only Bella.'

'Isn't Bella the headmaster's daughter?'

'Yes.'

'Let's hope she keeps it to herself.'

'She's a bit of a blabbermouth. Can we make cookies now?'

For the next few hours, we made tray after tray of cookies until everyone was covered head to toe in flour.

At five-thirty it was time to call it a day. Ruby dropped the girls home leaving me and Trent to tidy up.

'Thank you, Oakley. That was the most educational and funniest day I've had in a long time. I've seen Ruby in a whole new light. Maybe I should apply to be a teacher at Ruby's old private school.'

'A position at a private school sounds right up your alley. Ruby does come up with funny things.'

Trent paused in the doorway and twisted around with a glint in his eyes. 'If only my girlfriend hadn't finished with me, we could have basted the turkey tonight. I don't suppose you—'

I pushed Trent out the door. 'No, I don't. The only turkey I'm having will come tomorrow, with stuffing balls and chipolatas.'

'Shame, you don't know what you're missing, though no chipolatas, more Bratwurst and I wouldn't mind stuffing—'

'In your dreams, Trent, did you hear me? In your dreams! Now go home and I'll see you at nine in the morning.'

'You can't blame a bloke for trying. Happy Christmas, Tinker Bell.'

'Believe me, you're very trying. Happy Christmas, Trent, enjoy your dreams.'

'I will, night, Tinker Bell.'

'Night, Trent, and thanks for your help.'

'You're welcome.'

Chapter Twenty
Christmas Day

My phone was flooded with texts and photos from my nieces and nephews at four o'clock Christmas morning; today was going to be a long day. I pulled the duvet over my head and fell asleep until Nutmeg jumped on me at six o'clock.

All three cats helped me open their presents, ripping off wrapping paper sprinkled in catnip and revealing their new climbing tree, scratch posts, and three igloo beds.

Shadows were cast across the drive as I closed the door at seven-thirty and headed back to the village hall. It looked so festive, especially with two Christmas trees. I switched the lights and heating on and headed to the kitchen to cook the turkey and make mulled wine.

On opening the fridges, I frowned at the amount of food. We were going to be living on buffet food for the whole of Christmas. I popped the turkey into the oven, left a vat of mulled wine simmering, and arranged the food on platters before returning them to the fridge.

At 9 a.m. the hall door swung open, and Ruby ambled in.

'Happy Christmas, Oakley. The hall smells amazing. What can I do to help?'

'I've collected a couple of bags of fir cones, added baubles and there's a box of battery candles. Would you mind spreading the table clothes and arranging the table decorations?'

'Of course.'

The hall door sprang open again, and Trent marched in carrying a large rectangular box and a couple of carrier bags.

'Happy Christmas, you two, I've brought something for the kids. Is there a table free where I can set it up?'

Ruby pointed to a table by the Christmas tree. Trent placed the box on top and slid out an extremely tall chocolate fountain.

'I've brought giant marshmallows, strawberries, bananas, pineapple, and rice crispy cakes; the kids are going to love it.' Trent's excitement mirrored a child twirling around in a candy store, I'd never witnessed that side of him.

'They will, especially the twins. I'm not sure how popular we'll be with the parents though.'

Trent sliced the pineapple. 'We can tell them it's part of their five-a-day.'

'We'll leave you to tell them that, and you can clear up the mess when it's been knocked over.'

'Always a pessimist, aren't you? No one is going to knock it over.'

'Did you not know I had psychic powers?'

'Really? Can you see me in your future?'

'Only in my nightmares.'

'At least I know you're thinking about me in bed.'

We were interrupted when the door crashed open, and Blossom and Poppy ran in jabbering.

'Guess what Santa brought us?' said Blossom.

'No idea, were you good?'

'Always. He managed to get a karaoke machine down the chimney. We've brought it with us, Dad's unloading it from the car.'

I grumbled, 'Doesn't your singing scare animals and older people? You might scare our guests away.'

'No, we won't, older people like kids,' said Poppy.

'They haven't met the two of you or heard your singing!'

Blossom and Poppy glared at me, poked their tongues out, and skipped outside.

My brothers and their families began arriving laden with cooked turkeys, and even Molly had remembered to cook the ham. Things were going to plan; this was going to be the best Christmas ever.

Harrison strolled towards me with a cooked turkey. 'All right, sis, the hall looks great.'

'Happy Christmas, Harrison. Where's Willow?'

'She said she's spending Christmas with her friends.'

'Oh! I have her Christmas present at home, I was going to give it to her later.'

'She'll be back after Boxing Day.'

'That's a shame. I was looking forward to seeing her open her present. Maybe I'll take a picture of it and text it to her later.'

'Good idea. Mum, Dad and Nan are in the car park. Have you seen the number of people parking their cars?'

'No.' I peered out of the window. 'Why are they parking in the hall car park? That's odd, they're chatting to Mum. Crikey, Harrison, they're following her to the hall.'

I rushed to the door and met my mum.

'Hello, darling, Happy Christmas, isn't this wonderful? Do you know, I've met a woman who has even more kids than me.'

'Mum, who are all these people?'

'The families who received the food parcels.'

'What do you mean families? Don't you make them for single, lonely, older people, not huge families?'

'No love, didn't I tell you I swapped with Cinthia this year? I made the parcels for the families, and she made them up for the older folk.'

'No Mum. You mean to say I have invited fifty families for lunch?'

'I'm sure they won't all turn up, dear.'

'But ... oh, never mind, I need to speak to Ruby and Trent.'

Trent sauntered towards me. 'Oakley, who are all the people?'

'It seems we've invited fifty families to lunch.'

Ruby's eyes widened as she took a deep breath. 'No! Don't you mean *you've* invited fifty families, and not *we've*? Now what are *we* going to do?'

'Open the other function rooms, I'll pay for them when I hand the keys back.'

'Good idea, but what about the food?' said Trent.

'Have we used the French sticks?'

'No,' said Ruby.

'Why don't we make French bread pizza?'

Trent added his two pennies' worth. 'I've a better idea, why don't we have a pizza-making competition? Saves us all the work. Your brothers could head up five teams and Santa could judge it.'

'Great idea, it'll keep the kids out of mischief until they spot your chocolate fountain, plus, I have a load of bun tins in my car. I'll pop home for the ingredients, and we can make a batch of cupcakes.'

Ruby quizzed me. 'Will there be enough room in the oven?'

'Yes, the pizzas won't take long to cook. The kids can decorate the cupcakes once they're cool; maybe we could have a cake-decorating competition?'

Ruby poked her head inside Santa's sack. 'Great idea. Oak, there's not enough gifts in the sack for the extra kids.'

'Thanks, Rubes, I forgot about Santa's sack, I'll see if the local garage has any sweets.'

'Okay. Trent and I will set up the pizza competition.'

'Thanks, I think we might just pull this off. See you shortly.'

Half an hour later I returned laden with baking ingredients, cake decorations and ten carrier bags of selection boxes. Soon the hall was fit to bursting with jolly people chattering to new friends. The kids were belting out Christmas songs on the karaoke machine, and I made batches of cupcakes ready for them to decorate.

Trent walked with a swagger towards Ruby and me and draped his arms around us.

'You know what, ladies, I think we've averted a disaster. Everyone loves the pizzas, and ...' Trent paused as the chocolate fountain tumbled across the table spreading chocolate everywhere. Chairs clattered in all directions and people jumped out of the way as the chocolate fountain tumbled to the floor. 'Sorry, ladies, seems my services are required elsewhere.'

Ruby grabbed Trent's arm. 'I'll help you.'

I noticed people diving out of the way as my nan and her walking trolly propelled through the hall like a Formula 1 racing driver.

'Come on, out the way folks, lady with an empty glass coming through. Oakley, you're slacking my girl. Any more wine?'

'Yes, Nan, I'm about to make another vat.'

'Good girl. You're still going to invite me to stay in your new house, aren't you?'

'Yes, Nan, there's a room with your name on it for when you visit.'

'Excellent! Now hurry up with that wine. I've met a handsome man and I need Dutch courage to invite him home for a drink.'

'Have you left Forever Spring Chickens?'

'This morning, now I'm raring to find myself a toyboy and try out this new hip. Trent has turned out to be a fine-looking chap. I've seen the way he looks at you.'

'We're friends, Nan, that's all.'

'Friends is a good way to start.'

'And end, Nan, I'm not interested in Trent.'

'Shame, love, if I was only a bit younger ...'

'That's disgusting, Nan. He's twenty-nine and you're eighty-four!'

'Just because you're eighty-four doesn't stop you from window shopping. I still have urges, love.'

'Nan, please, too much information. I'll bring your wine over.'

'Thanks, love. I'm sitting by the Christmas tree with my new fella.'

A text message beeped on my phone; it was Mackenzie.

Mackenzie: Hi Oakley, Happy Christmas, hope the party is going well?

Me: Hi Mackenzie, Happy Christmas, it's a long story, but we have around 300 guests!

My phone chimed; it was Mackenzie.

'Oakley, what happened?'

I put my phone on loudspeaker while preparing another vat of mulled wine. 'I accidentally invited fifty families instead of fifty single older people.'

Mackenzie laughed his head off. 'Jeeze, did you have enough food?'

'Yes, loads. We organized a pizza-making competition, and they made me my favourite Hawaiian pizza. We also had a cupcake-decorating competition, and a friend brought a chocolate fountain. I've eaten so much I'm not sure I'll fit into my kayak when we go surfing later.'

'Sounds great fun, though exhausting. Last time I used a chocolate fountain there was more chocolate on the kids than in their mouths.'

'Yep, we also have it on the floor, tables, and chairs.'

'Sounds about right. We're about to sit down to a quiet Christmas dinner. Hope everything goes okay, and you catch some brilliant waves later. Speak soon. Oh, hang on, Beau wants a word.'

'Happy Christmas, Oakley, hope you've not caused any catastrophes.'

'Happy Christmas, Beau. No, I've managed to avert one. Mackenzie can tell you about it later.'

'Ok great. My dad said he's really pleased you want to buy Catkins and he'll call you after Christmas. Sorry, gotta go, Lily is waving a tea towel in my direction. Have a nice Christmas, Oakley, I'll pass you back to Mackenzie.'

'Bye, Beau. Hi, Mackenzie, perhaps next Christmas we can go paddling or surfing at Whispering Pines?'

'Sounds great, it's a date. Happy Christmas, hope the surfs up. Bye, Oakley.'

'So do I. Enjoy your Christmas dinner. Bye, Mackenzie.'

A bellow of 'Ho, Ho, Ho' echoed as Santa Claus pushed the door open. He was engulfed by kids badgering him for presents, though the second Trent stepped in, the kids formed an orderly line. I wished I had that much clout with my nieces and nephews, kids seemed to be putty in Trent's hands.

While everyone's attention was diverted towards Santa, my brothers were rounded up, and we headed to the beach. Soon we were paddling through the surf in search of the perfect wave. The sea may have been the colour of frothy cappuccino, but the waves were three-to-four feet and clean. We paddled through the swash to the back with everyone's beaming faces illuminated by the sun's amber glow.

'This is the one,' shouted Harrison.

Nine kayakers paddled towards the beach accompanied by screams of elation as the first wave caught up with us. With my paddle positioned in a low brace, I edged my kayak, and with the lightest touch of a stern rudder, the fairy really was flying. The flight was short-lived though, as someone carved in front of me. Momentarily, I became friends with the ocean floor, before rolling up. Several other kayakers were attempting to roll, and when I gazed at the culprit mouthing the word sorry, of course, it had to be Trent. Always the centre of attention and showing off as normal; he was never going to change.

Once again, we paddled beyond the breakwater, waiting for the perfect wave. I nodded towards Poppy and Blossom who sandwiched Trent between them. As the wave approached from behind, Poppy paddled to the right, Blossom paddled to the left and I paddled across the front of Trent.

'Oops, sorry Trent, I don't seem to have the hang of surfing.'

'Tinker Bell, you ...' Trent's words dried up as he capsized, and after failing to get his angle right, he exited his kayak. With the next wave, his kayak floated onto the shore and Trent swam after it to a round of applause, accompanied by the word, 'swimmer.'

We managed to catch several more waves before the horizon swallowed up the sun, and moonbeams shone on the crests of the waves. The temperature plummeted as ominous grey clouds gathered above our heads.

'Do you know what? I think it's trying to snow. Look under the lamps.'

Snowflakes twirled and twinkled like butterflies fluttering around a buddleia. What a glorious end to the most wonderful Christmas Day surf. We returned to the hall where festivities were winding down.

'Have you had a good day, Nan?'

'Oh, love, it was the best, I think I've pulled myself a fella. And guess what? He still has his own teeth!'

I hugged her and giggled. 'You deserve a bit of fun, Nan. Are you coming with us to Flynn's house?'

'Sorry, love, my fella has invited me back to his house for a nightcap.'

'Sounds like he is after one thing, Nan.'

My nan giggled and nudged me. 'He might just get it if we can remember where everything goes.'

'Oh my gosh, Nan, I was joking.'

'I'm not love, I'm wearing my pulling pants.'

'Remember, Nan, there's more to life than sex.'

'At my age, love, you never know if you'll wake up the next morning. You have to take the bull by the horns and grab what's on offer.'

I leant over and kissed her cheek. 'Sounds like this bull doesn't know what he's letting himself in for.'

'I'll go easy on him. Bye, love, thank you, it's been a wonderful day.'

I watched my nan amble to the door where her new-found love was waiting for her. He helped her with her coat, held open the door, turned to me, and tipped his hat. Ah, what lovely man, I thought, though did he know what he was taking on with my nan and her pulling pants? I doubted it very much.

'Auntie Oakley, are you ready? We can tidy up all this mess tomorrow. Let's go home,' said Blossom.

Poppy grabbed my hand. 'Come on, we've got loads of Christmas cookies to eat.'

'Oh my word, Poppy, you and your stomach. I'll pop home first, feed the cats and see if Santa left you any presents at my house.'

'Presents! I was having so much fun I'd forgotten about opening presents.' Poppy turned to Flynn, 'Dad, hurry up, we've got to go to home to open the rest of our presents.'

'Okay, girls, but what about Trent? We can't leave him on his own on Christmas evening. Oak, do you want to invite him to join us?'

'No, you invite Trent, or he will get the wrong impression and think I like him.'

Flynn raised his eyebrows whilst shaking his head. 'Sometimes, sis, you are such a wuss.'

Before Flynn could ask, Trent strolled towards us with his goofy grin plastered to his face.

'Cheers for a brilliant day, it's been the best Christmas I've had in years. I know how much you were looking forward to spending the evening with me, but I've had another offer – my girlfriend sent me a text and wants to make up.'

'That's great news, Trent, hope you have a lovely evening. Do you want any leftover food?' I said, breathing a sigh of relief, although Ruby appeared disappointed.

Trent held a goody bag up. 'Thank you, I've got plenty. Enjoy your evening and thanks for inviting me to spend Christmas Day with you.'

Ruby rushed to Trent and kissed his cheek. 'You were wonderful, we wouldn't have managed without you.'

'It has been an enlightening few days, Rubes; I'm off to meet my girlfriend and baste the turkey.'

Ruby and I chuckled like a house of hungry hens, though no one else understood why. Ruby left with Flynn and the girls, while I headed home to feed my cats and load my car with everyone's Christmas presents.

Half an hour later, I knocked on Flynn's front door and the girls rushed towards me. Poppy grabbed my hand. 'Hurry, Auntie Oakley, you have to open your present first.'

Blossom pointed to the back of the Christmas Tree. 'There's your present behind the tree.'

'How on earth did Santa get that down your chimney? It's massive!'

'He didn't, his mate Amazon delivered it.' said Poppy giggling.

I tore the paper off revealing a green and blue double sit-on-top kayak; I was lost for words.

Poppy peeled the remaining paper off. 'It's from everyone, we chose a double for when you get a dog, it can sit in the front. Originally, it was for you to share with a boyfriend, but we thought it would be easier for you to get a dog.'

'I think you're right, thank you, it's the nicest present I've ever had. Would you like to see your presents?'

'Yes, where are they?'

'Look out the window at my car.'

The girls rushed to the window, peeped outside, and screamed.

Poppy rushed to the front door shouting, 'Dad, Auntie Oakley has brought us pink sit-on-top kayaks!'

'No! Really, sis, that must have cost you a fortune?'

'I'm not worried about the cost, I thought they could keep them at Catkins for when they visit. I've bought Willow one too, though I think she's still upset with me. I was going to text her a photo but forgot to take one when I popped home.'

'Send her a photo of the girls' kayaks and tell her you've bought her one too.'

'Good idea, girls, stand in front of my car and I'll take a photo and send it to Willow.'

Five minutes later my phone rang.

'Hi, Auntie Oakley, have you really bought me a sit-on-top to keep at Catkins?'

'Yes. You can come and stay whenever you like.'

'Thank you, I'm so sorry I was rude, I can't wait to come down and stay.'

'You know you're always welcome. Are you joining us at Flynn's? The girls are about to open the rest of their presents.'

'I'll be there in five minutes, please tell them to wait for me.'

'Okay, see you shortly.'

Everyone was stuffing themselves with cookies and slurping hot chocolate when Willow arrived. After opening the remaining presents, we settled down to play board games until I headed home at midnight; it had been the best Christmas day ever.

Chapter Twenty-one
Valentine's Day and Moving Home

Christmas was a distant memory as February the fourteenth fluttered in. Trent and his girlfriend were back together, and I hadn't seen him since Christmas. Madigan had accepted my offer to buy Catkins and today was my moving day. There was a lightness in my chest, and a spring in my step, and no one was going to wipe the smile off my face.

The past six weeks had been a whirlwind of packing boxes and many, many trips to the recycling centre. Contracts had been signed and in three hours my house would belong to Harrison and Molly, and a dilapidated old farmhouse would belong to me. Technically though, sixty percent of Catkins belonged to Rob the Builders and Sons, as I'd been unable to secure a mortgage until Catkins was habitable. My dad and brothers had obtained a bridging loan allowing me to purchase Catkins.

At 8 a.m. Ruby bounced out of her car, pulled her bright pink bobble hat down and wrapped her scarf around her neck several times. 'Morning, Oakley, couldn't you have chosen a warmer day to move?'

'Morning, Rubes, it's a bit nippy, you'll soon warm up loading the van.'

'I need something to keep me warm. Is Flynn still driving your car down with the girls?'

'Yes, do you want me to ask him to warm you up?'

Ruby gave me her dragon stare and ignored my comment. 'Do you still need a lift to the depot to pick up the removal van?'

'Yes please, sure you're brave enough to risk travelling with me at the wheel?'

'I've got a crash helmet; do I need accident or life insurance?'

'Both, and a hazardous activity extension. Flynn's returning the van later, would you mind travelling back with him?'

'What about the girls?'

'They're staying overnight with my parents.'

Ruby smirked, then smiled. 'That's fine, I'm sure his driving is better than yours. It's freezing standing here, are you ready to collect the van?'

'Yes.' I pivoted on the spot. 'Listen.'

'What to? I can't hear anything.'

'Lovely, isn't it? Hold out your hand.'

Ruby held her hand out as several bell clappers fell into her palm.

'Oakley, tell me you didn't cut them out of Mrs Rhymes' wind chimes?'

'Yep. The jingle-jangle of her wind chimes has ruined my sleep for years, and that's not all.'

Ruby's whole body was shaking. 'Stop making me laugh, what else have you done?'

'You know annoying, jet-propelled, leaf blower man?'

'You mean Mr Un-Popular who blew dust over our barbeque?'

'Yes, that's him. I tipped ten black bags full of old leaves into his garden after he left this morning. They're scattered across his pristine lawn. I've put up with that bloody leaf blower for four years.'

'Oh my goodness, Oakley, let's hope we leave before he returns. What about Slugman?'

'Don't worry, he didn't get left out. Remember when he threw that slug over the fence, and it landed in your wine glass?'

Ruby screwed her nose up. 'How could I forget? I almost swallowed it.'

'It would have been cruel if I'd collected real slugs and snails, so I've thrown loads of jelly slugs and snails over the fence. They're amazingly lifelike; it looks like his garden has been invaded overnight.'

'Gosh, Oakley, when I told you to be more spontaneous, I wasn't expecting you to take my words literally.'

'Serves them right, they've been the neighbours from hell. Come on, let's collect the van before you freeze to death.'

Ruby parked at the depot while I collected the keys to a bright, yellow-and-black van, sign written: Helping you BEE on your way. At least the family convoy couldn't complain they'd lost sight of us. While Ruby dashed back to her car and retrieved a case of CDs her mum had lent her, a text message beeped on my phone.

Mackenzie:	Hi Oakley, hope the house move goes smoothly. The keys to both houses are at the Lily Pad.
Me:	Thanks a lot, Mackenzie. I'm so excited, must fly though as my co-pilot is on her way and thinks I've driven a Luton van before! I've driven plenty of transits, so I'm sure it will be fine, but wish me luck!
Mackenzie:	OMG! Good Luck.

Ruby returned with the case of CDs.

'My mum said they're great for driving. Is it okay if I play one?'

'Yes, of course.'

Ruby slotted a CD into the player. 'Who were you texting?'

'Mackenzie. He was just letting me know where the keys are to both houses.'

'He sounds lovely and is kind to let you stay in his house.'

'He is. I can't wait to meet him.'

The engine purred as I slipped the gears into first, released the clutch and pressed the accelerator. However, Ruby growled as she was flung forwards and backwards hitting her head on the headrest. 'Help!' by the Beatles belted out of the speakers before the engine stalled.

Ruby rubbed the back of her head. 'Oakley, you do know how to drive a van don't you? We haven't even left the depot and you've already stalled it.'

'Of course, I was just trying to find the biting point.'

'I'd try a bit harder if I was you, and it would help if you released the handbrake. Anymore kangarooing and you'll find my biting point.'

I switched the ignition on. 'Sorry, Rubes, I'll try again.'

Every time the engine stalled the CD returned to the beginning, and 'Help!' must have blasted out of the speakers at least six times before we had even left the depot.

When we arrived at my house, a deafening chain of eager box lifters had formed a line. Within a couple of hours, the van was loaded, and the roller shutter door secured. My canoes and kayaks were fastened to my brothers' cars, and all that remained was for the cats to be ushed into their carriers.

'We'll get them, Auntie Oakley,' shouted Poppy as she scaled the stairs.

Blossom followed her, before screaming, 'Auntie Oakley, Nutmeg's gone.'

I cleared the stairs in record time to find Jasmine and Cinnamon, but there was no sign of Nutmeg. Adrenalin rushed through my veins as I dashed from room to room. Blossom and Poppy ran downstairs, searched the garden, and returned with expressions akin to Santa forgetting them at Christmas.

Blossom rubbed her eyes and cried, 'She was here half an hour ago, we came up to fuss her.'

'Did you leave the door open?'

'No, we checked before we left. It was shut, wasn't it, Poppy?'

'It was shut, Auntie Oakley. Blossom is right, we closed the door.'

'Okay, I believe you. Please can you go out into the garden and call her again, she can't have gone far.'

I beckoned everyone into the garden. 'Has anyone else been in the room other than Poppy and Blossom?'

They shook their heads.

'Is anyone missing?' I said.

Molly scanned everyone. 'Harrison's still not here, he popped home to fetch our lunch.'

I dashed next door and peered through the window, spying on Harrison munching a sausage roll. I popped my head through the open kitchen door.

'Caught you in the act, scoffing as usual. You're meant to be putting the food in the bag, not your big mouth. Have you been into the room with the cats?'

Harrison twisted around, spluttering pastry everywhere. With his mouth full he stuttered, 'About fifteen minutes ago, I packed their beds and toys into a box and loaded it into the van.'

Willow sneaked behind me eavesdropping. 'Dad, did you leave the room before you sealed the box?'

Harrison brushed the pastry crumbs onto the floor. 'Erm ... I don't think so.'

Willow shrieked, 'Dad, you did! Uncle Flynn called you to help carry the fridge.'

'So he did, I forgot. I was only gone for a few minutes, then I sealed the box and loaded it into the van. Nutmeg wouldn't have climbed into the box in that time.'

Willow screamed, 'Dad, you know how much she loves her bed; how could you not have checked?' She stormed out of the room and downstairs with us running behind her as she heaved the roller shutter up. 'Dad, which box did you pack?'

'Oh, love, they all look the same to me.'

Willow shouted to everyone: 'Shush, I'll call her. Nutmeg, where are you?'

We held our breath and listened, but alas there was no squeaky meow. I shook a packet of Dreamies, as Willow continued to call Nutmeg.

Poppy pointed to a box in the top far left-hand corner. 'Listen, I think I can hear her meowing.'

Within seconds, Willow climbed on top of the boxes and passed one down. We tore the lid open, and Nutmeg popped out like a jack-in-the-box. She arched her back and meowed for the Dreamies. With the crisis over, Nutmeg and a handful of Dreamies were placed into her carrier and loaded into my car next to Cinnamon and Jasmine. After whizzing around the house, and saying goodbye to every room, I locked my front door for the last time before handing the keys to Harrison.

'All yours now, big brother, I hope you'll be happy in your new house, though I'd watch out for the next-door neighbours, they're a bit of a rowdy bunch, especially the boys!'

Reuben shouted from the back of the car, 'Dad, aren't we the next-door neighbours?'

'Yes, we are. Auntie Oakley is trying to be funny.'

We headed down the slipway onto the motorway and the skies opened, turning the motorway into a lake.

Ruby glanced in the side mirror. 'It's lucky we have a yellow van or else the convoy would never find us with this amount of rain.' At that point, the Beatles blasted out, 'Yellow Submarine'.

Ruby wiped the steamed-up windscreen. 'I hope someone isn't sending us a message.'

I starred at Ruby. 'Don't worry, it'll be lovely and sunny in Cornwall.'

'We'll see, it always rains when I go on holiday to Cornwall.'

'It wouldn't dare rain today; not on my moving-home day.'

Chapter Twenty-two
Stuck Like Sardines

Ruby whooped as we crossed the Tamar Bridge into Cornwall. The rain eased, and sunbeams gushed out from behind clouds as Ruby popped in another CD. 'Here Comes The Sun' blasted out of the speakers, as Ruby and I smiled at each other and laughed. By the time we arrived at Whispering Pines my voice was hoarse from singing. After picking up both sets of keys, we met Flynn and the girls outside Mackenzie's house.

Poppy ran up the beach towards us. 'Auntie Oakley, you're so lucky. It's lovely here, isn't it Blossom?'

Blossom held her hand above her eyes scanning the harbour. 'It's so beautiful, I wish I lived here. We can come and stay with you, can't we?'

I reached for Cinnamon and Jasmine's carriers from the back of my car. 'Yes of course, as long as your dad agrees.'

After opening the front door and stepping in, Willow closed it before releasing Nutmeg, Jasmine and Cinnamon from their carriers and soon all three cats had settled on the window seat eyeing up cackling gulls.

Willow perched on the window seat beside them. 'It's breathtaking, Auntie Oakley. Is your new home far from here?'

'About a mile.'

'You're lucky. I hope you don't mind me staying when school has finished?'

'You can stay whenever you like.'

After settling the cats in, Ruby and I returned to the van and the convoy followed us along the track to Catkins.

Ruby sprung up and down like a baby in a bouncer. 'It's lucky you didn't hire a lorry; we'd have never squeezed through. What were you saying about raining? It's bucketing it down!'

Pins and needles were shooting down my fingers and hands as I gripped the steering wheel. The track seemed far narrower than when we last visited.

'Sorry, I'd forgotten how bumpy the road was. Don't worry, the tractors manage to drive through so it must be wide enough for us.'

Ruby let out a high-pitched squeal. 'Oakley, stop, we can't get through!'

'Rubes, the tractor manages, and it's much wider than the Luton van.'

'The tractor must go another way. Honestly, Oakley, you can't get through.'

'I'll try, or else I'm gonna have to reverse back, and I can't see behind me.'

'Oakley brake! The embankment has collapsed into the road!'

'But Catkins is around the next corner.'

'It doesn't matter where the hell it is. You can't get through.'

With my obstinate head screwed on, I ignored Ruby. 'I'll give it a go.'

I revved the engine up, released the clutch and let the van roll forward a few more paces.

'See, no problem.' With my foot hard down on the accelerator the tyres spun round, and round, and round, churning up a plume of mud. I accelerated again, but we didn't move.

Ruby folded her arms and glared down her nose in tune to the CD playing, 'I Should Have Known Better'.

'Oakley, you idiot, we're wedged in.'

'I'll put it into reverse.'

'What about everyone behind us?'

'I can't see behind us.'

Ruby's head seemed about to explode as she shouted, 'Reverse slowly then.'

'Okay.'

I revved the engine up. 'Rubes, we don't seem to be moving.'

Ruby wore her fiery dragon face. 'Now what are we going to do?'

'I'll squeeze out of the window and climb up the embankment.'

'You're kidding me, the embankment is as high as the roof.'

I glanced at my phone. 'Have you got any reception?'

'Nope.' Ruby grabbed my arm. 'What's that noise? It's a quad bike, isn't that Beau? Cor, he looks hot.'

'It can be tiring chasing the sheep.'

'I don't mean hot as in warm, you ninny, I mean he's the cat's meow, and full of rizz.'

'You what?'

'Do you know what your problem is?'

I sighed. 'No, but I'm sure you're going to tell me.'

Ruby faced me. 'You always want what you can't have, and when something's right under your nose, you ignore it.'

'How do you mean?'

'I bet you're still dreaming about that guy Woody from the River Dart.' Ruby paused. 'Am I right?'

I slouched into my seat. 'I was hoping to bump into him again.'

Ruby raised her voice: 'Oakley, he had kids and was married. Forget about Woody, especially when you've got a hot guy like Beau coming to your rescue.'

Beau swung his leg over the quad bike, smirking and shaking his head.

'Morning, Beau, we have a little problem.'

'You don't say, Oakley.'

'Sorry, Beau. I thought the tractors drive down the track?'

'No, there's another gate.'

Ruby was getting into the habit of looking down her nose at me today.

'Oh!'

Beau peered up both sides of the van. 'Suppose you need my help, anyone behind you?'

'Six cars.'

Beau raised his hands to his head. 'You're joking!' He paused and brushed his fingers through his blonde curls. 'They'll have to reverse to the main road, then I'll drive a tractor up as far as I can and attach a chain. When I knock on your rear end start the engine, leave it in neutral and once you're out of the mud, stop and I'll unhitch the chain. I'll shout left or right so you can steer around the bends. And Oakley ...'

I smiled my sweetest smile. 'Yes, Beau.'

Beau smirked. 'Has anyone ever told you that you drive them round the bend?'

'All the time.'

'Thought as much.'

'I'm really sorry about this.'

'That's okay, I'll add another meal to the list, at this rate, if you keep needing my help you're going to be broke in no time. I'll be about fifteen minutes.'

'Thanks, at least you're never going to go hungry with me around.'

Beau laughed, slid back onto his quad bike, and disappeared up the track.

Ruby cackled. 'He can knock on my rear end anytime. He's gorgeous, Oakley, like your knight in shining armour. Look at that bum.'

'Ruby! You're so crude. Don't you think of anything else?'

'What else is there to think about?'

'Who are you? Where has my shy reserved friend gone? Anyway, I'm pretty sure Beau thinks I'm a pain in the backside.'

'You are.'

We both burst out laughing as I reached for a flask and cake container.

'You're so rude to me, I'm not sure you deserve a slice of walnut cake and mug of coffee.'

'You know I love you really!'

I poured two mugs of coffee from my flask, sliced the cake and passed it to Ruby.

Ruby held her mug up to mine. 'Cheers, all I can say is there's never a dull moment when I go on adventures with you, Oakley.'

'Aren't you going to miss me?'

'I have a little adventure of my own planned.'

'You do? What?'

'My house is on the market and I'm moving to South Africa for six months to a year.'

I almost choked on a walnut. 'Doing what? When did this happen?'

'Just before you decided to move to Cornwall. I spotted a tender to design a school in Africa. I sent my design in, and they loved it; they want me to project manage the build.'

'Seriously, when do you leave?'

'June, though I have to find a team of builders and source the materials.'

'That's wonderful, seems we're both going on adventures. Why don't you rent your house out?'

'Because when I return, I'm moving to Cornwall to be close to my best friend.'

'You are? Even if I'm a pain in the backside?'

'Yes, I wouldn't expect you to be any other way.'

'Have you told anyone else?'

'What that you're a pain in the backside? They already know.'

'Very funny. I meant about your move.'

'Not yet, you're the first person. Depending on if we ever get out of here, my first viewing is arranged for tomorrow.'

A knock on the rear of the van interrupted our chatting. Within twenty minutes, with Beau's help and a lot of swearing, I'd reversed the van back down to the main road.

Ruby tilted her head towards me. 'You did well, Oakley, only ten words shouted that your mum wouldn't have approved of.'

'My mum doesn't approve of a lot I say or do. Come on, we'd better apologise to everyone.'

'I think you need to drop the word *we*.'

A round of applause exploded when we stepped out of the van, although I noticed my mum had remained in the car.

'Oakley, I'll take the tractor back to the farm and collect the quad bike and trailer. You'll have to unload everything from the van into the trailer and I'll run it up to Catkins.'

I unlocked the roller door on the van. 'Thanks, Beau, I don't know what we'd have done without you.'

Ruby marched with purpose towards Beau. 'I do – starved to death in the van.' She wrapped her arms around him and planted a kiss on his cheek. Beau smirked without kissing her back; Ruby was such a tease.

Everyone unloaded boxes from the van and loaded them into the cars. Lando, Harrison and my dad waited for Beau while the rest of us trundled down to Catkins.

The embankments were carpeted in nodding snowdrops signifying spring was just around the corner. The approach to Catkins was lined with an avenue of hazel catkins, and a sprinkling of daffodils peeped through the hedgerow. Pussy willow blew back and forth and reminded me of Cinnamon swishing her bushy tail.

We parked the cars and began unloading the boxes. My heart was pounding with excitement as I turned the key in my new front door. A positive energy surged through my veins, and I felt like the luckiest person alive as a whole new life awaited me on the other side of the door.

My mum coughed several times as everyone except her piled through the front door.

'Oakley, you're not seriously going to live here?'

'Yes, Mum, it's my new home.'

'I'm not taking a further step into this monstrosity.' She paused, and about-turned. 'I'll wait in the car.'

'What? Fine, Mum, I suppose we can manage without you.'

Poppy handed me a pile of post. 'Are there any Valentines cards?'

'I'm not sure, I'll open them later,' I said taking a box off Flynn.

'Which rooms will be ours when we stay in our holidays?' said Poppy.

'I thought you might like the two rooms where you can share the Jack and Jill bathroom.'

'I didn't realise you had people already living with you already. Who are Jack and Jill?' said Blossom.

Everyone in the room sounded like cackling geese as I tried to explain.

'Jack and Jill are not living with me, they're from the nursery rhyme. The bathroom has a door at each end that leads into two separate rooms, it's like sharing an ensuite.'

'I'd rather have my own bathroom; it's not nice sharing with Poppy. Can't she sleep in one of the barns? No one would notice the smell then,' said Blossom jumping out of the way as Poppy tried to push her over.

'No! Why don't you go and explore the house while we finish unloading the cars?' I said trying not to laugh, and thinking how lovely it was going to be to have the house to myself.

Molly shook her hands in the air, wrestling with the cobwebs. 'Oakley, you can't live in a smelly freezing house with no electricity.' She turned the tap. 'Oh my god, there's no water.'

'The water pipes from the spring are damaged. There's a couple of containers of water in the back of my car.'

'What about the toilets?'

'They flush, but you will have to fill the cistern up afterwards.'

'Oakley, how could you have bought this house?'

'Have you seen the views?'

'Sod the views, where are the shops?'

'The village shop is about a mile away, but the main shops are twelve miles away.'

'Twelve miles! I can walk to mine in five minutes.'

'It's lucky I've bought Catkins then, and not you.'

Molly huffed and disappeared to the toilet. A few minutes later her scream almost shattered the only intact window. Poppy and Blossom tore down the stairs and bumped into me in the hallway, as Molly stood outside the toilet zipping her jeans up.

Molly cowered behind me stuttering, 'There's a creature in the toilet.'

I peered down the toilet. 'It's only a toad.'

She sprung back against the wall and screamed again. 'Get it out of there.'

Poppy leant over the toilet, sniggering. 'I'll fish it out, Auntie Molly.'

However, Molly was already halfway up the stairs in search of another toilet.

Poppy placed the toad into a bucket. 'Poor toad, imagine seeing that huge bum blocking out the daylight.'

Blossom grabbed the bucket. 'It must have been like seeing an eclipse! I'll take it to the pond.'

'Girls, that's not a nice thing to say about your auntie. She can't help it if she is rather endowered in the rear-end department. Please pop the toad in the rockery by the pond, then swill the bucket with fresh water and take it upstairs for Auntie Molly.'

Blossom giggled. 'Didn't Jack and Jill go up the hill to fetch a pail of water? We're going up to hill to take a pail of water! Let's just hope no one tumbles down!'

Poppy snatched the bucket off Blossom. 'I'll take it to the pond, and you can fill it with water and take it up to Auntie Molly. When's lunch?'

'Oh my word Pops, you, and your stomach. There's a freezer box of sandwiches in the kitchen. First though free the toad and take the water to Auntie Molly and girls...'

'What now?' said Poppy elbowing Blossom as they simultaneously erupted into giggles.

'Make sure you both wash your hands and leave some sandwiches for everyone else! I'll see if the trailer has arrived.'

In the distance the drone of the quad bike intensified, and soon it was all hands-on-deck. Twenty trailers later, the van had been emptied and everyone mingled outside sipping drinks and gorging lunch, though there was no sign of Beau. After hugs all around everyone headed for home, except me; I was home.

I leant against the doorway breathing in my new surroundings. I still couldn't believe how lucky I was. I'd escaped the endless babysitting and was about to start a whole new chapter in my life. It may have been Valentine's Day, and I didn't have a date, but Beau had come to my rescue and that was enough for me. Although I could have stood in the doorway all night, the cats would have thought I'd abandoned them. The fish and chip shop beckoned me, followed by a long soak in Mackenzie's bath; what a perfect way to end a wonderful day. After loading the freezer box, and empty water containers into my car, I arrived at Mackenzie's house five minutes later. I was about to open the door when there was the familiar drone of a quad bike.

'Hi Oakley, have you finished for the day? Fancy treating me to one of the many meals you owe me at the Reel Them Inn?'

For a moment I hesitated, had I heard right? Beau one of the most handsome men I had ever met was asking me out on Valentine's Day. This really was the best day of my life.

'Would love to treat you. I was going to pick up fish and chips, but the pub sounds like a much better plan.'

'Great, I'll pick you up at around twenty past seven.'

'Thank you. Can't wait, see you shortly Beau.'

'See ya, Oakley.'

I could hardly contain my excitement as Mackenzie's front door sprang open, and I was engulfed in a gorgeous sweet floral perfume. What a lovely change from the musky damp pong at Catkins. Mackenzie's home was full of driftwood sculptures; I wondered if he'd made any himself, especially the mermaid posing on a rock on the balcony.

All three cats were curled up asleep on the kitchen window seat.

Though the moment I opened their food they weaved in and out of my legs. My phone pinged with a text from Mackenzie.

Mackenzie: Hi Oakley, hope the house move went okay & you've settled into my house?

Me: Hi Mackenzie, move completed, but van got stuck in the track, and Beau came to the rescue. What's the lovely smell in your house?

Mackenzie: Beau, loves being the knight in shining armour. My house smells of Sandalwood. Anything you need let me know. You must be shattered; I'll leave you in peace. Night Oakley.

Me: I'm going out for dinner with Beau, though. I'm so tired I could climb into your bed.

Mackenzie: Ha, ha, ha! You're more than welcome to climb into my bed! It's a long way to travel though.

Me: OMG! I meant on my own, in your bed here. You're very cheeky!

Mackenzie: Better not tell Beau you want to get into my bed.

Me: I won't! Sorry I'm filthy, the shower beckons. Enjoy your evening.

Mackenzie: Enjoy your Valentine's meal, my filthy new tenant!

Me: Will do. Good night my cheeky new Landlord!

A fuzzy feeling of exhilaration surged through my veins as I stepped into the shower and stepped out rejuvenated. I wound my hair into a bun and pulled out a few strands. After applying my make-up, I slipped on a smart black culotte jumpsuit. I appeared a little overdressed, but it was all I had in my bag.

At seven-twenty I peeped out the window with jittery anticipation, but there was no sign of Beau. Fifteen minutes later I checked again, but still no sign. I glimpsed my phone but there were no messages, maybe something had happened. It seemed like hours had passed when a text pinged at eight-fifteen.

Beau: Sorry, will have to take a rain check tonight. Forgot it was Valentine's night, all meals had to be pre-booked at the pub. I'm off to my parent's house for a roast. You can buy me a meal another night. Enjoy your evening.

My heart sank as I flopped onto the sofa with tears of disappointment brewing. I should have known it was too good to be true to have a real date on Valentine's evening. Though I wasn't going to let Beau know how disappointed I was.

Me: That's okay forgot it was Valentine's night too. I'll walk to the fish & chip shop and have an early night. Thanks for your help today. Enjoy your evening.

Beau: You're welcome. See you around.

After changing my outfit, I headed along the cobbled footpath to the fish and chip shop. When I reached the door, it was eerily dark, and dangling in the window was a sign displaying; closed Sundays, 8 p.m. Maybe this wasn't turning out to be the best day of my life after all.

My stomach grumbled as I trudged back to Mackenzie's house, and opened my car boot to see if there were any sandwiches left in the freezer box. Though all that remained was a strand of cress, and a litre of milk. It seemed tonight I was going to bed hungry. I carried the milk carton into Mackenzie's house, opened the fridge, and stood back dumbfounded, it was jam-packed with my favourite food. I reached for my phone.

Me: Hi Mackenzie. Who filled your fridge with food?

Mackenzie: Lily. I wasn't sure what you liked other than Hawaiian pizza, so asked her to stock it with my favourite food in the hope you liked it too.

Me: OMG! Thank you so much. How did you know my favourite pizza?

Mackenzie: You told me at your Christmas Party.

Me: You remembered, I'm impressed, thank you, how thoughtful.

Mackenzie: You're welcome. Weren't you meant to be going out with Beau?

Me: He cancelled. All meals had to be pre-booked because of Valentine's Day. Why aren't you out somewhere special?

Mackenzie: I'm on call. Nothing worse than being halfway through your favourite meal and having to leave it. Look in the bread bin by the microwave and help yourself to anything in the cupboards.

Me: Almond and chocolate croissants, and there's a chocolate shop above the microwave!

Mackenzie: Should keep you going for a couple of weeks.

Me: More like a couple of years!

Mackenzie: Sorry Oakley my pager is going. Happy Valentine's Day, enjoy your feast. Night.

Me: Happy Valentine's Day Mackenzie, thank you for being so kind and thoughtful.

Mackenzie: No worries.

With the pizza sizzling in the oven, there was no better time to open the mound of post. Amongst the numerous bills, and moving home cards were three unsigned Valentine's cards, no doubt jokes from my brothers. Though one card said 'Let's canoodle sometime' which wasn't the type of card one of my brothers would have sent. But for now, all I could think of was pizza and a long soak in the bath.

Chapter Twenty-three
Jezebel

For the past fortnight, following a day of hard labour at Catkins, either one of my brothers or my dad had accompanied me to the pub for dinner. The locals seemed a friendly bunch, except for a group of women huddled in a corner like witches hovering over a cauldron. When I walked past my smile wasn't replicated, instead they tutted, and with faces set in concrete, shook their heads in disapproval. It was obvious they were eavesdropping our conversations, though what they found interesting about the schedule of works at Catkins was beyond me.

One evening, when Flynn and I headed out of the pub one of the women hissed, 'Jezebel.'

Flynn peered over his shoulder and shouted at me, 'Come on, woman, time we hit the sack. Think we're over the honeymoon stage, it's time we ramped things up a bit. By the way, your touching up has worked a treat.'

Drawn-out gasps and grunts from the witches' corner rebounded off the walls while I hurried out unable to speak. Flynn was still laughing, as he dropped me at Mackenzie's house and left for home. My phone hooted as I switched the kettle on.

Mackenzie: Hi, Oakley, how are the house renovations going?

Me: Hi, Mackenzie, everywhere is a mess and my brothers never finish one job before moving onto the next.

Mackenzie: Sounds like builders. Have you been treating them to a meal at the pub each night? How are the locals?

Me: I have, though a group of women playing cards keep staring at me. Hope none of them are my clients.

Mackenzie: Sounds like Penelope and her harem. Sorry, they're our high-maintenance clients. Do they know you're the new vet?

Me: No. I smiled and said hello, but they kept giving me the evil eye.

Mackenzie: Have you been taking different men to the pub or back to my house each night?

Me: Yes, my brothers drop me at your place after the pub. OMG, you don't suppose they think I'm having affairs with lots of men, do you?

Mackenzie: Based on their own behaviour, and how well they know each other's husbands, I'd say they're jealous of how promiscuous you've been.'

Me: I'm meant to be fitting in, not turning my life into a soap drama. I'll stay away from the pub for a bit.

Mackenzie: Don't let them worry you. Probably watching for pointers. I'd love to see their faces when they find out who you are.

Me: Madigan and your dad will be fuming when they hear the rumours about me.

Mackenzie: R u kidding? They'll think it's hilarious. They're a right pair of jokers.

Me: Sound like my brothers.

Mackenzie: Have you seen much of Beau?

Me: No. He's been busy setting up FloBeau Water Sports Centre.

Mackenzie: Is there much more to do at Catkins?

Me: Still waiting for the kitchen units, a few cosmetic touches, and a huge amount of tidying.

Mackenzie: It will be worth it in the end. Can't wait to see the transformation.

Me: Me too. Thank you so much for letting me stay at your house. It would have been awful living in the mess.

Mackenzie: That's okay. Glad to have helped, and don't worry about the gossips, they'll get their comeuppance one day.

Me: Like when their husbands get together over a pint and find out how well they know each other's wives.

Mackenzie: Ha ha, something like that. Any problems let me know and I'll sort them out. Night, Oakley.

Me: Tee-hee! Thanks, Mackenzie. Night.

The following day the kitchen units arrived, and when I ripped the boxes open the units were turquoise instead of maple. I sent a

WhatsApp to my family to find out what numpty brother ordered the wrong units.

The doorbell chimed and lurking in the doorway, clutching a box, was Beau.

'Beau, come in, I haven't seen you in ages.'

Beau handed me the box. 'Oakley, I can't believe the difference in Catkins. Here, this is from Lily, it's a double chocolate fudge cake. It looks like you could do with a slice. What's wrong?'

'The kitchen units are blue; they're meant to be Canadian maple and now the kitchen can't be fitted next week.'

'Why don't you put the kettle on, slice the cake, and I'll look at the units?'

'Okay.'

When I returned, Beau was sitting on the floor, sniggering.

'What's so funny?'

'Look, watch this.' He peeled a blue covering back revealing a beautiful maple door.

I bent forward for a closer look. 'For crying out loud, what an eejit I am, they're not blue!'

'No, it's the protective covering.'

'I've told my brothers they're numpties.'

I glanced at my phone to see plenty of laughing emojis. I sent a reply confirming the units were in fact, maple. Beau grinned as he took a huge bite out of a piece of chocolate fudge cake.

'Seems I've come to your rescue again. What are you doing later? Fancy buying me dinner at the pub tonight?'

'Would love to, but I'm staying away from the pub. I've been taking my family there each evening and I've got an inkling the locals think I'm having affairs with lots of men.'

Beau's sniggering sounded like a dolphin playing in the sea. 'Let's give them something else to gossip about, they'll think you're leading me astray too.'

I giggled while stuffing my face with chocolate fudge cake. 'Shall I meet you there?'

'No, I'll pick you up, it looks more convincing.'

'Okay, it's a date,' I blurted out with too much enthusiasm, before backtracking. 'Sorry was acting the part already. Another slice of Lily's cake?'

'Don't mind if I do, then I'd better be on my way.'

Beau wolfed down the cake, slurped his tea and wiped his mouth on his cuff.

'I'll pick you up from Mackenzie's at seven-thirty.'

'Thanks, Beau, I'm looking forward to it.'

The minute Beau left I headed to Mackenzie's house to get ready. With most of my clothes still in boxes, once again I dressed in my black culottes, and made a special effort with my make-up and hair. At seven-thirty precisely Mackenzie's doorbell chimed, and Beau appeared looking fetching in a black shirt and black jeans.

'Wow, Oakley, you look gorgeous.'

'Thanks, you don't scrub up too bad either.'

'Come on, let's give the busybodies something to talk about.'

We headed to the Reel Them Inn and chose a table within earshot of the chinwaggers. Beau leant across the table and took my hand in his. His hands were rough with bitten nails encased in mud, and as I gazed into his eyes rather than feeling a sensation of electricity, I felt like bursting into laughter, but as Beau gazed into my eyes, his sparkled like the sun on freshly fallen snow. I bit my lip holding in the avalanche of giggles as he broadcasted to the pub the first time we met.

'I recall you took my breath away as you dropped to your knees.'

My bout of giggles felt like popping candy.

'Remember the next time we met? I fell head over heels, and you got downright filthy.'

Beau raised his eyebrows and smirked. 'All I can remember was you spreadeagled on all fours. I have to say, you looked quite sexy, but not as sexy as you look now. I love your outfit although it would be even better lying on the bedroom floor.'

Memories flooded back of my bedroom in my old house. I'd have needed a platoon of male visitors to justify that amount of clothes on my bedroom floor. We were interrupted when a young man placed our meals in front of us.

'Thanks, Dustin mate.' Beau lowered his voice. 'Have you met Oakley yet?'

The young man pushed his glasses back. 'No, though Mam did tell me 'bout her.'

'Oakley, this is Lily's youngest son, Dustin; my little heartthrob cousin.'

I held my hand out to him, but he ignored it. 'Hi, Dustin, nice to meet you.'

The edge of Dustin's lips quivered, and his face turned pink. 'All right. Enjoy your meal.' He about-turned and hurried back to the kitchen.

Beau picked up his knife and fork. 'Poor lad doesn't say a lot. Spends most of his time with his head in books.'

'I love reading, he'll surprise you when he comes out of his shell.'

'Yep, he sure is a shy one. He was a bit of a surprise baby. There's nearly fourteen years between him and his stepbrother, Mackenzie, so guess he grew up without any siblings at home.'

'I didn't realize Lily was Mackenzie's stepmum.'

'Mackenzie's real mum was one of my dad's sisters, sadly she died when Mackenzie was eight. A few years later, during my dad's birthday party, Aidan hit it off with Lily, my dad's other sister. I guess Lily is also Mackenzie's auntie.'

'Crikey, glad you explained that before I had too much wine.'

'I'll order you another glass if you like, before I take you at your house.'

'Don't you mean take me back to my house?'

'I'd happily take you anywhere. Do you know how to tell if your house is haunted?'

'No.'

'When I take you in the bedroom, you won't stop screaming.'

I was trying not to explode with laughter as Dustin collected our empty plates and stared at me as if I had two heads. It seemed we had attracted an audience of quivering shoulders, and lips could be heard tutting in disapproval. I couldn't contain my laughter anymore and retreated to the ladies where I dashed into the centre cubicle; it seemed there was no getting away from the gossips.

'Maeve, is that you in the end cubicle?'

'Yes, Pen.'

'Have you seen how young Beau has been acting with that woman?'

'I have, he's certainly smitten. Do you think we ought to warn him that she's a hooker and has been taking different men back to Mackenzie's house for sex?'

'Knowing Beau, that's all he wants her for. He's not like his cousin Mackenzie, who Lily said has met someone special. Mackenzie wouldn't treat women the way Beau treats women. Have you got any loo roll in there? There's nothing in this toilet.'

'Yes, there's a spare one, I'll throw it through the cubicles.'

A toilet roll zoomed in front of me and stopped, I gave it a kick into the next cubicle.

'Have you got it, Pen?'

'Yes, thank you, Maeve, brilliant throw.'

'Beau's a ladies' man, though I'm a little surprised he's chosen this woman. She's dressed more conservatively to the others, and she's so much older. I think he may have met his match with this Jezebel.'

'Perhaps he occasionally likes experimenting with older women rather than the girls; show him the ropes, so to speak.'

Maeve chortled. 'Perhaps he's into bondage. Wonder how mature he likes his women.'

'I know what you're thinking, Maeve, and I think seventy-two is probably a bit too old for him. Not sure your husband would approve.'

'He doesn't need to know.'

Pen giggled. 'The only thing I get tied up with these days is my tongue. Hurry up, Maeve, it's your round, I'll see you at the bar.'

'With a tongue as sharp as yours, I can't believe that. I'll be out shortly.'

I stayed in the toilet until they'd left, then I sneaked back to my table processing their idle gossip.

Beau quizzed me. 'You were ages, Is everything okay?'

'Yes, sorry, I was stuck in the middle cubicle with two gossiping witches either side.'

'Anything interesting?'

'No, not really. I'm a bit tired and have a long day tomorrow, so I'm heading home.'

'I'll give you a lift, maybe I could come in for a nightcap?'

'Thanks, but I can walk back, it's not far.'

'If you're sure? One of my mates is at the bar, so I'll stay for another pint.'

'Okay, though make it an orange juice or you'll be over the limit.

'You're right thanks, and thanks for the meal.'

'You're welcome.'

Beau headed to the bar, and when the gossips weren't looking, I slipped out the back door. I strolled under the twinkling lights alongside the harbour reminiscing the conversation between the gossips. I was in desperate need of some girlie advice, and soon I was lounging on Mackenzie's sofa with my phone in my hand.

Me: Hi Rubes, are you asleep? I need advice about men.

Ruby: Hi Oak, I'm awake now. Ooh a subject close to my heart. How can I help?

Me: I overheard things about Beau that I'm a bit worried about.

Ruby: Like what?

Me: That he's slept with a lot of women and is only interested in me for sex.

Ruby: So?

Me: What if that's the only reason he likes me.

Ruby: Then you have good sex and move on to the next one.

Me: But I want a steady relationship, I don't just want sex!

Ruby: Then play hard to get. If he is really interested in you, he'll wait. If not send him my way.

Me: I don't like playing games. I want a romantic relationship where we date a few times and get to know each other before anything else happens. I want to fall in love, Rubes, not just have sex and be let down when he moves on to the next girl.

Ruby: Well, if you have good sex maybe he'll want more, or perhaps you could try dating Mr Frosty, though even he'll let you down eventually.

Me: Very funny, that's not helpful.

Ruby: It's just sex, you should be grateful he has chosen someone like you. Night. x

Me: Cheers for that! Night. x

That was the last time I'd ask Ruby for advice on men. I crawled into bed using my contortionist skills around the cats, first kicking Jasmine off the bed, and then Cinnamon. My mind kept wandering back to the tittle-tattle. Surely Beau wasn't like that? He liked me for my personality, or that's what I told myself. But perhaps Ruby was right, and I should play hard to get for a while. I'd prove to everyone that Beau wasn't simply interested in me for a night of sex. They say a way to a man's heart is through his stomach; perhaps if I cooked him an amazing meal, he'd never want to leave me. I drifted off to sleep reciting menus that would ensure Beau was interested in more than sex.

Chapter Twenty-four
Bath Full of Crustaceans

The following weeks flew by, and despite Beau's pessimism, Catkins had not required the use of a sledgehammer. The kitchen was perfect, the wood burners were amazing, and the new bathrooms and showers were out of this world. New carpets had been laid, windows replaced, and everywhere had been decorated. The garden was full of birdfeeders and Lando made me three bird tables and a concrete bird bath. All that remained was to replace the old AGA with a modern Rayburn that would operate the central heating and heat the water. There was a twelve-week wait, so for now, to ensure I had hot water I would have to fill the AGA with chopped wood. My brothers had even installed a doggy shower in the utility room in anticipation of me adopting a dog. Harrison snapped masses of photos for their website before everyone waved goodbye and left me alone in my beautiful new home.

My excitement was bubbling over as I headed down to Mackenzie's house to collect the cats and introduce them to Catkins. With the cats secured in their carriers, we were ready to begin our new adventure. There was just one more thing to do, I'd whittled a gift for Mackenzie, and it looked perfect on the mantelpiece above his fire. I hoped he loved his driftwood gull that was the spitting image of Sidney, well I thought so, though it could have been mistaken for a crow.

Catkins' front door swung open with joints that were now quieter than mine. The cats slinked out of their carriers, ears back and eyes aglow. After exploring the house, Nutmeg claimed her spot at the top of the stairs.

With the hallway window slightly ajar, the liquid gold chirruping of sparrows interrupted the early evening silence. I glided upstairs to christen my rolltop bath that was big enough for two, but for now it was best I kept that to myself, I didn't want every Tom, Dick or Harry sharing my bath. I popped the plug in, turned the tap on, and dangled my hand under the running water waiting for it to warm up, but it was stone cold! What a numpty – I'd forgotten that without lighting the Aga there was no hot water other than the power shower.

A few minutes later, the Aga was roaring as high as the yowling echoing from the bathroom. I flew upstairs to find Nutmeg dangling her paw in the water, which was level with the top of the bath. Swiftly, I flicked the tap off as an almighty splash echoed, and Nutmeg fell into the bath. Who knew cats were such good swimmers? She swam to the other side, scrambled out, and skedaddled through the doorway followed by me clutching a towel. After rubbing her nearly dry, she continued washing herself in front of the Aga while I dashed back to empty the bath. On reaching for the plug, I shrieked, stepped back, and retrieved my phone from my back pocket.

'Sis, what's up? We only left an hour ago; you can't be missing us already?'

'Harrison, why is my bath full of shrimps and prawns?'

Harrison addressed everyone who were howling with laughter.

'Lads, I guess shrimp wontons are on the menu for tea.'

Lando shouted, 'You should be pleased they're not crabs, wouldn't look good if the new vet had crabs.'

'Very funny. How did they get into my bath? And what the heck do I do with them?'

Spencer shouted, 'Catch them and pop them in the wok with a stir fry.'

Harrison told them to shush. 'We fitted a new filter system; I asked Spencer to drain the tank but obviously he didn't. You'll have to turn the main tap off, drain the tank, then turn the water back on and the tank will refill with filtered water. Oakley, don't light the Aga without any water in the system.'

'I've just lit the Aga! If I drain the bath, the shrimps and prawns will die in the sewage tank. I can't kill them.'

'Sis, they're crustaceans, you eat them in your Chinese, catch them in a net, put them in your pond, and let the fish eat them. You'll have to let the Aga go out before you drain the tank, and sis, don't forget to check under your bed for monsters.'

'You're hilarious, Harrison. I only know five monsters, and I'm talking to the oldest one. Good night.'

With the water turned off, and the fire in the Aga dwindling, I scoured the barns and sheds for a fishing net. After returning empty handed, my only option was my flour sieve. I was halfway upstairs when the doorbell chimed and standing in the porch was Beau and Wolf.

'Hi, Oakley, are you busy? I've brought fish and chips and Chinese, but there's far too much for one. Fancy sharing it with me?'

'That's very thoughtful, Beau, as long as it's not prawns or shrimps, I've seen enough of them to last a lifetime.'

Beau's mouth dropped. 'That's a shame. I was led to believe you liked prawns and shrimps.'

'Have you been speaking to my brothers within the last half an hour?'

'I might have been. Why are you holding a bucket and sieve?'

'Follow me, I'll take you upstairs.'

Wolf disappeared into the living room, as Beau raced to the top of the stairs before I'd even cleared the first step.

'Ooh, I like a forward woman, that's one invitation I'm not turning down.'

Giggling, I marched up the remaining steps. 'Sorry to disappoint, we're only going as far as the bathroom.'

'Perfect. Maybe we could see if your bath is big enough for two.'

'That's what I thought.'

'You still haven't told me what the bucket and sieve are for.'

'You'll find out soon enough.'

I pushed the bathroom door open, and Beau followed me towards the bath.

'I've already filled it; you climb in first and I'll fetch you a towel.'

Beau rushed towards the bath peeling his fleece off, he leant over the bath and laughed his socks off. He threw me a look that was normally exclusive to my brothers.

'As tempting as sharing a bath with you is, that's one invitation even I'm going to turn down. Why don't you just pull the plug out rather than using a sieve and bucket?'

'Because they'll die. Don't look at me like that, everything deserves a chance of life. I'm not sending them to their death in the sewage tank if they have a chance of living in the pond, even if the fish eat them.'

By the look on Beau's face, it was obvious he had the same opinion about me as my brothers did. He headed to the door.

'Let's eat the food before it gets cold, we can deal with the bath later.'

'Okay, I am a bit peckish.'

While I searched through boxes for plates and cutlery, Beau arranged the foil containers on the table and unwrapped the fish and chips. When he removed the foil lids, every tub contained a prawn or shrimp dish, accompanied by a huge bag of prawn crackers.

'Sorry, Oakley, I rang Harrison from the fish and chip shop to check the plans for tomorrow. He said you were lonely on your first night at Catkins and could I keep you company. I ordered another portion of fish and chips and was on my way when he rang again.

He said how much you loved Chinese, especially dishes with prawns and shrimps, so I headed to the Chinese takeaway. I wondered why there was so much humour in the background.'

'Yep, that's my brothers for you, always trying to wind people up. I don't think I've had time to be lonely. Now do you see why I wanted to move. Come on, let's eat, it looks scrumptious.'

Twenty minutes later, Beau wiped his mouth. 'I don't know about you, Oakley, but I'm full to bursting.'

'Me too. Thank you, Beau, it was delicious. Are you ready? Let's head upstairs and rescue the prawns and shrimps.'

We caught them in the sieve, drained and refilled the system. I was returning from emptying the final bucket of crustaceans into the pond when I heard Beau calling me. He was standing in the hallway looking up at the ceiling.

'I think we have a problem.'

'Not another one.'

'The drainage pipe from the bath hasn't been connected to the outlet, look at the ceiling.'

I tilted my head back, not only was a bubble forming, but water was seeping down the beams.

'Freaking hell! My bloody brothers are useless. I'll call Harrison.'

'My darling sis, did you enjoy your tea?' Harrison's sniggering was on par to Muttley the dog from *Wacky Races*.

'The Chinese was delicious, and the fish and chips to die for, for once I didn't have to pick any bones out, other than the huge bone I'm about to pick out of you.'

Harrison's sniggering stopped. 'Why?'

'Who forgot to connect the drainage pipe from the bath?'

'Brenden connected it.'

I heard Brenden in the background. 'I asked Spencer to do it.'

Spencer argued, 'I told you I didn't have time, the old man said he'd do it.'

'Hold on, sis, we'll call Dad.'

There was an awful lot of clattering before Harrison returned to the phone.

'It seems no one connected the pipe, whatever you do don't pull the plug out.'

'It's a bit late for that now, you told me to drain the tank. Water is pouring through the ceiling.'

Harrison snorted down the phone: 'Oakley, why did you pick today to do as I told you? You've always ignored me and done your own thing. We'll be back tomorrow to fix it. Find your tools, drill a few holes in the ceiling and place buckets underneath. Sorry, sis, just can't get the staff these days.'

'I have two sets of tools; one is packed in a box in the barn, and the other is heading north in a blue-and-yellow van advertising they can fix anything.'

Harrison chuckled. 'You know the saying, "If at first you don't succeed try, try, try again!"'

'I'll second that, you're very trying, big brother.'

'We aim to please. Why not ask Beau if he has any tools you can borrow, save searching through the boxes? Sorry, sis, we're almost home. See you tomorrow, and don't forget to check under your bed for monsters.'

'Good night, Harrison.'

I turned my attention back to Beau. 'Guess this wasn't how you were planning on spending your evening?'

Beau winked at me. 'Probably best I don't tell you how I was planning on spending my evening.'

'I was planning on going to bed early.'

'So was I!'

'I won't ask who with. You don't by any chance have any tools in your car? I need to drill holes in the ceiling before it collapses.'

'You're in luck, I was repairing a couple of fences earlier, my toolbox is in the boot. I'll be back in a jiffy.'

'Thank you, I'll find my stepladders.'

I positioned the stepladders under the bubble as Beau returned with his toolbox.

'Shall I hold the bottom of the ladder?'

Armed with his drill, Beau stepped onto the first rung and peered over his shoulder. 'On one condition.'

I gripped the stepladder directing my gaze to anywhere other than his bum. 'What condition? You sound like my mum.'

'Keep your hands to yourself, and no ogling my bum.'

'As if! I've seen enough builders' bums recently to last me a lifetime.'

Beau steadied himself on the ladder and aimed the drill towards the outside of the bubble.

'I see, so now you're saying I've got a builder's bum?'

'Not at all, you have a sexy ... what am I saying? Make sure your bit isn't too small.'

Once again, Beau peeked over his shoulder. When he caught me gawping, he could have blinded me by the glint in his eyes.

'I can assure you, Doctor Breeze, there have never been any complaints about the size of my bit.'

I giggled, wondering if his bit was as big as his head.

He drilled a circle of holes allowing water to trickle through like a rainfall shower head.

'I'll drill a hole in the middle using my biggest bit.'

I held tightly to the ladder. 'Aren't there enough holes? We don't want the ceiling to collapse.'

'Trust me, the ceiling is not going to collapse.'

'If you say so, but I'm standing back,' I said releasing my grip, as Beau swapped bits and drilled a central hole.

'Oakley, can you grab the drill off me? I've only gone and got my bit stuck in the hole. I'll need to wiggle it around before pulling it out, and I'm struggling doing it one-handed.'

I sniggered, reaching up for the drill.

'What are you giggling about?'

'I was imagining the comment my friend Ruby would say about you wiggling your bit one-handed.'

'Ruby? The cute redhead? When's she visiting again?'

It seemed Beau *had* noticed her.

'Not for a while, she's going to work abroad for six to twelve months before moving down here.'

'Moving here? Great! I hope she doesn't get into as much trouble as you. I'm giving up, I've pushed my bit in too far and now I've lost it. Right, mind yourself, I'm coming ...' Beau's words tapered as an almighty rumble reverberated above. 'What the f–.' Beau slid down the ladder like a firefighter on a shout. He tripped over the bucket, grasped my arm, and skyrocketed us backwards onto the floor. The bubble burst engulfing us in a cloud of dust, filthy bath water, a sprinkling of dead flies, moths, spiders and mouse droppings. Neither of us spoke for fear of swallowing anything. Beau knelt up, wiped his mouth, and through the cloud of dust, held out his hand. Rubbing my eyes, I grasped it, and he tugged me to my feet. Beau mirrored a ghost at a Halloween party. Lines of dust dripped down his forehead and snippets of plasterboard peeped from within his blond curls. We dashed to the utility room, and fully clothed, stepped into the dog shower.

Beau held the shower head above me. 'Oakley, why have you got so much dog shampoo when you haven't got a dog?'

'I'm going to adopt one.'

'One! You've enough shampoo for a dozen.'

'Blame my mum, she taught me to be well prepared.'

Beau chuckled. 'So did mine, but there are easier ways to get a man into a shower. Now, I'll wash your back if you wash mine.'

I snatched the shower head from him. 'Turn round then. If you'd listened to me and hadn't been fiddling with your bit for so long, none of this would have happened. Maybe it was a deliberate ploy of yours.'

Beau stepped out grinning, wiped his face and removed his top. 'Do you know what? Most girls drop like flies at the thought of showering with me.'

'Have you considered changing your deodorant from fly spray?'

'No flies on you is there, Doctor Breeze? I'll have it known I use the best cologne; hold on, I have a bottle in my jacket pocket.' He reached for his jacket, sprayed himself in cologne before reading the label, and bent over in hysterics.

My gaze diverted from his eyes to his chest where barely a hair was visible, and as I gawked for a few more seconds, it became apparent he'd waxed his chest. I'd never met a man who waxed more of his body than me. My lady shaver felt inadequate by comparison.

'You'll never guess what my cologne is called: Fly Away! Think someone is giving me a hint? I've got a spare pair of overalls in the car; I'll get changed and help you clean up this mess.'

'Thanks, my brothers owe you a drink tomorrow.'

'I think they owe me more than one drink.'

'While you're fetching your overalls; I'll nip upstairs and change.'

Beau's glint in his eyes was suggestive. 'Need any help?'

'Think I can manage, thanks,' I said smirking.

Beau seemed to be undressing me with his eyes as he looked me up and down and puckered his lips. 'Shame, you don't know what you're missing.'

An hour later, the floor was gleaming and appeared as good as new, though I avoided glancing at the black hole above me.

'Oakley, have you seen Wolf? He's been very quiet.'

I stuck my head into the living room. 'He's lying on the sofa. Ah ... look how sweet he is on his back with his front legs behind his head.'

Beau growled, 'He's a working dog and isn't allowed on the furniture. Wolf, get down.'

Poor Wolf's dreams of chasing butterflies were rudely interrupted as he twisted and fell off the sofa. He picked himself up, and with his tail between his legs, wandered over to Beau. That was a side of Beau I hadn't previously encountered and didn't like.

'Sorry, Oakley, he isn't a pet.'

'Was it necessary to shout so loudly? Even working dogs deserve a day off.'

'I don't want Wolf going soft on me. Come on boy, time to go home.'

'Hold on a minute, you left your drill in the kitchen, be back in a jiffy.' I dashed back to the kitchen and rummaged through a cupboard for a dog treat I'd brought in anticipation of adopting a dog. I picked a Jumbone, hid it behind my back, and returned to meet Beau at the door. I passed Beau the drill.

'Thank you for the Chinese and fish and chips, it was thoughtful of you. Sorry about the bath and ceiling.' With my hand held behind me, I followed Beau to his car with Wolf's tongue nuzzling my fingers. Wolf sneaked the Jumbone, crunched and swallowed it in one almighty gulp and ran alongside me, swishing his tongue around his lips and gazing up at me lovingly.

'Oakley, I have eyes in the back of my head. You'll spoil him.'

'Everyone deserves a treat now and then, even dogs.'

Beau threw me one of his scowls before climbing into his car and disappearing along the track.

I headed upstairs and remembered Harrison told me to check under the bed for monsters. Before climbing into bed I peeked under the mattress. Phew, no monsters were lurking. However, there was a massive cardboard box full of presents, which I couldn't wait to open.

Chapter Twenty-five
Monsters Hiding Under My Bed

It was like Christmas. The first present was from my parents; practical as ever, a torch, candles, matches and a keyring tracker. No doubt my mum wanted to know my every move.

The next parcel was from my nan and contained a pair of homemade curtains covered in embroidered birds sitting in oak trees; it was beautiful.

My nieces and nephews had wrapped their present in layers and layers of wrapping paper like pass the parcel. A bar of chocolate fell onto the bed with every layer I unwrapped. When I removed the final piece of wrapping, a Friesian cow onesie stared at me, and a note read:

> *To Auntie Oakley,*
> *Don't wear outside,*
> *or the local farmer might milk you.*

In small writing on the bottom someone had written:

> *or slap your hide.*

And on the reverse:

> *Careful the local friendly farmer doesn't*
> *artificially inseminate you.*

Next was a gift from my brothers, the tag read:

To our little sis, who needs more
action in the bedroom.
We thought you could rise every
morning with a cock.

I tore the wrapping paper off, and images flashed through my mind of my brothers looking at sex websites, but I was relieved to see a digital alarm clock with an alarm wake-up call of a cockerel.

The final gift was from my four sisters-in-law. The box contained a set of new towels, various bubble baths and shower gels, plus a huge bar of chocolate. At the bottom of the box was an envelope containing a card signed by everyone, and inside the card was another envelope. I peeled back the gusset and was close to tears when a picture of the cutest puppy fell onto my lap; he looked like a cuddly black-and-white teddy bear. The card inside read:

Hello, my name is Paddington, I'm a four-week-old
sheepa-doodle, I've been informed you will be my
human mummy when I'm old enough to leave my
doggy mummy. I can't wait for you to come and meet
me. I'm living at Paw-Some animal rescue centre. Lots
of love, Paddington xxx

Time to WhatsApp my brothers and send a text to my mum.

Me: Found the new love of my life under my bed. Thank you so much for my lovely pressies. I'm so excited! Love Oakley xxxx

Harrison: Ha, ha, sis, told you to look under your bed for monsters! Paddington is going to be a little, or rather big, monster! He has a glint in his eye and will get into as much trouble as you do. See you tomorrow x

Mackenzie: Hi Oakley, did you mean to send me this text? Did you find Beau under your bed?

Me: Sorry, Mackenzie, must have sent text to you instead of my mum. No, Beau is not under or on top of my bed. The new love of my life is a puppy called Paddington; my family have adopted him for me. Found the photo under my bed. I'll send you a copy.

Mackenzie: His face is etched with trouble. He will have you twisted around his not-so-little paws. Assume you will take him to work? Everyone will fall for those puppy-dog eyes.

Me: I'll check with Madigan and your dad. Have you heard from Beau recently?

Mackenzie: I phoned him not long ago. Couldn't hear what he was saying as he was in the yard and the cows were mooing. Sounded like he'd ordered an Asian takeaway that was crushed and now he was watching porn in the bath. I didn't have a clue what he was on about.

Me: Beau meant crustaceans! My bath was full of prawns, no watching porn.

Mackenzie: That's odd I pour bubble bath into mine.

Me: Ha, ha, ha! Cold water tank was full of them as numpty brothers forgot to drain it after fitting a new filter. They also forgot to connect the waste pipe. Ceiling flooded. Beau drilled holes, pulled out his bit, and the ceiling collapsed.

Mackenzie: OMG! Beau brags that girls say the earth moves when he pulls out his bit.

Me: Hah, hah, hah! He's right!

Mackenzie: Have you been given any clients yet?

Me: I have a client visit at 10.30 a.m. on my first day. Your dad is transferring one of his clients to me.

Mackenzie: Do you know which client?

Me: Fanny Flocker.

Mackenzie: Fanny Flocker is your first client! This will be your initiation test. Believe me, many a vet has left after encountering Fanny Flocker.

Me: Is she that bad?

Mackenzie: Yes! A few tips: do not eat her rock cakes or drink her tea. Make sure you sit on a newspaper, wear your overalls and wellies. If you have long hair wear it up, change overalls before you get back in your car. Whatever you do stay upwind of her unless you have a gas mask with you. If you find a bowl festering with maggots leave it, she feeds them to the birds and will get upset if it's thrown out.

Me: OMG! I swallowed maggots when I was six.

Mackenzie: Yuk! How?

Me: My brothers used to drag me fishing with them and they made me warm the maggots in my mouth in exchange for a bar of chocolate. I sneezed once and swallowed ten maggots. They wouldn't give me the chocolate as they said I'd eaten their maggots.

Mackenzie: That's the most disgusting thing I have ever heard. Fanny's house is full of little blighters.

Me: Like what?

Mackenzie: Fleas, bedbugs, lice, mites, mice and rats. The dogs and cats aren't house trained so watch where you walk.

Me: You're making me itch.

Mackenzie: Sorry! You need to come up with a plan and get the upper hand of my dad and uncle by outwitting them.

Me: Good idea, think I need to put my thinking cap on! Appreciate the forewarning.

Mackenzie: That's okay, we need to stick together. Remember, never, ever walk behind Fanny as she has a wind problem! Hope I haven't put you off working for Madhatters! It lives up to its name.

Me: Not at all! I like a challenge.

Mackenzie: You've joined the right vets then. I'll leave you to chew over your ideas. Night, Oakley, sleep tight in your new home, and don't let the bed bug's bite.

Me: Ha, ha, very funny. Night, Mackenzie.

My first night in my new house was certainly a memorable one. I pulled the duvet up to my chin and drifted off to sleep with the picture of Paddington etched in my mind, accompanied by creepy crawlies.

Chapter Twenty-six
Penelope Pringle

The following morning, my brothers arrived bright and early and barged through the front door.

Harrison light-heartedly kissed me on the cheek. 'Mornin' sis, enjoy your Chinese?'

I grinned at him. 'It was delicious, Thank you.'

Harrison glared at the hallway ceiling. 'You made a right mess here.'

'No I didn't, the plonker who forgot to connect the pipe did.'

Everyone stared at Flynn.

'Don't blame me, Dad said he was connecting it.'

'Look, I don't care what numpty was to blame, can you fix it?'

Flynn playfully put his arm around me ushering me towards the kitchen.

'We can fix anything. But first things first, sis, you're slacking, put the kettle on, we're gasping, and a few biscuits wouldn't go amiss.'

'The kettle is already on.'

A few hours later the ceiling had been repaired, and after two mugs of tea each and an empty biscuit barrel, my brothers headed to their van. Harrison loaded his toolbox into the back.

'Right, we're off to see Beau about building the jetty, unless there's anything else that needs repairing?'

'No, but give it time. Say hi to Beau from me.'

'Will do. I've left a tin of paint for you to touch up the ceiling once it's dry.'

'Thanks, Harrison, and thank you so much for Paddington, he's adorable.'

Harrison jumped into the driver's seat. 'Poppy and Blossom chose him. If he gets into as much trouble as you, blame them.'

'I'm sure he'll be an angel.'

Opening the window, Harrison smirked. 'That's what we thought you were, until you started talking and walking. See ya, sis.'

'Very funny.'

He waved goodbye and I watched the van until it disappeared out of view.

Five minutes later, I parked by the village shop to restock my biscuit barrel. Though the aroma of freshly baked bread and coffee wafting from the Lily Pad changed my direction. The bell jangled as I entered the door and headed to the counter.

While I was waiting to be served, my ears pricked up like antennae, earwigging a conversation between Lily and the woman in front of me. Oh my word, it was the woman from the pub who called me a Jezebel. Maybe it was time I played a few games.

The woman leant on the counter. 'I'm in such a conundrum, Lily, and don't know which way to turn.'

'Mornin' Penelope, What's the problem?'

Penelope continued. 'The men's rugby game is tomorrow morning, and as you know, Wendy washes their kit every week. She called me ten minutes ago, very apologetic, and full of flu. You won't believe it, but the lads' rugby kits are festering in the boot of her car as she's not been well enough to wash them. My husband is away working and has taken my car. Do you have time to pick up the kits, wash them and deliver them to the rugby ground by half past eight tomorrow morning?'

Lily poured the lady a double espresso. 'Sounds like you need this rather than lemon tea. Sorry, I'm working till eight tonight, and it'll be a tad late to start washing kits then.'

'That's okay, I'll contact the WI members.' Penelope hesitated as if there was something else she wanted to say.

'Were there owt else?'

'There is, though you know I'm not one to gossip, so mum's the word. Did you see that woman last week who was staying at Mackenzie's house? It was like a Piccadilly Circus with the number of men coming and going. Fancy flaunting them at the pub each night. Did you know she was getting cosy with your nephew Beau? Unbelievable. It's just not the sort of thing that goes on in Whispering Pines. We were shocked at how brazen their conversation was.'

'Talking about what?'

Penelope leant closer and whispered, 'Stripping, buffing, baring all, and one night one of the men mentioned how easy it was getting laid, and then he started talking about a hard erection that went up much easier than he thought. He mentioned his little pecker and a huge pair of knockers. He ended the conversation about finally getting plastered.' Penelope paused and moved in closer. 'And one even said it didn't need as much touching up as he thought. Oh Lily, it was so awful, I thought I was going to faint. Thank God the Jezebel has moved out of Mackenzie's house, now maybe we can get a little peace and quiet, my poor heart couldn't take anymore.'

Unaware someone was behind her I staged a croaky cough.

She peered over her shoulder and jolted her head back, before stepping sideways and glaring at me.

'Well of all the—'

Lily interrupted her midsentence. 'Ey up, lass, usual coffee?'

'Thank you, Lily, that would be lovely.'

'Penelope, I'd like you to meet our new vet, Dr Breeze, who's joined Madhatters. Dr Breeze has just moved into Catkins.'

Penelope glared down her nose at me. 'Catkins isn't habitable.'

'It is now that Dr Breeze's family stripped it bare, erected scaffolding, plastered it and laid new floors. There was a lot of touching up too.' Lilly paused, and smirked. 'And there is a lovely pair of woodpecker door knockers. Dr Breeze treated them to a meal in the Reel Them Inn each night to thank them.' Lily threw me a crafty look. 'Oakley, Penelope Pringle owns the Pegasus Riding school and runs the local WI.'

Penelope shifted from one foot to the other and with her head hanging low held out her trembling hand.

I shook it and said, 'Lovely to meet you, Penelope. Dr Breeze is so formal, call me Oakley, though my middle names are Jasmine Bell, and my closest friends call me Jezebel. I've heard nothing but good things about the WI and I was even thinking of hosting a garden party this summer.'

Penelope gulped and muttered, 'That would be lovely, dear.'

'Maybe I could help with your conundrum? I'm not doing much today. Why don't I pick up the kits, wash them, and drop them at the rugby ground tomorrow morning at eight-thirty?'

Penelope brushed her hair away from her face as a strawberry flush spread from cheek to cheek.

'That would be lovely, thank you. I do apologize, I have a terrible habit of opening my mouth before engaging my brain.'

'That's okay, happens to me all the time. Would you like me to drive to your friend's house and pick up the rugby kits now?'

Penelope's flush transformed to relief. 'Thank you, that would be a huge weight off my shoulders. I will give you Wendy's address and let her know you'll be there shortly.'

'Do you think she'd like any groceries from the local shop? She might be running out of things if she hasn't been out for a week.'

'What a wonderful idea, I didn't even ask her if she needed anything. Oh dear, I am getting frightfully forgetful and selfish in my old age. I'll go out and call her.' Penelope wandered towards the harbour to call Wendy and Lily burst into laughter.

'Oakley, you do realise you just got one over on Penelope Pringle? I've never seen her so flustered. Personally, I'd have wanted to slap her one. That woman gets right on me pikelets. Pompous cow.'

I giggled. 'On your what?'

'Sorry luv, on me crumpets. We call um pikelets in Yorkshire. Is Jezebel really your nickname?'

'No, I made it up. It was funny seeing her squirm, but I feel a bit guilty about humiliating her.'

'She brought it on herself, love. You know what I think? – Madigan made an excellent choice hiring you. The minute you walked in the café, I knew you would fit in perfectly.'

'Thank you, Lily. Where I lived before, I just blended into the background. Here, I feel I've found my voice.'

Lily leant back, placed her hands on her rather voluptuous hips, and shrieked: 'You definitely have a voice, can't deny you that. I'm wondering what you will do next.'

'Nothing I hope.'

Penelope returned and gave me Wendy's address. Wendy had already phoned the shop and told them she would pay the bill later on her card. Laden with one of Lily's lemon drizzle cakes, I left the café with my head held high, and a long shopping list.

Penelope's grinding voice drifted in the breeze with her final words: 'Must go and tell everyone the news.'

She'd never change.

While daydreaming, I collected a trolly and wheeled it into the shop. Immersed in my own thoughts, I hadn't spotted the figure bent over in front of me until it was too late. I stared at the horizontal body that was now muttering expletives. He scrambled to his feet and twirled around, whilst I apologised profusely.

'You seem to be making a habit of apologising to me.'

'I'm so sorry, Beau, I wasn't looking where I was going, daydreaming as usual. Aren't you meant to be meeting my brothers?'

Beau brushed dust off his coat. 'They're working on the jetty so sent me out for refreshments.'

'Blimey, they've already eaten two packets of biscuits.'

'Now they're going to eat two more, plus, sausage rolls, pork pies and pasties.'

'They've always been greedy. Changing the subject, guess what? You won't believe who I bumped into in the Lily Pad?'

Beau smirked. 'It could be anybody, you have a habit of bumping into people.'

'I know, sorry. Can you guess?'

'No idea.'

'Penelope Pringle. She was saying awful things about me without realising I was behind her. You should have seen her face when she turned around and recognised me.'

'Bet she was embarrassed. Her head is so far up her jacksie—'

Giggling, I reached over and placed my hand across his mouth. 'Stop, someone might hear you.'

'Did she apologise?'

'Yes. She said she needs to engage her brain before her tongue.'

'She has a sharp tongue and is a terrible gossip.'

'I made her feel guilty, as I offered to wash the men's rugby kit.'

'Isn't it a bit late to be washing the rugby kit? We're playing at nine-thirty tomorrow morning. What happened to Wendy?'

'She's got flu. Don't worry, I'll deliver it to the rugby ground by eight-thirty in the morning.'

'If not, we'll be running around in our undies. Are you going to watch the game?'

Flirting, I raised my eyebrows. 'Yes, if the blokes are running around in their undies, but I've arranged to see my puppy at four o' clock.'

Beau smirked. 'I have an idea, why don't I pick the kit up from you in the morning, say around eight-twenty, and you can pop down later and watch the match. Perhaps afterwards we can have a spot of lunch, and then visit your puppy together?'

Crikey, that sounded like an actual date. Perhaps the gossips were wrong about Beau.

'Sounds like a brilliant plan, thanks Beau. I'd better hurry, I've got to fetch Wendy's shopping before collecting the rugby kits.'

'Try not to get too close, don't want you going down with flu or I'll have to nurse your brow and impress you with my bedside manners.'

'Already covered, I'm leaving the food on the porch.'

'Shame. See you in the morning, Jezebel, and don't ruin our rugby kits.'

'As if I'd do that. I'll have you know, I'm a dab hand at washing men's clothes. Remember, I have five brothers.'

Beau laughed and wandered towards the cashier while I commenced Wendy's shopping.

Half an hour later, I set off down the country lanes to Wendy's home; a remote cottage on the cliff tops overlooking the sea. I left the shopping bags and lemon drizzle cake on the porch and rang the doorbell. A hand waved from the upstairs window and Wendy's car's hazards flashed as she unlocked it. Two Persian cats were nestled together on a downstairs windowsill. Behind them two curious black poodles sprung up and down as if they were bouncing on a trampoline.

I was almost knocked sideways when Wendy's car door sprung open. Holding my breath, I loaded the kits into a crate and placed it into my car. That lot was going to need plenty of detergent.

After parking outside Madhatters, and manhandling the crate into the reception, Aidan rushed to greet me.

'Hi Oakley, you're early, I thought you started work on Monday?'

'Hi Aidan, I do, but I need a favour. Wendy was meant to be washing the men's rugby kits, but she has flu, and the match is tomorrow. Would you mind if I washed them in your industrial washers?'

'Yes, that's fine. Do you think you could do me a favour?'

'Yes of course, what would you like me to do?'

'Wendy's our Saturday receptionist, but as she's sick, I've been covering the phones. I need to get to an emergency with a black dog. Would you mind watching the phones for an hour until we close at one o'clock? Just pull the door shut when you've finished and pop the key through the letterbox.'

'No problem, I can answer the phone while the kits are washing.'

'Thanks, that's a great help. Your first appointment is on Monday with one of my clients called Fanny Flocker. I'm going to transfer her to you, she's a tad eccentric, but a kind soul, I'm sure you will get on brilliantly.'

'Thanks, she sounds interesting.'

'That she is. Sorry to rush but I need to get to this emergency. See you on Monday, Oakley.'

'Do you need any help with the dog?'

Aidan reached for his jacket and headed to the door. 'Thanks, I'm sure it will go down smoothly, it'll be hard putting it down, but the time is right. Thanks for watching the phones.'

'You're putting the dog down! Oh how awful. Will the owner be okay?'

'Yeah, they've been bottling it up as it's been brewing for ages. I'm sure they'll be feeling quite bitter, and there will be plenty of tears flowing as it won't be easy putting the black dog down. Don't worry about it, I'll see you on Monday.'

'Sorry, Aidan, it's awful having to say goodbye to an animal. See you Monday.'

Each washing machine groaned as it was stuffed with rugby kits on the verge of sprouting mushrooms. I reached for a large drum of detergent and decanted some into a jug. A sadness washed over me; it was awful having to put animals to sleep, you knew you were doing the right thing, but it never got any easier. Poor Aidan, I hoped the owner wasn't too upset, and the black dog passed across the doggy rainbow bridge without any further suffering.

With the machines set at thirty degrees, I left them performing their magic and ambled back to cover the reception. While glancing out of the window, I noticed a figure scurrying from one tree to the next, heading in the direction of the Reel Them Inn. That was odd, I could have sworn it was Aidan.

After twiddling my fingers for three-quarters of an hour, I returned to the utility room clutching the phone. Just as I was checking the washing the phone rang. I paused both machines and answered the call.

'Good morning, Madhatter's veterinary practice, how can I help you?'

A hoarse screechy voice replied. 'Hi is that Oakley?'

'Yes. How can I help?'

'Oakley, it's Wendy, thank you so much for washing the rugby kits; you're an angel. Could I trouble you for another favour?'

'Yes of course, what would you like?'

'Are there any tubes of furball paste on the shelf in the reception?'

'I'll have a look.' I wandered back to the reception and checked the dispensary.

'Yes, there's loads.'

'Oh, what a relief. Beau is delivering me a trailer of logs shortly. I asked him to pop by the vets and pick up a tube. Could you register it in the diary, and I'll pay for it when I'm back at work?'

'Of course. That's kind of Beau to bring you logs. How are you feeling?'

'A lot better now I've eaten a slice of lemon cake. Despite his reputation, Beau does love to help everyone.'

I peered out of the window to see Beau struggling to reverse the trailer.

'Beau's outside, I'd better go. Hope you feel better soon, Wendy. Bye.'

'Bye, Oakley, thank you.'

I disappeared into the utility room afraid that he might see me peeping through the curtains as he tried to reverse the trailer. The cycles on both machines had finished, and as I unloaded the kits into several black bags my ears were alerted to the dulcet tone of Beau's voice. It must be destiny that Beau and I kept bumping into each other. Even the mention of his name sent soft waves of affection throughout my body. I was positive he was simply teasing me when he said he wanted to get me into bed. Loaded with the bags, I kicked the utility door open.

'There you are, Oakley, did Wendy call?'

'Hi Beau, yes the furball paste is by the door.'

Beau picked up the paste. 'Do you want a hand with that lot?'

'That would be lovely, thanks. How are my brothers getting on?'

'Great, they've built the frame for the jetty and were nailing the planks when I left. They're going to fix a hoist on the end, so we are fully accessible to everyone.'

I opened the boot. 'What a wonderful idea. Let's hope they do a better job than connecting baths.'

Beau tossed the bags into the boot. 'I hope so. The kits smell lovely, at least something has gone right today. I'll see you tomorrow morning.'

I felt on top of the world.

'Told you I was a dab hand at washing clothes. See you in the morning, Beau.' I waved goodbye and headed home.

After stringing the rugby kits around Catkins and breathing in the delicate lemony perfume, it kick-started me into a serious spring clean. Following the ceiling collapsing, Catkins had been covered in a thick layer of dust and it was hard to relax until every room was sparkling.

Five hours later, there was more dust on me than in the rooms and the bath beckoned me. Following a long soak, I stepped out feeling refreshed and spotted the cow onesie hanging on the back of the door. It looked so comfy and cosy, and the one advantage of living on my own was, there was no one to witness me dressed as a cow. After throwing logs into the wood burner and Aga. I switched the telly on and curled up on the sofa wrapped in a teddy bear blanket. Within seconds, the relaxing perfume from the rugby kits had transported me into the land of dreams. Woody was still waiting for me, although this time Beau was arguing with him over who was going to hold my hand while walking Paddington. I snatched the lead, and Beau and Woody held hands and walked off together, leaving me with Paddington. Dreams could be so weird ...

Chapter Twenty-seven
Dog Flap

Light peeped through the sides of the curtains as I attempted to pull the teddy bear blanket under my chin. Though with three cats sprawled on top of me it was an impossible task. Something annoying kept sticking into my bum. I pushed Nutmeg off, reached behind me, and gasped – I'd grown a tail! What the hell? I sat bolt upright throwing Cinnamon and Jasmine flying. My boobs had dropped to my waist, and I had four rather large nipples. Where was I? Oh my gosh, I'd metamorphosed into a cow! Then I breathed a sigh of relief as realisation struck and I remembered falling asleep wearing the cow onesie. On reaching for my phone a shimmer of panic sizzled through my body. Dammit, I'd overslept! Beau was due in thirty minutes and boy would he take the mickey out of me if he saw me dressed as a cow.

I flew off the sofa, whipped the curtains back, and groaned like the tree branches twisting in the gale-force wind. With rain clouds strewn across the horizon, today didn't look too promising for standing on the sidelines of a rugby match.

The top of the Aga was stone cold, the log burner had long died, and both log baskets were empty. It really made me appreciate central heating, and I couldn't wait for the new Rayburn to be fitted.

There was just enough time to fill the wood basket before I showered and changed. I slipped my hooves into my wellies, tucked my tail in my front zip, and clutching the wood basket attempted to exit the porch door. An almighty gust of wind nearly lifted me off my feet like Mary Poppins as I struggled to keep hold of the basket. The door slammed behind me as I dashed across the garden to the barn. I darted inside and tossed a pile of logs into the basket before lugging it back to the porch.

Holding the log basket against me I tried to push the front door open with my foot, but it didn't budge. What an idiot I was, I'd forgotten to retract the catch and lock it. I dashed around the side of Catkins to the utility door, but alas, it was locked too. I really was a numpty. Why hadn't I at least changed out of the onesie before fetching logs? Any minute now, Beau was going to see a Friesian cow stampeding around my garden and the Scorpions resigned to playing rugby in their undies.

With my heart pounding, I raced around the house trying to spot an open window, but they were all shut. There was only one remaining option staring me in the face. I knelt down and peered through the dog flap. Surely it was wide enough for me to squeeze through, it appeared big enough for Wolf. I pushed the flap, but of course it was locked from the inside. I rushed back to the front door, returned with a log, and took drastic action.

Soon two pieces of the dog flap were lying on the inside of the utility room. Phew with the panic over, there was just enough time to change before Beau arrived. I knelt down and began crawling through the frame. Though no matter which way I twisted my hips, and wriggled, I was well and truly wedged. I tried crawling backwards, but this cow wasn't moving in a hurry. The udder had caught on something, which was impossible to unhook whilst kneeling on all fours.

Nutmeg wandered into the utility room and cocked her head back and forth. The expression on her face was a picture, I was positive she was thinking, why are humans so weird? Maybe if I removed the onesie I could squeeze through naked, though thinking about it, and actually instigating it, was easier said than done. Balancing on one hand, I pulled the zipper halfway, but it jammed in the end of the tail that was still tucked into the top. I tugged again, but it wouldn't budge, and at the worse moment possible the doorbell chimed, and chimed, and chimed. It seemed Beau wasn't a quitter. I'd never anticipated such a huge bout of humiliation zooming my way than I did at that precise moment.

A few seconds later, the base of my tail felt as if it was being torn off by a pack of wolves. Moments earlier, the tail had been caught in my zipper, now the zipper was in two and my boobs were exposed, could my day get any worse? It seemed it could as footsteps approached from around the corner, and the sound emanating from Beau must have woken every resident in Whispering Pines.

'Good boy, Wolf, what have we got here? Oakley, why are you crawling through the dog flap dressed as a cow?'

'Sorry, didn't I tell you about my dressing-up fetish in my spare time? What do you think I was doing? The front door slammed while I was collecting logs. I was trying to get back into the house, but the onesie has caught on something. I've tried to unzip it, but the zipper jammed in the tail. Wolf has pulled the tail out, and now I'm exposing my top half!'

'You do get yourself into pickles. I'll try and unhook the onesie.'

'Just don't look through the flap, my boobs are exposed.'

'I can't look, your bum is in the way; I'll feel my way down.' He placed his hand on my bum before twiddling the tail. After replacing his hand back on my bum, he lingered a little too long.

'Yep, that's my bum all right, I think you've fathomed that out, now move on.'

'Now, Doctor Breeze, this won't hurt a bit. I'm going to have to put my hand between your legs to feel what's going on.'

'You won't tell anyone about this will you? It's so humiliating.'

'Of course I'm not going to tell anyone. Now shush, I'm concentrating.'

I felt his hand and arm between my legs.

'What are you doing now?'

'I think you've caught a couple of teats on bent screws, and I don't seem to be able to release them. I'll have to cut your teats off. Have you got a pair of scissors?'

'In the kitchen drawer ... Oh, you can't get into the house.'

'Don't worry, I'll be back in a few minutes.'

There was a loud bang as the front door slammed shut, and standing inside the utility room was Beau displaying a grin that split his face as he stared at my boobs.

'Stop ogling me. Please can you throw me a towel from the tumble drier. How'd you get into the house?'

Beau threw me a towel. 'I used the spare key. Didn't you look under the mat?'

'No, who would be silly enough to leave a key under the front doormat?'

'Everyone around here.'

'That's not very security conscious. I'm getting cold, please can you hurry up and snip off my teats.'

'Yes, I know, I can see you're Friesian!'

I glanced down to see the towel lying on the floor, I reached for it and stuffed it back inside the onesie.

'Ha, ha, ha, very funny. Now turn around. Is it easier to go down on me from the front or do it from behind?'

Beau chuckled. 'Do what?'

I could feel my blood boiling. 'Cut the teats off.'

Beau sneered. 'I'd prefer to try it from behind, it's easier to control what I'm doing.'

'You're so cheeky, just get on with it.'

'Oakley?'

'What now?'

'A little observation. If you have a dog flap, why do you need two litter trays?'

'I locked the dog flap as the cats have to stay in for a couple of weeks.'

'Just one more thing.'

'Flippin' heck, Beau, now what?'

'Why are both your cat litter trays full of birdseed?'

'What do you mean?'

'Look.' Beau pushed one of the litter trays towards me and sure enough, it was full of birdseed.

'It was dark when I filled the trays last night.'

'I hope you haven't filled the bird feeders with cat litter.'

'I know, I'm a bird brain, but I'm not that stupid.'

'No comment. I'll pop round to your rear end, keep your legs apart.'

Once again, Beau felt his way down my bum and through my legs. I felt him tugging on my onesie as he tried to cut off one of the teats. He seemed to be taking an age.

'Why are you taking so long? Can't you do it without fondling me?'

'I have a little problem.'

'Oh my god, now what?'

'The cuff of my overalls has caught on a nail, see if you can reach back and unhitch it.'

'Are you joshing with me?'

'No.'

'I can't reach it. Please throw the scissors through the flap, I'll try and cut my own teats off.'

'Watch what you're cutting, my fingers are down there.'

'I know, stop twiddling them around in my crutch or I will cut them off too.'

'Sorry, I've got cramp.'

'Shush, listen I can hear a vehicle.'

'It's probably the postman. Wolf, fetch Frank.'

A few minutes later a cheery voice sniggered, 'Well, well, well, in my line of work, you often see couples making out, but I've never seen a couple taking doggy style so literally. And fancy trying it in a dog flap; I don't know, you young 'uns, and dressing up as a cow and a farmer; I've seen it all now.'

I could feel Beau's body shaking with laughter.

'Frank, mate, see if you can unhook my cuff, it's caught somewhere around Oakley's udder.'

'Frank, I can assure you we were not having sex, doggy style or any other style. I locked myself out and tried to get in through the dog flap. Beau was helping me, but the cuff on his overalls has caught on something between my legs.'

'If you say so, love, it's none of my business what you get up to. Why didn't you use the spare key under the doormat? I'm not sure I can help – got a bad back. Looks like a job for the fire brigade. Back in a jiffy.'

I let out a huge sigh, although bending in this position for such a long time, and with Beau at my rear end, it was fortunate I didn't let anything else out.

Beau commented, 'What's that smell? Oakley, you haven't—'

Before he had time to finish his sentence I interrupted: 'No! One of the cats is sitting on the litter tray, or rather the birdseed tray. Count your blessings you're not stuck down this end.'

Footsteps approached from behind us.

'What have we got here? *Moove* over Frank and let me take *stock* of the situation. Beau, mate, we're kicking off in twenty minutes, this is not the time to be getting jiggy-jiggy with a young heifer, although from this angle she looks like a mighty fine specimen, if you don't mind me saying; fine rump on her. What's happened to our kit? The lads are going to be running around in their undies.'

Beau chuckled. 'Oakley, I'd like to introduce you to my cousin Ashley, Mackenzie's older brother.'

'Hi Ashley, nice to meet you, your rugby kits are in the house. I can assure you, Beau has not been getting jiggy-jiggy. Please can you stop all the jokes and try and unhitch us.'

'Thanks. Sorry, I'll try not to make any more jokes, but I do talk *udder* nonsense, and things tend to go in one ear and out the *udder*.'

Beau groaned. 'No mate, you just talk a load of *bull*.'

Ashley unhooked Beau's cuff and snipped two teats off the onesie.

After a bit of manoeuvring, the dog flap frame released me, and I crawled into the utility room. After closing the door to stop the cats escaping, I raced upstairs to change.

When I returned the house was eerily quiet, other than Cinnamon yowling in desperation to use the litter tray. I opened the door, blocked the dog flap, and peered at the litter tray. I couldn't believe I'd mistaken the birdseed for cat litter. I really was an airhead. I wandered into the kitchen and spotted a note on the table.

Thanks for washing the kits, kick off is in fifteen minutes, see you shortly. Beau.

After all my efforts and he hadn't even written a kiss on the note.

Chapter Twenty-eight
Bubbles

L eaving the Aga and wood burners roaring, I dashed upstairs to shower as the cats munched their breakfast. I chuckled to myself as I read the name on the shower gel – Cowshed, Awake and Bracing – how apt. As the hot water sprinkled against my body, citrus fruit bubbles tickled my nostrils ensuring I was wide awake, although the thought of standing in a bracing wind on the sidelines of the rugby match gave me goosebumps. Furthermore, the notion of Beau and Ashley blabbering about my embarrassing mishap could see me running for the hills. I stepped out of the shower and reached for my towel; my phone pinged a text message.

Beau: Where are you? Hurry up you have some explaining to do.

Me: OMG! Now what?

Beau: This you will have to see for yourself.

Me: Okay, be there shortly.

With so many layers plastered to my body, there was more chance of me dying from heat stroke than embarrassment. And with the amount of rain hammering down, my dry suit would have been more appropriate than my jeans and jacket. A round of applause boomed as I stepped out of my car. When I gained the courage and peered up, the clapping wasn't directed towards me. In fact, no one had even noticed my arrival. I'd never witnessed so much hoo-ha at a rugby match. Thank goodness, for once, no one was laughing at me. As I weaved between the hordes of spectators to reach the front the laughing was amplified, and sounded like a pack of spotted hyenas. I squeezed between two spectators to see what the hoo-ha was. A shiver raced through my body and a gasp escaped from my mouth. The rugby pitch had been transformed into a lake of fluorescent shimmering bubbles. A forward from the Stingrays passed the ball underarm to another Stingray, but it slipped through his fingers and was swallowed by the bubbles. There was an almighty splash as the players dived under the bubbles searching for the ball. A Scorpion kicked the ball into the air and a rainbow of bubbles twinkled and danced. Children clapped their hands as they ran around the pitch extinguishing the bubbles. A Stingray slid past them on his front, and when he stood up, bubbles exploded from his backside. After spotting me, Beau slid towards me. Phew, at least he was grinning.

'Oakley, what the heck have you done to our rugby kit?'

I was at a loss for words, as thoughts scrambled in my brain and my chest tingled.

'I've no idea what's happened. I loaded the rugby kits into the washing machine, decanted the detergent, added it to the washing machine, and set it at thirty degrees. The phone rang so I paused the machine and ...' I gazed at Beau and my words dried up midsentence. I clamped my hand across my mouth, took a deep breath, and regained my composure. 'Oh Beau, I'm so sorry, I unloaded it before it had rinsed. That explains why it smelt so lovely and was quite damp, although there do seem to be an awful lot of bubbles from laundry detergent.'

Beau's eyes squinted with mischief as he choked back laughter.

'I've just spoken to my mum, she said there wasn't any detergent left; the container on the shelf was Fairy Liquid.'

A sudden compulsion to flee to the hills washed over me as I tugged my beanie over my face trying to hide the pink flush I could feel spreading from head to toe.

'Really? Oh my gosh, what a muppet I am.'

'Don't worry, it's the funniest game we've played against the Scorpions. They're the best team in the Southwest, and we had no chance in beating them. But who cares now, everyone is having so much fun.' Beau paused and pointed to the right of me. 'Ashley's wife, Rylee, is over there, why don't you go and introduce yourself and I'll see you in the pub later.'

'Okay, thanks, see you later.'

'Good, lunch is on you.'

'That's the least I can do.'

I ducked my head and walked away like a dog with its tail between its legs. I caught sight of Rylee, a petite woman with the most immaculate blonde bob I'd ever seen. When Penelope Pringle reared her nosey head, I was forced to duck into the crowd until the coast was clear and I sneaked towards Rylee.

'Hi, are you Rylee?'

'Yes, I assume you're Oakley? Ashley told me about the little incident you had earlier.'

'He did? Oh, how embarrassing. What with that and washing the kit in washing-up liquid, everyone will think I'm a complete scatterbrain.'

'Don't worry, it's better than being inconspicuous, Whispering Pines needs livening up. Hardly anyone watches the rugby games anymore, but thanks to you there's a huge crowd. This is hilarious, Oakley, it's the best match I've ever seen.'

'They do look as if they're enjoying themselves.'

'They are. So, how's it going at Catkins? Have all the renovations been completed? That house must take hours to clean, especially the dusting.'

Before I had chance to answer a girl interrupted us. Her eyes were the colour of the Caribbean, and blonde ringlets hung down to her waist.

'Hi Oakley, I'm Flo, Beau's sister. This match is hysterical. How are you getting on with my brother?'

I sniggered. 'So many questions; lovely to meet you, Flo. I'm getting on fine with Beau. Now, going back to Rylee's question, most of the renovations have been completed and as for the dusting, I've been at it for hours.' I stopped mid-conversation noticing prying ears a few feet behind us. 'I think nosey Penelope Pringle is earwigging our conversation, I'll speak a little louder. As I was saying, I've been at it for hours. Dusting has given me immense pleasure, hardly a marriage made in heaven, but I've never felt so fulfilled and satisfied.'

Rylee amplified her voice. 'I know how you feel, dusting gives me immense pleasure too. After a good going over in each room, it leaves me with an overwhelming orgasmic tingling.'

Flo's voice magnified twofold. 'I've not been home in ages; I think dusting's going to get real action in my bedroom.'

Encouraged by the girls, my voice intensified. 'By the time I'd finished with dusting, I felt like a right filthy scrubber. Who would have thought dusting would have caused me to get so hot and sweaty? Mr Muscle worked wonders in the bathroom, and I felt fully rejuvenated after my bath, though no doubt by tomorrow I will have to start giving dusting a good going over again.'

'Well I never, Rylee and Florence, shame on the pair of you. And as for you, Dr Breeze, fancy taking advantage of someone so young.' A gloating Penelope Pringle sighed heavily with her arms folded across her chest, and as she glared down her nose, she exhibited a fine impression of an English bulldog. She pointed a finger at Flo. 'Mark my words, I will be speaking to your family later.'

We glanced at each other and burst into spontaneous laughter, as Penelope Pringle stormed off in a huff and merged into the crowd.

Flo sniggered. 'What was that about? Why did she point a finger at me?'

My eyes scanned Penelope Pringle as she wound through the crowd. 'I have absolutely no idea. What about you Rylee?'

'I've no idea either, but something got her goat.'

Flo snorted. 'Nah, more like she's just a miserable, interfering old goat.'

Rylee put her arm around her cousin. 'Ignore her, shall we go to the pub for lunch after the game has finished?'

'That'll be great, are you joining us, Oakley?'

'I'm already meeting Beau in the pub. We can't stay long though, as we're visiting my new puppy.'

'You have a puppy? What breed?'

'A sheepadoodle. His mother is a poodle who had the hots for the local farmer's Old English Sheepdog. The puppy is called Paddington, and he'll be ready in four weeks' time. Would you both like to join us?'

'Would have loved to, but probably best not to disturb you love birds.'

I sniggered. 'Love birds. Who are you kidding? Beau thinks I'm a featherbrain. Flo, watch out.'

With seconds to spare, I pushed Flo out of the way while Rylee and I were tossed onto the ground. The Scorpion wingman slid towards us as the ball torpedoed from under his arm and knocked Flo to the ground too. Rylee and I laid giggling on the ground, whilst Flo attempted to stand up. The Scorpion was covered head to toe in bubbles, and without turning, muttered an apology, before dashing back to the game.

Flo squeezed my arm. 'Oh my gosh, he's easy on the eye. Number one, do you know what his name is?'

Rylee scrambled to her feet and held out her hand to me. 'That's Test, the Scorpion's wingman.'

'I'm not sure about one, I'd give him ten out of ten, and he could test me out any day.' Flo paused, grabbed my arm, and ducked behind me. 'Oakley, he's walking this way. Do you think he heard me?'

My thoughts were doing somersaults. Test? No, it couldn't be, surely not. The Scorpion caught my eye and jogged towards us.

'Well, if it's not Tinker Bell, I wasn't expecting to see you here.'

'Hi Trent, the feelings mutual.'

'Are the fairy bubbles your handiwork?'

'Afraid so.'

'I don't know, you and fairies.'

Flo tugged my arm and whispered, 'Oakley, introduce me.' I reached back to Flo and pushed her forward.

'Trent, this is Flo, her dad is the referee and my new boss.'

Trent beamed the biggest smile ever. 'I'd better behave myself then, don't want to get into trouble with my future father-in-law.' He winked at Flo and returned to the game.

'He's gorgeous and practically proposed. How do you know him? Why did he call you Tinker Bell?'

'I dressed up as a fairy on our club paddle. His name is Trent, I've known him since I was four. Be careful though, he thinks he's a bit of a ladies' man, and he's a complete show-off.'

'Is he seeing anyone?'

'I'm not sure.'

'Do you think he'll be joining us at the pub?'

'From the look he gave you, I'd say yes.'

As Trent tackled Beau the ball slid to the ground. He pushed Beau out of the way, dived on top of the ball and sprang to his feet and attempted to run.

Madigan shouted: 'Test-tickles, at last someone manages to hold onto his ball.'

The crowd roared with laughter.

'Oh my god, Oakley, did my dad just shout out testicles? He's so embarrassing.'

I couldn't stop giggling. 'I think he was meant to say Test tackles, but yes, it sounded like testicles. I think your dad has been castrating too many animals.'

Beau tackled Trent as he ran towards the line, Trent reached behind him and pushed Beau away.

'Test, excellent hand job,' shouted Flo.

I bent over in hysterics. 'It's called handing off, not hand job.'

'Is it? I always thought it was called a hand job.'

'I think you'll find that's something else!'

Soon the ball was gathering pace as it skidded through the bubbles. Trent slid along the ground like a snowboarder, grabbed Beau's curls, and yanked him to the ground.

Madigan blew the whistle and shouted, 'Test, your tackle is far too high, this is a warning, drop your tackle.'

Once again, the crowd roared with laughter.

'Oakley, I wouldn't mind tackling Trent. Does he like outdoor pursuits?'

'He's a PE teacher and loves outdoor pursuits. Be careful though, he's a bit of a rebel and never listens to anyone, and always has to do everything his own way.'

'Ooh, he sounds challenging, I love rebels, I've never done as I'm told.'

Why did that not surprise me? Flo was like an older version of Poppy and Blossom.

Trent threw Flo another smile, which honestly appeared genuine. The final whistle blew, and the game was declared a draw. Trent wandered to the far end of the field, with Beau and Ashley in hot pursuit.

Flo's eyes followed Trent. 'Who are the three girls they're talking to? Do you think one of them is Trent's girlfriend?'

I followed Flo's gaze towards the girls lapping up the attention. Were my eyes deceiving me? One of the girls looked like Trent's ex-fiancé, Scarlett, and her sidekick, Cordelia. Though looking through the rainbow of bubbles, they could have been anyone.

I turned to Flo. 'I've no idea who they are.'

Flo smiled and her eyes lit up. 'I'm soaked through. I'm going to nip home and find something nice to wear before going to the pub. Won't be long.'

I grinned remembering what it was like to be smitten with someone at first glance.

'We'll save you a seat next to Trent.'

Flo waved and ran towards the car park while both rugby teams disappeared into the club house to change.

'Oakley, are you ready to go to the pub?' Rylee enquired.

'Yes, but I need to tell Beau where I am.'

Rylee's phone beeped.

'It's a text from my hubby, everyone has decided to eat at Neptune's Nook, as Trent said he's buying the first round.'

'That's thirty minutes in the other direction. I can't go or I'll be late seeing my puppy. What about Beau?'

'I'll text Ashley and find out.'

Rylee's phone beeped.

'Beau said sorry, but he can't miss Trent buying a round of drinks. You can buy him a meal another night, and he'll see the puppy next time. I'd better call Flo and let her know the rugby teams are going to Neptune's Nook. I'll join you in the Reel Them Inn, but first I have to find my hubby as he wants to borrow my car. Why don't you go ahead and find us a table?'

'Oh, okay,' I said, trying not to sound too disappointed Beau wasn't joining us. Guess I wasn't going on a date after all. I left Rylee chatting on the phone to Flo while I wandered across to the pub. As I walked towards the bar someone called out my name.

'Oakley, Oakley, over 'ere, wanna join us?'

I completed a 180-degree turn and spotted Lily waving from the conservatory.

I waved back and wandered over. 'That would be lovely, thanks. I'm waiting for Rylee, then we'll join you. Can I buy anyone a drink?'

'I'm alright love, Dustin would love another Coke, and I'm sure Aidan could manage to down a bottle of Black Dog.'

I put my hands on my hips and puckered my lips. 'Bottle of Black Dog? Aidan, you scoundrel, I thought you were putting a black dog down!'

'I rarely put a Black Dog down.'

Lilly glared at Aidan. 'You haven't tried that old trick on Oakley, have you? Poor gal, ain't even started work yet.'

'Woman, I was gasping for a pint. Oakley was only watching the washing, although after today's performance she didn't watch it very well.'

'Don't think you can change the subject n' wriggle out of it! Fancy trying to pull the wool over Oakley's eyes! I think Oakley is on to you now, aren't you love?'

'I'll be watching him like a hawk.'

After returning to the bar, Rylee arrived, and we ordered our food and drinks. We headed to Lily's table, and I squeezed in one side of Dustin, and Rylee squeezed in the other. Dustin lowered his head allowing his hair to dangle over his shoulders, obscuring his face. Lily was her normal chirpy self, laughing about my misadventures, when a dark shadow was cast over the table. When we looked up, the rain had stopped, and the sun was glaring through the window lighting up the silhouette of Penelope Pringle.

'Lily, I wasn't going to say anything, but the goings on with your son have got to stop. He's got guilt written all over his face.'

Dustin dropped his fork and spoon. 'What goings on? I ain't guilty of nowt.'

Penelope towered over him. 'That's not what I heard earlier, son.'

Lily interrupted. 'Penelope, Dustin isn't your son, we're trying to have a quiet Sunday lunch. What you want to say can wait til tomorrow; and maybe somewhere less public.'

There was an eerie stillness as everyone held their breath anticipating Penelope's next move proclaiming Dustin's charges. It was like sitting in a courthouse waiting for the judge to pass sentence and shout 'guilty.'

Penelope sucked her lips in, took a deep breath, and leant over our table blurting: 'It can't wait. Dustin is having an affair with his stepbrother's wife, his cousin Florence, and Dr Breeze. It's an absolute disgrace.'

Lily and Aidan dropped their cutlery, gazed around the pub, and accompanied by all the customers, dissolved into laughter. Poor Dustin looked like he wanted to hide under the table.

Lily wiped the tears of laughter away. 'Penelope, seriously you think our pure innocent lad is seeing three women?'

Aidan had the biggest grin I'd ever seen. He patted Dustin on the back.

'All I can say is, good on you son; didn't know you had it in you.'

Penelope Pringle snorted and stamped her foot. 'I'm only telling you what I heard.'

Dustin sunk into the chair. 'Mam, I've not done nowt.'

'I know son, we'll sort this. Penelope, from whom did you hear this ridiculous notion?'

Penelope gazed at me over the rim of her glasses.

'Dr Breeze was talking at the rugby match. She said how Dustin had satisfied her, given her pleasure, and made her feel dirty, and she felt rejuvenated in the bath. She even called him Mr Muscle. Rylee said he made her feel orgasmic, and Flo said he was going to get real action in her bedroom. It's pure filth.'

Every head in the pub turned in my direction as Rylee and I dissolved into fits of giggles.

I pushed my chair back, stood up and faced the busy body.

'I'll admit it was pure filth, but Catkins is now spick and span, thanks to cleaning and dusting. We were talking about dusting, not Dustin.'

Penelope Pringle glared at me, huffed, about-turned and made a sharp exit.

Lily's face was a picture as her smile met her eyes. 'Oakley, you do bring out the best in Penelope Pringle.'

I turned to Dustin. 'Sorry about that, Penelope Pringle is an interfering busybody.'

Dustin's grin had the appearance of an extendable coat-hanger. 'I feel honoured that she would think someone like me could pleasure three beautiful women.'

'Don't undermine yourself, Dustin. If your glasses didn't keep slipping down your nose, and you stopped hiding behind those locks, girls would be flocking to you like ewes to tup's nuts. No, I mean pellets, that didn't sound right.'

Dustin laughed and blushed, as he twisted his fork in his last mouthful of spaghetti.

'The mop on my head might come in handy dusting your house.'

The pub erupted into laughter and Dustin turned crimson.

'Not only cute, but humorous. Rylee and I are going to see my new puppy, would you like to escort us, Dustin? We could walk out arm in arm; see what the chinwaggers have to say about that.'

Aidan wiped his mouth with the serviette. 'Go on, son, prove you're a man and not a mouse.'

Lily cupped her hands over Dustin's ears. 'You don't have to love. We love you just as you are.'

Dustin removed her hand. 'Give over, Mam!' He rose from his chair and shoved his hands into his pockets. 'It would be my honour to escort you, ladies. Maybe you can help me find a puppy too.'

Lily roared with laughter. 'Who's this young man? Where's my little boy?'

'Grown up, Mam. Ready, ladies?'

Rylee and I sniggered, linked arms with Dustin and strolled out of the pub with cheers of: 'Good on you, son.'

We strolled to my car. 'Sorry about that, Dustin, you don't have to join us.'

'I'd love to. I've always wanted to work with animals. It's hard living up to the reputation of my dad, Uncle Madigan, and Mackenzie. You see, I don't wanna be a vet; I'd rather be a nurse.'

'Veterinary nurses are just as important as vets. Neither could work without the other. Why not go to college? I can find out details of the courses if you like.'

Dustin's eyes lit up and his lips uncurled into a smile. 'Really? Sweet. I finish school in three months, cheers.'

'That's okay, you're welcome, now let's go and meet Paddington.'

We piled into my car and drove the short distance to Paw-Some Rescue Centre. We were guided into the puppy introduction room, and when the door opened, eight sheepadoodle puppies scampered in. One puppy kept climbing onto my knee.

An assistant entered the room. 'Everything all right? Handful, aren't they?'

'They're gorgeous. Do you know which puppy is mine?'

'Let me look at their markings.'

'Seems you have been chosen by your puppy.'

'This is Paddington? He's adorable.'

'He thinks the same about you.'

Paddington crawled up and licked my nose.

'Have all the puppies found homes?'

'No, there are still two available. Why? Do you want more than one?'

'No, I think one is enough, but I know two people who might each like one.' I gazed towards Rylee and Dustin.

'How lovely, let's take your information to see if you are ready for a puppy in your life.'

Dustin jumped in, 'My dad's Aidan Summers, he's a partner at Madhatters veterinary practice. I'm going to train to be a veterinary nurse. This is my sister-in-law Rylee; she is already a veterinary nurse at Madhatters. Oakley joins the practice tomorrow. Our dogs can play together at the practice.'

I laughed at Dustin's enthusiasm.

'Dustin, hadn't you better call your parents first and check they don't mind?'

'Okay, I'll go outside and call them, but they did promise me a puppy when I turned sixteen, and that was two months ago.'

Five minutes later, Rylee and Dustin returned, grinning.

'What did Ashley say?'

'He said I've only known you a few hours and you're a terrible influence on me.'

The assistant giggled. 'So, I guess we have no puppies left now. We had better go and complete the paperwork.'

Dustin hugged his puppy. 'Would it be all right for me to volunteer? It would be great work experience for me.'

'I'll speak to the boss, but I can't see it being a problem.'

'Sweet, cheers.'

After completing the paperwork, we said goodbye to the puppies. Dustin hesitated at my car. 'Oakley, would you mind if I joined you next time you visit the puppies?'

'Of course not, maybe we'll invite your mum as well.'

Dustin sighed and his hair fell across his face. 'Do we have to?'

'Why?'

Dustin brushed his hair over his shoulders as he slid into the car. 'People won't talk if my mum is with me, but if they see me getting into your car, I'll be the talk of the village.'

I giggled. 'Of course we don't have to invite your mum.'

Dustin sat back and clicked his seatbelt. 'Sick. I can't wait to see my puppy again.'

After dropping Dustin and Rylee home, I drove back to Catkins to make a batch of rock cakes for my initiation day. My hands were covered in dough when my phone beeped; it was a text from Beau.

Beau: Think you have a new admirer. Dustin was floating on cloud nine. Couldn't get a lot out of him, other than he had been out with you and was in love.

Me: Ah. How lovely, thought he seemed happy when I dropped him home. Glad his mum and dad approved.

Beau: They did? But he's only sixteen!

Me: I think he's old enough to accept the responsibility, it's time to break the apron strings with his mum.

Beau: I'm surprised at you, Oakley; I think he's far too young.

Me: Too young? Of course not. Changing the subject, I still owe you a meal or two, when are you free?

Beau: Don't worry about it, I'm sure you're going to be far too busy now. See you around.

Me: Oh! Okay, see you.

That was odd, why was Beau turning me down? Despite having five brothers sometimes I really couldn't understand men. But for now, there was no time to dwell on the workings of Beau's mind. I needed to bake the rock cakes and get ready for my initiation day tomorrow. Mackenzie told me I had to be two steps ahead of Madigan and Aidan, and after the black dog incident, I could see my work was cut out with that pair of scoundrels.

Chapter Twenty-nine
Fanny Flocker

I popped by the Lily Pad before my first day at work and left laden with a box containing a variety of doughnuts. I pushed the front door open of Madhatters, where I was about to begin a whole new chapter of my life.

Madge jumped up and grabbed the box of doughnuts. 'Morning, Oakley, welcome to your first day at Madhatters. Looks like we're gonna need coffee to go with these.'

'Morning, Madge. I'll put the kettle on.'

I followed Madge into the kitchen, handed her my tin of rock cakes, and whispered, 'Everything still okay for three o'clock this afternoon?'

The glint in Madge's eyes was enough to spark a match. 'Yes, mum's the word. The appointments between three and four o' clock have been rearranged. I'll hide the rock cakes in the back, don't forget to bring back a few of Fanny's rock cakes.'

'I won't forget, although I hope Fanny's free this afternoon.'

'Fanny won't turn down a cup of tea with her secret crush, Aidan. She makes us laugh; Aidan is a married man, fortunately, Lily thinks it's hilarious.'

Aidan sneaked up behind us. 'What are you ladies gassing about? Thought I heard my name mentioned.'

'Morning, Aide, I was telling Oakley about the little crush Fanny Flocker has on you.' Madge pointed to the box of doughnuts. 'Look what Oakley has picked up from your naughty wife.'

Aidan opened the box and helped himself to a doughnut. 'Oh, is that all? Everyone has a crush on me.' He paused, took a bite, and licked his lips. 'Delicious, you know how much I love nibbling my wife's doughnuts.'

'Don't be cheeky, or I'll tell Lily.'

Aidan sniggered. 'I think Lily already knows what I think about her shock absorbers.'

Madge picked up the broom and chased him out of the kitchen. 'Scram, before I shove this somewhere the sun doesn't shine.'

Now I could now see why they called it Madhatters!

Madge disappeared back to the kitchen and returned with a tray of coffees and tin of biscuits.

Madigan wandered in from his examination room. 'Morning, Oakley, great to have you on board. I'll let you get settled, Madge will show you our computer system, and don't forget you have an appointment with Fanny Flocker at ten-thirty.'

'I can't wait to meet her. Do I need to wear full overalls?'

Aidan perched on the corner of Madge's desk. 'What to see Fanny Flocker? No, of course not. Remember, we always oblige Fanny when she offers us a cup of tea, and her rock cakes are to die for.'

Madigan sniggered. 'You enjoy obliging Fanny don't you, Aide?'

'You know me, Mad, I'm an obliging fella. But it's high time I stopped being so selfish and let someone else enjoy her amazing culinary skills.'

Madigan chuckled. 'We all know Fanny needs to see an eye specialist because she fancies you. Is there anything else we need to tell Oakley before she meets Fanny?'

Smirking, Aidan dunked his biscuit in his coffee. 'She has excellent sight when it comes to me. Fanny is a bit, um, how do I put it, antiquated, and a little eccentric when it comes to her clothing attire. She's also a bit of a royalist, but don't worry, she's going to really like you, Oakley.'

Madigan placed his hand on my shoulders. 'What is there not to like about the newest member of our team? My son is quite taken with her. I've heard plenty of men have been frequenting the pub with her. Mackenzie can't wait to meet her and she's a dab hand at washing clothes.'

I pulled away. 'Stop you're going to make me blush.'

Madge intervened. 'Come on, love, let's leave these hooligans to their schoolboy humour and I'll show you the computer system before you head out to meet Fanny.'

A couple of hours later, dressed in my protective critter-biting clothes, I parked in a lay-by beside a sign displaying:

Welcome to Woolly Jumpers.
Proprietor and shepherdess: Francis Flocker.

The fields bordering the track were adorned with alpacas of every colour, and the cutest Valais Blacknose sheep I had ever seen. They mirrored big fluffy versions of Cinnamon and Jasmine.

I ambled towards the drive and checked my pockets to find two of my rock cakes wrapped in kitchen towel. Several whining and yapping dogs greeted me at the gate until a voice screamed: 'Quiet!' And an eerie silence fell over the farm. A tall willowy lady with long grey lank hair rushed towards me wiping her hands on a pinny. Following her were several kittens chasing a twig caught in her billowing flouncy skirt. The pattern on her skirt was a pasty green with brown squares, enclosed by lime-green circles. It was similar to the wallpaper I'd removed from my bathroom and reminded me of peering through my mum's old kaleidoscope. Fanny Flocker drew closer, and I was aware of an overwhelming stench. It was a cross between the men's festering rugby kits and mothballs. When she greeted me in an elegant soft voice, her persona didn't quite fit her attire. I noticed her fern-green eyes light up as she held her hand out.

'Hello, you must be Oakley, the new vet. How lovely to meet you, I'm Francis Flocker, but you can call me Fanny. Come into the kitchen out of the cold. I've put a brew on, then I'll show you the farm.'

'That would be lovely, thank you.'

The stench from the kitchen nearly knocked me sideways, and clutter was piled as high as the ceiling. The pong was emanating from a bubbling cauldron, which was sitting on an Aga bordered by Union Jack flags. I peeked into the cauldron to see a yellow slime with green streaks. It wouldn't have surprised me to see Fanny chanting, 'Double, double toil and trouble; fire burn and cauldron bubble,' while she dropped in a newt's eye and frog's toes.

Fanny sniffed the gunk. 'Sorry about the smell, there were ten different cheeses in the fridge. I've melted them together, and once they've cooled, I'll roll them into a ball. When I cut a slice, it will taste of ten different kinds of cheese.'

I peered into the pan of simmering gunk again; the smell was enough to make you wretch.

'What are the green streaks?'

'Mould, dear. Care for a rock cake with your brew?'

Despite my stomach churning I mustered up the enthusiasm to mutter, 'Yes please, I've heard nothing but praise for your rock cakes. Would you like me to slice and butter them while you make the tea?'

'Thank you, dear, the plates are ...' Fanny paused, and spun around. 'Erm ... where did I put the plates? I spent hours tidying this place and now I can't find anything.' Fanny giggled. 'Before I tidied things away, I could find everything.'

Was she for real? What the heck did the kitchen look like before she tidied it?

'Don't worry, I have a couple of plates in my bag.'

'You're very organised. As you can see, I'm getting there. You should have seen what it looked like before I tidied up.'

'Dread to think in this black hole,' I muttered a little louder than I'd intended.

'Sorry dear, did you say something? I've lost one of my hearing aids and can't hear anything in the right ear.'

I pointed to the pink bowl by the bread bin. 'Spread in the pink bowl?'

'Yes, dear, and the rock cakes are in the tin on top of that pile of newspapers. I'll take the tea through to the parlour.'

Standing on an old milking stool, I reached up for the tin of rock cakes that was sitting precariously on top of the mound of newspapers. As one of the stool's legs wobbled, the tin leaped out of my hands, clattered onto the floor, and fired rock cakes like marbles falling through the sticks of Kerplunk. Drat, now I'd have to get down on my hands and knees and liberate the escapees. With the last of the rock cakes returned to the tin, I wondered if I'd lost my marbles! The rock cakes were true to their name and not a single one had been damaged, though how the heck was I going to cut one for Fanny without losing my fingers? I delved into my pocket for one of my buttered rock cakes and placed it on my plate. I tried to slice one of Fanny's rock cakes, however the knife slipped and narrowly missed chopping off my fingers. Now what? My plan was backfiring. I'd have to give Fanny my other rock cake and hope she didn't offer me another one of hers.

Ambling through the hallway was like playing snakes and ladders. Newspapers were piled in columns like Stonehenge. One minute I was sliding forwards, and the next backwards while avoiding knocking the columns to the floor. On reaching the parlour, Fanny passed me a chipped bone china cup embossed with pictures of the royal corgis. I passed Fanny a rock cake and glanced inside my cup at the hot milk disguised as tea.

'Thank you, dear, they look nice if I do say so myself.' Fanny watched me as I bit into my rock cake. She nibbled hers, jolted back, and devoured it within seconds.

Contemplating my next move, I eyed up spider plants that were about to fall victim to a dunking of warm milk.

I licked my lips. 'Fanny, the rock cake was delicious. Thank you.'

In an instant, she was up on her feet and striding towards the door. 'I'll fetch you another one, dear.'

With no time like the present, I leapt up and poured the tea into a flowerpot. Fanny returned a few minutes later with another rock cake cut in two – how had she managed that? And how the heck was I going to eat it? My plan was well and truly backfiring now.

'You've finished your tea, dear; I'll fetch you another cup, you can't eat a rock cake without a nice cup of tea.'

When Fanny exited the room, I spotted the top window ajar; it was now or never. The last visible sighting of the rock cake was one half taking out a gnome fishing on the edge of the pond, and the other half narrowly missing a squirrel. Fanny returned with a fresh brew while I pretended to wipe the final morsels from around my mouth.

'That was lovely, thank you.'

'My, you were hungry; I like a girl with a good appetite. Do you know what, I think we are going to become bosom buddies. Here's another cup of tea. That's the tenth pot I've made with the same tea bag, and it still tastes as good as the first cup. Now, tell me about how you ended up in Whispering Pines.'

We were chatting like long lost friends, when I noticed the squirrel bashing the rock cake on the gnome's head. Unable to break it, the squirrel leapt onto the windowsill and smashed the rock cake against the wooden frame. Thank goodness Fanny had lost a hearing aid. I jumped up and positioned myself in front of the window.

'Why don't we continue this conversation while you show me around your farm?'

'But you haven't finished your tea, dear.'

'That's okay, I love cold tea; I'll drink it when we return.'

'Okay, I'll be back in a jiffy, my coat's upstairs.'

Sitting beside me, a black and white collie swished his tongue around his lips, and when I peered into my cup, it was empty. The collie stretched his front legs, sniffed the mound of newspapers, and lifted his leg. Oh my word, I had to get out of this house! It reeked. Before I could escape, a voice called from the bottom of the stairs.

'Oakley, dear, I think there is a bird trapped upstairs. I can hear it tweeting, would you mind following me and we'll see if we can find it?'

'Of course, I'm on my way.' I remembered Mackenzie's advice

to avoid being downwind of her, but right now there wasn't a lot of choice. I'd just have to keep my distance.

We were nearing the top step before it dawned on me that perhaps Mackenzie had been winding me up, so I hurried up behind her. Without warning she stopped, gripped the banister, and from beneath the many layers of petticoats trumpeted a raspberry that was off the Richter scale. A squall of at least twelve engulfed me in a rancid stench of rotten eggs, and the sulphur burnt my eyes. Fanny Farty Flocker didn't say anything as she shook her skirt, giggled, and proceeded to the top. Surely, even without a hearing aid, she must have heard that noise. It was far worse than all my brothers' flatulence problems put together. My underwater swimming lessons were tested as I held my breath, rubbed my eyes, and rushed towards the open window on the landing. A lesson learnt – trust everything Mackenzie says. When I reached the top of the stairs, there was no sign of the tweety-bird.

'I don't know, dear, maybe it's in the attic, I'll look later.'

'Are you sure you don't want me to look?'

She stepped back, aghast. 'Oh no, dear, it's a bit untidy. Come on, I'll introduce you to the animals.'

Fanny stepped into the porch and the bird tweeted again. 'It's followed us downstairs, what a clever bird, let's leave the door open for it to fly out. First, I'll show you the pigs, they're mainly woolly Mangalitsa, but I've also got Kunekune.' Fanny pushed the porch door open, and we were confronted by a spring deluge.

'I'll make a dash to the pig's house. Would you be an angel and bring my umbrella, it's in the holder in the corner behind you. I wash my hair on the first Monday of each month and I don't want it to get out of shape.'

I glared at her hair, which didn't look as if it had seen a brush in years. To be honest, it wouldn't have surprised me if the missing tweety-bird was nesting on her head. The half-open umbrella was pushed inside the holder. I gripped the handle and yanked it out, whereupon a muffled scream escaped my mouth as I was covered head to toe in mice. They scurried up the handle, leapt onto my shoulders and arms, and flew off me in every direction. I'd never seen so many mice and was glad I was wearing my wellies. Fanny rushed back to see what the commotion was and stopped in her tracks as mice darted out in all directions.

Fanny bent forward roaring with laughter. 'That explains why my cat, Socks, has been staring at the umbrella stand for days.'

'Sorry I screamed; they startled me when they leapt up.'

'They're wood mice, dear, probably having a nice snooze when you tipped them out of their bed. Let's wander down to the pigs, and the ducks' palace.'

A sign hung above the gate. Welcome to Ducking-Ham Palace. Several smiling pigs were sliding around in the mud as a variety of upturned ducks splashed in the pond; maybe I was related to all of them.

'Do you sell them for meat?'

Fanny stepped back and gasped. 'Oh no, dear, this is a rescue centre, and I don't eat meat, just lots of veg, especially Brussels sprouts. The Kunekune were brought by people who thought they wouldn't grow big, look at the size of them.'

'They're huge.'

'Yes, they're very comical, they'd follow me around all day if they weren't fenced in. Come on, I'll show you the sheep and goats.'

We wandered to the far end of the farm where a sign hung above a gate saying: Welcome to Bleating-Ram Palace. Tunnels, tyres and various platforms were scattered everywhere. One platform had even been decorated as a throne. Standing on top were two regal-looking Angora goats watching over three Pygmy kids jumping on a sunken trampoline.

'They're adorable, do they have names?'

'I'm a bit of a royalist, so have named them all after the royal family. The three Pygmy goats on the trampoline are called George, Charlotte and Louis. The two Angora goats on the throne watching over them are called Camilla and Charlie. The long-haired Pyrenean goats in the far corner are Kate and Meghan. The golden Guernsey is called Harry, and the Valais Blacknose ram is called Wills, they're both favourites with everyone.'

'They're gorgeous. I love your sense of humour. I could watch them all day, but I should be getting back to the practice, as it's my first day.'

'You're welcome to pop by and watch them anytime you like, dear.'

'Thank you, I will. If you're not too busy this afternoon, have you got time to pop by for a cup of tea or coffee at around three? I know Aidan would love to see you.'

'Sounds lovely, I can always make myself free for Aidan.'

I strolled back to the house alongside Fanny, ensuring I wasn't downwind of her. When we reached the front door, she hung her coat on a hook in the porch, and the mystery bird began tweeting again.

'It seems to be following you everywhere.'

'I know, it's been following me around for days.'

'Are you sure it's not stuck inside your coat?'

'No, the pockets are buttoned up, and they're not big enough for a bird, look.' Mrs Flocker undid the pockets, pulled out the liners and something tumbled to the ground. I picked it up and handed it to her. She stared at me in disbelief, and we dissolved into laughter.

'Oh, you angel, the batteries must have been low in my hearing aid, and it sounded like a tweety-bird. I was a bit sceptical when Aidan said you'd be my new vet, but you know what, I think us girls are going to get along just fine. I'll tell him he's found himself a good 'un in you, not only have you found my hearing aid you've also found the tweety-bird.'

'Thank you. Aidan was saying how much he loved your rock cakes, maybe we could have some with the tea?'

'Ooh, what a good idea. If you like, take the whole tin with you.'

As I reached for the tin, I chuckled to myself at the sight of an electric carving knife surrounded by rock cake crumbs.

'It's time I made tracks. Now, don't forget, three o'clock this afternoon for tea or coffee. I'm sure Aidan and Madagan can't wait to see you.'

'Looking forward to it. I had better brush my hair.'

I waved goodbye with visions spinning in my head of Fanny arriving with a brush stuck in her hair. After changing my overalls in a field, I drove home to check on the cats and slice Fanny's rock cakes, though without an electric carving knife that was probably going to be an impossible task. Maybe Lily had one I could borrow. I parked outside the Lily Pad and dashed in to see her.

'Ey up lass, how's it going?'

'Great thanks, Lily, though I need a favour?'

'Of course, Dustin was buzzing when he got home last night, he's like a new boy. Set his sights on being a veterinary nurse and talking about working at the rescue centre.'

I opened the tin of rock cakes. 'He'll be a brilliant veterinary nurse. Have you got an electric carving knife I could borrow please?'

'Yer why? You haven't made them have you?'

'No. It's a long story.'

We sat down with a coffee and sandwiches, and I revealed the story of my initiation test.

'Oakley, that's awful. I had no idea my family could be so underhand. I love a bit of double-crossing. Would you mind if I popped by for one of the rock cakes? I wana watch 'em squirm as they bite into Fanny's.'

'Of course, though I'm not sure there will be any Fanny biting!'

Lily flipped a tea towel at me. 'Silly girl, I meant Fanny's rock cakes. What have you got planned for your tea?'

'Nothing yet.'

Lily disappeared to the kitchen and returned with the tin of rock cakes and a large plastic container.

'Is lasagne all right?'

'Thank you very much, you are the kindest person I have ever met. Lasagne will go down a treat.'

I opened the tin of rock cakes to see Lily had sliced each one in two. I stood up and hugged her.

'Ah, get away with you girl.'

'See you later, Lil.'

'Ta-ra love.'

I arrived at Madhatters for afternoon surgery. My first client was a rather elderly, grumpy cat that needed its claws trimmed. Next was a muzzled dog that also needed its claws trimmed, followed by an angry parrot who told me to, 'Eff off' as I tried to trim its claws and beak. I felt more like a podiatrist than a vet. The final dog needed his anal glands emptied. That smell was even worse than Fanny's billowing skirts.

Madigan returned after a liquid lunch with Farmer Geddon.

'Oakley, good you're back. How was Fanny?'

'Fine, we got like a pair of old school friends. She is popping by at three for tea or coffee.'

'Did she offer you refreshments?'

'Yes, delicious rock cakes; she's an excellent baker.'

'She is? That surprises me. So how was the house?'

'Lovely, she's more house-proud than me.'

Madigan ran his hands through his hair. 'Really? She's turned over a new leaf.'

'How do you mean?'

'Oh, nothing, love, nothing to worry about.'

The practice door swung open, and Beau strolled in. He leant back on his mum's desk, smirking.

'Hi, Oakley, was Fanny missing Aidan? We've heard how he likes to keep her happy.'

Aidan threw a stuffed sheep at Beau. 'Enough of your cheek, young man. Don't forget how much she fancies you too.'

Beau smirked. 'Doesn't everybody?'

I picked up a tray of dirty mugs. 'Hi, Beau, Fanny was missing everyone. She is popping by shortly for tea.'

Madge appeared in the doorway and said, 'I'll pop the kettle on.'

I dithered on the way to the kitchen, earwigging a conversation between Beau and Aidan.

'Beau, what did you want to ask me about Dustin?' said Aidan.

Beau cleared his throat and growled, 'I bumped into Dustin yesterday. He was in a daydream and said Oakley dropped him home and he was in love and couldn't believe his mum and dad approved. Then Penelope Pringle mentioned something about Dustin.'

'Oh, is that all. Well, yes, Lily and I discussed it briefly and thought it was time Dustin grew up and took responsibility. Get him out from under our feet. The two of them will be very happy together and can join Ashley and Rylee for lots of nice walks. I think it will bring him out of his shell. As for Penelope Pringle, you know what a gossip she is.'

Beau continued to vent his opinion: 'It's none of my business, but don't you think he's a bit young? He's not even seventeen yet.'

'I'm sure you were much younger than Dustin when you got your first puppy.'

Beau raised his voice. 'Did you just say first puppy?'

Aidan sniggered. 'Yeah, what were you thinking? Oakley took Dustin and Rylee to see her new puppy. I thought you were meant to be going with her. Anyway, when they arrived two puppies were still waiting to be adopted. Dustin fell in love with one, and Rylee the other.'

'I see, so he's not in love with Oakley?'

Aidan snorted with laughter. 'Well that he maybe, who knows the minds of sixteen-year-old boys, but I think you'll find he is more in love with his new puppy. You didn't think he was seeing Oakley, did you?'

Beau raised his voice and snapped. 'No, of course not.'

That explained why Beau didn't want to go out for a meal again; he thought I was seeing Dustin. Fancy him of all people believing in gossip from Penelope Pringle. Maybe the jealously proved he liked me after all.

I returned to the reception as the practice door swung open and Fanny and Lily entered.

Lily perched on Aidan's desk. 'Fanny, looks like we're on time for tea.'

Madge headed to the kitchen and returned with the plate of rock cakes. 'Help yourself to one of Fanny's delicious rock cakes, it will go lovely with a cup of tea.'

I jumped up from my chair. 'I'll pass them round.'

Four of my rock cakes had been stridently placed on top of Fanny's rock cakes. I offered them to the ladies first before passing the plate to the men.

Madge bit into her rock cake. 'Well, I say, Fanny, you've surpassed yourself, these are the best rock cakes you've ever made. What do you think, Lily? Almost as good as yours?'

Lily sniffed the outside and nibbled the end. 'By 'eck, Madge, I think they're better.'

Fanny tentatively bit the end. 'Well, I never, by Jove, think I've got the knack of baking.'

Madigan, Beau and Aidan's rocks cakes remained untouched on their plates.

I nibbled my rock cake. 'Come on, boys, plenty more where they came from.'

Aidan raised his rock cake to his mouth and gnawed it like a mouse. Beau scrutinised his before chomping it like a beaver. Madigan reluctantly nibbled his like a rabbit. It was hilarious and I wasn't sure how long I could contain my laughter.

Madigan placed the remainder of his rock cake on his plate. 'Fanny, isn't that Farmer Geddon on the yacht in the harbour? He always had a soft spot for you.'

We turned our attention to the window to see someone waving from a yacht, and when we about-turned, all three men were brushing crumbs off their tops with no sign of the rock cakes.

Madigan picked his bag up. 'That was delicious, Fanny, now I must dash as I have urgent appointments.'

Fanny passed the plate to Beau. 'I'm sure Beau can squeeze in another one.'

Beau was already marching towards the door. 'Thanks, Fanny, I'm full. I'd better get back to the farm.'

Aidan gripped his bag under his arm. 'It was lovely seeing you, Fanny, but I have a house call to make at 4 p.m. I'm sure you will get along fine with Oakley.'

Before anyone had time to say anything, Madigan, Aidan and Beau had hotfooted it out of the surgery.

Fanny seemed shocked. 'Was it something I said?'

'Not at all. Would you like another cup of tea?' I said heading to the kitchen.

'Thank you, but I'd better get off home as it's feeding time soon. I've had a lovely day, thanks to you. Remember, dear, pop by anytime for a natter over a cup of tea. I might even bake more rock cakes.'

'That would be lovely, thank you, Fanny.'

As soon as Fanny left, Madge cheered. 'Well done, love, that'll teach the lads not to mess with you, but if they don't come back soon, looks like we're taking the afternoon clinic.'

'That's okay, Madge. The looks on their faces made it worthwhile.'

Lily walked towards the door. 'Right love, remind us never to cross paths with you. Mackenzie will be dead proud of you. I'd best get back to the café. Ta-ra ladies.'

'Bye, Lily, thank you for supporting me.'

'You're welcome lass.'

The rest of the afternoon sailed by without a hitch. Madge saw Madigan's clients and I saw Aidan's. When the last client of the day left at 6 p.m., there was still no sign of Madigan or Aidan.

'Oakley, you get off home, I can manage now. It seems the men have had their noses put out of joint. No doubt they're nursing their pride in the pub.'

'With plenty of black dogs.'

'And a couple of Famous Grouse. It's been a brilliant day, and you have fitted in like the missing piece from a jigsaw. See you in the morning.'

'Thank you, Madge, we make a real team. I've loved my first day. See you tomorrow.'

I headed home feeling proud of myself, and wondering how the heck I'd pulled it off.

The cats rushed to greet me, although they were probably more interested in their tea than hearing about my day. However, I knew someone who would be dying to hear about it.

> **Me:** Hi Mackenzie, I sailed through the first day, and I'm going back tomorrow.
>
> **Mackenzie:** I've been thinking about you all day. How did it go with Fanny?
>
> **Me:** I hope you don't get too bored whilst I tell you all about my day?
>
> **Mackenzie:** I'll never get bored and can't wait to hear all about it.

Twenty texts later I was worried Mackenzie was falling asleep!

> **Me:** So that was my day. How was your day?
>
> **Mackenzie:** Not as eventful as yours. I can't wait to return to the practice. I think you and I are going to make a good team.
>
> **Me:** We sure will. Though I'm worried Beau isn't going to be talking to me anymore.
>
> **Mackenzie:** He will, he doesn't give up that easily when there's something he wants.
>
> **Me:** How'd you mean?

Mackenzie: Doesn't matter it's not my place to say anything. Sorry Oakley I gotta go out. Catch up with you soon. Well done for today, I knew you wouldn't let them beat you. Enjoy your second day.

Me: Thank you, Mackenzie, enjoy your evening.

I wondered what Mackenzie meant by it wasn't his place to say anything, perhaps he'd tell me another day.

The microwave pinged and I settled down to eat a plate of Lasagna and salad before replying to the texts from my family. It had been a brilliant first day at work and I couldn't believe I had outwitted my new bosses, though I had better watch my back from now on, who knew what tricks they would get up to next!

Chapter Thirty
Regretful Words

The next few days flew by, and on Good Friday we were closing early at 4 p.m. when the practice door swung open and Beau ambled in.

'Oakley, are you busy tonight? We need to go over the itinerary for tomorrow.'

'Hi Beau, I've not seen you all week. I'm baking hot cross buns for the kids at the weekend, but you can pop over for tea if you like; say seven-thirty?'

'What's for tea? Are you sure it's edible?'

'Of course,' I said wondering what I could cook, and then I remembered watching MasterChef and blurted out, 'I'm cooking chicken thighs with mushrooms and bacon in white wine sauce with a cheese and crumb topping and rarebit on jacket potato skins.' Oh my god, what was I thinking?

Beau ran his tongue around his lips in a provocative manner.

'Sounds delicious, what's for afters?'

I noticed his suggestive grin as he raised his eyebrows.

'I assume you mean pudding? I could rustle up a pineapple and treacle upside-down pudding.'

'Sounds fantastic, can't wait, see you at seven-thirty.'

'See you later.'

My shift was about to finish when the phone rang. It was Mackenzie.

'Hi Mackenzie, how are you?'

'Hi Oakley, how's this week been? Any more initiation?'

'Great thanks, and no more initiation, thank you for warning me I had to keep one step ahead of them.'

'That's good, let's hope they keep it that way, though watch your back, mark my words they'll be conspiring something else. Is my dad about?'

'No, he's out on a call, have you tried his mobile?'

'Yes, but it was switched off. He's probably in the pub. Don't worry I'll catch up with him later. While I'm on the phone, I know it's a long way, but are you interested in driving up to Scotland next month? It's my thirtieth birthday in May, and I'm hoping to arrange a weekend paddling to the Driftwood Islands; Flotsam and Jetsam. It would be great to meet up before I move back in June.'

'Sounds great. I'll see if I can get the weekend off.'

'Invite your brothers if you like. Are you doing anything interesting tonight?'

'Beau's popping round for tea so we can discuss the itinerary for tomorrow.'

'What's he roped you into?'

'I'm teaching canoeing and kayaking to a bunch of kids on Saturday, and Beau said he'd teach me how to paddleboard.'

'Sounds fun. I'm sure you're in good hands with Beau.' Mackenzie hesitated. 'Would you mind if I gave you a bit of advice?'

'Of course not.'

'I know Beau is my cousin, and it's probably none of my business, but just watch yourself with him.'

'Whatever do you mean?'

'My mum said you two were getting close.' Mackenzie paused. 'Sorry Oakley, Beau has a reputation of being a bit of a ...' Mackenzie paused again and sighed.

I was annoyed now. 'A what, Mackenzie?'

He blurted out, 'He's a player when it comes to girls. He normally goes for much younger, more vulnerable girls; his last girlfriend was only seventeen. He doesn't care much for independent women as he likes to feel superior and be needed.'

'I see. So, I'm too old, not vulnerable enough, and too independent. Mackenzie, you sound like one of my brothers; they're always giving me advice.'

Mackenzie sighed again. 'Sorry, Oakley, I shouldn't speak ill of him, but I don't want you to get hurt. I've seen it time and time again. He chases after pretty girls like a cat chasing and teasing a mouse. He'll catch them, let them go, ignore them for a bit, catch them again, and play with them for a bit more until they bore him. Then he moves on to the next victim. I don't want you to be another notch in his belt.'

My head was exploding like an unpricked potato in a microwave. 'Mackenzie, you're comparing me to a mouse, and I'm a victim who he'll get bored of soon. Remember at the beginning of the conversation you mentioned it was none of your business? Well, it isn't. I'm a big girl and can look after myself and have no intention of becoming another notch in his belt. Sorry, I have to go.'

'I apologise if I'm out of line, he has to grow up one day. I didn't mean to imply you were old, boring or a victim, on the contrary, it's not you, it's him. Beau gets bored if he doesn't get the one thing he wants, and if he does get it, he moves on to the next one; it's a no-win situation, and he's left a string of heartbroken women behind. Hope the weekend goes okay. Bye.'

I shouldn't have been so rude to Mackenzie, but I didn't need another big brother giving me advice and telling me what to do. I gritted my teeth, took a deep breath, and growled, 'Men!'

There was no time to worry about it for now. I had to hurry home to impress Beau with my culinary skills. I was going to cook Beau such a fabulous meal that he'd fancy me in his heart long before his bed!

Chapter Thirty-one
Loose Bottom

An aroma of cinnamon and spice wafted around the house as several bowls of hot cross bun dough proofed on the rack above the Aga. With the dinner cooking, there was just enough time to find an outfit and have a shower before Beau arrived. I riffled through my wardrobe, pulled on a pair of skinny black jeans and and tried on a black silky top sporting a neckline of sparkling embossed diamonds. I peered into the mirror, crikey, I was far too overdressed. Just as I was about to change and dive into the shower the doorbell chimed. I peered out the window and took a deep breath; Beau was an hour early and I hadn't even had a shower.

Without changing, I flew down the stairs two at a time and on opening the door the stench was worse than Fanny Flocker's bellowing skirts. Beau reeked like a slurry, his blond curls were ruffled with whisps of hay, and his overalls were filthy.

Beau beamed and his eyes wandered from my head to my toes. 'Wow, Oakley, you look gorgeous. I'm not too early, am I? Couldn't remember what time you said.'

'Seven-thirty, as I was baking hot cross buns for tomorrow. Don't worry, they're proofing at the moment. Come in, although dinner isn't ready yet.'

'That's okay, I had to clean out the cowsheds before returning the sheep to the field after their hooves were trimmed. I was passing Catkins so thought I'd pop in early.'

I held the door open and took a deep breath as he stepped past me. That was odd, how did he know he was early if he couldn't remember what time I said? Only Beau would have the audacity to turn up for dinner wearing overalls and ponging like a muck spreader.

I placed a newspaper on a kitchen chair. 'Would you like a drink?'

'Yes, that would be lovely, tea please, I'm parched. Don't suppose you'd mind me trying out your new shower?'

That was a first. No one had ever arrived for dinner and asked to use the shower, most people showered at home before they went out for dinner.

'I was about to have a shower myself, but you go ahead, there's a couple of warm towels on the rail.'

'We can share the shower, if you like?'

The penny dropped – the unkempt look was a ploy to get me into the shower.

'Call me old fashioned, but I prefer to know someone a little better before sharing a shower,' I said, thinking how unromantic to share a shower with a bloke ponging like a muck spreader.

'It's only a shower, I'm not asking you to jump into bed with me, well, not before I've showered. Sure I can't tempt you? We've shared a shower before, so what's the difference?'

'I was fully clothed. Sorry Beau, you go ahead. Dinner's not going to be ready for about half an hour.'

Beau lowered his head, dropped his voice, and slinked away. 'Okay, thanks. Do you mind if I take my mug of tea with me?'

'Of course I don't. Watch out for Nutmeg on the top step.'

On entering the kitchen, my nostrils were tickled by an unusual aroma wafting from the oven. It wasn't unpleasant, it merely didn't smell like chicken, bacon and mushrooms in a white wine sauce. It reminded me of breakfast in an American diner where the bacon was covered in maple syrup. Maybe something had spilt in the oven from another meal. There was no time to worry about it for now, I still had to chop the salad for the starter. My multitasking was tested when I remembered the hot cross buns needed piping.

Ten minutes later, I placed the hot cross buns in the oven and shouted up to Beau.

'Oakley, did you call me?'

'Yes, sorry, dinner will be a little longer as I've just put the hot cross buns in the oven.'

'Oh, is that all, I thought you were going to say you were on the way to scrub my back.'

'Nice try, I'm not that easily led astray.'

'You don't know what you're missing.'

Ten minutes later there was a loud thud and I hurried into the hallway to investigate. My feet performed an emergency stop when spotting Beau leaning out of the doorway wearing the teeniest of towels around his waist.

'Beau, what on earth are you doing?'

'Checking nosey Penelope Pringle has gone.'

'What? You answered the door to her in that teeny towel? It's hardly bigger than a flannel. Did she ask for me?'

'She did, but when I told her where you were, she looked shocked and rushed back to her car. Very odd.'

'What exactly did you say?'

'Nothing really. I said I was taking a shower and dinner was taking a bit longer to cook as you had buns in the oven. Very odd. She slammed the door shut and dashed off.'

'Crikey, I bet she thinks I'm pregnant.'

'What! Why?'

'A bun in the oven means I'm pregnant.'

Beau turned abruptly from the door. 'It does. That explains why she slammed the door and hotfooted it out of here. But I said you had buns in the oven, maybe she thought you're having twins.' He closed the front door and sauntered towards me naked as the towel remained trapped in the door. He glanced down, and meandered back to the door and opened it. I honestly didn't know where to look when he bent over in front of me and picked up the towel.

'Sorry about that, I was going to ask if I could borrow a bath robe as my overalls are a bit too smelly to put back on.' Beau said.

My mind had turned to mashed potato and I didn't know what to say, or what to think, in fact, for once I was speechless and more embarrassed than him.

Beau raised his voice. 'Oakley, did you hear me? Can I borrow a bath robe?'

I gathered my thoughts, gulped, and murmured, 'Flynn's robe is on the back of the door, second bedroom on the right.'

'Great, I'll be back in a mo.'

After returning to the kitchen and picking up a cucumber, I glanced at my piping nozzle. Images bounced into my mind causing me to wince at the thought of pushing the cucumber through my piping nozzle. When I picked up two carrots and realized they were joined together with a baby carrot hanging in the middle, I was positively quivering. Was someone trying to tell me something? I was surrounded by images of men's bits.

How could I sit opposite Beau now? This was so embarrassing; all I'd be thinking about was how ginormous his appendage was. And any minute now my phone was going to ring enquiring if I was pregnant.

I placed the bowl of salad, including the carrot man bits, on the dining room table and returned to the kitchen. Surprise, surprise, my phone was ringing.

'Hi, Lily.'

'Hey up love, how's your evening going?'

'Fine, thank you.'

'That's great, and is Beau behaving himself?'

'Of course. Perfect gentleman.'

'Oh, okay, as long as he is taking care of you.'

'Oh my god, Lily, out with it. Stop beating around the bush.'

'It's none of my business, though sounds like my nephew's been getting a tad heated around your bush, you know what I mean.'

'Lily! We haven't even kissed.'

'Oh! Right, it's just Penelope said—'

I interrupted her. 'You should know better than to listen to Penelope Pringle.'

'So, you're not up the duff?'

'No!'

'Oh lordy, Penelope Pringle said you had a bun in the oven.'

'I have twenty-four buns in the oven, Lily, hot cross buns.'

Lily roared with laughter. 'I see, I should have known better and not listened to gossip. Sorry love. Night.'

'Night, Lily.'

I reached for the oven gloves as Beau returned with my brother's robe wrapped tightly around him. Talk about a sausage wrapped tightly in a roll. Beau was at least six inches taller than Flynn and any minute the sausage was going to escape out the side.

'Can I help you with anything, Oakley?'

I held my composure and muttered, 'Would you mind taking the side plates into the dining room?'

'No problem.'

Beau picked up the plates and a tomato rolled onto the floor. Without hesitation, he bent over and retrieved it. As he stood up, I turned away pretending I hadn't ogled the outline of his bum. It seemed to be getting awfully hot in the kitchen, and I could feel my face glowing redder than the tomato.

We retreated to the dining room and sat opposite each other. Beau piled his plate high with chicken thighs and potato rarebits. Like a dog waiting for a titbit, I watched the first mouthful enter his mouth. I was expecting a nod of approval, or a compliment, but instead his grimace looked as if he was suffering from extreme indigestion.

'Erm ... lovely, Oakley, your thighs are, how do I put it, rather unusual.'

I placed a forkful of chicken into my mouth and stared at Beau as my eyes welled up.

'Beau, it's disgusting, it's so sweet. I'm so sorry, I don't know what happened.'

Beau took another mouthful and grinned. 'Don't worry, it's edible if you eat a piece of garlic bread at the same time; you hardly notice the flavour.'

I felt like crying, what the heck had I done? Tonight was a disaster. My culinary skills were not going to fire me into Beau's heart, they were so bad I could see him fleeing into the arms of Penelope Pringle and her hareem. Out of manners, Beau finished his meal, but I couldn't eat another mouthful. I cleared the plates and returned to the kitchen. At least I could redeem myself with the upside-down pudding, even a complete novice couldn't make a mistake with that.

I tipped the cake upside down onto a plate and tapped the cake tin, but when I removed it the bottom of the tin remained on the cake. What a bird brain, I'd used a loose-bottom cake tin, and not placed it on a tray. The treacle and pineapple juice had seeped onto the chicken thighs sizzling below, that explained why it tasted so sweet. Now the cake was going to taste like chewing cardboard. I warmed treacle up, poured it over the top, and layered it with custard, hoping Beau wouldn't notice.

'I hope you have room for pudding. I have a confession – I accidentally used a loose-bottom cake tin, so pineapple juice and treacle leaked over the thighs. I'm so sorry.'

Beau smiled. 'Don't worry, it tasted fine. I'm sure I can squeeze in a bit of pudding.'

Five minutes later he'd devoured the whole bowl.

I collected his dish. 'I'll clear the table; do you want to make yourself comfortable in the living room?'

'If you're sure you don't want me to help you.'

'No, that's fine, I'll make coffee.'

'Don't worry about the coffee, I brought a couple of bottles of wine with me.'

'I'm not good with wine, half a glass and it goes to my head.'

'I'll pour you a full glass then.'

'Cheeky. I'll be back in a few minutes, make yourself at home.'

Doubt swept across my body like waves on a stormy ocean. The whole evening was spoilt and hadn't gone to plan. My mind was like a whirlpool. Seeing Beau naked was like knowing what was inside your Christmas present before you opened it, thus ruining the initial element of mystery and surprise.

When I returned to the living room, Beau sat grinning and handed me a large glass of wine. I sank beside him with an attack of the collywobbles. He stretched his arm around my shoulders, and despite showering, all I could smell was the pong of sheep and a muck spreader. I should be sizzling with electricity, instead my body felt chilly like the north pole of a magnet repelling against another north pole. There was nothing frosty about Beau's intentions, they were defiantly heading to the south pole. What was wrong with me? Ruby would be fuming. A gorgeous bloke was sitting on my sofa, throwing himself at me, and all I could hear were Mackenzie's words ringing in my head like an earworm. Beau reached for my glass and placed it on the table, he leant in and kissed me. It wasn't a romantic kiss like in a fairy tale, more a frantic floundering kiss of a man desperate to go further. There were no fireworks, and nothing ignited within me. Perhaps Ruby was right, soulmates were only found in fairy tales. Beau began nibbling my ears as his hands caressed my body. I didn't kiss him back, not that Beau noticed; he hadn't even come up for air. This was going too fast, and as Beau's hands fumbled with the zip on my jeans there was a hammer on the front door and the doorbell chimed.

Beau mumbled, 'Leave it, they'll go away.'

The doorbell chimed again, followed by further hammering.

'I'd better see who it is.'

Beau sighed and sat up. 'It'll be nosey Penelope Pringle again. Don't be long.'

On opening the front door, I stepped back in shock. 'Willow! How on earth did you get here?'

'Auntie Oakley, I'm sorry, please don't send me away, I've left home. I caught the train to Plymouth and then a bus to the village. I bumped into a boy called Dustin on the bus, and his mum just dropped me at your gate.

'Well, don't stand on the doorstep, come in. I'll put the kettle on, and you can tell me why you've left home.'

We headed towards the kitchen as Beau popped his head around the door.

'Think I'll make a move, Oakley, sounds like you ladies have some catching up to do.'

'Sorry, Auntie Oakley, how thoughtless of me, you have company.'

'That's okay. Beau, can we continue our evening another time?'

'Looking forward to it. Nice to see you again, Willow. Oakley, I'll see you at the Lily Pad, say 8 a.m.?'

'Yes, that's fine, see you in the morning. Night, Beau, and sorry about the awful dinner.'

'No worries. It was lovely sampling sweet juices from your loose bottom and nibbling your rarebits. Okay if I borrow the robe?'

Willow giggled, placed her hands on her ears, and began humming. 'Not sure I should be listening to this conversation.'

'I'll let Oakley tell you about it.' Beau closed the front door and Willow followed me into the kitchen giggling.

'Are you going to tell me what he was talking about or is it private? Why was he wearing a bathrobe? Or shouldn't I ask?'

'No, it's not private. I'll tell you about my awful dinner over a cup of coffee. '

Willow was in hysterics after hearing about my evening. 'Don't tell too many people you have a loose bottom.'

I swished a tea towel around her head. 'Come on you, we need to let your dad and Molly know where you are. They'll be worried sick.'

'I doubt that very much.'

I rang Harrison and put the phone on loudspeaker.

'Hi sis, what's up?'

'Hi Harrison, is Willow there, she's not answering her mobile.' I gazed at Willow who had a bemused expression etched on her face.

'Not sure where she is, I've not seen her today.'

'What do you mean you haven't seen her today?'

'She went out with friends last night, must have slept in. I popped out on a job at eleven, but there was no sign of her when I got back.'

'Is Molly there?'

'Yes, I'll pass the phone to her.'

'Hi Moll, everything okay with the twins?'

'Yes, two months to go, but I can hardly get the seatbelt around me.'

'It will fly by. Have you seen Willow?'

'Not seen her since she went to her friends yesterday evening. I took the boys swimming, but she wasn't here when we got home. Shall I ask her to call you later?'

'No, don't worry.'

'What did you want her for?'

'To see if she was interested in work experience at the practice.'

'Yes, I'm sure she'd be up to that. Try her mobile. Bye, Oakley.'

'Bye, Molly.'

Willow was curled up on the sofa with all three cats lying beside her.

'See what I mean, Auntie Oakley. They haven't even noticed I'm not there. Please let me stay. I can continue my course at the local college, and I've got money saved up for my board and I'll find a local job and—'

'Okay, you can stay.'

Willow jumped up, sending the cats sprawling to the ground as she rushed over to hug me.

'But there's one condition.'

'Oh, here we go, rules, you sound like Nan.'

'Drop the Auntie Oakley, you make me feel old, just call me Oakley.'

Willow giggled. 'Thanks, Oakley, is there anything to eat? Something smells lovely.'

'Oh my gosh, I've forgotten the hot cross buns in the Aga. Please can you throw me the oven gloves.'

I opened the Aga door and placed two trays of cinders on the drainer. Willow stared at me and laughed like a kookaburra.

'Would you mind if I cooked tea each night? Or maybe we could eat out?'

'Don't be impertinent, they looked great when they went in for twenty minutes, two hours ago. Let's take your bags upstairs. You can have the room at the far end of the hall, it's decorated in duck egg blue, and there's a new bathroom in the ensuite.'

Willow pushed the door open, swivelled around and hugged me.

'It's the nicest room I have ever seen.' She sank onto the bed, exhausted. 'It's so comfy and there is a desk by the window where I can study. Thank you so much, this is the best day of my life. I'll be quiet, you won't even know I'm here, and I'll look after the cats and cook the meals.'

'No need to be quiet, I don't think I'm cut out for a life of peace and quiet. I'll leave you to unpack. What would you like to eat?'

'Can you manage to make jam on toast without burning it?'

'I'll try my hardest. Afterwards, you can call your dad and we'll discuss the rules.'

'Rules? Now you do sound like Nan.'

'Nothing too drastic. Let me know where you are going, and what time you'll be home. Keep your room tidy, and you can do your own washing and ironing.'

'Is that it?'

'I'm sure I can think of more.'

'No, that's enough.'

'How long have you been planning to move here?'

'Since you announced at Christmas you were moving. I registered at the local college to finish my A levels and I've already applied to university. What's going on with you and Beau?'

'I'm not sure if we're compatible. I think we want different things.'

'Sorry about that, he's lush.'

'He is a bit old for you, so don't start getting any ideas.'

'I like Dustin, he reminds me of Superman.'

'More Clark Kent than Superman. I suppose you'll want to be Lois Lane.'

'As long as she gets her Superman in the end.'

Half an hour later, Willow polished off her toast, called Harrison, and passed the phone to me.

'Dad wants a word.'

'Hi sis, are you sure you don't mind Willow living with you? I'll transfer money into your account for her board and food and give her a monthly allowance.'

'Not at all. I know what it's like trying to study with five noisy boys driving me crazy.'

'But that's what boys are like.'

'Why do you think I spent most of my childhood in my treehouse?'

'We weren't that bad, were we?'

'You were. I was glad when you all started getting married and left me in peace and quiet.'

'Not for long, once we started churning out our own sprogs. You wait till you start churning out yours.'

'You make me sound like a cow. I'm enjoying my peace and quiet away from you lot and want to keep it that way.'

'I hope Willow staying with you won't ruin your love life with Beau.'

'I'm capable of ruining my love life on my own.'

Harrison laughed. 'You're too fussy, sis.'

'Goodnight, Harrison.'

'Night, sis, say goodnight to Willow.'

Willow cuddled Nutmeg. 'Is Dad okay with me staying with you?'

'Yes, he's going to send me money for your food and give you an allowance.'

'I'd rather stand on my own two feet; I'll find a job.'

'I'm sure you can find a job, but for now, you must be tired, why don't you have a bath and an early night? You'll have to amuse yourself tomorrow as I'm going to be working as an instructor on the opening day of the water sports centre.'

'I'll find plenty to do. I might walk down to the Lily Pad. Thanks, Auntie Oakley, sorry, I mean Oakley. I am kind of tired. I'll look for a job tomorrow.'

'We may have a Saturday receptionist's position coming up if you're interested. I'm sure Lily could find you shifts in the coffee shop, and Beau and his sister, Flo, may need help at the water sports centre.'

'Sounds wonderful. I know you don't want me to call you auntie, but you are the best auntie in the world. I promise I won't cause any trouble.'

'Well, as nieces go you are pretty much at the top, though trouble does seem to follow me around, I hope you haven't inherited my trait. Enjoy your bath and early night, and I'm sure you may find a cat or two sleeping at your feet. Night, Willow.'

Willow scampered upstairs with Nutmeg racing behind her as I picked my phone up to call Lily.

'Hi, Lily, thank you so much for dropping Willow at Catkins.'

'Hey up, love you're welcome. I hope it didn't spoil your evening with Beau?'

'No I think you did me a favour.'

'How's Willow? Dustin were right taken with her.'

'Great, thanks. She's living with me until she goes to uni. She's looking for part-time work, so if you need help in the café, please could you let me know?'

'Tell her to pop by anytime and I'll sort some shifts for her.'

'That would be wonderful, thank you so much. Night, Lily.'

'Night, love.'

Half an hour later, I peeped into Willow's room to find her fast asleep with all three cats lying next to her. For the first time in years, I had my bed to myself; what a luxury.

Chapter Thirty-two
Always Burp Your Dry Suit

Sunbeams sparkled through the catkins while daffodils nodded gently in the breeze and birds chirped high in the trees. What a fantastic day to open the water sports centre. It was the middle of April, and the temperature was due to reach a balmy twenty degrees. Although it was going to be a scorcher, instinct told me to don a full dry suit, rather than my wetsuit shorts and cag. Doubtless I'd be spending more time in the water than on top while teaching kids to paddle. Though with my indecisive head niggling me it wouldn't hurt to throw my shorts and cag into my dry bag.

Trying to zip the back of my dry suit up was akin to reaching that annoying itch between your shoulder blades – an impossible task on your own. With Willow sound asleep, my only option was to wait and ask Beau, who no doubt would be eager to help. I flung my dry bag onto my back and said goodbye to the cats. During the past week I'd dropped my canoe, kayak and paddles at FloBeau water sports centre. Today, I had time to enjoy the beautiful spring morning while ambling along the track to the Lily Pad.

The hedges bordering the track were teaming with life as they burst out of their winter dormancy. Spring arrived so much earlier in Cornwall. Sycamore and hazel were interwoven with blackthorn and hawthorn, whose white flowers were attracting a menagerie of flies. A cobweb sparkled in the sun as a spider eyed up his breakfast. The embankments were awash with bluebells, and celandines. The perfume wafting in the air was mind-blowing, it smelt just like my Christmas hyacinths. A ladybird fluttered its wings while searching for its perfect breakfast spot before landing on a dandelion. Woven amongst the flowers were the distinctive heart and oval shaped leaves of archangel. Its buttery yellow buds looked like yellow baked beans. They waited patiently for their turn to explode into a carpet of clustered golden belled flowers. I reached down and picked a dandelion seed head and began blowing the cotton wool seeds.

'He loves me ... he loves me not ... he loves me ... he loves me not ... he loves me ... he loves me not.' I blew again, and again, but several seeds remained in the dandelion head. Sighing, I tossed the head into the hedge, I'm sure it didn't mean anything; it was just a silly childhood myth.

Further along the track the air was saturated with the aroma of wild garlic as wood anemone peeped though decaying bark. I hesitated at the magnificent old oak tree that was now in full bloom. Branches hemmed in crisp lime green leaves swayed in the gentle breeze as a woodpecker drummed high on the trunk. I continued along the track as a cuckoo cooed in search of a mate, and a robin whistled a tune staking its territory. I leant over a five-bar gate reflecting on how lucky I was to live in such a wonderful place. Lambs frolicked in the warming sun. It was as if someone had tied pogo sticks onto their legs and given them a trampoline. A huge smile remained on my face for the rest of the journey.

Sitting in the car park beside the Lily Pad was a quad bike and trailer. Lily spotted me, waved, and rushed over.

'Hey up, love. I've packed the nosh for the weekend. I've included loads of bags of hot cross buns to replace yours. Beau's gone to meet the minibuses; he asked me to tell you to run the trailer up to FloBeau.'

'Morning, Lily, thanks for the buns, you're a life saver. Have you any idea how a quad bike works?'

'No, love, I suppose you sit your backside down, turn the key, and away you go.'

I leant over the handlebars. 'Not sure it's that straightforward, it has leavers and a pedal.'

'That's likely the accelerator, or throttle, or whatever you call it. Start the engine and see what happens.'

I slid onto the seat, turned the ignition, and was torpedoed across the handlebars.

Lily roared with laughter. 'Oh 'eke, it's got gears, looks like you shift it with your foot. Treat it how you would like to be treated by a man, with tender love and care. Maybe it needs a tad of warming up.'

'You do make me laugh, Lily. Most men treat me like I'm their next conquest. Next, you'll be telling me to caress the bodywork.'

'If it helps. I warm up if my hubby caresses my bodywork. Lucky your wearing canoeing gear and have a helmet.' Lily sniggered. 'Not that I'm implying you're going to end up in the harbour.'

'How difficult can it be to stay on a quad bike? Where are the brakes?'

'Try the handlebars.'

I pressed the levers on the handlebars. 'You're right, I think I have the hang of it, glad I'm only going up the track alongside the estuary.'

'So am I. Try not to go too fast, then you won't need to brake.'

'I'll try. Oh, I almost forget, could you zip the back of my dry suit up please?'

Lily wandered around to the side of the quad bike, pulled my zipper, and passed me my buoyancy aid and helmet.

Lily giggled. 'You certainly look the part.'

'Thanks. Wish me luck. See you later.'

'Have a good day, love. I hope my nephew behaves himself.'

I set off slowly along the estuary singing 'Just Around The River Bend', from *Pocahontas*. It was one of Poppy and Blossom's favourite films and reminded me so much of them. A family of quacking mallards disrupted my thoughts as they glided past with ease.

Blimey, was I that slow? I curled my fingers around the throttle, squeezed, and shifted into second gear. With a bit more acceleration, I found third, then fourth and fifth. Now I was motoring. Wouldn't Beau be impressed? But why was the next bend racing towards me so fast? Where were the brakes? Think, Oakley, think. My brain had transformed to ice cream freeze. The next bend was nearly upon me, when the ice cream melted and a voice in my head screamed, 'handlebars.' I yanked the brakes as hard as I could and the quad bike cornered the bend on two wheels, before righting itself and coming to an abrupt holt.

Not again. Three egrets took flight as I bid farewell to the quad bike and performed an amazing belly flop into the incoming tide. Rather than floundering underwater, I floated on the surface and the current sped me towards FloBeau. I twisted onto my back and gasped at the size of my body – it was ten times fatter than normal. What an idiot, I'd forgotten to burp my dry suit after Lily zipped it up. I resembled a giant octopus as I swam backwards with pathetic flaps of my hands and feet. This was so embarrassing; the kids would be in stitches when I arrived at the centre. I spotted another eddy, maybe if I swam into it and sneaked up the embankment no one would notice me. A familiar chorus of quacking sped past me upstream and offered me a split second of camouflage. I twisted onto my front in preparation of executing a doggy paddle into the eddy. However, I was presented with a bank of mud, and although I had an affinity with mud, I had no plans to visit it today. I was left with no option other than to drift into FloBeau and hope no one noticed me.

With the shoreline in touching distance, I grasped the rocks on the seabed and slithered through the seaweed akin to a hippopotamus. My first attempt at standing resulted in a tsunami of ripples and fully tested a tufted duck's snorkelling skills. My second attempt resulted in a huge crowd descending and at least twenty pairs of teenage eyes glared at me. Standing among them was Beau, looking rather fetching in wetsuit shorts and a rash vest. He sauntered towards me, about-turned, and addressed the crowd.

'Gather around everyone, I'd like you to meet your canoeing and kayaking instructor, Dr Oakley Breeze, who seems to have taken the scenic route.' Beau grabbed my buoyancy aid, yanked me to my feet and once again addressed the crowd. 'By the look of it, Dr Breeze had the full force of the wind behind her.'

The crowd screamed with laughter like a clan of cackling hyenas. I was speechless as Beau continued. 'Now a lesson to you all when wearing a dry suit. Remember two things, one, to zip it up, and two, to burp it, or you will end up looking like this.'

The crowd's laughter sounded louder than a clap of thunder. If anyone had pricked me with a pin and kicked me into the air, I'd have whizzed around like Harry Potter playing quidditch.

'Oakley, you won't get far with all that hot air. If you remove your buoyancy aid you can release the air through your neck seal.'

'I can't, my buoyancy aid pulls over my head and it's not going to get far with my trapped wind.'

My audience was in stitches and held their noses at the thought of me releasing my trapped wind.

'Bend over, I'll unzip your comfort break zipper and squeeze the air out of your bottom.'

I was positive the noise from my audience could be heard for miles around. This was so humiliating, and Beau seemed to be lapping every second up. He pulled the zipper across my hips and ran his hands up and down my body, releasing the air.

A boy from the crowd shouted: 'She doesn't look like the Michelin Man from the tyre advert anymore.'

Beau squeezed the remaining air out and pulled my zipper back. 'I can ensure everyone that Dr Breeze does not have a spare tyre.'

I stood up feeling much thinner. 'Thanks, I think that is enough fondling. What happened to the kids' group?'

'Postponed until midweek. Instead, we have the sixth form students from All Saints School. Oakley, where's the quad bike? You were meant to be bringing the food.'

'Around the corner. I'll nip back and get it.'

'Don't worry, looks like it's found you.' Beau shouted over his shoulder while walking back to the centre.

The quad bike trundled towards us as someone shouted from the seat: 'Hello, Tinker Bell, or should I call you Pocahontas?'

'Trent, what the heck are you doing here?'

'Flo rang and said a group had cancelled and asked me if I wanted to bring any sixth form students.'

'I thought you worked at the secondary school?'

'No, I changed jobs. I work at the private school now. Anyway, you certainly know how to make an entrance. Love the singing by the way.'

'You didn't see me, did you?'

'May have done. I was taking photos of egrets when they took flight. I thought it was the singing that scared them until someone shouted: "Shit!" Then a creature resembling the Abominable Snowman drifted up the estuary. I wandered back down the path and found a quad bike on its lonesome. When I peered upstream, the creature was being overtaken by a load of ducks.'

'Those ducks were runner ducks on a mission.'

'Looked like mallards to me. How'd you end up in the estuary?'

'I was testing the water temperature as I didn't want the kids getting cold.'

Trent grinned. 'An unlikely story if ever I've heard one.'

Flo appeared, readjusting her clothes. 'Oh my gosh, Oakley, you look like you've taken a dip.'

I sniggered at Trent. 'Taking pictures of egrets, who are you kidding? With the heat radiating from you two, I think it's time you both took a dip.'

We were interrupted as Beau slipped into his authoritative voice and shouted from the centre. 'Oakley, when you have finished chatting, do you think you can spare me a minute of your time to do some work?'

His voice reminded me of the way he told Wolf to get down from my sofa. He really did have a Jekyll and Hyde personality, and made me feel like I was a pupil at the school.

'I think I'm being summoned, I'll bid farewell to you lovebirds.'

'Run along like a good girl.' said Trent as he winked.

Beau talked rapidly while clenching his hands. 'I've split the groups into four. Flo and Trent will instruct two groups. You can instruct canoeing to a boys' group. I'll take the girls, and then after lunch, we'll instruct kayaking and stand-up-paddleboarding.' Beau sucked his lips in and raised his voice. 'And try not to drown the boys, it won't look good on our opening day.'

With my sweetest smile I fluttered my eyelashes. 'I'll try my best, Beaufort.'

Beau tapped my behind with his paddle. 'Dr Breeze, try not to come back covered in mud.'

'Me? As if ....' I wandered over to the lads who told me they didn't need training and preferred to paddle upstream. With a deep sigh, I moseyed back to Beau.

'Sorry, Beau. Can I have a word please?'

'Excuse me, ladies, it seems Dr Breeze can't keep away from me. Dr Breeze, how can I help you?' Beau replied, mocking me.

'The boys said they don't need training and want to paddle to the end of the estuary. Is that okay with you?'

'Fine, you can assess their ability as you paddle upstream, but keep an eye on the tide.'

'Okay, thanks. Sorry to disturb your training, ladies.'

I trailed the boys as they attempted to race to the end of the estuary. Their canoeing ability seemed as inflated as Beau and Trent's egos. They paddled from side to side, swapping paddle hands and leaving a pattern on the surface like a slithering snake.

'Lads, can we stop for a bit? Let me show you how to paddle the J-Stroke, then you can paddle in a straight line on one side without the need to keep swapping sides.'

'Sorry, miss, there's no time, we all need to take a leak and we can't get out here as the cliffs are too high.'

'We've only been on the water twenty minutes. Didn't your mum teach you to go before you left home? You're worse than my nieces and nephews.'

'Need it again.'

'All six of you?'

'Yep.'

'You'll have to wait until the end of the estuary.'

When we reached the top of the estuary, the lads hopped out of their canoes and galivanted into the woods, leaving the canoes floating in the shallow water. Something fishy was going on and not for one minute did I believe they all needed the gents. I'd give them half an hour before texting Beau. He would be fuming if I lost his clients. After lifting the bows of the canoes onto the embankment, I sank beside them and nestled my head on a pillow of moss. The sun warmed my face, and for a brief second, I closed my eyes, and within minutes I'd nodded off. What seemed like seconds later, I was awoken by a squawking magpie. I jolted upright, opened my eyes, and glanced at the time. Strewth, I'd been asleep for an hour and a half. Ahead of me, a culvert of mud stretched as far as the eyes could see. Beau was going to be fuming, the tide had disappeared and so had his clients.

My first day working at FloBeau was not going to plan. On hearing jabbering, I sauntered to the edge of the wood, and six lads, with voices like foghorns, emerged from the undergrowth. They were tripping over each other and talking gibberish. I needed to face up to my responsibility as the lads that were in front of me were drunk out of their faces. Beau was going to be livid.

'Lads, where have you been? I've been worried sick,' I lied.

One lad waved his arm in the air pretending it was the trunk of an elephant, and another held out his arms pretending to be a plane.

The lad pretending to be an elephant held up his hand. 'Miss, erm, Miss, erm, sorry Miss, forgot your name, I'll call you little birdy. Where's the water?'

'The water has been sucked up by a herd of elephants. Where the hell do you think it's gone? Have you been drinking?'

'Me? No, just 'appy, darling. Watch out, there's another elephant behind you.'

'Don't you darling me! Sit down and don't move an inch while I decide what we are going to do.'

They plonked themselves on the ground jabbering like a roof top of chirping sparrows. I had little choice other than to call for help.

'Tinker Bell, how lovely to hear from you. What's up?'

'Trent, I have a problem, don't tell Beau.'

'What's it worth?'

'You not losing your job.'

'Sounds serious.'

'The lads are drunk. They went off into the woods and are now talking gibberish, giggling and seeing elephants.'

'Tell me you're joking.'

'No! They didn't return for over an hour and a half. This can't ruin Beau and Flo's first day. Beau is going to blame me if anything happens to them.'

'No, he won't. It's my fault, I should have warned you to keep an eye on them. This isn't the first time they've been caught. They were suspended for a week last time. I thought that would've taught them a lesson. I promised the head it wouldn't happen again. She's going to want my head on a chopping board, and likely expel the lads. I'll paddle up and deal with it.'

'You won't get far; the tides gone out.'

'How far?'

'Dunno, all I can see is mud. I'll come up with my own plan, please don't say anything to anyone yet.'

'What do you have in mind?'

'All I'll say is, the lads may need hosing down by the time we get back.'

'Knowing you it'll involve mud. We'll be ready with the hose and buckets of freezing water.'

'Great, thanks. See you later.'

'See yer, Tink, and I'm sorry.'

'That's okay.'

'Right, lads. While you were having a leak and getting plastered, you'll notice there has been a huge leak here and the tide has disappeared. Did you play tunnel ball at school when you were younger?'

'Yeah, isn't that where you line up behind each other, pass a ball between your legs and the one at the back catches the ball and moves to the front?'

'Yes, so we are going to reinvent it in the canoes using my pole. The person at the back can pole through the mud to the front. Once at the front they pass the pole back to the next person, and so on until the last person has the pole. Then they pole to the front, and we keep repeating it until there is enough water to paddle.'

Their expressions of bafflement were a picture.

The elephant impersonator replied. 'You what? Let me get this right, you want us to stand up in the canoe and use a stick to move us to the front, and then pass the stick between everyone's legs to the last canoe?'

'Yep, it'll be fun.'

'We're gonna go arse over tit.'

'It's either that or I'll call the head at your school, and you'll likely get expelled.'

'That's blackmail.'

'I'd call it tit for tat.'

'You're bluffing. You wouldn't dare.'

I held my mobile in the air. 'Mr Test has given me your head's mobile phone number, I lied. Would you like a little birdy to drop her a message about your extracurricular activities?'

'No! But we haven't used a pole before. I'm paddling with my mate, what if we get stuck and fall in the mud.'

'You'll have a canoe each now I'm not paddling. If you fall in the mud, then we'll practise rescue techniques to get you back into the canoe. Everyone understand?'

'About as clear as the mud. What are you going to do?'

'We need an opening day video for the website; think how famous you'll be. I'll instruct you from the rocks while filming.'

Plane impersonator addressed the lads: 'Think we're being

stitched up, lads. Why don't we ditch the canoes and walk back across the rocks?'

'We can't, our parents will kill us if we're expelled,' said elephant impersonator.

'I guess we have no choice then.'

Seven canoes lined up behind each other in the mudflats while I scrambled up the rocks to film them. The elephant impersonator reached for my pole and stepped into my empty canoe.

'How difficult can it be?' he chanted to his mates.

He placed the pole in the mud, slid my canoe along the surface, and forgot to pull the pole out. My devious plan was working, and he climbed back into my canoe plastered in mud. An hour later, six muddy lads reached the water. I waded out to my canoe, helped the lad climb into another one, washed the mud out, and stepped in. I felt chuffed to bits that I'd got one over on them. That would teach them to return intoxicated, and for once there was scarcely a speck of mud on me; Beau would be so proud of me.

Paddling back to the centre took ages, and boy was I relieved when the jetty came into sight.

Beau paddled towards me with an expression that was normally exclusive to Ruby.

'Oakley, what the heck happened to the boys?'

The lads kept quiet and stared at me anticipating my reply.

'We had a lovely morning, didn't we lads? We were practising our rescue techniques in the mud, just in case we came across an injured gull.'

The lads nodded and agreed, while Beau relaxed and chuckled.

'I think you had better get cleaned up, lads. Apologies about Dr Breeze, she does have a magnetic gravitation towards mud.'

Elephant impersonator winked at me. 'That's okay, it was great fun wasn't it, lads? We won't forget this day for ages.'

'That's good to hear, I would hate to have bad reviews on our opening day. I was a little worried Dr Breeze wouldn't be able to handle you.'

'She handled us just fine,' replied the plane impersonator.

Beau smirked and turned his head as Trent, Flo and their group headed along the jetty with their arms behind their backs. Trent beckoned me to paddle to the left, before they ambushed the boys with buckets of water and the hose pipe.

Following lunch, we played a game of kayak water polo and practised standing up on the paddleboards, where everyone except me, took a dunking.

'I'm impressed, Oakley, not only did you handle the lads, but you have great balance.'

Beau addressed the group. 'Look at Oakley, everyone, it's her first time on a paddleboard and she hasn't fallen in yet.'

Within a few seconds a tidal wave of paddleboarders headed my way, and soon I was making friends with the seaweed again.

I clawed my way back onto my board. 'Thanks, Beau, you and your big mouth. Do you need me for anything else, or would you mind if I paddled down to the harbour?'

'There is one thing I need you for, but it wouldn't be appropriate here, maybe my tent later? Carry on from where we left off last night?' Beau flashed a smile to his audience of sniggering lads.

I raised my eyebrows glancing over the top of my sunglasses. 'You're staying in a one-man tent. I doubt there's room for you, me, your big mouth and mammoth—' Before I could finish the audience erupted into laughter. 'I was referring to his ego.'

Beau sniggered. 'I'm sure there'd be plenty of room on top of me.'

'I'm sure if you stuck your head out of the tent flap there'd be loads more room.'

Beau teased me. 'You don't know what you're missing, woman. Go and enjoy your paddle, don't paddle up the inlets as they become shallow when the tide's out, and you might fall off. Try not to come back covered in mud.'

'I'll try. See ya later.'

The visibility standing on the board was amazing, and although Beau told me not to paddle up any inlets, the one ahead beckoned an exploration; what harm could I come to?

I guided my paddleboard into the entrance and followed the windy creek towards the end. Ripples shimmered with dorsal fins as grey mullet darted to and fro, and mayflies hovered above. Standing on the paddleboard felt like I was walking on water submerged in nature. The channel narrowed and as there were no visible turning circles I was forced to paddle backwards. With a gentle stroke of my paddle, I dipped it into the water trying not to disturb the wildlife. All of a sudden, a huge mullet took flight, hitting me squarely on the back of my knee. I keeled forwards, dug my paddle into the sand, and tried to keep my balance. The paddleboard blasted behind me, leaving me in midair with only one direction to travel. Two seconds later I was well and truly submerged in nature. Mullet swam for their lives as I snatched the leash and retrieved the paddleboard. After clambering back on, I decided it was best that little mishap was kept to myself.

Before long, the estuary opened into the harbour, and I paddled towards the Lily Pad. I spotted Lily in the garden serving a customer.

I waved and shouted, 'Hi ,Lily.'

Lily waved and walked down to the beach. 'You look a natural. How did you get on with the quad bike?'

'We parted company.'

'Heck no! Where?'

'I was bucked off on the last corner and floated up the estuary like the Michelin Man, because I'd forgotten to let the air out of my dry suit. Would you believe it, the kids are not so little, they're sixth formers, so we're going to need more food.'

Lily rested her hands on her thighs and erupted in laughter. 'Bloomin heck! Doesn't sound like you're having a good day.'

'At least I'm still upright on my board, even if I am a little wet. Do you by any chance have any spare burgers or sausages?'

'I'll have a look in the freezer. Is everything alright with you and Beau?'

'Yes, but I've fallen out with Mackenzie.'

''How on earth did you fall out with my lovely stepson?'

'He told me Beau was a player and warned me off him.' I sighed. 'Sorry, Lily, I was rude and told him not to interfere in my life.'

'Oh 'eck, love. I'm not biased, but I'm sure he knows his cousin better than you.'

'I know, but I have five brothers giving me advice, I don't need another one. I like to find things out myself.'

'I can see that! Come on take a seat in the garden, girl you need chocolate.'

'Thanks, Lily, what should I do about Mackenzie?'

'He won't take offence; he likes you too much.'

'Likes me? But he has a girlfriend.'

'I know, but it doesn't stop him liking someone else.'

'Oh!'

A few minutes later, Lily placed a mug of steaming hot chocolate beside me, squirted cream on the top, covered it in marshmallows, and placed a huge chocolate choux bun beside it.

'Thanks, Lily, you're amazing.' I bit into the choux bun sending cream spiralling out the end and around my face. I wiped the cream and slurped my hot chocolate.

I stood up and hugged Lily. 'Thank you, Lily, that was delicious. I'd better get back or everyone will think I've drowned.'

Lily handed me a bag with burgers, sausages and buns. 'Don't fall in or everyone will have soggy buns.'

'I have soggy buns all the time. Mackenzie, Ashley and Dustin are very lucky to have you as their mum. Bye Lily.'

'Get away with you girl. Ta-ra love.'

The tide had turned when I launched my paddleboard and with a gentle twist of my paddle, the clubhouse appeared in no time. Pacing along the beach were Beau and Trent.

Beau rushed down to the water's edge. 'Oakley, where've you been? We were about to send out a search party.'

Trent lifted the front of my paddleboard onto the beach as I jumped off. 'Tinker Bell, it's seven o'clock, we were getting worried.'

I handed Beau the freezer bag. 'I'm sorry, Lily and I only catered for young children, so I paddled back to the Lily Pad and picked up more supplies.'

'Good idea, thanks, we're starving. The barbecue is lit, we can take turns checking on the food while we play football; it's girls against boys. Oakley, you're on the losing team. Trent and I are on the winning team called, The Conquerors. What do you want to name the losing team?'

'The Conquerors? The girls are going to kick your butts, isn't that right girls?' I said to a round of applause from the girls.

Beau smirked. 'The girls haven't got a cat in hell's chance of winning against us.'

'We'll see about that. The girls' team is going to be called Victorious.'

In between checking the food, we played football for the forty minutes. The score was four goals all. I made a dash forward and dribbled the ball into the penalty area.

Trent lunged towards me. 'You're going down, Tinker Bell.'

He stuck his foot out, missed the ball, and sent me tumbling to the ground.

'Penalty!' screamed the girls.

Trent held out his hand and pulled me up. 'Sorry about that, Tinker Bell, I was aiming for the ball but lost concentration from being in so close to you. I'll leave you to take the penalty, but you won't score against Beau.'

'Trent, you forgot I grew up with five brothers, I have penalty taking down to a tee.'

Beau skipped from one goalpost to the other while clapping his hands. I placed the ball in its position and paced back, ready to score the penalty and win the match for the girls.

Ruby's voice kept niggling at the back of my mind as she said, 'Be more like me, if you like Beau, miss the goal, let him be the hero rather than you. Boys don't like to be shown up by girls, and you won't get a boyfriend if you score the goal. Miss it, and he'll come running to console you.'

The girls cheered me on, and a split second before I released my foot, I hesitated, shut my eyes, and kicked the ball. When I opened my eyes, Beau was surrounded by lads hugging and patting him on the back.

Trent sauntered towards me with the ball. 'Better luck next time. Anyone would have thought you kicked the ball with your eyes shut.'

'No, just a lousy shot.'

Trent frowned. I could see he didn't believe me. I was expecting Beau to rush towards me, put his arm around my shoulders, and offer me commiseration. Instead, he remained on the spot, milking the attention for all its worth as the circle of admirers expanded. My plan hadn't worked, so much for listening to Ruby's voice. I wandered off feeling downbeat, and wishing I'd listened to my own voice and scored the winning goal.

Flo ambled towards me. 'Never mind, Oakley, at least it was a draw, although anyone would have thought the boys had won by the way they're acting. Are you staying for a bite to eat?'

'Sorry, Flo, I've left Willow for far too long on her own. Please say goodbye to everyone. Please tell Beau I had to go home.'

'Of course, thank you for your help, do you want me and Trent to walk home with you?'

'Thank you but no, it won't take me long to walk up the path. Is it okay to leave my canoe and kayak in the clubhouse? I'll pick them up during the week.'

'Of course. Thanks for your help today.'

'You're welcome, it was fun. Enjoy the rest of the weekend. I'll catch up with you during the week. Night, Flo.'

'Night, Oakley.'

Within ten minutes, I arrived at Catkins to find Willow sprawled on the sofa. Nutmeg was lying on a cushion by her head, Cinnamon on her lap and Jasmine across her feet. The fire was crackling in the background while she watched a film. We chatted for ages listening to stories about each other's day. It was lovely having Willow to chat to, and the cats adored her; maybe I wasn't cut out to live a life of solitude.

We headed upstairs to bed followed by the cats who couldn't decide which room to sleep in. Jasmine followed Willow, Cinnamon followed me, and Nutmeg took up her normal spot on the top of the stairs, guarding all of us.

Chapter Thirty-three
Paddington, Bailey and Daisy

The following week, Willow settled in and secured a part-time job at the Lily Pad. Saturday morning dawned, and we were both as excited as each other to be collecting Paddington.

'How much further, Oakley?'

'We're almost there.'

'I'm so excited, it's like all our Christmas's rolled in together. Is this the house?'

'Yes, Paw-Some Rescue.'

We parked the car, rang the bell, and were greeted by Neave, the owner who seemed as excited as us.

'Morning, ladies, the big day has finally arrived.'

'Hi, Neave, this is Willow my niece who's living with me. I'm not sure who is more excited.'

'Nice to meet you, Willow, come in, the puppies are in the play area. Watch out for the kittens.'

Willow nearly tripped over a pair of black-and-white kittens as they chased each other in the hallway.

'Oh, my goodness, Oakley, they're adorable.'

'Aren't they gorgeous? I love the white one with a black saddle and black tip on his tail.'

'I love the black one with a white heart and white tip on her tail.'

Neave popped her head around the door. 'Everything okay?'

'Sorry, we were admiring your kittens.'

'Gorgeous, aren't they? The dad is a Maine Coon, and the mum a Ragdoll. They're the last of the litter. If you know anyone who would like them, please let me know.'

Willow squealed with delight: 'Oakley, can we have them? I'll help look after them.'

'They're adorable, are you sure you want to part with them?' I said.

'Yes, they were born here as the owner couldn't cope with the prospect of eight kittens so handed the mum into us. The mum has been spayed and rehomed along with the other kittens; these are the only two remaining. I was secretly hoping you'd take them as they adore Paddington.'

'We'd love to adopt them, wouldn't we, Willow?'

Neave opened the hallway door and five sheepadoodles almost flattened us.

'Seriously! We'd love them. Which puppy is Paddington?'

'He's sitting at your feet.'

'Oh my goodness, he is the most adorable puppy I have ever seen.'

Paddington licked Willow's hand, and then mine. We fastened his harness and Neave handed us a carrier containing two mischievous kittens, alongside a bag with blankets, toys and kitten food. Bang goes my peace and quiet; in the last few days I'd acquired a puppy, two kittens, and a sixteen-year-old girl.

We returned home, settled the kittens into the dining room and closed the door. Nutmeg, Jasmine and Cinnamon sniffed the outside, before turning their attention to Paddington. He jumped up and down with excitement, keen to say hello to his new friends. Jasmine and Cinnamon turned their backs on him, and slinked upstairs, but Nutmeg boldly walked straight up to him and told him she was in charge.

'Willow, would you mind keeping an eye on Paddington while I feed the kittens?'

'Can I take him into the garden?'

'Yes, it's been a week since he had his last injection, but only for five minutes. Show him where he is meant to do his business. If he goes there, please praise him and give him a treat. Whatever you do, don't let go of his lead. I'll be out in five minutes. We need to think of names for the kittens. Do you like the names Bailey and Daisy?'

'I love them.'

'Perfect. Now remember, don't under any circumstances let go of Paddington's lead.'

Willow stood astride and pointed to her mouth. 'Oakley, read my lips; I am not going to let go of his lead.'

I handed her Paddington's lead. 'Cheeky madam.'

Ten minutes later, Willow stood in the doorway holding a dogless lead. Close to tears she wailed, 'Oakley, I'm sorry, I didn't let go of the lead, I tried to stop him, but he slipped the harness and ... he just jumped in.'

'Oh my word, Willow, jumped in where?'

Willow cried, 'He chased some ducks onto the island in the middle of the pond. Now he's doggy-paddling around the island and won't come back.'

'Don't worry, I'll grab my sit-on-top kayak from the barn.'

We carried the kayak between us and dashed down to the pond. Paddington was still swimming around the island chasing the ducks.

We dropped my kayak onto the embankment, and I banged my thighs with my hands. 'Paddington, come here boy ... Paddington ...' However, Paddington's mind was set on rounding up his new friends and he didn't pay me a blind bit of notice.

'Willow, please can you fetch his squeaky Donald Duck, it's probably still in the car. I'll paddle out, press Donald's squeaker, and once I get Paddington's attention, I can grab him and haul him onto my kayak.'

'Okay, I'll be back shortly.'

Willow returned a few minutes later and threw Donald Duck to me. I paddled towards Paddington and pressed Donald's tummy, prompting Donald to quack incessantly. Paddington raised his ears and doggy-paddled towards me at a faster pace than I could backpaddle. This was not going to end well.

Ten seconds later, my sit-on-top and I parted company, and it zoomed across the pond with Donald Duck as the only passenger. Paddington swam after Donald Duck, and I swam after Paddington while my kayak surfed to the edge of the pond. Willow grabbed Donald Duck and ran backwards, as Paddington charged out of the pond and followed her. I crawled up the muddy embankment praying no leaches had found their way under my clothes. A round of applause sang out, and when we looked towards Catkins. Beau and Dustin were howling in laughter like a pack of jackals. Bubbles was like a bouncing kangaroo when he saw his brother, and the two of them jumped on top of each other until Dustin managed to grab Paddington.

Beau sounded like a snorting pig. 'And you said Willow didn't have any of your traits. She certainly picked up the love of mud baths.'

Willow was mortified. 'Oakley, Dustin can't see me looking like this, I need a shower.'

I reattached Paddington's lead and harness while Willow dashed back to Catkins.

Beau's laughter subsided. 'Oakley, sorry to turn up unannounced, but Dustin and I wanted to see if Paddington was being as good as Bubbles.'

'He's been home less than an hour and as you can see, we've discovered Paddington, like his owner, gravitates towards mud and water. Beau, fancy following me into the shower in the utility room?'

Beau turned to Dustin. 'See, mate, one day you'll be as popular as me, and maybe women will be dropping to their knees and inviting you into their shower.'

Dustin shrugged his shoulders. 'No, you're all right I don't need to be that popular. I'll put the kettle on and make everyone drinks.'

'Thank you, Dustin, I would love a black coffee. If you peep into the dining room, you might get a nice surprise,' I said dragging Paddington towards the doggy shower.

'I'd love a mug of tea please, Dustin, but first it's time to have a shower with Oakley.'

Bubbles shadowed Paddington until I switched the shower on, then he made a sharp exit. Paddington jumped up and grabbed the shower head off Beau spraying him in filthy water.

'You've got a right one here, Oakley, not sure how you're going to keep Paddington in your canoe. I think this deserves another meal; fancy going out tonight? I'm sure Dustin will be happy to take care of Willow.'

'I'm sure Willow can take care of herself. What time?'

'Pick you up in a couple of hours. I thought we might give another pub a try.'

'Sounds great, I might have dried Paddington off by then. I can't stay out too long as it's Paddington's first night, and I have two kittens.'

'You what? Where?'

'They're in the dining room as I thought it was too much to introduce my cats to the kittens and a puppy in one day. I'll let my cats sniff around the door for a bit before I introduce them.'

'So, you have five cats, a gigantic puppy and a sixteen-year-old living with you?'

'Yes. I don't think I'm destined for a quiet life.'

'You're telling me. I'd best be off, see you in a couple of hours.'

I was feeling guilty leaving Paddington and the kittens on their first night and wished I hadn't said yes to Beau. However, Willow and Dustin assured me they would play with them.

Willow persuaded me to wear a skirt, and in record time, I was ready. Soon, Beau and I were speeding away into the night. He took me by surprise when he released his hand from the steering wheel and placed it on my knee. A few seconds later his hand skimmed under my skirt and began traveling up the inside of my thigh.

'Beau, watch out!'

He removed his hand and braked. 'What was it?'

'A deer was about to step out, you'd better keep your eyes on the road.'

'It was lucky you spotted it.'

For the remainder of the journey he kept both hands on the steering wheel.

The pub was a lovely chocolate-box thatch, lit up by twinkling fairy lights. We found a table by a blazing log fire and ordered our meals. This was turning out to be the best day ever. I nipped to the ladies, and when I returned Beau was texting someone. He placed the phone on the side of the table and started talking loudly about himself. I sat listening intently unable to get a word in. He only stopped talking when a young waitress delivered our food. He couldn't keep his eyes off her and peered over his shoulder as she returned to the kitchen. He swallowed a mouthful of food and picked up his phone. Smiling, he began texting again before shovelling more food into his mouth. I had no idea who he was texting and found it irritating and rude. The phone beeped again, he smirked, stuffed more food in his mouth and texted his reply.

With his mouth full he spluttered, 'I don't want a dessert, how about you?'

'No, I'm fine, I'll ask for the bill.'

The waitress left the bill in a saucer on the table. Beau scanned her like an x-ray machine; I could have sworn he was undressing her with his eyes. I picked the bill up from the saucer and headed to the bar to pay. When I returned, Beau opened his wallet and pulled out four five-pound notes and placed them on the saucer for the waitress.

I lifted my jacket from the back of the chair. 'Isn't that a bit much for a tip? That's more than fifty percent of the bill.'

'I know, but I didn't pay. She's been very attentive. Didn't you ever wait on tables?'

'No, but if I had I'd have been a bit suspicious of being given such a huge tip!'

The waitress returned to collect the plates, she glanced at me as she picked the saucer up and collected the money. When she counted the money, Beau's business card slipped out onto the floor.

The waitress read the business card and stared at him.

'I don't think I'll be needing this, sir.'

'Sorry, how did that get there? Must have been caught in my wallet. You keep it, you never know when you may need my services.'

She flicked the card onto the table. 'Never, sir, thank you.'

Beau sprang up like a cheetah and knocked over the remains of his pint, and his phone slid across the table in a direct path towards the open fire.

I leapt up, avoiding the deluge, and caught his phone with one hand.

'I used to field for my brothers at their cricket matches, they didn't nickname me the one-handed dolly for nothing.'

Without thanking me, Beau growled, 'I thought a dolly was an easy catch.'

'I'm no easy catch, Beau.'

'I'm beginning to realise that. Come on, let's go.'

'What about clearing the mess up?'

'The waitress can do that; I gave her a big enough tip.'

We climbed into his car, and I barely had time to fasten my seat belt before Beau wheel spun out of the car park. He raced through the lanes with music blaring, and neither of us spoke another word. I clung on to my seat belt and prayed nothing was heading towards us as he cornered each bend. I was relieved when he dropped me home in one piece, before speeding down the track, without even saying goodbye.

I opened my front door, and before heading to bed, checked on Paddington and the kittens; all three were sound asleep. Trying not to disturb Willow, I crept up the stairs and stepped over Nutmeg, who for once didn't flinch.

The landing light flickered on, and Willow appeared in her dressing gown with her hands on her hips.

'What time do you call this, young lady?' she said, trying not to laugh. 'It's past your bedtime.'

'Sorry, am I grounded? I promise I'll stay in tomorrow night and cook tea.'

'You're the one being punished, not me.'

'You're a cheeky madam, maybe we could go out for fish and chips.'

'I suppose I could let you off the hook, this time. Did you have a good evening?'

'Yes, it was great, I lied. How about you?'

'Wonderful, Dustin and I played with the kittens, and Paddington and Bubbles. Dustin even cooked tea. He's so kind and thoughtful.'

'He is, you're very lucky to have found each other. What time did he leave?'

'Lily picked Dustin up half an hour ago. I'm glad you had a nice evening; I'm going back to bed. Night, Oakley.'

'Night, Willow.'

I slid under my duvet, closed my eyes and Beau was not invited into my dreams.

Chapter Thirty-four
Foraging Weekend

Beau avoided me the following week, and that suited me just fine. Luckily, I was scheduled to work at Madhatters on Saturday so could avoid Beau for a bit longer. Following my last home visit on Friday afternoon, I popped back into Madhatters to find Beau leaning against the receptionist's desk; so much for avoiding him.

Aidan glanced up, swigging his coffee. 'Afternoon, Oakley, I wasn't expecting you back today. Beau was just telling me he's double-booked paddling this weekend so will have to cancel the foraging event. I know you're scheduled to work Saturday, but Madge said she'd cover for you if you wouldn't mind helping Beau Saturday and Sunday. You can take Monday and Tuesday off instead.'

Beau swivelled around, scowling at Aidan. 'I told you Oakley wouldn't want to paddle on a foraging weekend; it's not her sort of thing.'

I wanted to say no, I'd rather work at Madhatters, but I was so annoyed at Beau's attitude my brain was incapable of engaging with my mouth.

'Foraging sounds like fun. I'm sure Willow will be happy to have the house to herself, but I'm not going unless I can take Paddington.'

'I suppose that would be okay. Wolf will be coming too; you can swim after the pair of them when they go doggy-paddling.'

'Paddington has his own doggy buoyancy aid now. Where are we paddling?'

Beau handed me a copy of the itinerary, which included a map and a list of edible seaweeds. My eyes scanned across the route before wavering at the lunch stop.

'Thong-Weed Cove. Then paddling and staying overnight in Fucus Nookie. Really? Is this for real?'

Beau's facial features didn't flinch. 'Yes, both coves are named after seaweeds.'

I was having qualms about this trip.

'Seriously, there are seaweeds with those names?'

'Yes, and there's one called False Eyelash Weed and Little Fat Sausage.'

Beau turned to Aidan. 'Not sure she believes us, Aide, show her your map.'

Aidan pushed his chair back. 'Sure, I'll fetch it from my office.' He returned a few minutes later and pointed to the coves of Thong-Weed and Fucus Nookie. 'People found it hard to navigate between the rocks at high tide in Fucus Nookie, so the locals built a quay. The cove is a regular spot for a bit of ... what shall we say, a bit of nookie, so it was named Fucus Nookie.'

'Sounds like a wind-up to me. What will we be foraging?

'Seaweed, Sea beet, kale, crabs, and I'll bring along the fishing rods. Tents are banned, but you can bring a tarp. Phones must be switched off and only used in an emergency.'

'I'd better go home and get ready.'

'Remember, it's back to mother nature, we'll eat what we can forage and practise rubbing sticks together or use a flint – no matches or lighters.'

Aidan ushered me to the door. 'Fucus Nookie is quite sheltered; you might need protection as it can get pretty warm in the sun.'

Aidan nudged Beau. 'Though I'm sure my nephew has thought of that. I'll lock up, best you get home.'

Beau grinned and tapped his top overall pocket. 'Always have protection with me, you never know when I'm feeling a bit hot under my collar.'

'I like a man who's not ashamed to admit he carries protection. Mine's waterproof factor fifty and is especially good for sensitive areas. Trust yours is good for sensitive areas too, Beau?'

Beau leant back on the desk and warbled like a lark. 'Yep, Oakley, I guess you could say that, used it on sensitive areas plenty of times, and I've never had any complaints.'

Aidan swallowed his coffee down the wrong way, choked, jumped up and disappeared out the back.

'What time are we meeting?'

'Meet me at the boat shed around eight-thirty in the morning. I'd better check on Aidan. See you tomorrow, Oakley.'

'See you in the morning, Beau.'

I shouted out the back, 'Bye, Aidan, see you Wednesday.'

'Bye, Oakley, enjoy your weekend.'

Not trusting them one bit, I popped into the Lily Pad to speak to Lily. Willow was working behind the counter.

'Hi, Oakley, would you like a piece of shortbread? I've just made it.'

I helped myself to a slice. 'Thanks, it looks amazing.' I paused as my tastebuds tingled. 'That's the nicest shortbread I have ever tasted. I can see who is doing the cooking for our summer party. Do you know when Lily will be back?'

'No idea, she was meant to call, but she's left her phone in her apron pocket. Mackenzie just rang, he sounded lovely, he left a message for Lily that he needed advice about a girl.'

'Did he know who you were?'

'No, I just said I was helping out in my holidays.'

'I wonder who the girl is? It's none of my business, especially as I was so rude to him.'

'You could always apologise.'

'I will at the right moment. I have a favour to ask, would you mind house and cat-sitting for the weekend? I've been asked to work at FloBeau.'

Willow's eyes lit up. 'I'd love to, where are you going?'

'Beau needs an additional instructor on a foraging and canoeing weekend. Madge is covering my shift at Madhatters.'

'Are you taking Paddington?'

'Yes, Wolf is coming too.'

'Would you mind if Dustin stayed over?'

'Can you behave yourselves?'

Willow peered down her nose. 'Of course. We want to look at our college courses to see what books we need.'

'When did you grow up so fast?'

Willow giggled. 'When I left home. I'd better text Dustin, when will you be home?'

'With the incoming tide on Sunday.'

Willow handed me another piece of shortbread. 'This is for when you get home. I've left a vegan casserole in the slow cooker.' She wandered towards me and put her arms around me. 'Thanks for trusting me. We won't get up to mischief, Dustin isn't like that.'

'I know you won't. Thanks for tea, it sounds amazing. What time will you be home?'

'About six-thirty.'

'Great, see you later.'

'Bye, Oakley.'

I headed home wondering what advice Mackenzie needed about a girl, but I put it to the back of my mind as something else was niggling me. I hated going away for the weekend leaving Willow and the cats. My job description didn't include working overnight for FloBeau, and the last person I wanted to spend the weekend with was Beau, but as usual, I found it hard to say no when people asked for my help. I would have to speak to Madigan about working away at the weekends.

Willow arrived home and we devoured her delicious casserole. With my lack of foraging experience, it may have been my last meal until Sunday night. I retired to bed early in anticipation of what lay ahead, especially paddling with a giant puppy.

Chapter Thirty-five
Fucus Nookie

The sun beamed through my curtains as I rose early with a cock crowing. Despite a wave of guilt washing over me, I hid butter, and a lemon to accompany the fish and seaweed; I was sure Beau wouldn't notice. With hardly any packing needed, and just one dry bag Paddington and I were soon ready for our adventure.

After securing the Beast to the trolley wheels, Paddington jumped in expecting me to tow him. I tossed my dry bag behind him and lugged the whole caboodle towards the footpath. Following a commotion of lifting, pushing, and a lot of swearing, we were soon through the kissing gates and on our way to the boathouse.

A high-pitched shrill of giggling could be heard for miles as we rounded the final corner and spotted Flo and Trent.

'Mornin', Oakley, isn't the weather great? I think we're in for a scorcher, sorry we double-booked, at least you get to spend the weekend with my brother.'

'Morning, Flo, morning, Trent. The weather is perfect, and I can't wait to paddle to the coves.' I said ignoring the comment about spending time with Beau.

Trent called Paddington, rubbed behind his ears, and spun around.

'Oakley, are you still driving up to the Driftwood Islands in Scotland next weekend? It's a long way to drive on your own.'

'I'm not sure, but if I do go, I'm quite capable of driving up on my own. Why do you want to know?'

'Mackenzie invited me and Beau. Flo is working, and I'm a bit worried that now I'm taken, you won't be able to keep your hands off me.'

Flo nudged him. 'Oakley, please ignore him, I've not said anything, he just has a massive—'

Trent interrupted whilst sniggering. 'Don't tell her that, woman, there's no way she'll keep her hands off me now.'

Flo giggled. 'You sound like my brother. You have two things that are massive – your head and your ego.' Flo turned to me. 'Oakley, I'm not the slightest bit worried about you controlling yourself around Trent, especially if Beau is going.'

'Don't worry, Flo, Trent is quite safe around me.' I said without mentioning Beau.

Flo grabbed Trents hand. 'Come on, Mr Egotistical, we'd better get the kayaks ready. Have a lovely weekend, Oakley.'

'You too.'

It was obvious Trent was smitten with Flo, even though he glanced over his shoulder and blew me a sly kiss; talk about cheeky. The minute they were out of earshot, a blanket of peace and tranquillity wrapped itself around me, but it was short-lived as Wolf raced to greet Paddington and they danced around in the sea, yelping with joy. Wolf crept towards me shaking himself from side to side and soaking me in the process. Beau appeared from the footpath with a huge dry bag slung over his shoulder and another one hanging from his arm. It seemed a bit excessive for a foraging weekend.

'Oakley, sorry I'm late.' Beau paused, glared at me and raised his voice. 'Oh my god, can you not go anywhere without getting covered in water and mud?'

'Blame your dog who just shook himself in front of me.'

He handed me a paper bag and a cappuccino. 'Oh, sorry, I know this doesn't fit in with the ethos of wild camping, but I won't tell if you don't.'

I peeped in the bag to find two, warm, chocolate almond croissants. 'I don't mind you being late if you come bearing gifts like this. Where's yours?'

'Very funny. Scoot over and we can eat these before we head off.'

I wiped the crumbs off my top. 'That was delicious, thank you.'

'No worries.' He paused as Paddington shook himself in front of us. 'Oakley, how are you going to keep Paddington in your canoe?'

'I have a plan.' I pointed to the bow of the Beast where Paddington's duck was tied in firmly. 'He won't jump out without Donald.'

Beau shook his head. 'Oakley, he's just a dog. You spoil him too much.'

I rubbed Paddington's ears. 'He's not just a dog, are you Paddington? He's my best friend, aren't you boy?' Paddington licked my hand. 'See, he understands everything I say.'

'Sometimes, Oakley, I think you're as crazy as Fanny Flocker.'

'Well, us crazy girls have to stick together. Now, are we paddling today or not?'

'I'm ready, we're meeting the others at nine-thirty in the harbour.'

'We'd better get a move on then.'

We paddled down the estuary, to find an empty harbour.

'My mates are late, as usual. I'll give them a call.'

'What mates? I thought it was a group of twelve clients.'

'It was two groups of six, but one group dropped out this morning. Now it's just my mates from the Scorpions, their girlfriends, and two more girls.'

'I see, well, I hope they haven't got lost.'

Beau reached for his phone. 'So do I. I'll call them.'

He paddled further up the estuary, so I wasn't party to the conversation, though with the breeze blowing towards me, my ears picked up every word.

'Mate, we're in the harbour at Whispering Pines. Where are you?' Beau paused. 'You're where? That's miles ahead of us. We'll paddle along the coast and meet you at Thong-Weed Cove.' Beau sniggered. 'Tell her I'm looking forward to seeing her again too. He paused again. 'Hi, Lottie, glad you could make it, there's plenty of room in my canoe if you want to paddle with me. I'll teach you how to paddle tandem.' He hesitated. 'No, you won't get that wet. Oh, you don't like walking through seaweed, don't worry I'll carry you to the top of the beach.' He wavered. 'I've missed you too. See you shortly, Lottie.'

Beau returned to his canoe. 'Sorry about that, seems they're miles ahead, we'll have to catch them up.'

My ears were ringing from the news that Beau was looking forward to seeing a girl called Lottie. I felt my chest tighten and heat rise through my body, I guessed that explained who he was texting in the pub. Mackenzie was right, Beau wasn't interested in a relationship, he hadn't got what he wanted, and had given up, and moved on. What an eejit I was, Lottie was welcome to him. If it wasn't for the fact I was employed as an instructor for the weekend, I'd have gone home. The sprinkling of happiness I'd felt when I first met Beau had transformed into a dull feeling in the pit of my stomach.

'Oakley, wakey, wakey.'

I picked my paddle up and swallowed my tears. 'Sorry, I was miles away. Guess we'd better catch your mates up.'

What I really wanted to say was you effing arsehole I'm off home, but it wouldn't look good if I fell out with my boss's son. There were plenty more fish in the sea, but why did I always find the sharks?

We set off at an impressive speed, and I hardly had time to catch my breath between each stroke. At least I matched Beau's speed, so he couldn't complain about that.

'Oakley, have you got your sail with you?'

'Yes.'

'If we rig them, we'll be sure to catch up with the others.'

'Fine, but I am going to have to move Donald Duck.'

Soon we were gliding over the cat-whisker waves, and in no time arrived to find a deserted Thong-Weed Cove. Paddington and Wolf leapt out of the canoes and chased terns across the beach.

'Beau, where is everyone?'

'No idea, they should have been here by now; it's eleven-thirty. Maybe we missed them. Let's stop here for a bit and see if they catch us up.'

'How could we have missed them? Do you want a drink? I've brought the Kelly Kettle with me.'

'Maybe they were paddling through one of the caves. I'd love a coffee, thanks. I'll stroll to the end of the cove and collect driftwood.'

'Why? There's plenty of driftwood next to me.'

'It looks drier at the end of the cove.'

'You must have amazing eyesight. Did you bring a water bowl for Wolf? The dogs are thirsty.'

'Under the airbag in the bow.'

Beau meandered to the end of the cove, texting as he walked. He scrambled to the top of a rock, which seemed a strange place to search for driftwood. With plenty of driftwood at my feet, I gave up waiting and filled the Kelly Kettle. While I sipped my coffee, Beau remained glued to the rock and didn't return for half an hour.

'You've been gone ages, what happened to collecting driftwood?'

'What's wrong with the driftwood next to you?'

'Nothing, but you said ... oh, what's the point?'

'Let's head off now.'

'Are we not waiting for your mates?'

'No, I can't get any reception, they must have missed the entrance to the cove and carried on to Fucus Nookie.'

That was odd, how could he have been texting without reception?

Beau glared at me and ordered me as if I was Wolf: 'Oakley, come on, stop dilly-dallying around, let's go. Wolf, here.'

I was beginning to wish I'd gone home. It wasn't too late to paddle back and leave him to find his mates on his own. But my decisive head told me to stay, Paddington and Wolf were having so much fun, and Willow and Dustin wouldn't be too pleased to see me home early. If I stayed, I could warn Lottie what Beau was like; it was only one night, I'd just have to put up with him.

My arms were beginning to ache when at last Fucus Nookie came into sight. It was an amazing cove, splattered in rockpools with a quay rising to the top. After removing my shoes, I curled my toes and dug them into the sand. It was so invigorating as the sand massaged the souls of my feet. Without a word, Beau dragged his canoe to the top of the cove and disappeared with his phone. I slipped my trolley wheels onto the Beast and hauled it to the top. The bottom of the cliff was strewn with dead seaweed, which prompted my decision to set up camp after high tide. I settled down on my Therm-a-Rest chair and waited for Beau to return.

Beau wandered back along the beach. 'Oakley, why haven't you set up camp and started foraging for everyone's tea? You'll need to set up the fishing lines too.'

'It's a spring tide, I'll wait until after high tide.'

'No, that was last night.'

'Are you sure?'

Beau fetched the fishing rods from his canoe and handed them to me. 'Of course, you had better find bait for the hooks and light a fire.'

'What about your mates?'

'I'm going to the other end of the cove to see if I can find any reception.'

I checked my phone, which showed full reception. Beau wandered towards the cliffs while I collected wood for a fire. Paddington raced towards me carrying a child's plastic spade and dropped it at my feet. It brought back memories of burying my brothers in the sand. Right now, I'd like to bury Beau right up to his neck and leave his head poking out for the gulls and terns to peck.

Beau returned, whistling, and full of the joys of spring.

'My mates turned back as the girls didn't like the gale-force wind and huge white horses. Come on, let's paddle back and meet them. They've booked rooms overnight in a pub.'

I bit my lower lip and looked out to sea.

'The waves look more like Shetland ponies than huge white horses. I'm not paddling back now; you can go on your own, I'm staying here with Paddington, anyway, I doubt the pub allows dogs to stay in the rooms.' I said, deciding it was high time I started standing up to people and saying no.

Beau sighed. 'I guess it's getting a bit late to paddle back. I'll see what they say.' He wandered to the end of the beach, while I built a fire pyramid to cook the invisible fish. With a spark from my flintstone, the fire was soon roaring away.

He wandered back and was in a much cheerier mood.

'All settled, they've made other plans. I'll catch up with them later. I'd better feed Wolf.' He strolled to the stern of his canoe, retrieved the largest dry bag, fed Wolf, and left the dry bag on the rocks.

'Beau, it's past teatime. Are you coming fishing?'

'I'm not hungry, you go ahead and see what you can catch.'

How could he not be hungry? I was starving. My enthusiasm for catching fish and eating seaweed had long since evaporated; I'd rather have eaten the dog biscuits.

'Beau, where's the loud music coming from? Sounds like someone's having a party.'

'Not sure, seems to be coming from around the headland.'

The volume increased twofold as a boat appeared decorated top to bottom in fairy lights and revolving disco balls.

Beau grabbed the bow of his canoe. 'It's the Saturday night eighties and nineties disco boat. Remember the inflatable gull you found? Probably came adrift from that boat. I'm going to paddle out and say hello.'

'Great idea, I love a disco, shall we take the dogs with us?'

Beau had already dragged his canoe halfway down the beach.

'No, I won't be long, you can stay here with the dogs and catch fish for our tea.' He shouted from over his shoulder.

He paddled towards the disco boat in tune with Five Star singing; "Stay Out Of My Life" I reached for my binoculars, and as Beau circled the disco boat, I spotted him chatting to a group of people leaning over the railings. A woman caught the bow painter, tied it to the railings and Beau climbed on board. A Janet Jackson medley followed including, "When I Think of You", "What Have You Done For Me Lately?" and "Nasty!" Maybe someone was trying to send me a message. Whitney Houston followed with, "How Will I Know", which was one of my favourite songs, and in normal circumstances, would have seen me belting out the lyrics, though my heart wasn't in it today. The music continued blaring while I sat waiting for Beau to return.

"The Tide Is High" boomed out of the speakers, and when I glanced at my feet, the tide really was high, and my fire was about to be swamped. My childhood dam-building skills flooded back, and with the help from two slobbering dogs, sand flew everywhere. They were shovelling at such a rate that my scoops with the plastic spade were paltry in comparison. The dogs appeared to be digging for gold, or maybe a long-lost bone.

At last, the fire stood proud, like a castle surrounded by a high wall and moat. but even I couldn't hold back the tide. As Take That chanted, "Relight My Fire!" there was about as much chance of that as there was of me eating seaweed for my tea. Waves were in touching distance of the cliffs, and the last embers of the fire were extinguished. Both dogs jumped onto the quay, and I hauled the Beast alongside them. Wolf began barking non-stop, and I noticed Beau's dry bag was about to be washed into the sea. I timed the waves to perfection as I dodged them, retrieved it, and crawled back onto the quay.

The sun sank into the sea and the sky was transformed into a peach melba with splashings of lemon and orange. I checked my phone. Surely that couldn't be right? Beau had been gone for hours. With daylight dwindling, I scoured the boat with my binoculars. On a second sweep, I noticed Beau sliding back into his canoe. With my eyes glued to the binoculars once again I scanned the disco boat. Rather than paddling back to the cove, Beau passed his dry bag and paddle to a man on the deck. He climbed back onto the disco boat and between them heaved his canoe on board. The boat's engine started, in tune to Swing Out Sister singing, "Breakout!" and as it chugged into the distance, Green Day sang the lyrics to "Good Riddance (Time Of Your Life)". I listened to the remaining lyrics until they were out of earshot. They summed my life up completely.

I owed Mackenzie a huge apology, his words had been akin to an earworm niggling at the back of my mind; it seemed I'd had a lucky escape.

The tide turned and retreated, leaving mounds of decaying seaweed were strewn across the beach. A carpet of tiny crabs scurried in every direction; they were even more indecisive than me. Scooping the seaweed with my foot I cleared a space for my groundsheet, and seconds later it was smothered in hundreds of sandhoppers jumping like kids on a trampoline. Oh my word, the sandhoppers were more dithering than either me or the crabs. Surely Beau realised the beach would be teaming with creepy crawlies. I couldn't possibly sleep in the open with sandhoppers jumping all over me. Now what was I going to do?

My stomach rumbled, reminding me I hadn't eaten anything since breakfast, and the dogs' biscuits were becoming more appealing by the minute. Wolf barked, announcing it was long past his teatime. I opened Beau's dry bag and Wolf pushed his nose inside in the hope of sniffing a tasty morsel. He backed up, barked again, and the look on his face melted my heart. Beau seemed to have an awful lot of kit considering it was a foraging weekend. I reached inside and pulled out a small freezer bag. When I unzipped the top, Wolf pushed his nose inside. Despite the smell of Beau's kit, Wolf could sniff a sausage out anywhere. I threw each dog a sausage and hesitated at the remainder. Though as tempting as they were, I wasn't about to eat the dogs' treats. Hidden under the sausages was a package wrapped in greaseproof paper, and on opening it, I nearly fell backwards. What a scoundrel! So much for foraging – lying in front of me were two pasties and two slices of pizza, oh my days, and I was worried about sneaking a knob of butter and a lemon!

Before my hunger pains were quashed, I wondered what else was hiding amongst his kit. I put the freezer bag aside and tipped the remaining contents into the Beast. A tub containing a selection of Lily's croissants rolled out, followed by a bag of cheese tortilla crisps, a jar of salsa, a huge bar of chocolate, two cans of cider and then ... No! Really? How could he? What an arsehole! Sitting in the pile of goodies was a two-person tent. So while I was expected to eat seaweed, gut fish, and sleep among crabs and sandhoppers, Beau was going to scoff Lily's goodies inside his tent! To be honest, arsehole didn't hit the spot, however removing us from Fucus and replacing it with him, was a bullseye! I was relieved Willow had interrupted the night on the sofa, and thank goodness Mackenzie's voice had been niggling the back of my mind, it was high time I apologised.

Me: Hi Mackenzie, I'm so sorry I was rude. I should have listened when you told me about Beau. I realise now that you were just looking out for me. Sorry I was wearing my stubborn head and wanting to find things out myself; I always learn the hard way!

Mackenzie: Hi Oakley, that's fine I should have been more subtle. Is everything okay?

Me: It is now I've opened my eyes to Beau. Why do I always choose the wrong ones?

Mackenzie: Don't judge us all by Beau's actions. There are some nice men out there waiting to be found.

Me: I'm sure there are, but for now, they can stay in hiding. I've got Paddington to look after, plus I've adopted two kittens in addition to my three cats, and my niece Willow has moved in. We're going to build a chicken run and plant a whole array of vegetables. I'm organising a summer garden party and the fete. Combined with work, I think that's enough to keep me going for the moment!

Mackenzie: Sounds exhausting, you're doing a good job of fitting in. My mum told me about the kittens, and little brother Dustin is smitten with Willow. Will you still have time to drive up for my birthday next week? I'll understand if you're too busy. Though May is the perfect time to visit the Driftwood Islands.

Me: I'll make time if you're positive you're not angry with me for being so rude to you? I'll also have to check Willow is okay to cat and dog sit. If she is, I might ask Lily to keep an eye on her. Willow is a very capable sixteen-year-old, but I still don't like leaving her on her own for too long.

Mackenzie: I'm sure Lily would love to keep an eye on her. I've never been angry with you! More annoyed at myself for poking my nose in.

Me: Don't be, it showed you cared. I need to listen to advice and stop being so pig-headed! My mum says it's one of my many faults!

Mackenzie: Oh dear, are there more? Ha, ha, ha.

Me: Hundreds!

Mackenzie: I call it free-spirited!

Me: My mum tells me I need to rein my spirit in.

Mackenzie: Never! Or you wouldn't be you. Sorry, I'm on call and have a call waiting. Catch up with your soon. Night, Oakley.

Me: Thank you for being so understanding. Glad we're talking again. Night, Mackenzie.

An eeriness fell over the cove as the moon glistened on the sea. After erecting the tent and settling down to eat my feast, I peered behind to see Wolf lying inside the tent; this was one time I could guarantee waking up next to a smelly, hairy male with dog breath. I slid inside, my sleeping bag sandwiched between Wolf and Paddington. Within seconds, the rhythmic lapping of the waves sent me into dreamland. Woody was still trying to reach my hand, but as Mackenzie paddled towards me, it seemed he had a bit of competition. Though in reality, it was just my luck they were both already taken.

Chapter Thirty-six
Peace and Quiet are so Overrated

The following morning, the cackling and squawking of gulls awoke me and both dogs dashed out of the tent. I peered through the open door and a feeling of happiness shot through my veins. The horizon had been transformed to a pallet of soft apricot, pink and mauve wisps of clouds resembling the sails on a fleet of yachts. There was barely a ripple on the sea, and in the distance, two seal's heads peeped out, before disappearing and re-emerging closer. What an amazing landscape. High tide wasn't for another four hours, which left plenty of time for rock pooling following my morning coffee and croissants, and as for Beau, he was well and truly in my past.

I loved rockpools; they were like a portal into another world. Limpets and mussels clung to the sides of rocks while a common blenny darted into overhanging purple laver seaweed. A hermit crab scurried across the sand and as a tiny starfish moved out of its way the tentacles of a sea anemone were ignited. I was captivated by the tranquillity, until there was a loud splosh as Paddington plopped his ball into the pool. He scrutinised me from under his long eyelashes and woofed as if to say, 'What yer doing, Mum? Let's play a game.' I threw the ball as far as I could and watched both dogs charge after it. Wolf snatched the ball and gambolled towards me, while Paddington returned dragging a huge piece of kelp. I left them playing a game of tug of war and packed up the camp ready for our long paddle home.

After a few pitstops along the way, Whispering Pines harbour came into sight. I surfed the Beast onto the beach in front of the Lily Pad, and both dogs launched themselves onto the pebbles. Lily rushed to greet me.

'Hi, Lily.'

Lily held the bow of the Beast as I stepped out. 'Oakley, thank God you're alright, we've been worried out of our minds.'

'What? Why?'

'Aidan left about half an hour ago to pick Beau up. Beau said he became separated from you while waiting for his mates. He paddled off to look for them, but darkness fell, and he was picked up by a boat and taken back to the dock.'

Unable to speak, my mouth dried up as we found a table in the garden. I plonked myself down on a chair.

'Did he mention why I have Wolf? And why he didn't call me?'

Lily sat down beside me. 'No, he said you didn't have a phone and he weren't sure where you were. Why didn't he have Wolf?'

I stood up allowing the heat to radiate to my head, and my voice to travel.

'He left Wolf with me at Fucus Nookie while he paddled to a disco boat and didn't return.' I paused, took a depth breath, and put my hand into the front pouch of my buoyancy aid and raised my voice. 'I have a VHF radio and my phone. Lily, he knew I was at Fucus Nookie.'

Tuts, grunts, and huffs echoed around the café garden, and one lady told her children to cover their ears.

Lily's face was a picture; one side was fuming, and the other side trying not to laugh. 'It's pronounced Fewcus Nook Quay! Oakley, you'll frighten away my customers.'

A prickly heat radiated from my face as I sat down.

'Oh! How embarrassing! I'm so sorry.' I paused as heads turned and all eyes fixed on me. 'I do apologise, I'm new to the area, and have been misinformed of its pronunciation by a couple of local jokers.'

A woman with three children ushered them to the garden gate, before glancing over her shoulder and returning.

'Hi, I'm the local headmistress and the family over there are the local baker's wife and kids. Don't worry, people often pronounce it incorrectly, though not normally with such passion. I'd have words with those jokers if I was you.'

'I'm so sorry. I think heads will be rolling when I return to the practice. By the way, I'm Oakley Breeze, the new vet, it's lovely to meet you.'

The woman hovered at my table.

'The new vet! Nice to meet you too. No doubt we will be seeing more of each other. The vets visit at least once a month to talk to the children.'

'How wonderful, I love chatting to children,' I said, hoping to score Brownie points with the headmistress.

'I may need your assistance in a small matter involving hamsters, but we can talk about that another time. I'll be in touch soon.'

'Hamsters? Oh, okay, I'll look forward to it.'

The woman ushered her children to the car park, followed by the other mums.

'That were Mrs Pecker, can you imagine the nicknames the kids give her? Her husband is the local vicar; his name is Benedict. No doubt she'll wanna tell you the story of the hamster murders.'

'Poor woman. Hamster murders? Sounds revolting, how could anyone harm a hamster?' I dropped Beau's dry bag beside Lily. 'Would you mind returning Beau's dry bag? And can I leave Wolf with you? I can't face Beau.'

'Of course, I'll let Beau know Wolf is with me.'

'Look on the bright side, if Beau had stayed at Fucus Nook Quay, I would have slept in the open and feasted on seaweed.'

'Why didn't you take a tent? Everyone knows you can't sleep in the open at Fucus, too many sandhoppers and crabs. What happened to the food I gave Beau for you to share?'

'It was a wild foraging weekend, and we weren't meant to take food or tents. When I fed Wolf, I found Beau's tent and loads of food. No doubt he was going to share it with his girlfriend, Lottie.'

'I'm lost for words, love. I know he's my nephew, but what a rascal.'

'Don't worry, I believe in karma; something will happen in the future to pay him back. On the positive side, I've made up with Mackenzie. I'm hoping to drive up to Scotland next weekend to paddle to the Driftwood Islands. Would you mind keeping an eye on Willow for me?'

'Course I'll keep an eye on Willow. Mackenzie is a good lad he wouldn't treat you like Beau. Shame he's met someone else, the two of you would go together like strawberries and cream. By the way before I forget, Madigan said to tell you the contractors are tarmacing the track to Catkins next weekend, so no more bumpy journeys.'

'At last, the potholes were turning into craters. As for Mackenzie, we're just friends. I'm staying away from men for the foreseeable future. Thanks for looking out for Willow, have you seen her and Dustin?'

'They've taken Bubbles for a wander, should be back around six. Ta for looking after Wolf.'

'That's okay, he's no trouble, unlike his owner. I'm off home for a long soak in the bath to eliminate any covert sandhoppers. Bye, Lily.' I turned to Paddington. 'Come on, boy, let's go home.'

Lily beamed and stroked Paddington, who was reluctant to leave his best pal Wolf.

'See ya, love.'

Paddling up the estuary with the incoming tide was effortless, and when I arrived at FloBeau I was thankful it was deserted. With the wheels attached to the Beast, it was a long old slog up the track home.

I opened the front door and was pleasantly surprised to see a vase of flowers on the kitchen table with a note from Willow and Dustin. Paddington was greeted by Bailey, Daisy and Nutmeg, but Jasmine and Cinnamon still eyed him with superstition. I was halfway up the stairs when Flynn rang.

'Hi, Flynn, how are you and the girls?'

'Hi, sis, we're fine thanks. I have a huge favour to ask. You know Ruby is going to South Africa to project manage the school?'

'Yes, she leaves shortly.'

'Well, she's asked me to join her and head up a team of builders.'

I sank onto the stairs. 'Seriously? For how long?'

'I'm not sure, could be up to a year. The thing is, the girls don't want to come, and their mum doesn't want them, and—'

I butted in: 'Oh my gosh, of course I'll have them.'

'It will be for less than a year, and I will come back and visit. Ruby and I are planning on buying a piece of land close to you and submitting plans to build our own house.'

'Did I hear right? You and Ruby? When did that happen?'

'She was supportive when Kate walked out, but we didn't want to take things further until the divorce was finalised at Christmas. When the opportunity came up for Ruby in South Africa, I didn't know where the relationship was going until she suggested I joined her.'

'Oh, Flynn, I'm so happy for you both, and I'll take good care of the girls until you return.'

'I know you will, sis, they love you so much. You're more like a mum to them than their real mum.'

'Well, I practically brought them up while Kate was at uni. Are they happy about you and Ruby?'

'Yes, they love Ruby, after you.'

'Have you told them yet about staying with me?'

'It was their idea! They miss you, Willow, Nutmeg, Jasmine and Cinnamon, and they can't wait to meet Paddington and the kittens.'

'After the weekend I've had, this is the best news ever. Willow will be so excited; she misses them loads.'

'It won't cause any problems with you and Beau, will it?'

'Beau is in the past!'

'Sorry, sis, the right guy is out there somewhere, you just have to stop looking so hard. I know it's short notice, but we're leaving in three weeks. The girls were going to stay with Mum until the end of the school year, but when I rang Whispering Pine's primary school, Mrs Pecker, the head teacher, said the girls could start in three weeks.'

'Perfect, I can drop them off in the morning and they can either meet me or Willow after work.'

'Thanks, sis, I knew you wouldn't mind. No doubt you'll hear from Ruby shortly.'

'Okay, I can't wait to tell Willow. Bye Flynn.'

'Thanks so much, sis. Night.'

A second later Flynn rang again.

'Sorry, sis, but I have two monsters here that want to say something.'

'Auntie Oakley, thank you so much, we're so excited to be coming to live with you,' said Poppy.

'Aren't you sad your dad is going away?'

'Yes, but we can facetime him. We're more excited about coming to live by the beach. We can go paddling in our new kayaks, live with Willow and play with Paddington and the cats, and Auntie Oakley ...'

'Yes Blossom?'

'We'll be good, promise.'

'Aren't you always?'

'Yep. Bye, Auntie Oakley.'

'Bye, girls.'

I climbed into the bath, nestled down in the bubbles and my phone rang again.

'Hi, Rubes, you're a dark horse.'

'Sorry, I've been dying to tell you, but until Flynn's divorce was finalised, we couldn't say anything.'

'That's okay, I suspected something was going on, but when you flirted with Beau, I wasn't sure.'

'Sorry about that. I wanted Flynn to wake up and make a decision. I was fed up keeping quiet about our relationship. I thought if I made him jealous, he might react, but he didn't. So, I gave up and put in the tender for South Africa; I knew he wanted to branch out from the family business and was hoping he'd join me. It worked, but I wasn't expecting the girls to stay behind.'

'They'll be fine with me until you're home. I've made up with Mackenzie, are you going to be free to paddle in Scotland next weekend?'

'I've nearly finished packing so should be free. Beau invited your brothers ages ago, though I wasn't sure if you would still be going. I can't wait as we have lots of catching up to do. How was the weekend with Beau?'

'He's seeing someone else. He paddled to a disco boat and left me and the dogs alone all night.'

'The rotten skunk. I'm so sorry, Oak. The right one will come along when you least expect it. Sorry, gotta run, I'm having tea with Flynn and the girls.'

'Give them a kiss from me. See you next weekend, my future sister-in-law.'

Ruby chuckled. 'See ya, Oak.'

I heard the front door slam, and the sound of footsteps racing upstairs.

'Oakley, are you up here?' yelled Willow out of breath.

It seemed my dream of a life of solitude was very much a figment of my imagination.

'I'm in the bath!'

Willow shouted through the door. 'I've had a text from Blossom and Poppy. Is it true they're coming to stay with us?'

'Yes, for a while. Do you mind?'

'Of course not, they're like my little sisters. This is so exciting; I feel like I have a proper family. How was the weekend?'

'Fine,' I lied. 'Did you have a nice weekend with Dustin?'

'The best. Thanks for trusting me.'

'Were the cats on their best behaviour?'

'About as good as the twins! Daisy was hanging off a branch on the oak tree and Dustin had to climb up and rescue her. Then we lost Bailey and found him asleep among the towels in the tumble drier. I must have left the door open while helping to rescue Daisy. It was lucky I didn't switch it back on. We need to keep a close eye on those two.'

I watched Bailey, who was balancing on the edge of the bath and dangling a paw in the bubbles as he attempted to catch my big toe.

'I'm sorry I left you both to look after them, I shouldn't have gone away for the weekend.'

'We didn't mind, but then Bailey climbed up the tree and got stuck. Dustin was at the top of the ladder, and nearly fell off laughing as Bailey must have climbed down when we fetched the ladder. I spotted him sitting in the bird bath while Dustin was calling his name from the top of the ladder.

'The little devil. Maybe I should cancel next weekend away for Mackenzie's birthday as you'll have Paddington to look after as well.'

'No don't cancel, we'll be fine. Paddington can play with Bubbles.'

'Well, if you're sure, but they'll be no more weekends away after that, especially with the twins arriving. We have our summer garden party to organise, and we've been roped into helping at the village fete.'

'I'm so excited, this is going to be the best summer ever. Can I cook tea?'

'Yes, but try not to burn the food.'

'I haven't inherited that trait.'

'Glad to hear that. You can cook more meals from now on then.'

'Poppy and Blossom can help me.'

'Remind me to order more fire extinguishers.'

'I will. We can place them in different parts of Catkins, then move them to the kitchen when you're cooking.'

'Very funny! It's lucky there's a door between us. Now hurry up and cook my tea girl, I'm starving.'

'It'll be ready shortly.'

I reached for my phone to text Mackenzie while keeping an eye on Bailey, who was now trying to pull the plug out.

Me:	Hi Mackenzie, Guess what? Peace and quiet are about to be shattered in my household.
Mackenzie:	Hi Oakley, Why?
Me:	My eight-year-old nieces are staying with me while my brother is working abroad for up to a year.
Mackenzie:	Peace and quiet are so underrated! Do they like animals? Can they paddle?
Me:	They love animals and canoeing and kayaking. Though they never stop jabbering!
Mackenzie:	They sound enchanting. A life without jabbering would be so dreary.
Me:	It would. Somehow, I think my destiny is meant to be a hullabaloo of calamities.
Mackenzie:	Sounds perfect!
Me:	You're right. I'm looking forward to next weekend, can't wait to meet you. Willow is cooking my tea, how lucky am I? Night, Makenzie, so glad we're speaking again.
Mackenzie:	You're welcome, Enjoy your tea. Hope Willow hasn't burnt the kitchen down. Looking forward to meeting you next weekend too. Night, Oakley.

When I opened the bathroom door, the aroma wafting upstairs was sublime. Bailey scampered downstairs, jumped over Nutmeg and she didn't flinch, but as I stepped over her, she swiped my leg with her paw.

Laid out on the table was a huge dish of tikka masala, rice, onion bhajis and vegetable samosas. With Willow doing the cooking, I just had to train Poppy and Blossom to do the washing, ironing and housework and I could put my feet up for the next year. Although that was probably one dream that was never going to come true!

Chapter Thirty-seven
Return of the School Nemeses

A week passed, and I could hardly contain my excitement on the evening before travelling to Scotland. Beau still hadn't contacted me; Lily said he was too ashamed of the way he'd behaved. I certainly wasn't going to contact him, even if it was going to be awkward paddling in Scotland.

During my two days off and the evenings over the past week, I'd designed a spraydeck for Mackenzie for his birthday. Flo gave me the measurements of his canoe and I used a similar pattern to the one I made for my solo canoe. The opportunity to use mine hadn't arisen yet, but as I'd inherited my Mum's moto – to always be prepared – my spraydeck was packed inside my car. You never knew when a squall might be on the horizon, though I hoped my spraydeck wasn't going to be christened this weekend. Once I knew Mackenzie's sitting or kneeling position, I could finish making his. With my indecisive head screwed on I was worried he may hate the colour and never use it. But hey-ho, it was the thought that counted, at least it was a safer bet than baking a birthday cake.

I left home early on Thursday morning, and after an overnight stay in a B&B in Penrith. I was the first to arrive at Trent's uncle's campsite the following afternoon. Positioned either side of the entrance were two old yellow-and-white-striped dory boats filled to the gunwales with summer daisies. Cables from the back of the boats were attached to wakeboards with statues of cats surfing. Etched onto the hull of each boat were the names James and Nancy, and a sign said: Welcome to Kittiwake Camp Site. I parked at the top of the campsite and noticed another sign declaring: Gone fishing, catch you later!

A lady resting on a nearby bench looked up from behind a pair of retro cat-eye-framed glasses. Her hair was arranged in a 1950's beehive and was as black as liquorice, and her lips were painted fuchsia pink. She brushed her skirt down and headed towards me, while I opened my window.

'Mornin' lassie, are you looking for a pitch?' Her voice sounded far older than her façade, which implied she'd walked off a casting for the movie, *Grease*.

'Morning, yes, I've already booked, do you know if I can pitch my tent anywhere?'

The lady pointed to the bottom of the field. 'Plenty of spaces lass, though I'd pitch in the corner behind that hedge. It's a long way from the facilities, but you should be protected from tonight's storm.'

'Storm? The forecast said it was going to be a lovely weekend.'

'We have our own localised mini-climate. Main forecasters don't always get things right here.'

'Okay, thanks for the advice.'

'You're welcome, lass.'

After erecting my one-person bivy tent, I secured a tarp over the top for added protection. While my Therm-a-Rest self-inflated, I wandered along the beach collecting driftwood to light my Kelly Kettle. When I returned to my tent, my phone pinged a text from Flynn.

> **Flynn:** Hi, sis, really sorry, none of us can make it this weekend, too busy packing and the rest are working. Hope you have a nice time.

Me: Oh what a shame! Was looking forward to catching up. X

Flynn: Stop off here on your way home. Girls would love to see you.

Me: Okay, love too. X

I peered over the hedge as two cars, laden with canoes, screeched into the campsite. Two girls jumped out and dashed to the ladies as Beau and Trent opened their doors. I headed in their direction, and froze; were my eyes deceiving me? The girls emerging from the ladies looked like my nemeses from school, Trent's ex, Scarlett, and her sidekick, Cordelia, the only two people I truly disliked in the world.

Scarlett and Cordelia were the 'It' girls at school. With their immaculate long blonde hair, Barbie-doll figures, and cosmopolitan clothes, they oozed confidence and self-esteem. They sucked the air out of any room as love-struck boys gasped at their beauty and swarmed around them like bees above a lavender bush. The girls strutted like a pair of displaying peacocks. They drew attention to themselves and bullied and pushed anyone over who dared cross their path. A hareem of bewitched girls were enraptured by their every word and obeyed their every command. At fifteen, Scarlett ensnared Trent into her tangled web, and quickly they became the couple everyone idolised, except me. They were engaged at eighteen, only to split up three weeks later when Scarlett cheated on Trent. I hadn't seen the girls in over ten years, though on reflection, maybe it had been them at the rugby game.

Scarlett fluttered her Cleopatra eyelashes before opening her big mouth.

'Hi, Oakley. Surprise! Bet you didn't expect to see us again?'

'No, you were the last people I was expecting to bump into.' Although it felt more like a collision than a bump, this was one serpent that would forever be a venomous snake; I'd have to watch my back with her.

She dazzled her gleaming white teeth and tossed her hair over her shoulders.

'We bumped into Beau on a disco party boat. Poor lamb drank a bit too much and had to stay with us in our hotel.'

That explained what happened to Beau last weekend!

'Anyway, must dash, Beau will be getting lonely without me.'

The girls tottered back in their skimpy vest tops, short skirts, and flimsy sandals, hardly suitable attire for a canoeing weekend. Trent ambled towards me.

'Trent, how could you have invited them on this weekend?'

Trent peered at the girls. 'I didn't! Beau met them at the rugby game. I had no idea they were going to be here. He invited them to paddle to Fucus Nook Quay, but they returned because the sea was too rough, so he arranged to meet them on the disco boat.'

'Seriously? So he had no intention of paddling back to the cove? Oh my god, I'm such an idiot.'

'He's the idiot, not you, I only found out this morning that I was paddling with Cordelia, and believe me, I called him something stronger. We had to pick them up from Cordelia's parent's house near Ullapool. Please don't tell Flo that Scarlett is my ex, I'll tell her myself.'

'Fine, but they had better not ruin the weekend. Can they even paddle a canoe?'

'Beau said he taught them how to hold his paddle last weekend.'

'I bet he did!'

Trent smirked. 'What time are Ruby and your brothers arriving?'

'They've cancelled, so we're just waiting for Mackenzie. Have you met him before?'

'No. I hope he's not like his cousin. Right, can't stand here chatting all day, I have tents to erect. By the way, what you are doing for tea tonight?'

'Aren't we going to the pub?'

'No, sorry, the girls are cooking us tea, but they've not included you.'

'Doesn't matter, I'll go to the pub with Mackenzie. The last thing I want to do is watch Scarlett and Beau swooning over each other.'

Trent scanned the campsite. 'Where's your tent?'

I pointed to the bottom of the field. 'I'll show you. I've pitched it where it's more protected from the elements.'

We wandered to the bottom of the field and Trent peered over the hedge.

'There's a storm forecast tonight, so I've fixed my tarp across the top of my tent.' I said knowing full well he wouldn't believe me.

He gazed into the horizon and exclaimed, 'What storm? I've not heard anything. Watch out, looks like Scarlett was listening and is heading our way.'

Scarlett marched straight up to Trent and butted in, 'I'm not staying by Oakley, it's too far to the toilets.'

Trent's scowl suggested he'd taken lessons from Ruby. 'It's more protected, and the toilets aren't that far from Oakley's tent.'

Cordelia joined in babbling like a spoilt child. 'I'm not walking on my own in the dark. I want to camp under the streetlamp. Come on Lottie let's find Beau.'

The girls marched back to the top of the field, or rather hobbled in their silly heeled shoes.

'Sorry, Oakley, looks like you are on your own until Mackenzie arrives.'

'I'd rather be on my own than listen to their whining. Need any help with the tents?'

'No thanks. Beau and I have our one-man tents, and the girls have a new fast-erect tent. Apparently, with a bit of pumping, it can be erected single handily in under eight minutes!'

I glanced at Trent and giggled, as he raised his eyebrows.

'Oakley, don't even go there!'

'I have no intention of ever going there, I've been telling you that for years! I'm going to make a coffee; hope the tent erection goes well.'

'By the time your kettle has boiled the tent will be erected.'

'We'll see.'

I turned to leave and noticed Beau with his head buried inside the boot of his car. He unloaded a tent the size of a hotel and didn't look up, as he dropped it onto the floor and wiped his brow. The tent didn't appear to be the fast erect tent Trent was expecting.

I called Mackenzie and left a message on his answerphone. With my binoculars around my neck, and a mug of coffee, I couldn't wait to see my afternoon's entertainment.

Beau carried the tent to the front of the shower block. Cordelia stamped her feet and dragged it under the streetlamp. Scarlett lugged it back to the shower block, whereupon Cordelia hauled it back under the streetlamp. Scarlett confronted Cordelia head on. There was an amazing catfight as they faced each other, hands on hips, throwing accusations. Trent intervened and threw a coin into the air, resulting in Scarlett storming off into the arms of Beau. I should have felt a twinge of jealousy, however, I felt sorry for Beau getting involved with that wild cat. This was more entertaining than a soap opera.

Trent opened the tent bag and scratched his head, followed by a lot of cussing, before dropping the tent on the ground. The girls sat back, filing their nails while Beau and Trent put their heads together. I could only imagine what was being discussed. Trent raised the canvas above his head, revealing a faded, two-tone blue tent; not the cosmopolitan tent I had envisaged. In fact, it appeared at least a hundred years old. It reminded me of my grandad's tent that leaked if you brushed against it in a storm. With my ears pricked, I caught the tail end of the argument. It seemed Scarlett had been worried she'd damage her nails, so asked the postman if he could take the tent out of the garage and load it into the car. He must have picked up the wrong tent. The effing and blinding continued, and after several pole changes, at last, the frame was up. Now all they had to do was fathom out how to lift the canvas over the top.

This was the funniest entertainment I had seen in years. The boys knelt down, allowing the girls to climb onto their shoulders and the boys scrambled to their feet. Scarlett screeched like an owl and nearly tumbled backwards, she grabbed Beau's blond curls, and in return, he howled like a dog. This was hilarious! The girls attempted to heave the canvas over the top of the frame, but when Scarlett broke a nail, she threw a hissy fit, and Beau toppled over sending her tumbling to the ground. She jumped up and ran crying to the ladies with Cordelia running behind her. Maybe it was time to add my two pennies' worth. I sauntered towards Beau and Trent trying not to giggle, thus revealing I'd been spying on them! Beau glanced up and headed to his car.

'Need any help with your erection, Trent?'

'Okay, so it's taking a little longer than eight minutes. If you think you can do any better, be my guest. '

'This tent is like my grandparents' old tent. You erect the frame halfway and throw the canvas over it before fully erecting the legs.' I ambled towards the frame, pushed a small button on one of the legs, twisted it and pulled it in half. 'See, all the legs have internal connecting spring coils, which enables you to bend the legs inwards and lower the frame so you can draw the canvas over the top before you raise it.'

'I'm impressed; not just a pretty face!'

After re-erecting the tent my way, it was ready for the inner bedrooms to be hung. I riffled through the tent bag.

'Trent, where's the rest of the tent and groundsheet?'

'There's nothing left in the bag. I'll check the car.'

'The bedrooms clip onto the inside of the frame, and once pegged down, help to prevent it blowing away during a storm. They'll need a groundsheet too.'

'There's nothing in the car. Don't worry, it's only for one night and there isn't going to be a storm, so they'll be fine. They can use my spare groundsheet.'

Scarlett and Cordelia emerged from the toilets and strutted towards me, and without a word of thanks, entered their tent.

Scarlett popped her head out of the door. 'Beau, honey, be a darling and fetch our bags, airbeds and camp kitchen from the car. Oh, and can you pump the beds up too?'

A sudden tightness like indigestion you couldn't shift washed over my body. Surely Beau wasn't going to obey her commands. Scarlett had Beau twisted around her little finger, and without hesitation, he did exactly as she'd asked.

'Afterwards, honey bunny, could you assemble the camp kitchen, and I'll cook you a lovely meal.'

This was too painful to watch. The tightness in my body had transformed to suppressed laughter witnessing Beau falling into her web. My stomach and ribs were aching from an explosion of giggles that was brewing inside me; it was time for a swift exit.

I made my way back to my tent and footsteps crunched on the gravel path behind me. When I glanced over my shoulder, Beau was jogging behind me.

'Oakley, wait. I want to apologise about last weekend. I didn't mean to stay overnight and leave you on your own. I fell asleep on the boat after having too much to drink. When I woke up, we were back at the dock.'

Oh my word, what was this guy like? He could win the top award for stretching the truth.

'Funny that, so, after you heaved your canoe onto the disco boat, you immediately fell asleep seconds before the boat lifted anchor?'

'How'd you know I heaved my canoe on board?'

'Beau, honey, – isn't that what you like to be called? – there is a modern invention called binoculars. I was getting worried about you, and my stomach was rumbling.'

Beau looked at his feet. 'Oh! Sorry, and, sorry I left Wolf with you. Thank you for taking good care of him, he loves you. Did you catch any fish for your tea or eat seaweed?'

'No need. While I was foraging in your bag for food for Wolf, I came across your stash of goodies that were washed down with a can of cider. Amazing what you can find whilst foraging, especially the tent!'

Beau looked down to the ground, shuffled his feet and kicked a stone. 'Sorry, Oakley, I don't know what to say.'

'I do. Go back to your girlfriend, you'll need all the luck in the world with that one.'

Beau drew in a deep breath and sighed. 'Sorry about Lottie. I didn't realise you knew each other. She's nice once you get to know her.'

'Her nickname at school was Scar, not Lottie. She caused a lot of damage and left her mark wherever she went.'

'She's changed since you were at school. You'll love her once you get to know her more.'

'I doubt that, Beau. Scars rarely change that much.' I paused, noticing Scarlett waving at us. 'It looks like you're needed again.'

Scarlett placed her hands resting on her hips. 'Honey bunny, come on, less chat please, I need your help.'

Beau waved and grinned. 'Guess she has another job for me. Poor girl, she's not independent and strong like you, Oakley. She's never been camping, and it's all a bit daunting. I'd better get back.'

'Yep, best you run along like a good boy, honey bunny.'

Beau twisted around and it appeared Trent's scowl was contagious. How could he be so gullible? Scarlett had been camping loads of times, though on recollection, she'd never helped. She was back to her old tricks. Casting a baited line, catching her man, and reeling him in, only to throw him back when she was bored. In fact, she sounded just like Beau. She was as transparent as a window, and Beau had fallen through it; they were welcome to each other.

Chapter Thirty-eight
Egg on Their Faces

Mackenzie still hadn't rung me, and with last orders on the horizon, I could feel the hunger pains rampaging in my stomach. I sent a quick text message to check he was all right, and a few minutes later my phone rang.

'Hi, Oakley. Didn't you get my message?'

'Hi, Mackenzie. No, what message?'

'I left a message with the girl who answered Beau's phone. Sorry, I can't make it tonight. I had to carry out an emergency caesarean on a dog and I can't leave her and puppies overnight.'

'I didn't get the message. How is the dog and the puppies?'

'They're fine, she had twelve pups, so it was all-hands-on-deck! I wonder why the girl didn't tell you I'd called?'

'It's a long story, I'll tell you another time. Glad the dog and puppies are well. When will you be here?'

'Sometime tomorrow. I'll catch you up at Flotsam Island. I'm sorry about the pub. Are you too late for last orders?'

'I'll be fine, thanks, don't worry. You'd better get back and check on the dog and puppies. I'll see you tomorrow.'

'Can't wait to meet you. Can I ask you something?'

'Yes, of course, anything,' I said, wondering if he knew Beau was now seeing Scarlett.

'Could you buy two litres of milk in the morning as the shop might be closed by the time I arrive?'

'No problem.'

'That'll be great, thanks, you had better get something to eat. See you tomorrow.'

'Look forward to it. Bye, Mackenzie.'

I put on my detective head wondering who had answered Beau's phone. The boys were scoffing a full English breakfast in the entrance of the girls' tent. A huge saucepan of baked beans remained bubbling on the gas stove, alongside it were the remnants of a pan of scrambled eggs.

In my most sincere and sweetest voice, I said, 'Wow, that looks delicious. Sorry to disturb you. Beau, are there any messages on your phone?'

Beau shovelled a forkful of black pudding and sausage into his mouth. 'No, why?'

'Mackenzie called you.'

'No he didn't.' He peered up and saw the look on my face. 'Hold on a minute I'll have a look.'

Scarlett cast an eye towards Cordelia, who turned her head and ignored her.

Beau scrolled through his phone. 'That's odd, he rang at three-thirty, but he didn't leave a message.'

Trent placed his knife and fork down. 'He'd better hurry up the pub stops serving food in fifteen minutes. Have you spoken to him, Oakley?'

Time to lure Scarlett and Cordelia into my web.

'A few minutes ago. He said he asked a girl to pass a message on.'

Trent twisted around to Scarlett and Cordelia. 'Did either of you take a message from Mackenzie?'

Scarlett's eyes were smouldering with spite and vengeance.

'We haven't spoken to Mackenzie, have we Cordelia? Shame if he can't make it tonight. Poor Oakley won't have any tea, and all we have is a pan of baked beans and leftover scrambled eggs.'

I turned to address Scarlett. 'Mackenzie asked me if we minded waiting as he doesn't fancy paddling to Flotsam on his own.'

Scarlett took the bait. 'He didn't say that did he, Cordelia?' She glared at Cordelia for backup, though Cordelia continued looking the other way. Scarlett blurted out: 'He said we're not to wait, he'll meet us later.'

'I thought you said you hadn't spoken to him,' said Trent.

'Silly me, must have slipped my mind.'

Trent placed his plate on the ground and wandered into the middle of the campsite with his phone glued to his ear. A few minutes later he returned.

'Oakley, can I have a word. My aunt and uncle have ordered you the catch of the day with chips, no charge, and should be ready in ten minutes.'

'Seriously? Oh my goodness, thank you Trent.'

'The pub is called, Off The Hook. You can join them at their table in the window.'

'Thank you. Enjoy the rest of your evening.'

Footsteps caught me up on my way back to my tent, and as I peered over my shoulder, Trent was following.

'Oakley, sorry about Scarlett and Cordelia. I'd watch your back with them. Does Mackenzie really want us to wait?'

'No. I made it up.'

Trent sniggered. 'You, sneaky vixen. Do you know what? You've changed since you moved.'

'How do you mean?'

'Not such a walkover; feistier and more sure of yourself, it suits you.'

'Thanks, I'll take that as a compliment. Remember there's a storm forecast tonight. Check the guys and pegs on the girls' tent.'

Trent laughed. 'One thing hasn't changed, still the pessimist! Enjoy your tea with my family. Please tell them I'll see them on Sunday night.'

'Will do, see you later.'

The meal in the pub was delicious, and Trent's family were extremely welcoming. It was late when we left the warmth of the wood burner and headed into the night. The wind nearly took the pub door off its hinges as Trent's uncle held it open. A flash of lightning lit up the sky as pebbles pummelled against the sea wall. I counted six before a rumble of thunder. We said our goodbyes, and I legged it towards the campsite.

The trees buckled and strained, with their groans of pain carried away in the eye of the storm. My pace accelerated as I dashed into the toilet block. The pitter-patter of raindrops amplified and bounced off the roof like marbles jumping on a trampoline. I hovered in the doorway, anticipating the right moment to dash to my tent. All of a sudden, a scream as eerie as a fox searching for a mate, echoed from within the girls' tent. A bolt of lightning illuminated the campsite as the canvas on their tent ripped in two. Like a deflating balloon, half the tent skyrocketed into the horizon. With the next gust of wind, the other half took to the wing and spiralled down the campsite. I stood glued to the spot as the tent twisted like tumbleweed blowing in a desert. It would have been cruel if I laughed out loud, instead my giggles brewed inside me like a coffee percolator boiling. The girls remained in their sleeping bags as light from the streetlamps illuminated their cucumber-green facemasks. I was nearly overcome with laughter as their beauty routine had been enhanced by leftover baked beans and scrambled eggs; talk about egg on your face! The camp kitchen and two empty saucepans lay on top of them as Trent and Beau arrived at the scene. Despite the incessant rain, the girls remained motionless with their faces set like concrete. Beau scooped Scarlett over his shoulder and headed into the shower block. He returned minutes later, hitched Cordelia onto his shoulder and joined Scarlett, while Trent bundled their kit into the back of his car. Beau slinked back from the shower block as I ambled out of the toilet block.

Baked beans and scrambled eggs dripped off his top and he muttered: 'I could hardly get a word out of them. I've left them crying in the showers. Oakley, are you going to be all right in your tent?'

'Fine, thanks. My tent's protected from the wind.'

'Guess we should have listened to you and pitched our tents by yours. I'm going to sit in my car and wait for the girls. See you in the morning.'

Trent took my arm. 'Oakley, I'll walk back with you to your tent.'

'Trent, don't be silly, the weather is awful; go back to bed.'

'No, I need to walk back with you.'

We walked halfway in silence, battling against the wind and rain, until Trent stopped.

'Are we out of earshot?'

'Yes, why?'

There was no need for a reply as Trent bent over and brayed like a donkey. Even the sound of the wind and rumbling of thunder didn't camouflage his whinnying.

'Did you see their faces?' Trent was in hysterics. 'They were covered in baked beans and scrambled eggs. We'd offered to clear the dishes, but they said they would wash them in the morning.'

I started laughing too. 'I don't think I can ever look at a baked bean again. Maybe they'll go home now.'

'I don't think Scarlett will leave her beloved Beau. Sorry, I should have believed you about the storm, at least you're well protected in the corner, unlike my tent. Any room in yours?'

'Sorry, it's my one-man bivy tent.'

'That's fine, I can be the one man. We could practise a bit of canoodling.'

'Someone sent me a Valentine's card mentioning canoodling. It wasn't you, was it?'

Trent's eyes twinkled. 'May have done. If you get too cold, you know where I am.'

'Trust me, I'm never going to get that cold. Remember, you have a girlfriend called Flo!'

'I know, but she's not here and you are. Can't blame a bloke for trying.' Trent wandered towards his tent before looking back and waving.

Trent and Beau were as bad as each other. At least the mystery of one of my Valentine's cards had been solved. I stripped off under my tarp, tossed my wet clothes aside, and crawled into my tent. My phone rang just as I had snuggled down into my sleeping bag.

'Hi, Oakley, sorry to ring you so late, did you manage to get something to eat?'

'Hi, Mackenzie, yes thanks, had a delicious meal in the pub with Trent's family.'

'Oh, did Trent go with you?' Mackenzie sounded disappointed.

'No, Scarlett and Cordelia cooked him and Beau a full English breakfast. You will never guess what happened to the leftover baked beans and scrambled eggs.'

'No, what?'

'Scarlett and Cordelia were plastered in them when their tent blew away.'

I could hear Mackenzie laughing. 'Jeeze, tell me more. Are you okay?'

'Fine, thank you. It's going to take ages to tell you everything that has happened.'

'I don't mind, I've got plenty of time to listen. I'm in my sleeping bag lying on a sofa next to the dog and puppies.'

'I'm in my sleeping bag too, just don't fall asleep until I've finished the story.'

'I'll try not to.'

I spent the next hour talking about my day. Mackenzie was such a good listener; although he may have fallen asleep while I rabbited on.

'How's the dog and puppies?' I said, hoping he was still awake.

'They're a greedy little bunch. Jeeze, do you know the time? It's half past one! I think we had better go to sleep.'

'I'm wide awake now!'

'Try counting sheep.'

'Sheep are my nemesis. I'll count cats.'

Mackenzie sniggered. 'Night, Oakley.'

'Night, Mackenzie, and happy birthday.'

'Thanks, but it's not my birthday until tomorrow.'

'It is tomorrow!'

'Of course, it's Saturday.'

'See you this afternoon. Have a good journey.'

'Enjoy your paddle across to the islands.'

'I will. Night.'

'Night, Oak, and don't let the bed bugs bite.'

'Oh my god, now I have visions of sandhoppers in my sleeping bag.'

Mackenzie sniggered down the phone. 'Lucky sandhoppers. Think of something else you wouldn't mind hopping into your sleeping bag and nibbling you.'

'I have something in mind.'

'You do, who?'

'He's big, hairy and showers me in kisses.'

'Beau or Trent?'

'Neither, Paddington!'

'You make me laugh, it's time to go to sleep! Night, Oakley.'

'Night, Mackenzie.'

I snuggled into my sleeping bag listening to the howling wind and rain pelting against my tarp. I was very glad I'd pitched my tent on the other side of the hedge.

Chapter Thirty-nine
The Light Went Out

The rich melodious chirring of grasshoppers awoke me early; thank goodness they were outside the tent! I snuggled into my warm sleeping bag as the rhythmic tinkling of the waves lapped on the shoreline. The acoustics were hypnotising me back to sleep, until I remembered how far away the toilet block was. I dressed, crawled out of my tent, and with my washbag under my arm, dashed along the path towards the ablutions.

Steam was rising from the paving slabs as the sun warmed the remnants of last night's storm. On passing the boys' tents the snoring was akin to a walrus sucking clams; another good reason for pitching my tent on the other side of the hedge.

On returning to my tent, the snoring had intensified; it seemed the boys were not early risers. Fifteen minutes later, all I could hear was the sizzling in my frying pan and whistling of my kettle. With a mug in one hand and a plate piled high with mushroom sarnies in the other, I headed to the beach and found the perfect breakfast spot to watch the new day dawning.

The amber glow of the sun rose higher and dispersed last night's rain clouds. Sea grass swayed in the breeze, and the sky was transformed to a flawless summer blue as terns and gulls darted across the cliffs. What a fantastic day for canoeing. I glanced over my shoulder to see the boys were up at last. With my mug of coffee in my hand, I sauntered over to see what the plans were.

'Morning, lads. You could both snore for England; sounded like a couple of snorting walruses sucking on clams when I passed your tents.'

Trent sniggered. 'Not us, we slept in our cars.'

Scarlett popped her head out of Beau's tent and the look she gave me was like lightning striking.

Trent whispered, 'I think you'd better keep out of her way today, Oakley.'

'With pleasure. I'll wait for you on the beach.'

'You'll have a long wait. Beau is cooking the girl's breakfast, and they're eating it in bed.'

'Thought they'd had enough breakfast in bed last night.'

Trent chuckled. 'Don't remind me, not sure I can eat scrambled eggs or baked beans again without laughing.'

'Me neither. See you later, Trent.'

'See yer, Tinker Bell.'

After packing everything, I tossed my dry bags into my canoe and wheeled it to the beach. I glanced up momentarily as the sun disappeared behind clouds resembling the milky froth on top of a latte. Drat! Milk! What a scatterbrain. I'd forgotten to buy Mackenzie's milk.

I dashed up the campsite and spotted Beau sitting on a chair with his head in his hands.

'Morning, Beau, how long are you going to be? Have I got time to nip to the shop? Mackenzie asked me to buy milk.'

Beau looked up, and with his elbows on his knees, cupped his chin in his hands.

'Morning, Oakley, at the rate these girls are taking to get ready I think you have enough time to milk the cow. I'm beginning to wish I hadn't invited them.'

'Probably best I keep my mouth shut on that subject.'

Beau sighed. 'I'm sorry, Oakley, I haven't behaved very well. Somehow, I can't envisage Lottie on the back of a quad bike while Wolf rounds up the sheep.'

That vision made me giggle. 'She's more of a wolf in sheep's clothing.'

'Erm ... I'm beginning to see that, maybe I should have listened to you.'

'Maybe. Do you want anything from the shop?

'No thanks. Have you seen the size of the freezer bag Lottie packed? Wouldn't be surprised if it didn't sink my canoe. I'll ask Trent if he needs anything. Bud, did you remember milk?'

'No, forgot, mate, the girls asked me to pick up four litres, plus two for us.'

I butted in: 'Six litres of milk seems an awful lot, won't that make the canoes a bit heavy?'

'Tinker Bell, always the worrier. It'll be fine, we can distribute it between our canoes and even out the trim.'

'Still seems excessive to me.'

Beau reached for his wallet. 'Here's the money. Do you want a hand carrying the milk?'

'No thanks, I can manage. See you shortly.'

While wandering to the shop, I was greeted by a man slouched on a bench. His face was tanned and weathered with a long, white bushy beard covering his yellow oilskins. When he grinned a mouthful of white teeth reflected in the sunlight.

'Mornin', lass.'

'Morning.'

'I noticed you walking up from the campsite. Staying long?'

'We're canoeing to the Driftwood Islands for the weekend.'

'Have you seen the forecast? Gonna be a storm coming in later, can feel it in me bones. Cows over yonder been sitting down all mornin' and there was an early red sunrise.'

'Really?' I spun around and gazed out to a calm sea.

'I thought after the storm last night it was meant to be a lovely weekend, with light winds no more than force two.'

'Sea state changes as the wind gets up, specially round that there headland. A squall is coming in, best leave paddling until tomorrow.'

'Every where's so calm.'

'Now lass, listen, the barometer dropped this morning. Have you heard about the calm before the storm? You don't wanna be paddling around the headland of Flotsam above a force five. The waves can get over three metres and the wind buffets them off the cliffs. If you're paddling canoes, you're likely to sink! Got any deck covers with you?'

'I made a spraydeck, but left it in the car, do you think I should take it?'

'Not much use in the car, love. Always trust my instincts.' He chuckled to himself. 'And the cows up yonder. I'd say it was going to get up to at least force six to seven. Make sure you have a leash on your paddle, and keep a spare handy, just in case.'

'Seriously? Thanks for the advice. I'll tell the others, but I doubt they'll believe me. Maybe your oilskins are more appropriate than my shorts and t-shirt.'

The man smiled. 'Wouldn't be without me slickers. Don't listen to your mates, know your own mind love. You'll be the one laughing when the storm arrives. Heed what I've told you.'

'Thank you. I will.'

The man stood up and wandered towards a little boy waving from the top of the hill.

I pushed the shop door open and scouted around for milk. The fridge was empty except for boxes of goats' milk. I approached the man behind the counter.

'Excuse me.'

'All right, hen, how can I help you?'

'Is this all the milk you have?'

'Delivery is late, love.'

'Okay, thank you. I'll take the goats' milk.'

Laden with the milk, I totted back and met Trent at the top of the campsite.

'Oakley, what's taken you so long? We were going without you.'

'Sorry, I was chatting to a man about a squall coming in.'

'There isn't a squall coming in! You don't change, do you?'

'He seemed genuine.'

Trent grabbed my hand and dragged me towards the shoreline.

'Does it look like a squall is on the way?'

'Not really. But that's why it's called a squall.'

Trent raised his voice. 'Stop worrying, it will be fine.'

I handed the milk to him. 'Sorry they only had goats' milk. I'll be ready in a mo. I'm just popping back to my car for something.'

'Fine, but hurry.' Trent turned and shouted to Scarlett and Cordelia who were waiting by my canoe. 'While Beau and I move the cars to the car park, can you two please find room for the milk in the canoes?'

'Of course, Trent darling,' Scarlett said in her sweetest voice.

On my return, I was shocked to see Scarlett and Cordelia wading in the sea holding my canoe.

Scarlett passed me my buoyancy aid as I leashed my dry bag containing my spraydeck.

'Oakley, as you're paddling on your own, we thought we would help you with your canoe.'

Cordelia grasped the stern. 'We'll hold on to it while you climb in.'

'Thanks,' I said half-heartedly.

This was out of character, even a cold-blooded lizard like Scarlett couldn't warm up that quickly.

I pulled my buoyancy aid on and stepped into my canoe, which seemed to be sitting quite low in the water. With my backside perched on the kneeling thwart, and my feet tucked under, I paddled towards the first wave, but it was akin to manoeuvring a ferry with a single blade. As the wave approached, I sank my paddle over the top and punched my way through. The next wave caught the bow and propelled me backwards to the beach. The girls' laughter zoomed over my head as I repeated the stroke again, and again. It was relentless, like pushing your shopping trolley the wrong way on an escalator. At last, I reached beyond the break water.

Screams echoed as both girls faced the full force of the waves. They paddled past me, false eyelash free and faces so green I could have sworn they were still wearing their cucumber facemasks. The wind strength increased, and the tandem canoes had developed a great rhyme and were barely visible. Although the waves were simply cat's paws, paddling solo was like being sucked into a vat of treacle.

My mobile meowed from within its waterproof bag. It was Mackenzie.

'Hi Oakley, how's it going?'

'Hi Mackenzie, slowly; I can't keep up with the others and my canoe feels like I'm towing a whale.'

'Oh dear, did you pack too much? Where are you?'

'No, I packed lightly. I'm ferry gliding across to the foot of Flotsam Island, then we're paddling up the west side before beaching at the top.'

'Probably strong undercurrents. I should be on the water in a few hours. I'll meet you at Flotsam headland.'

'Keep an eye on the weather. I think there might be a storm brewing.'

'Will do. You'd better try and catch up with the others. See you later.'

'Bye, Mackenzie.'

When the first stop at Flotsam Island came into sight, I was relieved to see the others had waited for me in the eddy.

Beau peered behind. 'You all right, Oakley? You seem to be struggling.'

'I'm fine, thanks. My canoe seems awfully heavy, and the bow keeps dipping.'

'Do you want us to wait while you reload it and alter the trim?'

Scarlett twisted around. 'We haven't got time for Oakley to reload her canoe. She should have checked it before we left.'

'Don't worry, I'll manage.'

Beau reached for my bow. 'If you're sure. I could always try and make room in my canoe for something.'

'Thanks, don't worry, I'm sure your canoe is as heavy as mine.'

'Not really. Considering there are two of us it feels fairly light.'

I paddled past Beau and Scarlett as Trent pivoted around.

'What's wrong? Why can't you keep up? Scarlett and Cordelia have been managing.'

'There are two of you in each canoe. And I think I must have packed the kitchen sink again.'

Trent smirked. 'I know your motto, packing for every eventuality.'

'Yep, you never know when something might come in handy.'

Beau pointed to the ominous black clouds. 'Come on, enough about what Oakley has packed. Looks like she might be right, and we are heading into a storm.'

I paddled back into the shore. 'I'll be about five minutes, I'm going to fasten my spraydeck, or my canoe will become a bathtub.'

Beau appeared interested. 'Where did you get a spraydeck for your canoe?'

'I made it out of ripstop nylon and coated PVC.' I opened the bag and revealed a bright pink spraydeck.

'Oh my word, it's Barbie-doll pink,' sniggered Beau.

Scarlett raised her voice in annoyance. 'What's wrong with pink, it's my favourite colour?'

Beau didn't reply.

Trent paddled towards me and examined my handiwork. 'What worries me more is that Beau knows what Barbie-doll pink is. Showing your feminine side, mate. I'm impressed, Oakley, the stitching is brilliant.'

'Thanks, at least my canoe won't fill with water.'

Trent picked up his paddle. 'It's not going to be that bad. We'll be at the head of Flotsam before the storm hits us. We can't wait any longer for you, you'll have to catch us up.'

Both canoes steamed ahead while I attached my spraydeck and slotted my phone and spare paddle into pockets on the deck.

Beau shouted behind him. 'Are you all right, Oakley?'

My reply was drowned by the squall and lost forever on the crest of the waves.

The hum of the wind amplified to a steady drone, like an orchestra warming up before a performance. The height and gradient of the waves increased, and as the swell rose and fell my canoe was glued to the surface. The tandem canoes had disappeared in a veil of mist, and I was left to face the merciless sea on my own.

A symphony of waves ricocheted against the cliff, and as the white horses reared up against each other, it was comparable to striking cymbals. With the full force of a westerly gale in my face, the cross winds were making it impossible to paddle. All I could do to survive was to put in low braces to keep myself upright. I shivered as a sudden sense of fear raged through me, and I realised the severity of my situation. Froth-fuelled waves buffeted me from one side to the other and bounced off the spraydeck; it was like being inside a washing machine. Without my spraydeck, I would have been floating in a bathtub, or worse, sitting at the bottom of the ocean. Salty spray licked my face and burnt my eyes while I clung onto my paddle with arms like jelly. Thank goodness I'd fastened my paddle leash. This wasn't fun anymore; the enjoyment had long gone. I was in a perilous situation at the mercy of the sea. My only option was to turn around and surf the waves back to the eddy at the bottom of the island. Timing was imperative, the last thing I wanted was to broach a wave sideways and capsize my canoe.

There was a loud meow from my phone. I brushed the spray away from the case and pressed answer.

'Hi Oakley, are you busy? Can you spare me a few seconds?'

'Hi Molly, I'll call you back later.'

'Oh, but it will only take a second, it's very noisy at your end, sounds like you are at the laundrette. I'm trying to give Tom his worming tablet, but he keeps spitting it out. Harrison is holding him, is there another way to give him the tablet?'

Like a bolt out of the blue, a clap of thunder echoed, and instantaneously it was followed by a streak of lightning.

'Oakley, what was that noise?'

'Don't worry, only a thunderstorm. Have you got any cheese?'

'Yes.'

'Break a few bits off, roll into balls and hide the tablet in it.'

'Good idea. Reuben's fetching the cheese.'

The skies opened showering me with warm rain that washed the salt out of my eyes. I peered over my shoulder to see a humongous wave breaking on the crest.

'Molly, I'll have to call you back. I have a big wave coming up my back end.'

'Big Dave is coming up your back end! Oh my god, Oakley, the kids are here! I'll hold until you've finished. Tom must have his worming tablet. Oakley, that's amazing he's eaten the cheese. Oh no he spat the tablet out.'

'Molly, you need to get your ears tested. If you have any cream cheese crush the tablet up, mix it into the cream cheese, and paste it onto his paws and he'll lick it off.'

I glanced behind and began paddling like a wind-up toy as the wave picked up the stern.

'What was that? I've got to paste the cream cheese onto his balls so he can lick it off? You removed his balls! I'll paste it onto his legs instead. Guess what? It's working, yep, he's licking it off his legs. Oakley you're a genius. Have a lovely day with Big Dave, bye.'

With no time to say goodbye, I prayed today wasn't the day I entered the pearly gates. At least my mum wouldn't bite my head off when she saw the state of my house. I was also wearing clean, presentable knickers and had remembered to shave my legs.

The sea was relentless, as yet another gust of wind hit my canoe and pivoted it sideways. It felt like a pair of hands had lifted the bow and was pushing me at an alarming rate backwards towards the cliffs. Any minute now my body was going to be smashed to smithereens and devoured by millions of crustaceans. My canoe was torpedoed between a set of rocks, and as a scream escaped my mouth, the light went out.

Chapter Forty
Magical Spell

A couple of minutes ago, I was positive my makers were reaching out to me, however, as if by magic, I was still very much alive. My canoe was cocooned backwards inside a narrow tunnel. Ahead of me the sea was ferocious, yet behind me, there was an air of serenity. As my eyes adjusted to the darkness, iridescent tendrils of light danced like fairies under my canoe. The glow was hypnotic, it was as if someone had waved a magic wand and chanted abracadabra as they magicked the Northern Lights into the tunnel. I reached behind me, and using my fingertips, gripped limpets masquerading as climbing holds. Following several elbow brushes, and few expletives, I heaved myself backwards into the light at the end of the tunnel.

I was magnetised into an open roofed cavern, the size of the London Palladium. The expanse that encompassed me was breathtaking and glancing towards the sky was akin to gazing into another galaxy. Any minute now I half expected someone to shout, 'Beam me up Scotty!' Rays of light reflected on a pool of water and transformed it into a tapestry of shimmering green sequins, laced in silver. As I leant over the side of my canoe, my reflection bounced back, like *Alice Through the Looking Glass*. I peered up scanning the cavern; it was like paradise. A horseshoe beach was sprinkled in rock pools, and as the tide lapped gently on the sand, I thought how lucky I was to have it to myself.

A beach of pure white sand bordered a sheer cliff face, where spray from a cascading waterfall created a rainbow. Out of the corner of my eye, I noticed something darting behind the rainbow; maybe I wasn't alone after all. Rubbing my salt-laced eyes momentarily blinded me. As my vision improved, I couldn't miss the sinister neon-green eyes the shape of builder's bricks, peeping through the waterfall. A shiver ran throughout my body, giving me the heebie-jeebies. Yet, when I closed my eyes and rubbed them again, the creepy eyes had disappeared.

Oakley, pull yourself together, I chastised, it's simply a figment of your overactive imagination.

I paddled to the beach and stepped onto sand resembling icing sugar. With visions of the creepy eyes flouncing in my mind, memories of Scottish mythical creatures temporarily blurred the visions. What if the eyes belonged to the famous redcap or the mean goblin that lived in ruined castles? Oh my word, there were ruins of a castle at the top of Flotsam! Or perhaps it was a creature from Hogwarts. Pull yourself together Oakley, I reprimanded myself for thinking such utter nonsense.

Despite Beau, Trent and the girls being pains in the neck, thoughts turned to their safety. Crikey, and what about Mackenzie? Surely, he wouldn't be silly enough to paddle during a storm? With no reception on my phone, thank goodness I had the back up of my VHF radio that was stowed in the front pouch of my buoyancy aid. I didn't need rescuing, but at least I could let people know of my whereabouts, and check the others were safe. Though when I opened the pouch, a few expletives escaped my mouth; someone had swiped the radio! There was nothing I could do to help the others, but at least I could help myself. In no time at all smoke spiralled through the open roof, signalling my location.

I returned to my canoe to collect my tent; however it had disappeared including my sleeping bag, Therm-a-Rest, and clothes.

Instead there was eight litres of goats' milk and a box of wine. Hidden behind the deflated air bag was the girl's monstrous freezer bag, two containers of water, and a ton of pebbles! No wonder my canoe was weather cocking, it was a miracle I wasn't naming my canoe, the Titanic! On the flipside, their devious plan had backfired as I wasn't going to be starving tonight, though how on earth I was going to use eight litres of goats' milk was anyone's guess.

Scattered across the beach at the end of the cavern was enough driftwood to construct a shelter, though it meant walking past the waterfall. I advanced with caution, peeped through the mist and was relieved to see no sign of glowing eyes. On my return, loaded with armfuls of driftwood, I hesitated again in front of the waterfall. Feeling sceptical the neon-green eyes were not a figment of my imagination, I dropped the wood and clambered up the rock face. A small cave had formed behind the waterfall, and cowering at the back, two pairs of neon-green eyes reflected in the mist. I couldn't help smiling, or rather laughing at myself, as a pair of kids bleated. No redcaps or goblins, just baby mountain goats. They must have fallen off the cliff, and although they didn't look injured, the poor things appeared half starved. They must have been ravenous, and I had just the thing – eight litres of goats' milk; talk about karma!

Before long, a saucepan of steaming goats' milk was warming while I tied the fingers on my paddling gloves, leaving just the thumbs free. I pierced a hole in the thumbs, and after filling the gloves with milk, I crawled into the cave behind the waterfall. Soon both kids had full tummies and followed me back to my camp.

My flat-packing construction skills were fully tested as I stood back admiring the tepee assembled from driftwood. It stood tall for just two minutes before toppling to the ground when the larger kid backed into it. Not to be outwitted, shelter number two was soon constructed.

The smaller kid headbutted the larger kid, and before long they were making a heck of a din, skipping and bouncing across the beach. I could only think of two names for them; Ant and Dec, seemed quite apt. I hauled the gigantic freezer bag out of my canoe and tugged the zip open. Oh my days, there was enough food to feed a family for a week. After slicing an onion, I tossed the peelings onto the fire and left it to dwindle before cooking my tea.

The sparkling pool beckoned me, though without my swimming costume it appeared a bit of skinny-dipping was in order. Armed with my mask, fins and snorkel, I hobbled over knobbly pebbles until my feet sank into the sand. Dressed in my birthday suit, a feeling of liberation tingled my body as the sun's rays warmed my back. I slipped my feet into my fins and fitted my mask and snorkel. As I moonwalked backwards into the sea, I prayed there were no critters that enjoyed nibbling wobbly bits. Thank goodness no one could see a white bottom bobbing up and down, they might have mistaken me for a beluga whale.

The array of sea life was spellbinding, and all concept of time disappeared. I could have stayed there for hours, though when salty water leaked into my mask I was forced to surface. On removing my mask and rubbing my salty eyes, my hair sprawled over my shoulders. When I scanned the beach ... that was odd, the fire was still roaring. It should have dwindled by now, unless of course my shelter was on fire!

The salt continued stinging my eyes, and rubbing just made them worse. I trundled blindly towards the fire, then froze, rivetted to the spot! What the hell! From within the plume of smoke, perched on top of a rock, was the silhouette of a mysterious man. Flipping heck, how long had he been watching me? Anchoring the fins to my chest, each boob fitted neatly into the foot holes. I held the mask down below, and armed with my weapon, a rubber snorkel, I edged closer. The man jumped off the rock, and with a cheeky smile etched across his face, ambled closer. Dressed in surfing boardshorts, shortie cag, beachball cap and sunglasses, he held a towel towards me. Seconds later the grin changed to a grimace as he dropped the towel and spun around.

'Hi, Oakley, I've been paddling up and down the island looking for you.'

'How'd you know my name?' I said nearly dropping the mask as I held the fins closer to my chest.

'I'm Mackenzie!'

'Oh my word, Mackenzie! How on earth did you find me? No! Don't turn around!' I shrieked as I interrupted him as he was about to turn and speak. 'Please can you throw the towel behind you.'

With meticulous precision, he walked backwards throwing the towel directly in front of me.

'I've been following your tracker signal. But despite beeping, there wasn't any sign of you. I was getting quite worried and beginning to think you'd drowned!'

'I thought I was going to drown. It was a fluke I ended up in here. I forgot about the tracker my mum gave me, trust her to lead you to me. How did you know how to find me?'

'Beau contacted your brother Harrison who gave us your tracker details. I've let him know you're safe.'

'Really? At least the others are safe, and I guess big brothers have their uses. Thank you for letting him know I'm okay.' I said dropping the snorkelling gear and wrapping the towel around me. 'You can turn around now, I'm decent.'

He twisted around, grinning. 'I'm so sorry about earlier, I had no idea you were skinny dipping. I didn't see anything, honest. My sunglasses make things appear quite dark. I wasn't expecting you to dress in your birthday suit for me.'

Goose bumps swept across my body as I shivered. 'Very funny! Happy birthday, Mackenzie! I wouldn't have been skinny dipping if my swimming costume hadn't been stolen.'

'Who do I thank?'

'For what?'

'Stealing your costume.'

'Probably Scarlett, who is Beau's next victim. Has the storm subsided?'

'It's not so gnarly. The others were washed across to Jetsam, but they had no idea where you were. Beau was quite impressed with Scarlett as she had a VHF radio, which he used to contact the authorities.'

'That confirms who stole my radio then. Do you have one?'

'Yes, I picked up their message on mine. Then I spotted a plume of smoke billowing above the cliffs, and there was a whiff of burning onions. The RNLI were about to launch a search party, but I cancelled the shout when I found you.'

'Oh my god, I've caused so much trouble. Guess it was lucky I lit the fire and threw the onion skins on before I went swimming. I should have listened to the man who told me not to paddle. How'd you find the tunnel?'

'Quite by accident. It was as if someone picked up the stern and pushed me between some rocks into a tunnel. With the next wave, I was washed into the cavern. Who was the man who told you not to paddle?'

'I don't know, he was dressed in yellow oilskins and sitting on a bench when I went to fetch the milk. He warned me about the storm, but the others wouldn't believe me. He said he lived on the hill; I will check it out when we get back.'

'Good idea, we can thank him. Beau wasn't happy with you because you pinched their food, milk and water.'

'Erm ... not quite correct. Someone, or rather Scarlett, replaced my gear with their food, milk, water and a mountain of pebbles. No doubt she was hoping I'd drown.'

'Really? That's awful! I think Beau needs to know about that although karma has a way of working things out. I guess they're the ones going hungry tonight.'

'They are, but we're going to feast like kings!' I said trying not to drop the towel.

'Is there any food left?'

'Plenty, I've not started it yet. Fancy joining me for a birthday banquet? There's also a box of wine in my canoe.'

'Sounds great, I'm starving.'

'Would you mind if we continued this conversation whilst I wasn't wrapped in just a towel?'

'Don't mind me, you can remove it if you like.'

'Cheeky! I'm going to change behind the boulders. The only clothes I have is what I was paddling in.'

'I've got a spare fleece if you get cold.'

'Thanks, do you like the shelter I built?'

Mackenzie put his hand across his mouth to hide his smile.

'Erm ... it's interesting. It's lucky I have my tent. Makenzie paused as Ant and Dec bleated from within the shelter. 'Oakley, why are there are a pair of kids in your shelter?'

'That's Ant and Dec!' I shouted from behind a boulder.

Mackenzie roared with laughter. 'Why have you named the kids Ant and Dec?'

I ambled towards him, pulling my hair back into a ponytail. 'It's Saturday night, and my kit has been taken away. Plus, as we're about to eat food that theoretically isn't mine, technically it's a takeaway. One kid is bigger than the other, so the names seemed fitting.'

Mackenzie rested his hands on his hips and bent forward laughing. 'You're so funny. By the way, you look just as lovely dressed as you did wrapped in a towel.'

'Thanks.' I felt myself rubbernecking him, he was even more ravishing than Beau. Strands of mahogany brown hair peeped from under his baseball cap and a chinstrap beard framed the contours of his face. I had no idea what colour his eyes were as he was sporting a pair of smart black sunglasses.

'Oakley, would you mind doing me a favour? If I lean forward, could you pull my cag over my back, it's a bugger to get off on your own.'

'Stripping seems to be a trait in your family.'

He flashed me a cheeky grin. 'At least I wasn't wearing my birthday suit when we met for the first time. Maybe you'd like to perform an encore later?'

I sauntered towards him. 'You have as much chance as Fanny Flocker making a batch of edible rock cakes. Now bend forward, Dr Summers, this won't hurt a bit.'

Mackenzie chuckled as he bent forward and stretched his arms towards me.

'Do you mind if I hold on to you, or I'll fall backwards?'

'I don't know, you boys, any excuse to grasp a woman's hips.'

'I was aiming for your waist, not your tits, unless of course that's where they are?'

I snorted as I giggled. 'I said hips not tits! And no, they're not at my waist, yet.'

Tugging the bottom of the cag up to his shoulders was like helping Poppy and Blossom out of their dry suits, though on the other hand, Mackenzie was worse. When I drew his cag inside out and over his shoulders, Mackenzie mumbled something about still wearing his sunglasses. He let go of my hips, bashed me with his elbow, and sent my sunglasses flying through the air. I lost my balance, fell backwards onto the sand, and a split second later, Mackenzie landed on top of me. Still cocooned inside his cag, he scrambled to his knees and wrenched it over his head. I was enveloped in a sensual aroma as he offered me his hand.

'I'm so sorry, I'm a bit accident prone. I'll try not to cause any further catastrophes.' Without our sunglasses, our eyes met for the first time, revealing he had the most amazing sparkling Aegean blue eyes. He gazed at me with a puzzled expression and repositioned his sunglasses. 'Are you okay?'

My body was shuddering with giggles as I retrieved my sunglasses. 'Fine, thanks, you're as accident prone as me and we haven't even opened the wine yet. Would you mind warming the kids' milk and I'll start tea?'

'No problem, fancy a glass of wine?'

'Just a small glass please. Beau served me a huge glass; I think he was trying to get me drunk!'

'What happened between the two of you?'

'He's moved on to Scarlett now, they're welcome to each other.'

'His loss.'

While Mackenzie bottle-fed Ant and Dec, I chargrilled the

sausages and burgers. I handed Mackenzie a plate piled high with food.

'Wow! Thanks, that looks delicious.'

'You're welcome.' I reached towards him with my glass of wine. 'Happy birthday, Mackenzie. Sorry it's not how you were expecting to spend your birthday.'

Mackenzie leant towards me and toasted my glass.

'Cheers. Are you kidding? This is the best birthday ever.'

I sank beside him with my plate balanced on my knees. 'I haven't given you your present yet.'

'I wasn't expecting a present. What is it, an encore of the birthday suit?'

'No! You said you didn't see anything!'

'I didn't, that's why I want an encore.'

'Sorry, no encore. I've been making you something, though it's not quite finished yet, and I'm not sure if you will like the colour.'

'You have? No one has ever made me anything before.'

I passed Mackenzie his present and he tore the paper off.

'You've been making me an orange spraydeck for my canoe!' He jumped up and unfolded it. 'It's the most amazing present I have ever had. Now I'll be able to paddle on grade four rivers without bailing every second. How'd you know the size?'

'I asked Flo what canoe you had.' I said standing up.

Mackenzie reached out and hugged me.

'Thank you, you're very clever, I love it and can't wait to see it when its finished.'

Maybe now was a good time to ask about his girlfriend, as he'd not mentioned her.

'You're welcome, what did your girlfriend buy you?'

He drew his eyebrows together. 'What girlfriend?'

'Your mum said you'd met a special girl.'

'Did she? Oh, the blabbermouth. No, I don't have a girlfriend.'

I smiled to myself as we finished the feast, and as the sky darkened, we settled back to watch the sunset.

Mackenzie jumped up and tossed a few more sticks onto the fire.

'Are you warm enough?'

'I'm a bit chilly.'

'Take a pew closer if you like.'

As I shimmied closer. The sensual aroma of his cologne was intoxicating. We could dispense with any small talk; his cologne was enough to seduce me. With our shoulders touching I yearned for him to wrap his arm around me as we gazed at the twinkling stars. Venus, the goddess of love, reflected on the surface of the pool as the moon hemmed the ripples.

'Are you warmer now?'

'Still a bit chilly,' I lied.

Mackenzie repositioned himself behind me and slide his athletic legs either side of my body. He cocooned me against his torso and wrapped his arms around me while I relaxed my head against his shoulder.

'Feel better?'

'Much, thank you.' A wave of warmth fizzled throughout my body, and as Mackenzie clasped my hands in his, my pulse intensified; maybe this was how love felt.

'I don't know about you, Oakley, but I could sit here for an eternity.'

'Me too, it's the best day I've ever had.'

'As comfy as I am though, it's nearly dark and I think we'd better erect the tent and stoke the fire before we lose the light.'

'Good idea. Do you mind if I borrow your fleece?'

'Of course not. It's in the orange dry bag in my canoe. Would you mind fetching the tent as well, it's in the huge yellow bag. I'll collect some more wood for the fire and clear an area for the tent.'

Glancing into Mackenzie's canoe made me laugh; he carried even more kit than me! A feeling of déjà vu struck as I zipped up the fleece, and when I tugged the tent out, something spiralled onto the beach.

I gazed at it in disbelief and shouted through the smoke, 'Mackenzie, where did you find this?'

'I forgot about that. I've been meaning to throw it away, just kept forgetting.'

Tears were prickling at the back of my eyes. 'Did you find it in a river?'

'No, it was in the footwell of my kayak when I drained half the river out.'

'Was this before Christmas on the River Dart?'

'Yes, why?'

Tears began trickling down my cheeks. 'It's my fairy shoe!'

Mackenzie dropped the wood and rushed back. 'You're kidding me! You're the fairy I rescued from the river?'

I stepped back, unable to find any words other than, 'Yes.'

Mackenzie grabbed my arm. 'I can't believe it's you! I thought there was something familiar about you when your sunglasses fell off. The last time I saw you, you were covered head to toe in mud and your face was a rainbow of smudged make-up.' Mackenzie chuckled, paused and brushed a strand of hair out of my face. 'You were the special girl I told my mum I'd met. I thought I'd never see you again.'

Tears of happiness gushed down my cheeks. 'Sorry I didn't recognise you, the last time we met you had a full beard, croaky voice, and I thought you were married.'

'I was growing my beard for Decembeard to raise money for bowel cancer. I'd nearly lost my voice from shouting at the lads the day before, and no I'm not married. I thought you were married! Wasn't that your husband who I met in the café? He said you'd taken his daughters home to your mum as she had tickets to see *Cinderella*.'

'That was my brother Flynn! The girls are my nieces who are coming to live with me. Who were the children in your car?'

'My nephews and niece. My sister went into labour early and asked me to pick the kids up from the Santa train. I had to stay and look after them for a couple of days while she was in hospital; that's why I missed your interview.'

I slumped down onto the sand. 'So, I've been dreaming about Woody, and he was right under my nose.'

Mackenzie sank down beside me. 'You've been dreaming about me then?'

'Don't let it go to your head, I may have been having nightmares. Why are you called Woody? Nothing crude I hope?'

Mackenzie leant back, laughing. 'Nothing crude. My mates named me Woody because I enjoy sculpturing driftwood.'

'So do I! Did you make the sculptures in your house?'

'Yes, did you like the one of the mermaid?'

I sniggered. 'Yes! I think you spent a lot of time sculpting certain parts.'

Mackenzie rubbed his palms together and smiled. 'I enjoyed that bit, I'm good with my hands.'

'Why doesn't that surprise me?'

We wandered back to our camp as Ant and Dec charged around bleating for more milk.

'I'd better fetch another carton of milk from my canoe.'

'Okay, I'll erect the tent.' Mackenzie hesitated. 'I've only got one sleeping bag, we may have to share body heat.'

'I'm sure I can live with that.'

Was I dreaming? And any minute now I was going to wake up and realise I'd fallen asleep alone in the cavern? Though it felt so real, and on glancing through the grey smoke drifting from the fire, was the silhouette of one gorgeous man who was definitely not a figment of my imagination.

Briefly, the moon peeped behind from the clouds, casting shadows that danced like fairies in a fairy ring. With my next step, I tripped over the tip of a camouflaged rock and landed face-down in the sand. All I could hear was Mackenzie laughing and calling my name.

I knelt up, giggling and spitting sand out. 'I think the wine went to my head.'

Mackenzie was shaking with laughter as he dangled a towel in front of me. 'You only had half a glass! You're such a lightweight! Here, take my hand.'

He extended his arm, unclenched his fingers, and grasped my hand. Our eyes laced together as he drew me into his fine physic.

He captivated me in his smile while his fingers caressed the outline of my face, before circling the contours of my lips. His eyes glowed unspoken love before he cupped my chin in his hand. Time stood still when his lips as soft as rose petals brushed against mine. The sky was showered with meteorites; it was as if someone had sprinkled a handful of sparkling diamonds from the moon. We could have been the only people left in the world while we gazed towards the universe and listened to the fire crackling. There was no need for further words as a magical spell was cast upon us. And while I melted into Mackenzie's arms, Woody paddled into my heart ...

About the Author

I first stepped into a canoe when I was four, and from then on developed an affinity with water, whether it was frozen or liquid! I grew up in the countryside, and from an early age loved gardening, nature and wildlife. I could often be seen climbing a tree or walking home with an injured animal or bird; I even kept frogs in my bedroom!

Aged nine I started ice-skating lessons, though with a lack of transport in the countryside I was unable to continue skating until I bought my first car aged eighteen. From that moment I could be seen skating five nights a week at the former Bristol Mecca ice rink or roller skating on Weston-Super-Mare sea front.

During my teenage years I worked weekends to save money for water sports holidays in Exmouth. During these breaks I learnt to paddle a kayak, sail and windsurf. Ten years later I can vividly remember an autumn evening, standing on the edge of the River Yeo in Congresbury and gazing at the cold murky water with cows as our spectators. The instructor had just told us we were going to practise our capsize drill for our one-star kayaking certificate. As much as I loved water the thought of going upside down, exiting my kayak and crawling up a muddy embankment did not seem too appealing! However, I did it and came up smiling, covered in weed! I wasn't aware of it at the time, but that was the turning point in my life, and the start of something very special.

I've paddled many amazing rivers and coastal stretches of the UK and Greece. I've met some incredible people along the way, and have been extremely lucky to see amazing spectacles, and camp in remote and wonderful locations.

You are probably wondering: did I always want to be a writer? Well the answer is no. As a child I loved writing stories and reading, especially Famous Five books, but writing as a career had never been an option. My English teacher said I had an amazing imagination, but unless I learnt to spell or talk in class, I would never amount to much! I wanted to be a marine biologist, a vet, or a famous ice-skater, but they were simply pipe dreams. Instead I followed other paths. It was while I was self-employed helping older people to remain independent in their homes that the idea of writing a book came into my mind. I used to cheer people up with funny stories, and one day a client suggested I share them with the world. Since then I have been writing every minute of my spare time, and absolutely love it.

I live in a rural location with my three rescued cats, and I still continue to rescue animals and birds.

Paddle into My Heart is the first book in a trilogy. Oakley will be enjoying a lot more adventures, and no doubt getting herself into a lot more mischief!

Paddleintomyheart@btinternet.com

Facebook: Jenny Dutton romcom author

Printed in Great Britain
by Amazon

58434016R00209